The Cassandra Complex

Tor Books by Brian Stableford

Inherit the Earth
Architects of Emortality
The Fountains of Youth
The Cassandra Complex

The Cassandra

Complex

BRIAN STABLEFORD

A Tom Doherty Associates Book • New York

THE CASSANDRA COMPLEX

Copyright © 2001 by Brian Stableford

Edited by David G. Hartwell

A Tor Book
Published by Tom Doherty Associates, LLC
175 Fifth Avenue
New York, NY 10010

www.tor.com

Tor® is a registered trademark of Tom Doherty Associates, LLC.

Library of Congress Cataloging-in-Publication Data

Stableford, Brian M.
    The Cassandra complex / Brian Stableford.—1st ed.
      p. cm.
    "A Tom Doherty Associates book."
    ISBN 0-312-87773-0 (alk. paper)
    1. Twenty-first century—Fiction. 2. Forensic scientists—Fiction. 3. Missing persons—Fiction. 4. Biotechnology—Fiction. I. Title
    PR6069.T17 C375 2001
    823'.914—dc21   00-048018

First Edition: March 2001

Printed in the United States of America

0 9 8 7 6 5 4 3 2 1

For Jane, and all victims of the Cassandra Complex

Acknowledgments

The plot of this novel is loosely based on a short story entitled "The Magic Bullet" that appeared in *Interzone 29* in 1989. I am grateful to David Pringle for publishing that story, and to Gardner Dozois and the late Don Wollheim for reprinting it in their respective annual collections of the *Year's Best Science Fiction*.

I should also like to thank Jane Stableford for proofreading services and helpful commentary, and the late Claire Russell and her husband, Bill, for their great kindness and for the part their ideas played in shaping the background of the story.

The book by Claire and W. M. S. Russell to which the text refers, *Population Crises and Population Cycles,* was published by the Galton Institute in 1999. The book by Garrett Hardin to which the text refers, *The Ostrich Factor: Our Population Myopia,* was published by Oxford University Press in 1999.

The Cassandra Complex

PART ONE
The Mouseworld Holocaust

When Lisa first heard the noise, she wasn't sure whether it was real or not. She didn't think she'd been asleep, but she couldn't be certain. Sometimes, like all confirmed insomniacs, she fell asleep without realizing she had done so—and sometimes she dreamed without actually falling properly asleep.

If the sound had been one of breaking glass or splintering wood, she would have sat up immediately to reach for the phone, but what she had heard—or thought she had heard—was the noise of the front door opening without any force applied to it. That should have been impossible. Both locks had combination triggers as well as swipe slots, and they were supposed to be unhackable. Lisa lived alone, and was not inclined to trust the combinations to anyone else. A member of the police force had to take such precautions very seriously, even if she was a lab-bound forensic scientist who ought to count herself lucky to be clinging on to limited duties now that she was past the official retirement date.

Because it seemed so unlikely that she had heard what she thought she did, Lisa remained quite still, straining her ears for further evidence. She let four or five seconds pass before she even opened her eyes to take a sideways glance at the luminous display on the screen beside her bed. The timer told her it was five minutes to four: the darkest and quietest period of the cold October night.

Then a second noise drew her eyes to the door of her bedroom. There was a certain amount of light filtering through the closed curtains, but she lived on the third floor, too far above the level of the streetlights to obtain much benefit from their yellow glow. The door was shadowed, and she couldn't tell for sure whether it was opening until she saw the pencil-thin beam of light sneaking through the widening crack—the beam that was guiding the person whose quiet hand was pushing the door open.

Lisa immediately pulled her bare right arm out from beneath the duvet, reaching for the handset suspended beside the screen. She thought she was moving fairly swiftly, but the intruder's beam had already caught the movement of her arm. Even as her hand made contact, she saw the silhouette of the gun barrel that had been raised to catch the light.

"Don't touch it!" The voice that spoke was filtered through some kind of distorter that made it sound robotic.

Lisa snatched her hand back, and immediately felt ashamed of her obedience.

"Shit," said a second voice, sounding from the hallway.

"Shh!" said the first intruder, who was now well into the room, holding the gun no more than a meter from Lisa's face. "Get on with it. She won't make any trouble."

Lisa had been in the police force for more than forty years, but she had never had a gun pointed at her. She didn't know how she was supposed to feel, but she was fairly certain that she wasn't afraid—puzzled and annoyed, but not afraid.

I ought to be able to identify the weapon, she thought. It was absurdly irritating that the only thing she could see in the beam of the light was an unrecognizable gun. It looked heavy and old—not exactly an antique, but not the sort of dart gun that had recently become fashionable among the young. It could easily have dated back to the turn of the century, maybe even to the period before the handgun ban that had preceded her recruitment to the police force. She knew that she would have to give Mike Grundy an exact account of what was happening, and that Judith Kenna would read her statement with utter contempt if there were nothing she could say for sure except that she had been threatened with a gun whose make she could not name.

As the other intruder moved inquisitively around the room, a second slender guide light briefly picked out the head of the one who was threatening Lisa, outlining an almost-featureless oval helmet. Lisa knew that the two must be dressed in matte black, probably in one-piece smartsuits whose unbreakable tissue-repellent fibers would leave no clues for forensic analysis. In order to be a successful burglar in the age of scientific detection, you had to be extremely careful to leave no traces. That wasn't the purpose of smart textiles, but it was a happy side effect as far as the criminal classes were concerned.

"What are you looking for?" Lisa asked. Because it was such a cliché, the question seemed far more foolish than it was. She had nothing worth stealing—nothing, at any rate, that justified the kind of risk the burglars were taking or the kind of expertise they must have employed to hack her unhackable locks.

"I think you know exactly what we want, Dr. Friemann," the distorted voice replied. The bedroom walls had neither eyes nor ears, but the other room was fully fitted and the bedroom door was still open. The speaker obviously didn't care about the possibility that the pickups in the other room would record the voice for analysis by Lisa's colleagues in Sight & Sound. Presumably, therefore, the voice distorter was no mere frequency modulator.

Do I know what they want? Lisa wondered. *If they're professionals, it must be work, but I don't bring work home, Anyway, I don't have anything to do with AV Defence, or even with industrial espionage. Even if there is a war on, I'm a noncombatant.* Her eyes tracked the movements of the second intruder, whose attention was now concentrated on the desk fitted into the corner to the left of the window. That was her main homestation. Her flat had only two rooms, apart from the kitchenette and the bathroom, and contemporary fashion dictated that if there wasn't an already allocated space, the best site for the main homestation was in the bedroom, not the "reception room." Having been brought up before the turn of the millennium, Lisa—who had little need for a room in which to receive visitors—always thought of her other room as the "living room," although the siting of the homestation ensured that she spent far more time in the bedroom.

The second intruder was already pulling wafers and sequins off the unit's shelves, sweeping them into a plastic sack without making any attempt to discriminate between them. A few old-fashioned DVD's went with them. Most of the stored information was entertainment, and most of the text and software was public-domain material that Lisa had downloaded for convenience in the days when downloading had been convenient. It was all replaceable, given time and effort, but some of it was personal, and much of that was private enough not to be stored in the unit's web-connected well or duplicated in Backup City. It wasn't the sort of stuff for which people kept remote backups—not even people who were far more conscientious about such things than Lisa was.

When the shelves had been swept clean, the searcher started poking in the cubbyholes and emptying the drawers.

"None of it's worth anything," Lisa said. The comment was as much discovery as complaint, because she realized as she watched the hidden corners of her life history disappearing into the sack that there was very little whose loss she had much cause to regret. She had never been the kind of person to attach sentimental value to digital images or documents.

"Be good, now," said the robotic voice, contriving to sound bitter and angry in spite of its manifest artificiality. "Stay quiet and stay alive. Play up and you might not."

"Why?" Lisa asked softly. She was genuinely puzzled. Even as an agent of the state, Lisa had rarely roused anyone to bitterness or anger; only one person had ever threatened to kill her, although her testimony in court had convicted more than a dozen murderers and more than a score of rapists. Save for that one exception, the convicted and condemned had always recognized that she was only reporting what the evidence revealed. Hardly anyone nowadays blamed messengers for the news they brought, although it was conceivable that the national paranoia that was increasing day by day while the Containment Commission dithered might yet bring back the bad old days.

"You'll work it out," her adversary informed her. "If we don't have what we need, we'll be back, and next time—"

Lisa never got to hear what would happen next time if the burglars didn't have what they needed, because the speaker was abruptly cut off by the telephone bell. It wasn't a particularly strident bell—Lisa never needed much waking up—but the tension of the situation made it sound louder than it was.

Lisa's eyes were immediately drawn to the screen, where the caller's number was displayed in red above and to the left of the time. She recognized the number immediately—and so did the person on the other end of the gun.

"It's Grundy's mobile," the robotic voice reported to the busy searcher. "Probably headed for the university."

"If I don't answer it," Lisa pointed out, "he'll know that something's wrong."

"He already knows," the distorted voice told her. "Fifteen minutes more and he'll know exactly how much is wrong. Believe me, Dr. Friemann, when I tell you that you won't be very high on his list of priorities."

That's what you think! Lisa retorted silently.

The telephone continued ringing.

"Finished," the searcher reported. "If it's here, I've got it."

Lisa didn't make any conscious decision to be brave. If she'd made a conscious decision at all, she'd have taken into account what the gun wielder had already told her about the possibility that playing up might put her life at risk. It was something deeper, something more reflexively desperate, that made her lunge for the handset and snatch it from its cradle.

"Help me, Mike!" she yelled. "Intruders on premises. Now, Mike, *now!*"

"Shit," said the searcher again.

"He's at least four miles away," said the burglar with the gun. The artificial voice still sounded bitter, but there was more contempt in it than anger. "The first three miles of that are in the blackout. The routine patrols have all been diverted. No help can reach you in time, Dr. Friemann."

Lisa was still holding the handset to her mouth. Mike Grundy was saying something, but he must have been holding his own handset too far away for a decent pickup, perhaps because he needed both hands to drive. He seemed to be cursing, but the word "blackout" leaped out of the incoherent stream like a weird echo.

"I need help, Mike," Lisa repeated, speaking more calmly now that it seemed she wasn't about to be shot. "Alert the station. The burglars are armed. They must have a vehicle downstairs, but for the moment, they're still here, taking time out to sneer."

Some movement of the weapon or a slight change of the dark figure's attitude must have spoken directly to Lisa's subconscious mind, because she jerked her face back, away from the handset, a full second before the gun went off.

The bullet hit the earpiece.

The impact plucked the handset from her loosening grip without breaking any of her fingers, but Lisa felt plastic shards scoring the flap of flesh between her thumb and forefinger and drawing jagged slits along her inner forearm. She saw the blood spurting even before she felt the shock. The pain must have been intense, if only for a moment, but she was far more aware of the fact of pain than of any actual feeling, and the fact seemed trivial by comparison with frank wonder that she had turned her head out of the way in time.

She had no time to curse before the gun fired again.

The screen beside the headboard shattered. Then the weapon fired twice more, its wielder having swiveled through a hundred and forty degrees. The entire homestation seemed to explode—but Lisa was still conscious, still very much alive.

"Nobody cares about *you*, you stupid bitch!" the distorted voice hissed in her ear. "Miller never cared, and no matter what he promised you, you'll be dead soon enough. I wouldn't do you the favor of shooting you. Let's go."

The final remark, Lisa knew, was addressed to the companion

who had emptied her shelves and cubbyholes; it was unnecessary, because the second burglar was already exiting the room as fast as was humanly possible. The gunshots must have awakened the Charlestons, whose bedroom was directly below Lisa's, and maybe the Hammonds below them. The burglars wouldn't necessarily have a clear run down the three flights of stairs—but the inhabitants of Number 39 were a law-abiding lot. The two young tearaways on the ground floor were the kind who'd have a dart gun stashed behind a radiator, and John Charleston had always given the impression of being a man of hidden depths, but no one would impede the escape for more than the time it took for wise discretion to get the better of foolish valor.

"Morgan Miller never made anyone a promise he didn't intend to keep," Lisa remarked as the burglar with the gun disappeared into the darkness of the living room. "Not his style at all." The last words, at least, were too quietly spoken to be audible as the two intruders raced through the door that had the supposedly unhackable locks. They must have come up the stairs almost silently, but they went down like thunder, even in their muffled shoes.

Lisa leaped out of bed and ran to the window, not caring that she was naked as she snatched the curtains open. She hoped to catch a glimpse of whatever vehicle the thieves had arrived in, but they hadn't left it parked in the road outside the block of flats. She lingered for a couple of minutes, but she didn't see the fleeing burglars make their exit. If they'd come in by the front door, they'd obviously made provision to use a different exit.

The shooter had told the truth about the blackout. If Mike had started out from his own house in response to an alarm call, he'd have driven straight into total darkness, because all the lights on the farther side of Oldfield Park were out, at least as far to the north as Sion Hill. There had been a major power failure—or major sabotage. The town center was out, although the glow on the far side of Lyncombe Hill suggested that Widcombe still had power.

Lisa didn't go to her own door, partly because she wanted to be certain there was nothing else to be seen in the flat—and no useful information to be gained there that might make her statement seem less ridiculous to Judith Kenna's censorious eye—and partly because she was still naked. As soon as she switched on the light in the living room, however, she saw the word that had been sprayed on the inswung door and knew it must have been put there before the two seeming professionals had hacked her supposedly unhackable locks.

The word was "Traitor."

It made no sense at all. Professional spies didn't pause in their work to spray insults on the walls of their victims. Even kids bent on pure vandalism rather than on profitable theft rarely used spray paint, because sprays were too promiscuous and carefully tagged; the contaminated clothing of the perpetrators would be ample evidence to secure conviction.

In any case, who on earth was she supposed to have betrayed? What awful secret did the burglars think she harbored, buried somewhere in her personal-data stores—and why did they think she had done them an injury by keeping it?

Lisa picked up the phone on the living-room table and was slightly surprised to find that it was still working, in spite of the comprehensive trashing of the bedroom systems. She punched out the number of Mike Grundy's mobile.

"I'm okay, Mike," she said as soon as he answered. "Four shots fired, but it's mostly property damage. I'm bleeding where shrapnel cut my hand and scraped my arm, but they didn't shoot to kill."

"I'll be there in two minutes," Mike told her. "I was already on my way to pick you up. You're not the only one to be targeted tonight—all hell is breaking loose. How bad's the bleeding?"

"Not bad," Lisa assured him, inspecting her hand while she said it. "It doesn't need gelling—not if the hospital's blacked out, at any rate. I'll wrap it up." She was still aware that it was hurting, as hand injuries always did, but it was still the fact of pain of which she was aware, coupled with a peculiar mental detachment. She told herself that it was hurting because of the density of the nerve endings, not because of the seriousness of the wound, and that it would heal easily enough. Then she told herself that she ought to be glad. If Judith Kenna had had her way, Lisa would have retired from the force without ever seeing *action*. Now she had been threatened and shot at, as well as embroiled in whatever kind of hell it was that was breaking out all over the western reaches of the cityplex.

"Do that," Mike said tersely. "I'll need you at the university. Firebomb in the labs. At least one person injured—one human, that is. Maybe half a million mice dead."

Lisa felt a shiver run through her body, but told herself it was delayed shock caused by the fact that she'd just had a gun pointed at her, not to mention that the gun had gone off—four times.

"Is it Morgan?" she asked querulously. "How bad is he?"

"I don't know yet," Mike told her. "Do you have any reason to think it might be Morgan?"

Lisa was all too keenly aware, even as she issued a reflexive denial, that the gun-wielding burglar must have mentioned Morgan Miller's name deliberately. *Everything* that had been said to her, in fact, must have been said for a reason, however perverse the reason might be. In a world whose walls were growing eyes and ears in ever-increasing quantities, only fools were incautious—and it was difficult to believe that anyone capable of opening her door could be a fool. They had painted TRAITOR on her door *for a reason*.

Lisa wanted time to think, but she didn't want to hang up the phone before she'd told Mike Grundy the most obviously interesting and most evidently sinister of all the things the person who'd shot at her had taken care to let her know. "The one who was holding the gun recognized the number of your mobile when you called," she said. "Whoever they are, they seem to know a hell of a lot more about us than we know about them."

It wasn't until after she'd said it that Lisa realized it might not be the cleverest thing for a person to put on the record when she'd just found the word TRAITOR sprayed on the door of her flat by someone who'd known the secret combinations of both its locks, especially when she desperately needed the goodwill of her superiors to be allowed to go on working.

TWO

Lisa dressed, cursing the clumsiness forced on her by the torn hand. She pulled on a pair of tights and an undershirt made of smartish fibers, but force of habit remained strong, and the tunic and trousers she put on next were the same dead kind she always wore on the outside. Although the undershirt soaked up the evidence of her arm wounds easily enough, the blood still flowing copiously from the tear in her hand immediately stained the cuff of the tunic.

For once, she admitted that it really might have been wise to embrace the new generation of smart fibers more wholeheartedly. She probably would have, if she hadn't grown so sick of hearing people recite TV-hatched slogans over the years that her natural stubbornness had intensified her determination not to be railroaded by the lords of fashion and the prophets of doom. The new police uniforms issued the previous year were only five years behind the times, but CID and lab workers had the privilege of lagging even farther behind if they wished, and she'd taken that opportunity even though she'd known it lent fuel to Judith Kenna's conviction that she was past her use-by date.

In order to prevent the problem from getting any worse, Lisa fetched the first-aid kit from the bathroom. She hadn't opened it for years, and it didn't have any kind of dressing adequate to take proper care of the problem, but she found an absorbent pad that would fit over the awkwardly placed cut on her hand and managed to tape it on with old-fashioned adhesive tape.

Having dressed the wound as best she could, Lisa made a concerted effort to collect herself mentally. She thanked the good fortune that had helped her resist the temptation to fight her insomnia with drugs. She'd been having trouble sleeping for some months, but she hadn't resorted to medication because she didn't believe that insomnia deserved to be reckoned as an illness. She had addressed the problem as a straightforward challenge to her powers of self-discipline: a rebellion of her treasonous flesh against the stern empire of her mind. Her method of fighting the sleeplessness had been to instruct herself not to worry about it, because a woman of sixty—sixty-one, now that her birthday had come and gone—didn't need that much sleep anyway. She had also informed herself that lying still in the darkness was, in any case, sufficient to garner most of the benefits that sleep was supposed to confer. Even so, she could easily have weakened on a dozen occasions, and last night might have been one of them.

She went downstairs to meet Mike Grundy at the front door of the building—to save time, she told herself. The crime scene would have to be examined, sooner rather than later if there were staff available, and the spray-painted legend would be duly noted; but for the time being, she wanted to concentrate on the big picture, of which the raid on her premises seemed to be a relatively trivial facet.

John Charleston and Robbie Hammond must have been lurking inside their locked front doors, listening for clues to what was going on. John peeped out as she passed by, then threw his door open wide. By that time, Lisa was halfway down the next flight. Robbie had taken his cue from the sound of the door opening. They seemed absurdly like bookends as they peered at her, one from above and one from below.

She didn't stop. "Police emergency," she said in what she hoped was a reassuring tone. "All safe and secure upstairs. SOCO will probably get here before I come back. No cause for alarm."

"Was that gunfire?" was the only question either of them managed—but by that time, she'd raced past Robbie Hammond and was well on her way to the front door. She didn't bother to answer him. She left the two of them to meet one another halfway and discuss the matter between themselves.

Mike's black Rover was already coming around the corner, and she hardly had time to stop before it was beside her. She used her left hand to open the door.

"It's okay," she assured him as his eyes were drawn to the patch-work dressing on her right hand and the bloodstain on her cuff. "Stings a bit, but it's fine. Drive. The university, not the hospital."

He nodded and put the car back into gear. He had to do a three-point turn to get out of the cul-de-sac, and the screech of his brakes probably woke up more people than the four gunshots had, but he was back on Cotswold Road inside of ten seconds. Ordinarily, he'd have crossed Wellsway on to Greenway Lane, but Greenway Lane led into the blackout, so he headed south to use Bradford Road and Claverton Road. It was a longer way around, but it was probably safer.

Why black out that part of the grid? Lisa wondered. *It doesn't cover the university or the flat—only a couple of miles in between. Are they just trying to cover their escape routes, or is there a third scene we don't yet know about?* She didn't raise the point with Mike, though, because he was already talking urgently.

"The live feeds to the security TV's were doctored," he reported, "but the digicams themselves weren't damaged, so the wafers should tell us what actually happened. The alarms went off when the sprinklers kicked in, but the system couldn't do more than contain the fire and stop it from spreading. Apart from the one room, damage is limited. The injured man was shot with one of those dart guns that everybody and his cousin seem to have nowadays, but they dragged him way down the corridor before leaving him, so he shouldn't have inhaled too much smoke—hopefully."

"You said *half a million* dead mice?" Lisa queried to make sure she'd taken the right inference.

"That's right," Mike confirmed. "The bombs were in the room you always called Mouseworld."

"Why would anyone want to bomb *Mouseworld*?" Lisa asked. "All the AV research is on the upper floors, in the containment facility. All the sensitive commercial stuff is there too—what there is of it nowadays."

"Maybe they couldn't get access farther up and hoped the fire would spread through the ceiling," Mike suggested. "It won't make much difference—the Ministry of Defence is sending down a team of spooks from London. I know we aren't supposed to say there's a war on, but there *is* a bloody war on, and until they know this isn't that kind of hostile action, they have to assume it is. Whatever your people pick up tonight is likely to be taken out of their hands tomorrow, in the interests of national security. I'm likely to be left high and dry too, looking just as foolish. The chief inspector's on her way to the scene, but that won't help either of us."

"I suppose not," Lisa agreed. Chief Inspector Kenna hadn't taken any great pains to support Mike through his recent divorce, and hadn't seemed to approve of the fact that Lisa had tried to help him, even though they'd been friends and colleagues for more than twenty years. Kenna seemed to think they were both dinosaurs, their methods and instincts equally out of date. "On the other hand," Lisa added, "you and I know the territory better than anyone—and I'll probably know the victim too. The men from the Ministry will need our help."

"I know that and you know that, but will they?" Mike countered. "The spooks are coming by helicopter, but it'll take a little while for them to assemble at the point of departure—they probably won't get here until nine or ten this morning. We're trying to contact Burdillon, Miller, Chan and the other members of the department, but that won't be easy at this time of night, even if it weren't for the blackout. If the bombers could cause that to simply cover their tracks . . . who the hell are we dealing with, Lisa? What were they after at your apartment?"

"I don't know," Lisa said, wishing there were some way to display her sincerity more clearly, even though Mike Grundy was the one person in the world who wouldn't dream of doubting her. "They seemed to think I would know, but I don't. I don't have a clue. All I know for sure is that they recognized your phone number, and that they took time out to tell me that Morgan's promises couldn't be trusted, even though he never made me any, and that the one with the gun was tempted to shoot me even though that probably wasn't in the plan . . . and they spray-painted 'Traitor' on my door."

She hadn't really planned to let that out just yet, but the flow had built up a momentum of its own. Mike turned to look at her, even though his eyes ought to have been glued to the patch of visibility that the headlights carved out of the road; this far out of town, the streetlights were so sparse that they might as well have been driving in the blackout.

"That's crazy!" he said. "Why would *anyone* do something as stupid as that?"

"Why would anyone do something as stupid as bombing Mouse-world?" she countered. "That's what *I* call crazy. What kind of ter-rorist would target a room full of mice?"

"The mice could have been innocent bystanders," Grundy pointed out. "On the other hand . . . well, there may be a real plague war on now, but hobbyist terrorism has been a plague of sorts since '22, and I don't suppose the talk of curfews and all other contain-ment precautions the commission's considering will have pleased the flackers, whackers, and code-busters. Must be a big gang, though, to hit three hard targets with such precision—assuming that the black-out really is theirs. Maybe they want to make us believe they're hob-byist terrorists, although they're not. Maybe they're using crazy doodles to obscure their real agenda. Some of these so-called private-security people . . ." He left the sentence dangling.

"Maybe," Lisa concurred. "The blackout—"

She broke off when Mike cursed. An old red Nissan had zoomed across his path as he approached the junction of North Road and Ralph Allen's Drive, even though it was his right of way. He kept his foot on the accelerator regardless. He had switched off the com-puter's warning bell, but it took only three seconds for the dashboard screen to bring up a red-lettered message stating that although the primary responsibility for the near miss lay with the other vehicle, the person in charge of the Rover was nevertheless guilty of "con-tributory negligence."

Lisa wondered what conditions were like in the town center. The roadside digicams were self-contained and battery-powered, so they hadn't been disabled by the general blackout, but they weren't equipped to see in darkness as intense as that which had descended in the wake of the power cut. There were plenty of kids on the new estates west of the campus who might figure that this was the ideal time for joyriding. It might not be just teenagers, either—all the drivers in England tended to take whatever opportunities they found nowadays to exceed the claustrophobic legal restrictions on their speed and movement, no matter what their onboard computers dumped into their black boxes. Mercifully, it was nearly five o'clock in the morning and there wouldn't be many honest citizens on the roads, except for those driving delivery vans. The vast majority of people tucked up in their beds wouldn't know when they woke up that there had been a blackout.

Lisa was about to resume her observation about the blackout when Mike's phone rang. He snatched the handset up and pressed it to his ear. Lisa cocked her own ear as if to listen, although she couldn't possibly make sense of the slight leakage of sound. She had to wait for him to put the phone down again to receive the news.

"It's not Miller," he said tersely. "The body in the corridor, that is. The wafer from the corridor's best-placed eye shows Ed Burdillon going in after the bombers. They shot him—but they didn't leave him to burn. He's been taken to the hospital, but the paramedics reckon he'll be okay. He's unlikely to have been a preselected target, given that the perpetrators took the trouble to drag him clear before the bomb went off. Probably just unlucky—wrong place, wrong time. On the other hand . . ."

Lisa's stomach had lurched in response to the news that a man she had known for nearly forty years had been hurt, but not as much as it might have done had the man been Morgan Miller.

Edgar Burdillon had been head of the Department of Applied Genetics for nearly twenty years; in the eyes of far too many half-baked, anti-GM fanatics, that made him personally responsible for the rape and near murder of Mother Gaea, secret plans to manufacture a super race, high unemployment, the torture of innocent animals, and the attempted usurpation of the female prerogative. Now that the government was openly considering stringent containment measures, there would be hundreds of crazies ready to assume that he was also fully involved in developing the weapons that would be used to fight the First Plague War. Ed's days as a fashionable media pet were a long way behind him, but he had never been shy about issuing propaganda for biotechnology. He had been attacked before, but only at the nuisance level of egg-throwing, poison-pen letters, and acid on the hood of his car. Morgan Miller had suffered as much—and Chan Kwai Keung still had Hong Kong connections, which would make him personally responsible in the eyes of some madmen for at least one of the epidemics that the governments of Europe and America would soon be trying their utmost to "contain."

Lisa blinked as the Rover hurtled across what had once been Claverton Down toward the industrial park erected when the old quarries had been filled and leveled. The multitudinous lights of the campus were already vivid in the gloom. The Applied Genetics building was just north of the Avenue, and she could already see the flashing blue lights on the fire apparatus gathered on the south side of the campus. The pall of smoke above them was stained an ugly shade of pink by that fraction of the sodium light it reflected back to the ground.

It can't be anything I've given him, she told herself while she ran through a mental list of the tasks she had thrown Ed Burdillon's way during the last year in her capacity as a pen-pusher. Yes, there had been investigations concerned with DNA polluted by "viral anomalies," but there had been nothing that looked remotely like hostile action. The MOD had undoubtedly sent work to the department, for which Ed would have taken personal responsibility, but whatever the half-baked might think, England's green and pleasant campuses were not awash with GM weapons capable of wiping out the population of a cityplex the size of Bristol in a matter of days. Viruses simply weren't tough enough to wreak that kind of havoc in a world where civilized people were willing and able to observe elementary standards of hygiene, and their much-touted propensity to mutate was a thousand times more likely to render them harmless than to increase their lethal force. Bacteria designed for immunity to common antibiotics were slightly more dangerous, but every household armed with bleach and detergents was a virtual fortress—and Burdillon had been a virus man through and through ever since the early days of magic bullets.

They came at me too, she reminded herself. *They were looking for something in my files.* Even after scrupulous reexamination, however, she couldn't find a likely link. Almost all of the work she had subcontracted to the university labs during the last three decades had had to do with problematic DNA sequences gleaned from everyday crime scenes. Not even any mass murders, let alone any sensitive industrial espionage. If Ed and she had somehow contrived to get under the skin of some rival establishment—which would presumably be a megacorp rather than a foreign government nowadays—she certainly had no idea of how they had done it.

As the Rover zoomed past a baker's van carrying the morning quota of bread to the circus-starved masses, the driver made V signs at Mike, not caring in the least that he might be en route to an emergency. If he had known exactly who Detective Inspector Grundy was, he would probably have redoubled the vehemence of his gestures.

"And you!" Lisa muttered, loudly enough to startle herself. Mike glanced at her, but made no comment.

They were almost at the campus gate; the headlights had picked out the red-and-white stripes on the barrier.

The security guard didn't wait to inspect the passcard Mike was fumbling from his pocket—he presumably figured that anyone in a black Rover who wanted to get in must have a legitimate mission. Reporters always drove brightly colored Italian cars and never got out of bed at five o'clock on an October morning.

Lisa wondered whether the team that was flying out from London by helicopter might be just for show, but it seemed unlikely. Until they had more information about the motive for the attack, the Ministry of Defence would be obliged to treat the incident as a possible threat to national security. Even if some lunatic fringe organization like the Defenders of Mother Gaea or the New Luddites were to own up to the crime campaign before noon, the MOD would probably want to remain involved, if only to keep a heavy foot on the toes of the Special Branch. Hobbyist terrorists were perversely unwilling to accommodate their missions and objectives to the neat divisions of responsibility set out by the last wave of institutional reorganizations.

It had been some months since Lisa had last visited the university in person, but the campus still felt more like home than her actual home. She had only to visit it twice or three times a year to maintain the force of impressions stamped on her psyche nearly forty years before, when she'd started her course of postgraduate study under the supervision of Dr. Morgan Miller.

Ed Burdillon had been merely one of the troops in those days, with not a gray hair on his head, and Chan had been in his second year of post-doc, patiently waiting for opportunity to come knocking. In those days, she had driven to the campus from a brand-new high-rise in Bathampton Warren on a 50cc motorcycle. She'd spent the best part of three years in a lab just along the corridor from Mouseworld, in and out of it all the time. It was easy enough to imagine someone working late one night, tracking a particularly tricky 3-D electrophoretic migration pattern, hearing noises and going to investigate. . . .

Except, of course, that Ed Burdillon didn't work just along the corridor from Mouseworld. He worked on one of the floors above, in a Level 4 biocontainment facility. He might have heard the noises through the floor—but if it had been only noise, he wouldn't have thought too much about it, because he couldn't have known that Security was unwittingly watching tapes instead of live transmissions. He must have seen something—perhaps a black-clad figure in a helmet like the one Lisa's assailant had worn—and realized that Security wasn't on the ball. To fix the digicams, Lisa thought, the bombers must have had an inside man—but how had they sneaked him in? Even the humblest lab assistants had to be positively vetted these days if they were to have access to the biocontainment facility.

The flashing blue lights were all around them now. Mike slowed down before braking, but Lisa had reflexively put out her right hand; the pressure of her fingers on the dashboard reminded her that she still hurt and that even the slightest shock could renew her awareness of her pain, taunting her with her fragility.

Mike, in a fit of unaccustomed chivalry, had already run around the car to open the door for her. "Let's go," he said tersely. "Better find out what we can before the men from Ministry take it out of our hands."

It was probably going to be worse than that for her, Lisa realized. She wasn't likely to have just the case taken out of her hands. Everything the intruders had said and done for the benefit of the recording devices in her living room had been calculated to imply that she knew far more about this than she actually did. Painting TRAITOR on the door was presumably mere underlining, made for mocking emphasis. She would have to be treated as a suspect by the men from Ministry, at least to begin with—and wouldn't Judith Kenna love *that*?

THREE

Lisa paused in the doorway of Mouseworld, content for the moment to look inside without actually stepping over the threshold. There were too many people there already.

She placed her right hand against her sternum, not caring that the blood oozing from the dressing would stain the front of her tunic. The pain of the rip was definitely a feeling now as well as a fact, and the fumes were making her head ache. To make matters worse, the tiredness she'd been unable to cultivate while she lay awake in bed had now descended upon her like a pall. She had never felt less like throwing herself into her work.

The stink was the worst of it—but that was partly because the smoke spiraling from every direction in the hectic airflow made it difficult to see. The sheer faces of almost undifferentiated blackness might as well have been mere shadows. Oddly enough, there seemed to be hardly any warmth left in the cavernous space; the sharp autumn air circulating through the blown-out windows had carried away most of the heat, even though oily smoke still seeped from the molten remains of the plastic faces that were once cages housing small animals.

Lisa had to squint and concentrate hard to make out the vaguest outlines of the thousands of tiny corpses within the walls of shadow. Most of them must have been roasted rather than burned, but it was only in her imagination that the chorus of five hundred thousand agonized mice sounded obscenely loud. Mice weren't equipped for screaming and within a couple of seconds, the intense heat and smoke must have robbed them of what voices they had.

The central H Block had suffered worst of all. It didn't require an expert to guess that the incendiaries—of which there must have been at least two—had been placed in the coverts of the H-shaped area.

The main experiment, involving the four mouse "cities" arranged around the walls of the room, had run for decades. It had been famous in its way, but it had been regarded as a mere curiosity—a kind of scientific folly—even in 2002, when Lisa had arrived, shortly after her twenty-second birthday, impatient to be trained in all the hot new techniques of DNA analysis. She had already joined the police force, and had gone through basic training of a sort during the summer months.

If the Mouseworld cities had been a folly then, what were they now in 2041? The passage of time had lent them a certain dignity, although all the claims made over the years for their renewed relevance rang slightly hollow to those in the know. The human population explosion had indeed produced all the dire effects that prophets such as Morgan Miller had predicted, but careful analysis of the physiological tricks that the mice of Mouseworld had mastered had made not a jot of difference. Those humans who followed the mouse example had needed no help to do so, and those who were Calhounian rats through and through could not have been changed by any plausible intervention.

Half a dozen firemen were wandering around aimlessly, two of them still in full breathing apparatus and two others carrying huge axes in a fashion suggesting they were longing to get on with the job of clearing the debris off the staircases and catwalks—a job that would have to wait until the Fire Investigation Team had made a meticulous inspection of the site, probably in company with experts from the Bomb Squad. The axemen had taken their masks off, although the SOCO workers operating under the supervision of Steve Forrester were fully suited.

Lisa still outranked Forrester, in theory at least, but she wasn't his line manager; he was the up-and-coming heir-apparent to the entire department. He came over as soon as he noticed her, but it was a token gesture.

"Nothing much for us here," he said. "I sent Max and Lydia with Burdillon in the ambulance—we might get something from his clothing, if we're *very* lucky. As he came through the door, he was shot and fell sideways to his right. One of the bombers got ahold of his jacket and dragged him thirty meters down the corridor. His jacket was dead and the bomber was wearing smart gloves, but there's still a possibility that something stuck."

When Lisa nodded an acknowledgment, Forrester immediately turned away. Although the senior fireman must have deduced by now that she was police, he wasn't in any hurry to talk to her. She was, after all, a middle-aged woman, even if her passcard did state that she was a doctor of philosophy as well as an inspector. She seemed to have held the rank of inspector forever; three reorganizations of the relationship between forensic-science officers and the main body of the force hadn't succeeded in solving the problem of a grotesquely inappropriate and largely tokenistic ranking system.

When the senior fireman finally condescended to approach her, Lisa stepped over the threshold and moved to the left of the door so they wouldn't be in the way.

"Your mice, were they?" asked the officer as he squinted at the fine print on her card, having rubbed his eyes to clear away the last few smoke-induced tears. His hair was dyed black. The fire service, like the police force, was an institution in which youth and physical fitness were traditionally held in great esteem; they seemed destined to be the nation's last bastions against the quiet revolution of gray power. Lisa wondered whether the fireman viewed the prospect of premature redundancy with the same vaguely nauseating apprehension that had become her own mind's rest state.

"Not ours," she told him. "We still subcontract some animal work to the university, but the vast majority of the mice in here weren't on active service anymore. Those that weren't in the cities—the ones in the central block, that is—were mostly obsolete models and other GM strains preserved as library specimens. All current work is conducted on the upper floors."

The fireman nodded sagely, although he probably didn't have a clue as to what she meant by "obsolete models" and certainly didn't care. "Good doors, fewer windows up there," he said approvingly. "Certain amount of damage outside but not much in. Parallel labs on this floor came off worse, even though heat always tries to go straight up. There was a *lot* of heat, but it didn't last long. They used a fierce accelerant, but most of the local material was decently retardant. Whole thing was a matter of *Bang! Whoosh! Bob's your uncle.*"

Lisa thought about that for a moment or two. "Did the bombers expect it to spread upstairs?" she asked. "Were they hoping to destroy the whole wing?"

"Don't know what they expected or hoped," the black-haired man replied punctiliously. "Not my job to speculate."

"I'm just trying to understand why they put the bomb in here," Lisa said, struggling to remain patient in spite of her stinging hand and aching head. "Might Mouseworld have been the most convenient point they could reach in order to launch an attack on the high-security facility above it?"

"Maybe," said the fireman dubiously. "They certainly had easy access here—door was unlocked, not broken open. Then again . . . has to be off the record, because I'm not the man supposed to swear to it in court, but *I* reckon there were four devices, placed low down to blast in all four directions. Never saw anything like *this* before"— he waved an arm at the blackened walls, presumably referring to the vast arrays of interconnected cages—"but if I had to guess, I'd say the bombs were placed to make sure they got all the animals, and nobody gave a damn about the rest of the wing or anything upstairs. Why would anyone do that, hey?"

The fireman was trying hard not to sound anxious, but there had to be at least as many rumors running around Widcombe Fire & Rescue Station as there were around East Central Police Station. Loyal public servants weren't allowed to say there was a war on, but they all knew full well that millions of people were dying of hyperflu in Mexico, North Africa, and Southeast Asia, and not because their chickens' resident viruses had been possessed by some kind of mutational madness.

"It's a mystery to me," Lisa admitted tactfully. "Who would want to assassinate five hundred thousand redundant mice? If there are any significant experiments running at the moment—and I doubt there's anything much concerned with infective viruses—those animals are upstairs, locked in steel safes surrounded by moats of bleach. There was nothing dangerous here; the lab assistants only wore masks and gloves because of the regs. All the mice on the outer walls were part of a famous experiment that had been running since before you and I were born."

"Doesn't do to be famous nowadays," the fireman observed. "Even if you're only an experiment. Hear about that TV weathergirl got whacked last week? Don't care what they say about the impending frustrations of containment—world can't get much crazier than it already is."

"Do you have any idea of what kind of devices were used?" Lisa asked, knowing she ought to ask the questions Mike Grundy would want answered, even if the investigation would be taken out of his hands before noon. "Have you seen anything like them before?"

"Better ask the experts," the black-haired man told her cautiously. "Most of the arson I see is kids with cans of gasoline or beer-bottle Molotovs."

"You mean that this was a professional job?"

"No such thing," he said contemptuously. "Nobody makes a living torching things. Anyway, every common or garden lunatic can decant cordon-bleu bomb-making instructions from the net. Kids only use gas cans because they're lazy and because gas gets the job done—if they wanted to do it the fancy way, they could easily find out how."

"Why was *this* job done the fancy way?" Lisa persisted. "What was accomplished here that couldn't have been done with a can of gasoline and a match?"

"One-hundred-percent mortality," he said succinctly. "Like I said, all the local materials, apart from flesh, are decently fire-retardant, so the structure held up far better than the inhabitants.

As you'd expect. Nothing's fire*proof*, of course, but labs in tall build-
ings have to observe the regulations. Mind you, fancy accelerants
aren't easy to buy or cook up in the kitchen, so it's unlikely to have
been actual *kids*. Some organization, I'd say. Some intelligence too.
If I were you, I'd assume—at least to start with—that what they
wanted to do was what they actually did. They certainly made sure
they didn't leave a single living thing alive."

Lisa looked up at the blackened wreckage looming eighteen or
twenty feet above her on three sides. She remembered the labels that
had been proudly pasted atop each vertical maze: LONDON; PARIS;
NEW YORK; ROME. There was no trace of them now—they, at least,
had not been made of fire-retardant plastic. The mouse cities weren't
Edgar Burdillon's experiment and never had been—he had always
regarded them as something of a space-wasting nuisance, so there
was a certain sour irony in the fact that he had gone to their defense
and been hurt in consequence. It was difficult to specify exactly
whose experiment the cities were now that their original founders
were long retired. They were simply *the* experiment—a hallowed
tradition, not merely of the Applied Genetics Department, but the
university's entire bioscience empire. So why, Lisa wondered, should
she feel such an acute sense of personal loss as she stared dumb-
founded at the ruins? Was it because the stability of the mouse
cities had somehow come to symbolize the stability of her own
personality—essentially undisturbed save for a couple of "chaotic
fluctuations" way back in the zero decade?

Lisa couldn't believe that any terrorist organization could possibly have a grudge against the mouse cities. Their size made them the
most conspicuous victims of the attack, but their destruction could
have been the unfortunate byproduct of a determination to destroy
some or all of the other mice kept in the lab complex: the library
specimens in the central section. *If so, which ones were the bombers
most likely to have been after—and why?*

The GM strains in the H Block had been the detritus of hun-

dreds, maybe thousands, of mostly discontinued experiments. Lisa
doubted that anyone currently active in the department was
acquainted with the nature and history of more than a few dozen of
them. There would be a supposedly complete catalogue on the computer, of course, but every data bank had to be kept up to date, and
everybody knew that records of that kind never matched reality with
any exactitude, because errors accumulated over the years and no
one could ever be bothered to sort them out—especially if nobody
cared passionately about the accuracy of the data. The animals in the
tightly sealed biohazard units on the upper floors would be comprehensively documented, but not these. It was possible that nobody
would ever know for sure exactly what had been lost.

The fireman had turned away while Lisa was thinking, and she
couldn't see any need to call him back. Someone was coming up the
corridor behind her and she put her head around the door to see
who it was, after briefly rubbing her smoke-irritated eyes.

Lisa recognized the campus security guard responsible for the
building. He'd been around almost as long as she had. His name was
Thomas Sweet, although Lisa realized with a slight shock that she'd
never actually had occasion to address him by name. He knew her
only as an occasional visitor, but she obviously seemed to him to be
a sympathetic figure—a possible ally against all the uniformed men
and "the slings and arrows of outrageous fortune." The deeply
mournful look brought forth a faint but heartrending echo in her
own being.

"Miss Friemann?" he said desolately. "Is that you?"

"Yes," she said, unworried by the fact that he hadn't called her
"Doctor," let alone "Inspector," although she certainly wasn't
unaware of it. "What happened, Mr. Sweet? Have you collected the
wafers from the security cams?"

"Gave them to a DS," Sweet assured her. "DI Grundy wants to
run through them again, but I've taken a peek and the bombers are
all wrapped up. Won't have left much evidence for you, thanks to the

so-called smart fabrics they were wearing." His own uniform was thoroughly dead, and Lisa guessed that his private wardrobe was even farther behind the times than her own.

"We'll get something," she said, trying to sound optimistic.

"Wasn't my fault, Miss," Sweet insisted. "They hacked into the system and sent false pictures to my VDU's. They had smartcards, you know—didn't trigger a single alarm."

"How many were there?" she asked, unable to remember whether she'd already been told.

"Three of them. Heads inside helmets—purpose-built, not ordinary motorcycling helmets. Looked like they were pretending to be SAS commandos. Only one thing I could make out for sure."

"What was that?"

"They were women. Two of them, at least. Third might have been a man—probably was, judging by the way he dragged the prof along the corridor like a sack of potatoes, but not the ones with dart guns. Doesn't make much difference these days. Remember that evil bitch you banged up after the Dog Riots thirty years back? What was it she called herself?"

"Keeper Pan," Lisa said automatically, slightly surprised by the readiness of her memory.

"Let her out again soon enough, though, didn't they? *Animal Liberation Front!* Is *this* what they call liberation?"

For the moment, Lisa thought, Animal Liberationists were probably the least likely suspects. Even in their heyday, animal libbers had used firebombs only against people. Mice were right at the bottom of their hierarchy of deserving species, way below pigs and rabbits, but they were innocents nevertheless. Keeper Pan and her friends would never have firebombed Mouseworld. Lisa did, however, pause to wonder whether the person who'd shot the phone out of her hand could possibly have been a woman. It had been too dark to judge the shape of the black shell-suit, but there might have been something else that would give her a clue, if only she could focus her memories. . . .

"He had a lot of stuff in here, didn't he?" the security man went on. "Stuff from way back—been inoculating mice with voodoo for forty years, they say, trying to work magic. Never came to anything much, though, did it?"

After a moment's confusion, Lisa realized that the *he* in Sweet's statement wasn't Edgar Burdillon, but Morgan Miller.

"Did they try to get into any of the other labs or offices?" she asked sharply.

Sweet shook his head. "Came straight here," he said. "Seemed to know exactly what they were doing. Didn't go to the upper floors at all. Why would they want to burn Mouseworld, Miss Friemann?"

"I don't know," Lisa said, marveling at the absurdity that the casual shooting of a once-eminent scientist did not seem bizarre at all by comparison with the destruction of a classic experiment in animal population dynamics. The fact that Ed Burdillon had been driven away in an ambulance, his life endangered by toxic fumes, hardly seemed to have registered with the old man.

"I tried to call him," said Sweet—still presumably referring to Morgan Miller. "So did the police. He isn't answering his phone."

"Is he away?" Lisa asked.

"Not that I know of," the security guard replied, still shaking his head in disbelief. "I tried Stella too, but everyone sets their answerphones these days, day and night alike. Too many nuisance calls, I guess."

Lisa knew that Stella Filisetti was Morgan Miller's latest research assistant. She didn't know if Morgan was screwing her, but she assumed that Sweet believed he was. It had been Morgan's habit since time immemorial, and he wasn't the kind of man to give up on his habits while there was still breath in his body.

Morgan had been seventy-three years old on his last birthday, but the last time Lisa had seen him, he'd assured her that he was "as fit as a flea." Seventy-three wasn't old these days, no matter what Police Admin and the top men at Fire & Rescue might think. The university certainly hadn't tried to force Morgan to retire, even though the younger members of the department were sometimes wont to say, with a sneer, that he hadn't produced a single worthwhile result in thirty years.

"I'm sorry, Miss," Thomas Sweet went on. "Maybe I should've called you too, but I didn't have your number. I dialed 999 to get the fire department and the police, then I tried Professor Burdillon's office. Couldn't get through, of course—I didn't know then that he'd gone downstairs. I tried Dr. Miller and got no reply, so I tried Stella, then Dr. Chan. No reply from any of them. Not *one*." He seemed deeply resentful of his failure, as if he suspected that he would be held responsible for it.

Their conversation was interrupted by another new arrival: a woman in her mid-thirties, with short-cropped hair and a raptorial attitude. Lisa had been hoping to see Mike Grundy before Judith Kenna found her, but it was too late now.

It didn't seem to have occurred to the chief inspector that there were times when a professional smile, however sardonic, wasn't entirely appropriate. "Mr. Sweet," she said mildly, "DS Hapgood would like another word with you."

She waited for the security guard to go through the doorway before continuing. "It's good of you to race out here to give us the benefit of your special expertise, Dr. Friemann, but you really should have remained at the other crime scene. Senior officers ought to set an example in procedural matters, don't you think? I see that you're hurt too. Is that a *bandage* on your hand? You really ought to have seen a doctor before rushing off like that—Detective Inspector Grundy seems to have been extremely irresponsible."

"Don't blame Mike," Lisa said frostily. "My home first-aid kit's ancient, but the dressing will do the job just as well as a fancy sealant. It's just a slight cut in an awkward place, plus a few scratches on my arm. There was nothing I could do at home but trample on evidence—and I *do* have special knowledge of this location and the victim. When the men from the Ministry of Defence get here, they'll want to talk to me."

"I'm sure they will," the chief inspector purred. "Have you formed any conclusions?"

"Not yet," Lisa admitted, wishing there were some vital clue in plain view whose significance she alone had been able to see. Desperate to even the score, she said: "Have you managed to figure out why they blacked out the center of town?"

"I think so," said Kenna, her smile becoming smug as well as sardonic. "I presume they did it partly to provide getaway cover for the vehicles carrying the bombers and your own intruders, but the main reason must have been to cloak the third—and probably most important—part of their scheme."

Lisa suppressed a curse and managed to sound completely neutral as she said: "Which was?"

"The abduction of Dr. Morgan Miller," the chief inspector informed her.

ou might have done better to go to that crime scene rather than this one, given that you're familiar with his house," the chief inspector went on while Lisa struggled to absorb the news. "As I said, DI Grundy seems to have acted rather recklessly in bringing you here without waiting to get a better view of the whole picture. You might still be able to advise the investigating officers as to what has been taken from Dr. Miller's house, but it's too late now to think of sending you over there before the MOD team arrives. The intruders destroyed his main homestation, just as they smashed yours, but they seem to have removed at least one obsolete machine. They haven't taken all his sequins, wafers, and diskettes—but that's probably because they'd have needed a van to transport them in."

"Abduction?" Lisa echoed, still fixated on the first sentence of Kenna's little speech. "Morgan's been *kidnapped?*"

"I very much doubt that they intend to hold him for ransom," the younger woman replied insouciantly. "I think it's far more likely that they want him to tell them something before they kill him, don't you? I don't suppose that by any chance you have any idea of what it is they want to know?"

"No," said Lisa shortly, then realized she'd been wrong-footed again.

"Well," Kenna said, relishing the carefully hoarded line, "you obviously didn't know him quite as well as you thought you did. And he evidently didn't confide in you quite as much as the people who went after him thought he did. Mr. Smith will be disappointed."

"Who's Mr. Smith?" was the only counter Lisa could improvise.

"Peter Grimmett Smith is the MOD man who'll be taking charge of the investigation. He'll be working closely with us, of course. I daresay he'll find plenty for DI Grundy to do. I'm not so sure that we'll need much more from *you* once you've been debriefed, though—unless you can exercise your memory sufficiently to remember some little secret you and Dr. Miller might have kept between you. One that might help to explain four firebombs, two burglaries, two cases of malicious wounding, and an abduction." The professional smile had vanished now.

It hadn't occurred to Lisa until the conversation reached that pitch of sarcasm that Judith Kenna might honestly believe that she was concealing something. Nor had it occurred to her that the dislike Kenna had never tried to conceal might run deeper than mere irritation and ageism prejudice—but she considered the hypothesis now.

Twenty years ago, Judith Kenna had served a brief term as one of Mike Grundy's sergeants, and now she was his boss. Kenna had guessed, of course, that Mike must have told Lisa that he had screwed her way back when, but however embarrassed the chief inspector might be about that particular *little secret*, it surely wasn't grounds for a serious hate campaign. Kenna had doubtless also guessed that while Mike had been sleeping on Lisa's couch following the breakup of his marriage, he hadn't always stayed on the couch—but what difference did that make? Lisa couldn't believe that mere jealousy was a factor—but if not jealousy, what? Was it just that Lisa wouldn't play ball when Kenna had begun trying to hasten her toward retirement? Or was it just that Kenna's ego was so insecure that she didn't want to have anyone around who was older, wiser, and independent-minded?

Knowing that she had to say *something*, Lisa eventually said: "If there was any secret, it was between Morgan and Ed Burdillon. Are you *sure* he's been abducted?"

"Of course not," the chief inspector replied. "There are signs of a struggle, but that would be easy enough to fake. Are *you* suggesting that Morgan Miller might be the man behind all this—the one who sent bombers to the university and burglars to raid your flat?"

"Don't be absurd," Lisa retorted. "I was wondering if he might have been away when the burglars came to call. Have you got the abduction on tape?"

"Probably not," Kenna told her. "Unfortunately, Dr. Miller's house doesn't appear to have any security cameras, not even in the hallway or on the porch. It's a very old house—and he's a very old man. Twentieth-century habits die hard, as you obviously know. The street cams will have picked *something* up in spite of the blackout, but it won't be much and they probably won't prove anything one way or the other. Tracking the getaway will be very difficult indeed."

"This is crazy," Lisa said helplessly. "It doesn't make any sense."

"It certainly doesn't," agreed the chief inspector. "But whoever did this had reason enough to send at least seven people to formulate a plan of extraordinary complexity. *They* think it makes sense—and we have to figure out what sense they think it makes. Continue your inquiries, Dr. Friemann—but don't go back to the labs with Dr. Forrester. Mr. Smith will want you close at hand when he arrives, and for some time afterward. We'll probably need you to look through Miller's house in the hope that you can give us some information about the items that have been removed, but Mr. Smith will have to decide when. In the meantime, ask one of Fire and Rescue's backup paramedics to treat your hand and arm."

Having given these instructions, Judith Kenna turned on her heel and left. Lisa watched the chief inspector walk back along the corridor, moving with quasimilitary rigidity. While she was still standing there, dumbly, the remaining firemen pushed past her, reeling up two flabby hoses as they went. It wasn't until they'd all disappeared that Mike Grundy shuffled around the corner where he'd presumably been waiting out of sight.

"Sorry," he said. "Didn't realize quite how much shit had hit the fan—the news about Miller's house being turned over only just came through. What the hell's going on, Lisa?"

"I don't know," Lisa said, wishing that she did. *You'll work it out*, the man—or woman—who'd shot her had said. *If we don't have what we need, we'll be back, and next time. . . .* Now Lisa wished that she'd heard the end of that sentence. There was another that seemed even more ominous in present retrospect. *Nobody cares about you, you stupid bitch!* the distorted voice had informed her. *Miller never cared, and no matter what he promised you, you'll be dead soon enough.*

But Morgan had never promised her anything: not love, not marriage, not partnership, not wealth, not even a substantial share of his meager wisdom.

Whatever information she was supposed to have must still be safe and secure in Morgan Miller's mind—but if his captors thought they were going to beat it out of him, they had another think coming. Lisa was convinced that if there was one man in the world who would never give in to pressure or temptation, it was Morgan Miller.

"I suppose it isn't likely to be personal," Mike mused, carefully leaving out the inflection that would have made it into a question. "Whoever did this was attacking Applied Genetics, not Burdillon. Why else take the trouble to drag him clear of the fire? If their reason's political, they'll probably want to brag about it, but if not . . ." He trailed off temptingly, but Lisa had no other suggestion ready.

She wondered if it was possible that the bombers had gone after Mouseworld simply because it was a classic experiment, a living legend. Extreme Gaeans, way out on the green end of the spectrum, might conceivably believe that hitting Mouseworld might help them make a point about the *real* London, Paris, New York, and Rome and their plight within the context of the *other* war that dare not speak its name: the war for the salvation of the ecosphere. But what, if so, was the motive for Morgan's abduction?

She recalled then that Thomas Sweet had told her that Chan Kwai Keung wasn't answering his phone, and that he hadn't been able to get a hold of Stella Filisetti either. It was possible that the register of crimes patiently listed by Judith Kenna would expand even further before daybreak. Chan lived way out in the country, so it would take time for Mike's men to check out his address, but Stella Filisetti probably lived closer to the campus. The men sent to bring her in for questioning should be reporting shortly. The true magnitude of the crime would be evident soon enough.

Mike was still waiting for a comment.

"If their target really was the cities, and they're doing it to make a point," Lisa said hesitantly, "they'll have to ram the point home somehow. Maybe Kenna was wrong about the ransom demand—maybe we'll get one as soon as the TV news people wake up."

Mike immediately picked up the thread of the argument. "We have to be looking at some kind of organization with an inside connection," he said. "They had a smartcard pass and the combinations of all the doors they needed to get through. In a way, *that's* the weirdest thing about the whole operation. They got through your door, and Miller's, just as easily. They also switched off the power to a substantial slice of the city, and they knew my mobile-phone number. That's a *lot* of inside information, Lis—and it's from at least three different insides, unless . . ."

"Unless it's *our* inside information," Lisa finished for him. "They're trying to set me up with this 'Traitor' crap, aren't they? Why would they do that, if not to distract attention from someone else?"

"You don't suppose it could be Ms. Kenna, do you?" He wasn't serious. He had seen Lisa's mood darken again, and he was trying to compensate.

"No," she said, for form's sake. "Not her—but not Morgan, either. Not me and not you and not Ed Burdillon. But it has to be someone who knows more than he or she should about at least three of those five and the places where we live and work. If it's not someone close to us, it must be one hell of a hacker. The Gaean Libs are rumored to have high-powered hackers in the ranks, but all the best poachers turn gamekeeper as soon as they can. If we've been hacked to that extent, it's far more likely to be someone working for one of the megacorps. But what would convince a megacorps that a quiet backwater like the fourth campus of a provincial university has any secrets worth stealing? That would be one hell of a mistake—if it *is* a mistake."

"If it *is* a megacorp op," Mike observed glumly, "the MOD won't get to the bottom of it. Not that they'd tell us if they did. Can't be, though. Mayhem and kidnapping isn't the megacorp way. They already own the whole fucking world, thanks to the big smash-and-grab raid that fucked up the Eubank, the Fed, and everybody's pension funds. Their carpetbaggers can buy anyone they want for next to nothing, even out of a university. Especially out of a university. Where else can you and I go—if Kenna manages to ease us out—but straight into the pocket of the Cabal?"

It was all true, Lisa conceded. Ever since the great stock-market *bouleversement* of '25, a handful of megacorporations had gradually taken effective control of the world. The power of national governments had been on the wane for a century, but the engineered crisis had administered the coup de grâce. The "gray power" everyone talked about was just ballot-box power; no matter how it contrived to expand the legally sanctioned work opportunities of the over-fifties, it couldn't conjure up any new employers. If you wanted to work, you had to take your begging bowl to the megacorps, and if you had a valuable secret of any kind, you had to sell it to the megacorps. It was no good trying to play one corp off against another, because they all worked as a team. The broadsheets called them "the Ultimate Cartel," but that was just politeness; the tabloids were right to prefer "the Cabal." Megacorp publicity claimed that the substitute term had arisen because tabloid editors were as illiterate as their readers, not because anyone had knowledge of an actual secret conspiracy, but everyone with half a brain took that as one more sign of their undoubted guilt.

Mike Grundy's gaze had wandered. Lisa followed it, tracking across the appalling blackness of the spoiled walls and the crude stumps of what had been the projecting sections of the central H Block. The stink was still appalling. No matter how hard the cold wind blew through the empty window frames, the foul odor kept on renewing itself, emanating with seemingly relentless fervor from the roasted fur of half a million mice.

"Let's get out of here, Lis," Grundy said. "There's nothing we can do. Want to sneak a look at the security tapes before they're commandeered?"

"Kenna told me to get my cuts properly cleaned and dressed," Lisa replied uneasily. "Given her deep-seated conviction that I'm too firmly stuck in the past to be useful to today's go-ahead police force, it might have been a bad idea to let her see me sporting a Stone Age dressing and multiple bloodstains on my dead sweatshirt."

"The Fire and Rescue paramedics are downstairs," Mike said. "We can share the elevator."

Lisa was by no means reluctant to be hustled back to the gaping doorway, but she couldn't resist the temptation to take one last panoramic look at the ruins of Mouseworld.

"Seventy years," she murmured. "Eight hundred generations. All gone in a momentary holocaust. Hideous."

"You can say that again," the detective muttered—but he didn't mean what she meant. He wasn't a scientist. He didn't understand. It wasn't his fault, of course, but it was a gulf between them nevertheless. There had always been a gulf between them, even when they were at their closest, in the traumatic weeks after Helen had thrown him out. At the time, Lisa had thought it was the specter of Morgan Miller that had held her back from any fuller engagement with Mike's need or his wayward emotions, but now she realized it had been something more fundamental.

They were both detectives, in their different ways, but they had never had the same goals. Mike was a man who thought in terms of offenses and results, while Lisa thought in terms of puzzles, clues, and solutions, but even that wasn't the heart of it. Mouseworld had meant something to Lisa, not merely as a symbol of the world's historical predicament—which it had been set up to be—but as a symbol of humankind's well-meaning, ill-directed, and ineffectual attempts to come to terms with that predicament. To Mike, it was just a mess of mice, which had stunk to high heaven even before it was torched.

ike Grundy's subordinates had commandeered Thomas Sweet's
office, partly for the sake of the video surveillance cameras and
partly for the sake of the percolator. When Grundy turned up, with
Lisa still in tow, a constable in plainclothes immediately poured each
a cup of coffee. Lisa hesitated before accepting hers, but the residual
smoke and fumes had parched her throat and she knew that the caffeine would help her fight off the inconvenient tiredness. She took
the cup. Grundy poured milk into his own cup and then offered the
carton to her, but she shook her head.

"There's nothing much on the tapes," said the sergeant who'd
been patiently running them through. Lisa had never met him
before, so she assumed that he was part of Judith Kenna's infusion of
new blood. Grundy introduced him as Jerry Hapgood.

"Three individuals, five-seven, five-nine, and five-eleven," Hapgood went on. "Two definitely look woman-shaped—can't really tell
about the tallest one, although it took serious muscle power to tow
Burdillon to safety without hardly slowing down. Both of the women
were armed, one with a real gun and one with a silly dart pistol. The
one with the real gun—looks like an antique, probably been mothballed for fifty years—covered Burdillon while the other turned to
fire, so they must have had a plan of sorts for dealing fairly gently
with anyone who interrupted them. They sailed through all the
doors, and they knew the routines of Sweet's people well enough to
be in and out without giving them any opportunity to interrupt."

The bleeper attached to Grundy's waistband went off and he
plucked the phone from his belt. After identifying himself, he listened for a full two minutes, saving up the expletive until there was
a suitable gap in the information flow. Lisa knew by the way the DI's
eyes sought out her face that the news was expected, but disappoint-

ing. She had guessed long before the phone was back in its holster.

"They all got away," Mike reported glumly. "Traffic picked up the trace of a likely vehicle moving away from your place, but it headed straight into the blackout. Same with the van that took the bombers away from the campus."

"Both stolen?" DS Hapgood asked, obviously assuming that the question was merely rhetorical.

"Actually, no," Grundy said. "Both registration plates came up 'No Record.' Not even write-off salvage—never issued."

Lisa couldn't see that it helped much. If the perpetrators had put false plates on their own vehicles, that gave her people a chance of matching up forensic evidence if ever the vehicles could be traced—but if they'd used stolen vehicles that they'd subsequently dumped, they might have left evidential traces in them, even if they'd torched them, and time was of the essence. "Anything at all on the people who took Morgan?" she asked.

The question was addressed to Mike, but it was the sergeant who took it upon himself to answer. "Nobody saw or heard a thing," he said. "Detached house, nice neighborhood, four in the morning, power out—what do you expect? We still don't know for sure that he was taken. He was definitely at home the previous evening, but he could have gone out under his own steam after the blackout."

"Why would he do that?" Lisa countered.

"How would I know?" Hapgood said, seemingly stifling the temptation to add an insubordinate expletive by way of punctuation. "According to Sweet, the guy was the next best thing to a comic-book weird scientist. Obsessive-compulsive type."

From the corner of her eye, Lisa saw Mike Grundy wince. The sergeant obviously wasn't yet party to all the relevant gossip.

"His work was reckoned as an obsession only because he never found what he was looking for," Lisa observed calmly. "If his particular Holy Grail hadn't proved quite so elusive, his single-mindedness would be called commitment and he'd have a book-length entry in every encyclopedia on the net."

"Holy Grail?" Hapgood queried sarcastically. For a detective, he was surprisingly slow on the uptake.

"The prize," she said. "The panacea."

"A cure for hyperflu?"

Lisa supposed that it was a natural guess, even though the hyperflus had been around for only seven years. "Not a cure for a specific disease," she informed the young man wearily. "Not even for a whole class of diseases. Something even more basic than that. A general-purpose, targetable transformer that would make *all* gene therapies easier to administer and more precise. When he started out, cancers were still a major killer and everyone was trying to tailor virus transformers to take them out—'magic bullets,' the jargon used to call them. Morgan was working at the most fundamental level, trying to design a vector that could take any DNA cargo into any type of specialized cell and deliver it to any chromosomal address, according to need or demand. If he'd found it, it would have provided a method of attacking all genetic-deficiency diseases, all cancers, and most kinds of injury. One-shot medicine—just turn up at the clinic, list your symptoms, get your tailor-made injection, go home cured. A vector like that would have had other functions too, but the main incentive was medical. As individual solutions to specific problems turned up year after year, though, the pressure to develop a multipurpose delivery service eased off.

"In the end, Morgan seemed to most of his colleagues to be searching for a solution to a problem that no longer existed. It didn't lessen his determination to find it."

"And did he?" asked the sergeant, fishing for a motive.

"No," Lisa admitted. "And even if he had, it wouldn't be worth kidnapping him to get it—not unless someone's dreamed up a brand-new killer app that no one else managed to think of during the last forty years."

"But that kind of research *is* war relevant, isn't it?" Mike put in. "If Morgan had found it, it would provide a general defense against biowarfare agents, wouldn't it?"

"Actually, no," said Lisa. "We already have defenses against the individual hyperflus and their kin—the problem is that they mutate so quickly and so promiscuously that they keep one step ahead of our immune systems. Morgan's new delivery system wouldn't get around that problem. Nor would it fortify us against the *next* wave of biowarfare agents, which will undoubtedly be transformers themselves. If this mess has anything to do with Morgan's research, it must relate to something he found by accident—but if Morgan had discovered *anything* relevant to biowar defense, he'd have handed it straight to the MOD. He wouldn't even have asked for a quid pro quo. Obsessive-compulsive he might be, but he's not conscienceless, and he would *never* try to play political or commercial games with something that might save lives."

"According to Sweet," DS Hapgood put in, "he was nutty about overpopulation. Just like the Gaean Libs. Always argued that plague war was inevitable, and not entirely a bad thing, Sweet said."

"That's right," said Lisa. "Morgan always said that everything that's happening now had been inevitable for nearly a century, and easily foreseeable to anyone with half a mind at least since the days of his childhood. He's always argued that the coming collapse would have an upside as well as a down—but that doesn't mean he regards it as any less hideous and tragic than it seems to be working out to be. He'd never have admitted to obsession, but he always pleaded guilty to being a victim of the Cassandra Complex: the sense of powerlessness and world-weariness that comes from knowing that terrible things are going to happen without anyone being able to prevent them. The Gaean Libs and other pious econuts might be prepared to tell the world that the death of millions of people is a blessing and exactly what Mother Ecosphere needs, and that we all deserve everything we get, but Morgan Miller despised that kind of sanctimony. If he'd stumbled across a cure for hyperflu, he'd have done everything he could to get it to everyone who might benefit from it. Believe me, *I know.*"

She became uncomfortably aware that everybody in the room was staring at her, embarrassed by the intensity of her polemic. Jerry

Hapgood had finally got the message, and he shut up—but Mike Grundy had heard that kind of sermon far too many times to give it his full attention, and he was still mulling over the conversation he and Lisa had had at the door of Mouseworld. "What if it weren't a new means of defense?" he asked quietly. "What if it were a new means of attack?"

That, Lisa had to admit, was a horse of a different color. If Morgan *had* had a secret, and a powerful motive for keeping it. . . .

"This is all rather hypothetical, isn't it?" said Judith Kenna's voice from the doorway of the surveillance room. "Wouldn't you be better employed helping the constable scan the tapes, DS Hapgood? Have you seen the paramedic yet, Dr. Friemann?"

"It was my fault," Mike put in quickly. "We were sidetracked."

"I needed a cup of coffee more than I needed sealant," Lisa said. "Given that you ordered me to stick around instead of going back to the labs with Steve or to Professor Miller's house, I thought I'd be best employed in helping to fit the various pieces of the puzzle together. If your people are trying to establish Morgan Miller as the prime suspect in this affair, they're barking up the wrong tree, and if I can direct them to more profitable lines of inquiry, I might be able to save you a great deal of work."

"How many of the mice in the burned-out lab belonged to Morgan Miller?" Kenna asked abruptly. The eyes that she fixed on Lisa had a distinctly predatory gleam.

"I doubt that there were more than a couple of hundred involved in current experiments," Lisa told her. "Stella Filisetti will probably be able to give you an exact number, and a full account of any transformations Morgan had carried out on them."

"What about mice left over from old experiments?"

"I don't know," Lisa admitted. "He probably had a hand in designing twenty or thirty disease models, and at least as many strains transformed for other purposes."

The predatory gaze switched targets, focusing on Mike Grundy. "Do we know for sure that Miller went home yesterday evening?"

the chief inspector asked. "The officers at the house have surely confirmed that much?"

"Yes," he acknowledged.

"Is there any evidence that anyone else was present? Did he have any visitors, apart from the unwanted ones?"

Lisa inferred the question meant that Stella Filisetti wasn't at home, or anywhere else that she could be easily located. Mike seemed to hesitate between a straightforward negative answer and the more honest rejoinder that although nobody had reported any such evidence, he didn't really know. Eventually, he said nothing. Instead, he picked up his mobile and called the officer at the scene for an update. There was a long pause while they waited for a response.

Then, "No," he reported. "The street cams show that he came home alone, and they don't show anyone else approaching the house while the power was still on. Although there's no video or audio record, it looks as if he was in bed, asleep, until something woke him. The debris suggests a relatively brief fight—either they hit him a lot harder than he hit them, or they put him out with tranquilizer-loaded darts. They hacked his locks as easily as they hacked Lisa's. Nobody had to be inside to let them in. One of the items taken seems to have been an ancient PC; the other may have been a more recent stand-alone."

"They were probably looking for something that he didn't want to put on a networked machine," Judith Kenna concluded. "Something he might have backed up on a wafer or a sequin that he gave to you, Dr. Friemann. That's the way it looks, isn't it?"

"Morgan never gave me any backup wafers," Lisa said. "If that's what the people who burgled my flat were looking for, they were mistaken."

"Or misinformed," Kenna pointed out. "They must have had confidence in their source, don't you think? They must have thought it was *necessary* to secure all three targets: the mice, the data, the backup. But there might, of course, have been *four* targets."

She presumably meant Stella Filisetti—but Mike Grundy was

quick to say: "Or five. We still haven't established contact with Dr. Chan."

"But it must be significant that Miller's computers have been taken," Kenna countered, "and that Dr. Friemann's backups were cleared out. If Miller isn't the perpetrator, he's certainly the key. Do you suppose, Dr. Friemann, that he might have placed a wafer or a sequin on your shelves without your even knowing it?"

"Not recently," Lisa replied coldly. "He hasn't visited my home for over a year."

"Of course," the chief inspector said with a perfunctory nod. "You've . . . moved on since then."

Lisa clenched her fists reflexively, and regretted it when pain flared up in the wound she'd only just grown used to protecting.

"Morgan would never do something like that," she said.

"But he could have discovered the codes to your locks easily enough, if he'd wanted to?"

"He wouldn't have wanted to," Lisa insisted. She barely prevented herself from naming the one person who *did* know the codes to both her locks—but Judith Kenna already knew that name.

"Do you know the codes to *his* locks, Dr. Friemann?" Kenna went on inexorably.

For a moment, Lisa considered raising the possibility that Morgan might have changed his codes, as everyone was supposed to do at regular intervals, but she knew full well that he wouldn't have done any such thing, anymore than she had. "Yes," she said finally. "And I could have told the bombers how to get into the labs, at least as far as Mouseworld—but I didn't. Neither did Morgan."

"I'm merely trying to fit the pieces of the puzzle together," Judith Kenna assured her vindictively. "You see, I can't think of anyone else except you and Morgan Miller who had ready access to *all* the necessary information. The missing research assistant might well have been able to tell someone how to open Miller's locks, but I presume that neither she nor Dr. Chan could have told anyone how to get through yours."

"That's not all they did," Mike Grundy pointed out. "They blacked out half the town. Anyone who could hack their way into *that* system could hack any number of locks. If Miller, Chan, or Burdillon had found something that someone else wanted to get a hold of, we'll have to look a lot farther than their friends and colleagues. We ought to backtrack their communications—trace every phone call and every e-mail, internal and external. That's where we'll find the clue to what this is all about—because that's where the people who did all this must have found their motive."

"I'm afraid that *we* won't be able to do any such thing," Kenna informed him—and she really did seem slightly regretful. "The MOD has already placed all those records under a security blanket. If we're lucky, they might let us in on whatever they find—but that will depend on how much help they think they need. If Morgan Miller is still being held in the area that was blacked out, they'll probably let us help them find him—and get him back, if possible—but if the people who have him manage to smuggle him out and away, we'll be out of the loop. I'd like to ensure that that doesn't happen, if possible."

Lisa realized that Judith Kenna would far rather that this turned out to be a local operation, and that it really was Morgan or one of his friends and colleagues who was behind it. If a megacorp *were* behind it, the likelihood was that Morgan would never be seen again and that no one outside the secret meeting places of the Cabal would ever know where or why he had been taken.

She really would like it best of all if I were involved, Lisa thought. *She'd rather find one of her own officers guilty—if only slightly—than get nothing at all. Always provided, I suppose, that the officer in question was due for retirement anyway. And if any stray mud were to stick to Mike—well, I guess she'd just grin and bear it. And grin again. Unfortunately for her, I really didn't do it—and unfortunately for me, I really haven't got a clue to who did, or why.*

SIX

I f you've finished your coffee," Chief Inspector Kenna said to Lisa, "I'll walk you to the paramedic station."

"I can find it on my own," Lisa assured her.

"I'm going the same way," the younger woman pointed out. "The helicopter from London should be here soon, and I need to make sure there's enough clearance in the parking area to let it land."

As they walked out of the building into the cold dawn air, Lisa said: "You don't really think I had anything to do with this, do you?"

"I certainly don't think you're allied with the perpetrators," Kenna assured her. "But the fact that they decided to include you in their set of targets suggests that you do have *something* to do with it, wouldn't you say?"

"Everyone is supposed to keep important data backed up at a remote location," Lisa said. "I'm one of Morgan Miller's oldest friends. Maybe they just assumed that he'd keep backups at my place—not realizing, I guess, that Morgan doesn't do very many of the things that everyone's supposed to do."

"Perhaps they did," the chief inspector admitted.

They had drawn level with the small ambulance that had trailed the fire engines; its two staff were sitting inside looking bored, having not had a single significant case of smoke-inhalation to treat. The young woman who leaped out in response to Lisa's gesture with her towel-enshrouded hand seemed glad of the opportunity to do something.

Judith Kenna looked carefully around while the paramedic unwrapped the bloodstained dressing and peeled back the sleeve of Lisa's undershirt, tut-tutting all the while.

"I know it probably said 'Sterile' on the package," the paramedic said, "but this patch must be thirty years old. You really ought to get a modern medical kit—and the fabric of this undershirt isn't nearly smart enough to cope with gashes like these. There are much better ones on the market nowadays."

"Dr. Friemann was at home," the chief inspector put in, anxious to deflect any implied criticism of the facilities at her station. "You know how it is with home kits—you never replace them until you use them up. And I don't suppose responsiveness to injury was uppermost in her mind when she bought the undergarment."

Lisa grit her teeth and said nothing.

The paramedic tut-tutted again over the various wounds before reaching for a tube of sealant. "You'll never get the stain out of that tunic," she observed. Her own uniform, unlike Judith Kenna's, was made of ultramodern fibers that were presumably as expert at mopping up blood as they were at mopping up sweat and tears.

Lisa tried to take the criticism as stoically as she was taking the treatment, although the anesthetic effect of the sealant couldn't offer much protection to her self-esteem. In the hope of deflecting the censorious gaze of Judith Kenna's eyes from her hand, she said: "On the other hand, if the kidnappers were just guessing where Morgan might have kept his backup wafers, they probably wouldn't have contented themselves with raiding my place. If Morgan had found something recently, they might have been more likely to look for it at Stella Filisetti's place." She was fishing, to find out whether Kenna knew whether or not Morgan had been screwing his research assistant. When Kenna didn't bite, Lisa added: "Unless, of course, it was Stella who told them my flat was the more likely hiding place."

"How well do you know Stella Filisetti?" Kenna was quick to ask.

"Hardly at all," Lisa admitted. "I've only met her a couple of times. Morgan never told me anything about her, except for a few passing remarks about her radfem sympathies."

"Some of the nicest people I know are radfems," the chief inspector commented mildly. "None of them pose any threat to national security."

"I didn't mean to imply that he disapproved," Lisa said swiftly.

"You have radfem acquaintances yourself, I believe," Kenna added.

Lisa had to stop herself from asking the chief inspector where that tidbit of information had come from. Instead, she said: "I've known one or two." Her first assumption was that Kenna must be talking about Arachne West—but then she remembered that she had had more recent and much longer-enduring contact with another proud wearer of the label, and wondered how significant the chief inspector's choice of the word "acquaintances" had been. Arachne West had almost qualified as a friend once—but Helen Grundy never had.

If Helen was numbered by Kenna as one of those radfems who were "among the nicest people I know," Lisa thought, that might go a long way to explain why she was so down on Mike—and why she might disapprove so strongly of Lisa's having taken Mike in for a while after Helen threw him out.

"All done," said the paramedic brightly. "None of the cuts is bad enough to need syntheflesh—just peel off the sealant in three or four days. How'd you do it?"

"Somebody shot a telephone receiver out of my hand," Lisa said laconically. "It could have been worse—at least the shooter waited until I'd taken it away from my ear."

The young woman grinned as if it were a joke, then went back to join her partner.

"Is Stella Filisetti a suspect?" Lisa asked the chief inspector.

"We're treating everyone as a suspect until we know otherwise," Kenna replied predictably, "including your friend Sweet. Security people usually have ways of accumulating information on people with whom they come into regular contact."

"He's another casual acquaintance," Lisa said. "But it would take a master of disguise to seem that stupid if he were actually the criminal mastermind who planned all this."

Kenna was still watching her closely, speculatively, if not actually suspiciously. The chief inspector was obviously not convinced that Morgan Miller hadn't entrusted her with a precious backup wafer, perhaps containing the secret of the Ultimate Weapon of Biowarfare. Lisa realized that it might not be easy to persuade Kenna that the burglars had simply made a mistake—understandably enough, given that she couldn't quite convince herself that they had *simply* made a mistake.

If a mistake had been made—and it had been, Lisa silently insisted—it couldn't have been simple. The reasoning that had led the would-be burglars to her must be as convoluted as it was powerful. The fact that she was Morgan's oldest friend wasn't enough. Nor was the fact that she had once been his mistress. There had to be something else. But if they suspected that she and Morgan had discovered a biowarfare weapon *together*, when were the two of them supposed to have done it? Surely nothing that they had worked on back in the first decade of the century could possibly have any relevance to the hyperflu epidemic, or whatever agent of the apocalypse would follow in its train.

Or could it?

Lisa was grateful to realize that Judith Kenna was no longer looking at her. The chief inspector had been distracted by the distant sound of a helicopter's throbbing engine.

"That'll be your Mr. Smith," Lisa observed, hoping her relief didn't show too clearly. "He's made good time."

"Yes, he has," the chief inspector agreed, her tone finely balanced between satisfaction and regret. "I'll have to brief him. You'd better wait with DI Grundy."

All but one of the fire engines had now been withdrawn, so there was plenty of space in the parking lot for the chopper to set down. Lisa watched four men climb down from the belly of the aircraft. They were all wearing black overcoats, which seemed as distinctive as a uniform—much more so, in fact, than the relatively casual shell-suits of the paramedics, let alone Mike's plainclothesmen.

Lisa had had contact with MOD field operatives on numerous

occasions, but she didn't recognize any of these men. She couldn't even guess which of the many available sets of cryptic initials might be used to identify their department. They looked like businessmen, but that wasn't inappropriate to the kind of work they would be routinely engaged in. The government for which they worked was not one of those conventionally regarded as a mere puppet of the megacorps, but its supposed independence meant that its dealings with the corps were all the more intricate and challenging. The only way to compete with crocodiles, or even to avoid becoming crocodile food, was to cultivate crocodilean habits.

Lisa thought she identified Peter Grimmett Smith even at a distance, and her guess was confirmed when she saw him shake Judith Kenna's hand. He was a tall, dark-haired individual, handsome in a stately sort of way. He seemed to be tired and fractious. Lisa was perversely pleased to note that he must be in his sixties, easily old enough to be the chief inspector's father.

Poor Judith, she thought. *Just can't get away from the older generation. Mike, me, Sweet, the senior fireman, and now the man from the Ministry. Is his expertise past its use-by date too, I wonder? Is this his last mission before he retires to the old bee farm? If he's waving the flag for gray power, he's really going to jangle her nerves, especially if he succeeds in getting to the bottom of all this while she's still flummoxed.*

She wondered briefly whether the spook's name really was Smith, but decided that it probably was. No one used Smith as a nom de guerre anymore; it was too *twentieth century.* The Grimmett, which presumably served to distinguish him from all the other Peter Smiths on the civil-service roster, was a bit of a giveaway.

Lisa was tempted to hang around and watch, but the advent of daylight hadn't banished the relentless wind and she'd neglected to put on her own black overcoat before leaving home. She retreated into the building and went back to Sweet's office, where Mike Grundy's men were still impatiently gathering information and trying to judge its significance. Sweet had rejoined them, but no one seemed to be restricting their conversation in case he might be an enemy keeping tabs on their progress.

"They've got to be local," Jerry Hapgood was saying. "The blackout proves that."

"No, it doesn't," Mike told him. "The blackout only proves that they were clever enough to know they couldn't transport Miller crosscountry without being tracked, unless they could work a concealed switch. We don't know that they didn't bring him out of the blackout before Powergen got its act together—and even if they bring him out now in the trunk of some commuter's car or the back of a pickup, we don't stand the slightest chance of intercepting him, even with real containment measures about to come into force."

"This whole containment thing's a joke," once of the PC's observed. "It'll all be show no matter how far it goes, so that the government can pretend they're doing *something*. When hyperflu arrives, if it hasn't already, there'll be no way to pin it down. If we don't have a cure soon, it'll run riot."

Lisa knew that the PC was right. Even the strictest imaginable containment strategy would leave far too many loopholes where a cityplex like Greater Bristol was concerned. The inhabitants of the Outer Hebrides might manage to control traffic between the islands and the mainland carefully enough to keep out viruses, but Britain was far too overcrowded and far too *busy*. If the First Plague War really were shaping up to be World War Three—and it was difficult to see how the viruses could be offset before the epidemic was worldwide—then the Bristol cityplex would eventually find itself in the front line. So-called pre-containment measures couldn't keep Morgan Miller in the East Central area any more than they could keep hyperflu out of it if his well-organized captors wanted to remove him.

"The men from the Ministry are here," Lisa said, although she knew they must have heard the helicopter. "They'll be taking over the thinking and planning."

"Doesn't mean they'll carry the can if Miller slips through the net," Hapgood pointed out. "Always blame the messenger—isn't that the thinking?"

"Better not let the chief inspector hear you talking like that," Mike Grundy observed as he moved away from the group to stand closer to Lisa. "Okay, Lis?" he asked, nodding toward her sealed cuts.

"Fine," she told him. "Numb now. Did you manage to get a team out to my place?"

"Yes. Nothing yet. The burglars' vehicle was parked on the school grounds, but there's nothing there that might help us to identify it. Your neighbors say they didn't hear anything until the shots were fired, and they didn't come out of hiding in time to see anything. The paint on the door might have trapped a fiber or two, but it looks as if the bullets they fired into your equipment might be our best bet. Together with the dart in Burdillon's body, they're the only solid evidence we have. If we can trace either one of the handguns, we're away . . . but how far we'll get without the telephone records, I wouldn't like to say. You look tired. You can't go home, but you should get some sleep—can I return the favor you did me when I was between residences?"

"Kenna wants us both here, at least until Smith says we can go," Lisa told him. "Anyway, given her attitude, it might not be a good idea for me to stay at your place. Does she know Helen?"

"God, I hope not," Mike said. "Why?"

"Just something she said. Stella Filisetti has radfem connections."

"*She* might know Helen, then," Grundy observed. "I doubt that Kenna would get involved with any kind of organization or movement outside the force, however respectable—and with people like your old friend Ms. West still around, radfem isn't respectable yet. Kenna's far too principled to associate with the Arachne Wests of this world, and getting palsy-walsy with Helen would be only one step removed. No matter how determined she might be to persuade me to retire quietly, I doubt that she'd go to Helen for ammunition. Anyway, that's all water under the bridge. Do you think Filisetti's the insider? Any particular reason, apart from the fact that she's not at home?" He didn't add: *and probably screwing your old boyfriend.* He was too scrupulous.

"If Morgan discovered something interesting," Lisa observed, "Stella would be in the best position to know about it. If he took precautions to conceal it from her, that might have made her all the more curious. The only flaw in the theory is that Morgan *couldn't* have discovered some state-of-the-art biological weapon by accident. That's the stuff of cheap technothrillers—and he wasn't doing that kind of work. If it really is cloak-and-dagger business, we'd do better to focus our attention on Ed Burdillon and Chan. Do the security wafers indicate how Ed became aware of their presence?"

"No. Do you think *he* might have been the inside man? They could have arranged to knock him over to give him an alibi of sorts."

"No," said Lisa. "Ed's straight. So's Morgan. Neither of them would have tried to hide something useful to national security, or even something valuable in purely commercial terms."

"Unless they had a good reason," Mike pointed out, "or the temptation was so great that even an honest man could be corrupted. Everyone has his price."

"Not Morgan. And it's still the stuff of cheap technothrillers."

"It's their script, not ours," Mike reminded her. "If they're crazy enough, they probably think like a cheap technothriller. Anyway, remember what you said earlier about the Cassandra Complex. Morgan Miller has spent fifty years preaching that a population crash is inevitable, even though everyone with half a brain can see that we can't carry on increasing our numbers without completely fucking up the ecosphere. He's been suffering all the while from feelings of impotence and bitter frustration. Just suppose that after those fifty years, he suddenly found there was, after all, a way that he could *do* something. If Morgan were offered a way to stop playing Cassandra, couldn't he be tempted? If he were offered a means of *taking a hand*, mightn't the chance to set aside that awful feeling of futility have been irresistible?"

"Morgan's not behind this," Lisa assured him. "I'd know."

"Would you?" he asked, so softly that the other men might not have been able to hear him even if they were listening hard, "or is it just that you can't stand the thought that you might not . . . that he'd let Stella Filisetti in on it, but not you?"

"There were *two* women," Lisa reminded him grimly. "And that's just here. Maybe *all* of them were women—the fact that Sweet's convinced that no woman could have dragged Ed Burdillon away from Mouseworld at a trot only means that he never met Arachne West, or any other Real Woman. If you think it might have been Morgan or anyone working for him who shot the phone out of my hand, wait till you hear the tape from my living room. The way he—or she—spoke Morgan's name is enough in itself to establish that he's a victim."

"Don't rule anything out, Lisa," Mike urged in the same low tone. "Just think about it. We need this result, you and I. If we can get one over on Kenna while the MOD man's watching, we'll have arms and armor—but if we come out of it looking bad, we'll both be on the scrap heap in no time."

"Morgan's a victim, not a conspirator," Lisa insisted frostily. "As am I. Not to mention half a million mice. Which is, if you care to think about it, the oddest thing of all. Why kill the mice, Mike? If there was some amazing secret hidden in Mouseworld, why not simply steal the mice that contained it? Why kill them all?"

"I can't answer that," Grundy whispered—and for the first time, Lisa realized just how frightened he had become. "I can't make sense of any of it yet. I can see Kenna's ax coming down on my neck, but I can't see any way off the block. How's that for a Cassandra Complex? The only one who can get us out of this with our careers intact is you, Lis. Even if the fools who came to your flat had it completely wrong, they think you know what's going on. They must have a reason to think that, and you're the only one who stands a chance of figuring out what it is. Whatever it is, Lis, *you* have to get to the bottom of it—and you have to face up to whatever it turns out to be. All I'm asking is that you don't leave any stone unturned, no matter how uncomfortable it might be—not just for your sake, or mine, but for Morgan's. If he *isn't* behind it, they're going to kill him as soon as they have what they want—and the longer he holds out on them, the worse they'll hurt him."

Lisa was tempted to tell Mike that he couldn't have it both ways—that she couldn't consider the possibility that Morgan might be responsible for this mad caper while simultaneously motivating herself with the thought that he might be in mortal danger—but the complaint died on her lips. Whichever one of the two possibilities was right, she *did* have to solve the puzzle as quickly as was humanly possible, and she *was* the person best placed to do so. If she failed, everybody might suffer.

Probably, she thought, that was why the intruders had come to her apartment—not to rob, but to discredit her; to do as much as they could to earn her the mistrust of Peter Grimmett Smith and his merry MOD men. If so, she had to hope that Mr. Smith wouldn't fall for it—and whether he did or not, she had to bend every atom of her intelligence and of her knowledge of Morgan Miller's life and work to figuring out exactly what kind of mess he had gotten himself into.

first Interlude

THE POLITICS OF mOUSEWORLD

The tour that Morgan Miller gave Lisa when he welcomed her to the department began with the lab space in which she would be working and the parallel spaces occupied by her fellow research students, then progressed to his own territory. There was far too much for her to take in all at once, and too many names to remember, but it was obvious from the start that Miller was a misfit. It wasn't just the fact that he was the only person except for the departmental secretaries who wasn't wearing a white coat; it was the slight wariness haunting the attitudes other people struck when they spoke to him. Some of them, Lisa assumed, must have been working cheek-by-jowl with him for years, but not one of them gave the impression of actually knowing him.

Miller was not a tall man—his height was almost exactly the same as Lisa's—but he gave the impression of being loftier than he was. His frame was slim and his face rather gaunt. She guessed that he was in his late thirties, but there was a stern agelessness about his hard features that suggested he wouldn't look substantially different in twenty years' time. No one would have described him as handsome, but the narrowness of his jaw made the upper half of his face seem uncommonly wide, exaggerating the width of his forehead and making his dark-brown eyes seem a trifle overlarge. When he had been a child, Lisa thought, those eyes must have seemed plaintive and adorable, but now that he was a man, they seemed intimidatingly cool and contemplative. The whole ensemble gave the impression of a penetrating intelligence quietly lurking in the depths of an unusual mind. Had he not possessed such a luxuriant head of dark-brown hair—which certainly wasn't a wig—Miller might have have resembled a stereotyped cartoon egghead, but there was something about him that resisted submission to any kind of category.

It wasn't until the end of the tour that he took her into Mouseworld. He ushered her through the door with a wry smile, as if he were ashamed to have to stoop so low as to use it as a kind of punch line but had no alternative. It was an awesome sight, and it stopped her in her tracks for a moment. Miller had obviously seen similar reactions many times before, and the wryness of his smile twisted his thin lips into an unclassifiable grimace.

"Four hundred and fifty thousand, give or take ten percent," he said, anticipating the question that had indeed sprung unbidden to Lisa's lips—although she had not actually intended to voice it, because she knew how lame it would sound. "That's in the one big experiment distributed around the four walls. The mice in the central block are taking part in several hundred different enterprises of considerably more importance, so we take care to give them all the space they need. Ours are in this sector here."

Miller moved toward the central H-shaped complex, but Lisa didn't move with him, even though she had noted that he'd said "ours" rather than "mine." She couldn't take her eyes off the walls.

The four cities were not identical in terms of their layout—London had to accommodate the door to the lab, Paris was interrupted by two large windows, Rome by two smaller ones, and New York by a huge cupboard—but all four were "open" in the sense that all of the internal partitions contained doorways and all of the rooms had openings in the floor and ceiling, connected by ladders to the floors above and below. Although each city's space was divided into dozens of floors and each floor into hundreds of compartments, every mouse could get to any location within its own city, always provided that the other mice in the sector would permit it to pass.

Lisa observed that the automatic feeding mechanism was simple in its basic design but amazingly intricate in its construction, making a supply of food pellets and water continuously available to every compartment. She also saw that each compartment had its own built-in cleaning system, equally simple in design, which continuously replaced the sawdust-like matrix that soaked up the urine. The system must have been wondrously efficient, because the stink, though distinct, was by no means nauseating. Such quasiclinical observations were, however, utterly overwhelmed by the impression created by the restless mice as they swarmed in vast numbers through the mazy complexes, like wheat fields blown by a wayward wind, or an ocean stirred by lashing rain and turbulent eddies.

She had never seen anything like it, nor had she ever imagined anything like it. She had never seen life in such awful, chaotic profusion.

"It must cost a fortune," was the observation she actually made when she finally found her voice, but it was a ridiculous understatement of her actual response.

"Compared with what?" Miller retorted wryly. "A cyclotron? Ofsted? Back in seventy-four, the university's one and only computer filled a dedicated building and cost millions—Mouseworld must have seemed trivial by comparison. But you're right, of course. The start-up cost was far too high even in the context of thirty years ago, at the optimistic height of one of the rosier interludes of the old boom/bust cycle. Fortunately, the population explosion was a hot topic then, thanks to Paul Ehrlich and a few other best-selling alarmists. There were big grants to be had. That was before the ostrich factor took hold."

It was the manner in which he spoke that kept everyone at a distance, Lisa realized. It wasn't that he was contemptuous, or hostile, or unduly arrogant—but there was something in his manner that emphasized a detachment so extreme as to constitute *removal*. She knew it wasn't the kind of trait that most women would find attractive, but most women didn't consider themselves natural-born forensic scientists. Why, she wondered, didn't he wear a lab coat?

"Ostrich factor?" she queried, while her captive eyes roamed the four walls of Mouseworld, refusing even to see the central block, where all the compartments were neatly separated from one another and at least one mouse in ten was a Morgan Miller, gloriously secure in its own abundant personal space.

"Head in the sand," Miller told her. "If we refuse to see the problem, it doesn't really exist. The phrase is Garrett Hardin's, but the book that contains it didn't get anywhere near the best-seller lists, thus proving its own thesis. You should come along to my third-year lectures on the population dynamics module—I kick off with an introduction to the neo-Malthusians in three weeks time. It's usually rather lively, even nowadays, when little short of a neutron bomb can be relied upon to raise the majority of students out of their appalling apathy. No offense intended."

"None taken," she assured him. She knew what he meant. She'd taken undergraduate courses in Practical Transgenics and Bioethics— topics that raised a storm wherever the chattering classes gathered for a dinner party or paused to gossip in Waitrose or the GP's waiting room, but couldn't even raise a ripple at home. Anyone who bothered to sign up for such courses was already numbered among the converted, and the students were relentlessly agreeable in the face of their teachers' preachings. It was almost as if they were members of some beleaguered cult.

"I'm assuming that you're an exception," Miller said, perhaps intending to pay Lisa a compliment. "I suppose that as a policeman, you'll at least be uncommonly dutiful, if not overly willing to challenge authority."

That seemed to Lisa to be marginally more offensive than the remark for which he'd issued his offhand non-apology. "I'll come along to your lectures," she assured him. As a postgraduate, she was obliged to attend a quota of second- and third-year courses in order to make up ground that had fallen outside her own undergraduate specialties. Those that her supervisor taught had to be on her list, if only for diplomatic reasons.

"If you cared to set an example and ask some searching questions in the seminars, I'd be grateful," he said. "It might save me from having to go quite so far over the top in the hope of eliciting a response. Feel free to be as aggressive as you like. It's a postgrad's responsibility to play the Judas goat, after all."

It wasn't, but Lisa didn't know whether he was joking or being provocative, so she didn't laugh and didn't rise to the bait. "Twenty-eight years is a long time to run an experiment," she said instead. "And the running costs can't be trivial. Even if the food's cheap, equipment maintenance and waste disposal must consume quite a budget."

"Animal population dynamics is a difficult field in which to do experiments," Miller agreed, seeming to lose half an inch of height as he bowed to the force of her fascination with the four cities and slumped into patient resignation. "Even organisms that can get through a generation in thirty days or so have to be observed for years if you're to get any worthwhile data about the way their populations respond to changes in circumstance. Anything with a yearly life cycle is out of the question for lab work, although there are teams all over the world that send people out every spring to collect data on wild populations of all kinds of species, and have been doing so for twenty years and more. Most of what we know about mammalian population dynamics in nature is based on the records kept by hunters and fur trappers, and the data is prejudiced by the fact that the killing of their members by humans is by far the most important variable impacting on the populations. Lab-based observations are virtually restricted to rats, rabbits, and mice—and if you think the running costs of *this* setup are an unacceptable burden, imagine what it would cost to keep a similar number of rats or rabbits."

"So why keep them in such large numbers?" Lisa asked.

"Because you can't do experiments on the effects of overpopulation with small numbers," Miller observed, without loading the comment with more scorn that was actually necessary.

"I see," Lisa said, wishing that she'd seen it a little earlier.

"The American experiments set up in advance of this one were all terminated after a couple of years," Miller told her, perhaps by way of repentance. "Even when they began to produce interesting results, the practical and political difficulties of keeping them going were insuperable. The whole point of this one was to build something sustainable over the long term, in the hope that it would clarify some of the puzzles Calhoun and McKendrick had to leave unsolved."

"And has it?" Lisa asked, determined not to be forced into a humiliating confession that she had no idea of who Calhoun and McKendrick were. Fortunately, Miller knew perfectly well that she was a biochemical geneticist whose background in population biology was likely to be exceedingly sketchy, and he didn't try to make her look foolish.

"Calhoun was one of the first people to investigate what would happen to a population limited only by space," he said. "His experiments gained a certain anecdotal notoriety in the sixties, when even I was but a child, but that overestimated both their scope and their importance. To simplify brutally, he put a few rats into a fairly spacious but limited complex, gave them as much food and water as they needed, and did what he could to keep pollution within reasonable limits. The population did pretty much what he expected it to do: rose exponentially to a peak, then collapsed again. When the crowding became unbearable, the rats' social system—such as it was—completely disintegrated. They fought continually and destructively, began to eat their own young, and showed every known symptom of environmental stress: ulceration, heart disease, hair loss . . . you name it, the observers saw it. It was never really intended as an experiment in the scientific sense, of course. If I remember correctly, Calhoun was working for the National Institutes of Health. It was a demonstration—a parable to supplement the natural parables of the lemming and the snowshoe hare."

"I read about the snowshoe hare," Lisa put in helpfully. "They're responsible for the lynx cycle in Canada—and the lemmings are famous. There used to be a cinema ad that showed them pouring over a cliff, but I can't remember what it was for."

"It was an antismoking ad," Miller reminded her. "People misunderstood the lemmings for a hundred years, just as they misunderstood the lynx cycle. The myth was that the lemmings were committing suicide, just like smokers who wouldn't stop. There were all kinds of crackpot theories. One suggested that some atavistic instinct was forcing them to follow an ancient migration route to land that had been inundated by the sea. In much the same spirit, people tried to correlate the lynx cycle with the sunspot cycle, as if that would somehow provide an explanation. Even within the scientific community, there was a well-established myth of predator-prey cycles suggesting that the number of lynx pelts recovered by the Hudson Bay Company's trappers varied cyclically because of the feedback effects of the trappers' own activity, or because every time the lynx numbers increased, they sent the populations of their prey into steep decline. All nonsense, of course. The lynx population and the snowshoe hare population went up and down together—the population crashes that caused the hares to decline were entirely independent of the intensity of predation, but every time the hare population crashed, the lynx population crashed too."

"But they can't have been in the same situation as the experimental rats," Lisa pointed out, glad for an opportunity to show that she was on the ball. "They had unlimited space."

"That's the curious thing," Miller agreed. "You'd think so, wouldn't you? The snowshoe hares had all of Canada, the lemmings all of Siberia and Scandinavia. You'd think that the limiting factor controlling their population size would be the availability of food— but it wasn't. When the cases were actually investigated, it immediately became obvious that the peak populations could endure the winters, despite the scarcity of food. The populations didn't collapse until the spring, when food was becoming much more abundant."

He paused, inviting Lisa to catch on. She had to hesitate for six or seven seconds, but then she figured it out. "The mating season," she said.

"Exactly," Miller conceded, favoring her with a smile of pure but not particularly abundant generosity. "They could tolerate the density of population when their attention was fixed exclusively on the business of survival, but when the breeding season came around, the males became fiercely territorial. It wasn't the absolute limitation of space that was important, but the perceived limitation. The competition for territory became so intense so suddenly that the animals couldn't handle the consequent physiological stress. Their systems became permanently adrenalinized. Snowshoe hares are relatively meek, so they just drop dead in droves, mostly from heart attacks. Lemmings aren't—when they get into fighting mode, they simply can't stop. The lemmings that died in the last couple of so-called lemming years were mostly killed on the roads, and human activity has had such a profound effect on their numbers that there'll probably never be another, but the lemmings that had attracted the most attention back in the famous lemming years were the ones that carried their territorial squabbles to the limits of the available territory. They fought on clifftops for every last meter, sometimes to the death. Suicide wasn't a factor, although sheer frustration was."

"And all these examples became parables in the sixties and seventies because everybody thought that something of the same sort was going to happen to us," Lisa finished for him. "I see."

"If only," Miller said. "What actually happened was that a few strident alarmists began telling people that something of the sort was bound to happen to the human population if we didn't take measures to prevent it, and take them *soon*. For five years or so, a few people listened, and grew anxious—and then even they decided that by far, the easiest way to stave off the anxiety was not to listen to the alarmists. So they played the proverbial ostrich and stuck their heads in the sand. They were encouraged to do it by economic theorists who thought that economic growth was the only worthwhile goal of collective human endeavor, and that population growth was good because it facilitated economic growth. Ironically enough, the original founders of Mouseworld were also anti-alarmists."

Lisa hadn't been expecting that, and she couldn't take advantage of the pause that Miller left for her to pick up the baton and carry the argument forward.

"After Calhoun's demonstration," Miller continued, "other researchers tried to repeat his experiment using mice, which were more convenient by virtue of their smaller size. McKendrick was one of those researchers. The other experiments duplicated Calhoun's findings, and so did some of McKendrick's populations, but McKendrick also found some exceptions. Some of his mouse populations didn't exhibit the standard boom/crash scenario. They adapted their behavior to a much higher population density than their wild cousins were used to. There was still a certain amount of nastiness, but they managed to limit their breeding without overmuch cannibalism, and the increase in mortality that helped bring the two into equilibrium was achieved without overmuch fighting."

"I get it," Lisa said. "Mice are meek, like snowshoe hares, while rats are more like lemmings."

"That's part of it," Miller agreed. "But it's not the whole story. Snowshoe hares may be meek, but they still go through boom-and-crash cycles. Nobody knows for sure, but the more important distinction might be that when rat numbers explode in the wild, they're usually cut back by disease—as witness the Black Death. Calhoun's rats were flea-free, of course, so they didn't suffer the same check. Plagues of mice are more commonplace than plagues of rats, especially in limited spaces, but there doesn't seem to be an external limiting factor that kicks in—not reliably, at any rate. For that reason, mice seem to have evolved their own internal limiting mechanisms. Because the mechanism is activated only under exceptional circumstances, which may occur only once in a hundred or a thousand generations, a lot of strains lose it to genetic drift—but enough retain it to gain a selective benefit when the conditions do arise. The same is true of some insects that became human commensals as soon as the first agriculturalists began cultivating wheat and rice. The grain beetles, for whom a field of wheat was Utopia and a granary Seventh Heaven, have relatively efficient internal mechanisms of population control, which can stabilize their populations and protect them from the devastations of boom/crash cycles.

"Storytellers in search of more reassuring parables argued that if mice were smart enough to avoid the worst effects of overpopulation, ultrasmart humans ought to be able to do it too. They chose to ignore the fact that it wasn't intelligence that was enabling McKendrick's luckier mice to do what they did. They also chose to ignore the fact that humans haven't gone through nearly enough generations since the first human population crisis to begin to develop the kind of facultative response that the luckier mice possessed."

"And these are lucky mice?" Lisa asked, waving her hand in a broad semicircle to encompass as much of Mouseworld as she could.

"They are now," Miller confirmed. "To begin with, all four populations boomed and then crashed, and then went through the whole cycle again—but after the second crash, the more adaptable mice had come into their inheritance. Since then, all four populations have stabilized. Imagine that: London, Paris, Rome, and New York, all marching in step toward a common goal! Inspiring, in its way, but no real cause for congratulations. The mice have been intensively studied, of course, to see exactly how they work the physiological tricks that allow them to stabilize their populations, in the hope that science might provide for humans what natural selection probably hasn't— but given that we *are* so smart, it seems ridiculous to try to duplicate the admittedly imperfect methods of mindless mice, don't you think?"

"I don't know," Lisa said. "It depends. If intelligence produces a political solution to the problem, that would be a triumph. But if it doesn't . . . mightn't it be a good idea to have a biological solution as backup?"

"If only it were that simple," Miller replied sadly—but he didn't seem in the least scornful of her suggestion. "Alas, if our intelligence is inadequate to facilitate a purely social solution, it can hardly be expected to facilitate the social application of a biological one. People who refuse to use contraception for the sake of the common good are hardly likely to accept institutionally imposed sterilization, are they?"

"Actually," Lisa said, grateful that the training she'd recently undergone was useful for something, "that's not as obvious as it seems. People accept policing to the extent that they do because they admit the necessity of restraint and want it imposed uniformly and fairly. All motorists routinely break the speed limit and park their cars wherever they can, and they all get mad if they're caught by radar or ticketed by a traffic officer, but they all accept the fundamental necessity of speed limits and parking restrictions."

"That's a fair point," Miller conceded, "and the comparison is probably more relevant than it seems, given that so many people seem to care at least as much about their cars as their children. I can see that you'll be a considerable asset to my seminars on the neo-Malthusians. Maybe you can take them over next year. But you mustn't allow yourself to become too entranced with Mouseworld. Whatever its running costs may be, they're trivial compared to the time it can soak up. Whatever you do, don't volunteer to help with the counting or the data processing. As far as the production of interesting results is concerned, the cities ran into the law of diminishing returns ten years ago. No matter how long they may continue, each hour invested in their observation will produce less and less reward as time goes by. You and I, Lisa, must concentrate our attention on events on a much smaller scale. DNA is the key to everything: all biological understanding and all biotechnological possibility. Can we move on now?"

She couldn't help noticing that it was the first time he had spoken her name. She was slightly ashamed of herself for caring, but she figured that she could probably forgive herself, if the need arose.

In spite of Morgan Miller's advice, Lisa couldn't help being fascinated by Mouseworld. She was relieved to discover that she wasn't the only one and that its captivating influence wasn't confined to fledgling research students. Chan Kwai Keung was already in his second year of postdoctoral study, having committed himself to the long rite of passage by which aspiring university scientists had to spend the early phases of their careers working on short-term contracts for derisory salaries. His stature was a little shorter than Morgan Miller's, and no slimmer than Lisa's, but he moved with an economical grace that made him seem far less obtrusive than either of them. He always had a book in his hand, but Lisa suspected that the habit had as much to do with an obsessive need to have a kind of retreat permanently available as with any desire to cultivate an image as the most studious apprentice in the department's junior ranks.

Chan, unusually, had already tried the more lucrative option of working for one of the big pharmaceutical companies in the field of animal transgenics, but had decided that he would rather work in the public sector. Most of Lisa's fellow postgrads thought he was mad, and the fact that he loved to sit and read in a tubular-framed chair in a corner of Mouseworld greatly encouraged that opinion. When Lisa asked him why he had returned to the public sector, he murmured something about finding it difficult to breathe while wearing a gag, adding a gnomic comment to the effect that the air in Mouseworld was naturally bad, and therefore good, rather than unnaturally bad, and therefore worse.

On the subject of Mouseworld itself, by contrast, his voice elevated itself to a normal conversational level and his manner became noticeably less self-effacing.

"Morgan has a jaundiced view of the experiment," Chan explained late one afternoon when Lisa contrived to distract him from his reading sufficiently to indulge in a long and languid conversation. "He considers that it has made its point and has no further utility, but that is because he has a very limited view of its achievements. He does not appreciate the true value of its spin-off."

"People do tend to be cynical about spin-off," Lisa pointed out. "I don't suppose it's true that the only spin-off the U.S. space program ever generated was the nonstick frying pan and the stretch-fabric bra, but the fact that people say it's so is revealing in its way."

"I did not have that kind of technological spin-off in mind," Chan admitted, "but even in that arena, Mouseworld has made its contribution. Had its original designers only thought to patent the automatic feeding-and-cleaning system, they might now be on the threshold of a fortune. The apparatus recently built for harvesting human growth hormone from the urine of a population of transgenic mice is a straightforward modification of the architecture of Mouseworld."

"You're taking the piss!" Lisa said, her suspicion tempered by pride in the quickness of her wit. "On an industrial scale?"

"Indeed not," Chan replied, although the faint grin playing at the corners of his mouth suggested that he was not a man who could always resist the temptation to improvise a straight-faced tall tale. "Sheep like Dolly and Polly and calves like Rosie may grab all the headlines, but milk is by no means the only bodily fluid that can be augmented with the aid of transplanted genes. The bladder has many advantages as a bioreactor, partly because urine is continually produced by male as well as female animals, but mainly because it is much less chemically complex than milk, thus making separation of the desired protein much easier.

"Although it is not yet fashionable, I believe that the urine of mice has greater potential as a pharmaceutical carrier than most of its rivals—certainly more than the semen of pigs and probably more than the fluid secretions of rubber trees. Milk is, admittedly, in the running, but my belief is that it will prove to be too difficult and too time-consuming to produce breeding populations of transformed sheep, goats, and cattle. If milk ultimately wins out as the carrier of choice, the rabbits, whose use has been pioneered by the Dutch, will probably win out as producers; what they lack in terms of the prolific production of milk, they make up in terms of the prolific production of more rabbits. They too are kept in facilities whose architecture owes something to the inspiration of Mouseworld."

"Which the designers failed to patent?"

"Alas, yes. The world was very different then. The so-called 'Green Revolution' was planned and carried out by workers in the public sector, who published everything and ignored the niceties of intellectual property rights. The biotechnological revolution, on the other hand, is being planned and carried out by employees of large corporations, which only publish ads and slogans and try very hard to claim intellectual property rights to everything—including their ads and their slogans. If you look with educated eyes, you can see it happening in Mouseworld, as the privileged inhabitants of the central H Block become increasingly anonymous and furtive, hiding secrets into which no one but each mouse's master manipulator is supposed to know. That is more the kind of spin-off I had in mind when I first raised the issue."

"Professor Miller doesn't seem to have much sympathy for the notion that the four cities are an accurate parable of the human predicament," Lisa told him.

"Perhaps he is insensitive to the deeper subtleties of the parable," Chan suggested. "He tends to think of the mice in the central block as something separate from the cities, so when he speaks of Mouseworld as a parable, he only has in mind the population problem, but the population problem is not all there is to Mouseworld, any more than it is all there is to the human world. I am not saying, of course, that every other aspect of the human world is mirrored in the confusion of that magical H—but I do say that those with the eyes to see it will find more mirrors there than they might expect."

"The models," Lisa said, to demonstrate that she was on the ball. "Around the walls, the more or less healthy masses, but in the ghetto, the seriously sick."

In the wake of the Human Genome Project, there had been a boom in the use of transgenic mice as "models" of every known human genetic-deficiency disease. All kinds of gene-based diseases that were difficult to investigate in living human patients could be inflicted on "knockout mice" by deliberately damaging the relevant gene in mouse embryos, which could then produce true-breeding populations of mice, all of whose members were victims. Where variant forms of a still-functional gene were responsible for pathological symptoms, the variant forms could be transplanted from humans into mice in place of the deleted native version, with only a little less trouble. The development of the diseases could be tracked much more closely in model mice because specimens could be killed and dissected at every relevant stage, and the populations also provided valuable preliminary testing grounds for possible treatments and cures.

"That's right," said Chan, bowing his head slightly to acknowledge her alacrity. "But you must follow the analogy farther."

She tried. The evening sun, which was shining in a margin of clear sky but lit abundant clouds from below, was filling the room with a peculiarly fiery light. Where it reflected from the transparent-plastic faces of the cages, it was more red than gold.

"You mean that the models are temporary residents in Mouse-world," she ventured eventually. "The business is booming now, but it'll be a short-term thing. As we find the treatments and the cures, the models will become obsolete—and in the human world too, the genetic-deficiency diseases will begin to disappear."

"If only it were that simple," Chan lamented. "Alas, we shall probably be required to keep the models long after their human analogues have become mercifully extinct. Already there are redundant models mingled with the others, mere library specimens sustained in case they should someday become necessary again. Naturally enough, you are thinking of the most obvious applications of the new technology—the battle against Huntington's disease, Duchenne muscular dystrophy, phenylketonuria, and all the other crippling conditions our new model armies will allow us to defeat. Those models are, of course, the ones that wear their names with pride. But what of the others?"

He paused so she could prompt him, but she was still distracted by the temporary play of the unusual light as it filtered through the few portals left to it by Mouseworld's architects. The pattern of the reflections that redirected the mellow beams into the corners of the vast room seemed quite amazing. Some of the compartments now had faces resembling rose-tinted lenses; others seemed to be ablaze with the glory of Armageddon.

The tenor of the conversation made it remarkably easy for Lisa to imagine Mouseworld as a human world writ small, its seething masses confused by all kinds of myths and apocalyptic imaginings. People fixated on dates had become particularly agitated in December 1999, and again in December 2000, but the lack of any outrageously peculiar event on the thirty-first of either month had only made them look even harder for signs of apocalypse in the everyday world, which continued on its stubborn course regardless of their hopes and fears. How many of them had seen, or even heard of, Mouseworld? How many had wondered whether the plague of people might be the mysterious Fourth Horseman of Revelation? Momentarily lost in these imaginings, Lisa had to bring herself back to earth with a bump in order to ask: "What others?"

"What of those new subspecies that hide their transgenic lights behind carefully placed smoke screens?" Chan continued seamlessly. "Are we so naive, you and I, that we take it for granted there are no mice in Mouseworld designed to model human factors whose problematic aspects are far more controversial than fatal diseases? Are there gay mice in Mouseworld? We suspect so—but you and I cannot pick them out, because they are closeted, carefully unlabeled by their investigators. Are there mice whose makers dare to hope they will be more intelligent than their common kin, mice whose makers hope they will be stronger than their common kin, mice whose makers hope they will far outlive their common kin? Yes, yes . . . undoubtedly. But which? The strangest thing about the H Block that lies at the very center of Mouseworld is that its society is subject to all kinds of *hidden hands* whose motives and methods are unclear. Is that not a telling mirror of the world in which we live? Is it not testimony to the true momentum of history, the fundamental paradoxicality of progress?"

"This is a university, not some top-secret research establishment in the Arizona desert," Lisa reminded him. "The people who are doing these experiments will publish the results in due course."

"Will they?" Chan asked. "They feel strongly about it, for the most part—Morgan Miller more strongly than most—but the culture in which they operate is not merely more powerful than they are, but more powerful than they can imagine. The universities are already adopting, explicitly as well as implicitly, the same habits of confidentiality, the same obsessive interest in intellectual property, and the same blatant cupidity as their commercial rivals—and could not help so doing once they accepted the view that they were indeed *rivals* of the biotechnology companies. Yes, the H Block was planted in the dead center of Mouseworld, surrounded by the proud relic of an earlier age—but while the cities continue to pour forth a cataract of data open to everyone who cares to look, what do the H Blocks produce? A vast series of tentative trickles, whose multifariousness serves to conceal their incompleteness. Thus the esoteric future emerges from the exoteric cradle of the past."

"In that sense," Lisa observed, "the deeper analogy surely doesn't go far enough. All the work in here is being carried out with the aid of research grants, except for the kind of stuff people like me are doing just for practice. It all has to be accounted for. There's nothing *sinister* going on here. Compared with the real world, it's a bit of a children's playground, or a Utopian enclave."

Chan smiled at that. "Of course it is," he said. "It is a mirror of our dreams and ambitions rather than the ugly reality of the world as it is. Or should I say *your* dreams and ambitions? It is, after all, a thoroughly Western image."

Although she knew little or nothing of Chan's personal history, Lisa knew immediately what he meant. In China—which had recently reclaimed Hong Kong from its former colonial masters—the population problem was not being left alone to find its own solution. There, if nowhere else, was a government that was not content to hope that the crisis would somehow be averted, or that the aftermath of the human depopulation crisis would follow the pattern now set by the mice of Rome and London, Paris and New York. China was the nation that had weathered more population crises in its own history than any other, and perhaps the only one whose leaders had really learned anything from the bitter experiences of their forebears. But Chan Kwai Keung was not in Hong Kong now. He was in England, where prosperity obscured all anxiety about a population whose increase had not yet been eliminated by the continual decline in the birth rate. In England, the most common view was that the population explosion was a "Third World problem" that did not apply to the developed nations, where women were marrying later and an increasing number were choosing not to marry at all.

Lisa herself had no intention of marrying or of having children. She could not imagine why so many women became broody, and she fervently hoped that no such misfortune would ever befall her— although even she was sometimes disposed to wonder whether this was evidence of something lacking in herself, some element of instinct lost to casual mutation. *How many of us,* she wondered, *are nature's knockout mice—and what, if so, are we modeling? The spectrum of human potential, or the range of potential folly?*

"The architects seem to have taken as much care to isolate London, Paris, Rome, and New York from the rest of Mouseworld as our own governments have taken to isolate West from East and North from South," Lisa agreed, "but at the end of the day, all the mice in the world have common problems. The ecosphere has its boundaries, but we all draw on the same resources and we all piss into the same pond. If the population boom does turn to a catastrophic collapse, it will affect all of us. No matter how we guard our individual cages, we'll all go down together when we go."

"There you are," said Chan lightly. "If we only look with educated eyes, we can see all manner of parables in this awesome confusion. Now that we have penetrated the darkest secrets of DNA, we are in some danger of forgetting that the actual actors in the world's drama are not disembodied genes, but firmly embodied organisms. Forensic science may deal almost exclusively in the future with the DNA extracted from smears and stains, but the criminals it convicts will all be whole organisms. Their genes may betray them, but cannot accurately define them."

"That's very good," Lisa said, meaning the compliment sincerely. "This place is by no means short of would-be philosophers, but you're the real thing, aren't you?"

"Very much so," he assured her. "So is Morgan Miller, in his own contradictory way. And so are you, if I may say so, despite your strange ambition."

"I like the idea of solving vexatious problems," she told him. "I like the idea of catching evildoers."

"Common criminals will always get caught," Chan told her, his voice retreating to a whisper and taking on an unaccountable chill, "but most evildoers, alas, go unrecognized and unchallenged. Perhaps it would be different if we were able to recognize the evils extrapolated in our own actions, but we are little better than mice as natural mathematicians—or, for that matter, as natural moralists."

"Maybe," said Lisa, still responding to his lightly veiled criticism of her chosen vocation, "but we have to do what we can, don't we?"

"We should," he agreed as the light of the setting sun added a hint of flame to his polished flesh, "and perhaps we shall."

PART TWO
The Ahasuerus Ambush

L isa's first interview with Peter Grimmett Smith took place in a ground-floor seminar room. The setting would have seemed incongruous in any case, but it happened to be a room in which she had once chaired population-dynamics seminars for Morgan Miller. It had been redecorated and refurbished long ago, but the smart bioplastic on the floor bore exactly the same pattern as the dumb vinyl that it had replaced, and it was easy enough for her mind's eye to substitute a lumbering TV-and-video and a primitive OHP for the station electroepidiascope that had replaced them.

The chairs were very different, being tastefully upholstered in a smart fabric whose soft texture and maroon hue could hardly have contrasted more strongly with the old gray-plastic monstrosities, but at the end of the day, a chair was just a chair: something to sit on. The desk across whose teak-finish surface she faced the man from the Ministry of Defence was likewise just a desk, similar to any number of desks that had formed barriers between her and the world during years past.

Smith looked almost as tired as Lisa felt, although he, like Mike Grundy and Judith Kenna, must have had the opportunity to get *some* sleep before the alarm bells began ringing. The apparent tiredness took the edge off his interrogative manner. "For form's sake, Dr. Friemann," he said, "I have to ask you whether there's a possibility that the people who ransacked your apartment early this morning could have found any classified material." He wasn't quite as good-looking at close range, and the harsh light of the seminar room exposed every sign of his age.

"There was nothing classified for them to find," Lisa assured him truthfully. "Nothing in the least sensitive, in fact. Everything work-related stays at work, in the office or the lab."

Smith nodded. Lisa was reasonably certain that he believed her; even Judith Kenna had to concede that she had a hard-won reputation for method, discipline, and good organization. "Do you have *any* idea of what these people might have been looking for?" he asked. He gave the impression that he was asking again purely for form's sake, knowing exactly what the answer would be—but she knew it might be a ploy, to set her at ease while he developed his suspicions more subtly.

"I'm not sure that they were looking for anything," she said pensively. "They may have been putting on a show. It's possible that the real purpose of their visit was to leave that stupid message on my door."

She noticed the ghost of a smile on the MOD man's face. "Why would they do that?" he asked.

"I think they might have been trying to discredit me," she said. "Perhaps they think that I'm the most likely person to figure out what's going on here, because I probably know Morgan Miller better than anyone else in the world does and I certainly care more about him than anyone else in the world does. I think they wanted to set things up so the people in charge of the investigation wouldn't entirely trust me and might decide to keep me on the sidelines just in case. Have they succeeded?"

"They might have," Smith told her with apparent frankness, "if the circumstances hadn't been quite so awkward."

Lisa raised her eyebrows, waiting for an explanation, but all Smith said was: "Considering your record, Chief Inspector Kenna doesn't seem to have a very high opinion of your abilities."

"I can't help that," Lisa said. "It's what we twentieth-century leftovers used to call 'a clash of personalities.' Does she say I can't be trusted?"

Smith shook his head. "Not at all. She did make some vague observations about lack of objectivity—something about it not being helpful to be so closely involved—and obsolescence of expertise. I got the impression that obsolescence of expertise might be one of her favorite phrases." He made a slight gesture with his right hand, intended to draw attention to the gray hair that an unwary youth cultist might have taken as a symptom of his own impending obsolescence.

"I strongly disagree about the helpfulness of my past involvement with Morgan Miller," Lisa said flatly.

"Good," Smith said. "As for the other thing . . . well, I find myself confronted with a desperate shortage of up-to-date expertise. Every biologist we had on call is working full time on the emergency. I need an adviser who knows her way around Morgan Miller's field, and there's at least a possibility that expertise as out of date as his will be the most useful kind. In brief, Dr. Friemann, I need your help far too desperately to worry too much about the fact that someone on the other side took time out to write 'Traitor' on your door. Time is pressing. Whatever reason they had for snatching Miller, we have to get him back quickly if we can, and we have to take whatever action may be necessary if we can't. Are you willing to be seconded to my unit?"

"Yes," she said, "I certainly am."

Lisa hadn't expected it to be quite as easy as that. She guessed it wasn't just Peter Grimmett Smith who had found himself short of resources; his employers probably thought they were scraping the bottom of the barrel by appointing him to investigate. From the viewpoint of the MOD, this was a minor distraction—a nuisance they would have been glad to leave alone, had they only dared.

On the other hand, she couldn't let his willingness to take her aboard lull her into a false sense of security. The fact that he needed her didn't mean that he trusted her.

"In that case," Smith said, "I have to impress upon you that everything that passes between us from this moment on is confidential. You don't repeat it—not even to Chief Inspector Kenna or Detective Inspector Grundy. Is that clear?"

"As crystal," she said. "What have you got that Kenna hasn't?"

He nodded, presumably approving her businesslike attitude.

"We commandeered Miller's phone records," he said. "Two calls leaped out screaming—both made within the last week, both to institutions he'd never contacted before, both asking for appointments to visit. And before you ask—no, we didn't have his phone tapped. He put a tape on the calls himself."

That wasn't easy to believe. "*Morgan* set a tape to record his own phone calls?"

"Not a permanent one. He just activated his answerphone during those particular calls. As if he wanted to make sure there was a record. As if he knew he might need one—even though he only asked for appointments to visit. He got the appointments within minutes, but that's not surprising. He's a biologist of some standing, even if he hasn't published much recently."

"Who did he call?" Lisa wanted to know.

"The first call was to the local offices of the Ahasuerus Foundation."

Lisa had heard of the Ahasuerus Foundation. It had been set up by some buccaneering sleazeball who'd made a fortune playing the stock market during the Great Panic of '25, ostensibly to sponsor research into technologies of longevity and suspended animation. At least a dozen similar outfits had been set up during the last half-century by aging millionaires offended by the thought they couldn't take their ill-gotten gains with them.

"And the other?"

"That's a little weirder—some crackpot outfit in Swindon called the Institute of Algeny. Algeny apparently—"

"I know what the word means," Lisa told him.

Smith raised his eyebrows slightly. "Perhaps you could explain it to me," he said mildly. "The on-line dictionary wasn't very clear."

"It was a coinage of the 1990s that never really caught on, although Morgan approved of it. It was derived by analogy with alchemy. Alchemy was a pseudoscience of inorganic transformations that assumed all metals were evolving gradually into gold, and might be given a helping hand to fulfill their aspirations if only the art could be properly understood and mastered. Algeny is an organic equivalent that assumes all organisms are striving to better themselves, and that we're already in the process of mastering the art that will allow men to become supermen."

Smith nodded. Lisa's explanation had obviously added a measure of enlightenment to what he'd learned from the dictionary. "So the most obvious thing that the two institutions Miller contacted have in common—" he began tentatively.

"—is a strong interest in technologies of longevity," Lisa finished for him.

"Miller's not a young man," Smith observed. "Do you think he was a potential buyer?"

Lisa considered the possibility, then shook her head. She felt that a shadow had fallen over her, and knew it must show on her face. "He was deeply ambivalent about the process of growing old," she admitted, "but he was a lifelong enemy of narcissism. He thought that declining sperm counts and the changing demographics of the developed countries were both good things, even if they were too little too late, because it's better to have more older and, hopefully, wiser people around than lots of hungry children. It would have gone against his conscience to seek self-preservation in a world whose population was way past the long-term carrying capacity of the ecosphere."

"A seller, then," Smith said.

Lisa shook her head to that too. "No," she said softly. "I don't think so."

Smith didn't bother to point out that there didn't seem to be an obvious third alternative—unless the Ahasuerus Foundation and the Institute of Algeny had something less obvious in common. "Neither institution is British," he commented, watching closely for Lisa's reaction. "The Swindon outfit's European Union, but its headquarters are in Germany. Ahasuerus is American."

"Intellectual activity is as global as commerce nowadays," Lisa pointed out. "In any case, the EU and the USA are the best of buddies, united against the menaces of hyperflu, international terrorism, and illicit economic migration."

"True," said Smith in a tone that suggested it wasn't the whole truth. The MOD probably figured that the nation's friends needed more careful watching than its enemies did.

Lisa waited for the MOD man to continue—which he did after a contemplative pause. "So tell me, Dr. Friemann," he said, "what would a man like Dr. Miller do with a new technology of longevity if he happened to stumble across one while playing games with genetically modified mice?"

Lisa didn't open her mouth to begin a reply, because she knew full well that she wouldn't be able to finish the first sentence before doubts consumed it and spat it out. She needed more time to weigh the possibilities and to recalculate her assessments of the situation as she had so far found it. She shuffled uncomfortably in her seat, not because the chair was badly designed, but because the ambience of the seminar room had begun to call forth fugitive memories of long-past pressures and intellectual discomforts.

As long ago as 1999, she knew, a gene had been discovered whose modification extended the normal life span of a mouse by a third. It had triggered an assiduous search for more, which had still been in full swing in 2002, but Morgan had never deigned to participate. He had correctly predicted that the equivalent gene in humans would turn out to have been activated already by the processes of natural selection that had extended the human life span in the interests of parental care. Was it conceivable, she wondered, that even though he hadn't been in the hunt, Morgan had nevertheless contrived to stumble upon a transformation that allowed mice to live *much* longer than their natural spans without exposing them to the long-understood rigors of calorific restriction? If so, it *might* have provided a motive powerful enough to inspire his kidnappers—and maybe a motive powerful enough to take the precaution of destroying every single mouse in Mouseworld.

Lisa wondered if Morgan's paranoia about overpopulation might have been sufficiently intense to stop him from publishing an experimental finding that might have made the problem even worse—but she quickly rejected the hypothesis. As she had already told Peter Grimmett Smith, Morgan wasn't that kind of man. Nor was he the kind of man who would automatically seek custodians for any kind of secret inside such fringe organizations as the Ahasuerus Foundation and the Institute of Algeny—in which case, why on earth had he contacted them? The fact that he *had* might have persuaded someone—someone who didn't know him as well as she did—that he might have a secret worth stealing. In these troubled times, even a hint might have been enough to move someone to take desperate measures to steal his secret.

"Do you think someone inside one of the two organizations had Morgan snatched?" Lisa asked.

"It's an appealing hypothesis," Smith conceded. "If not, perhaps someone in one of them forwarded the information to some interested third party."

"An unfriendly foreign government?"

"Perhaps."

"Or the Cabal?"

Smith frowned. "We don't use journalistic terms like that, Dr. Friemann. We're rather old-fashioned in the Ministry. We still use phrases like 'private enterprise' without the slightest hint of sarcasm. But, yes—I suppose it's possible that whatever Dr. Miller told the people at the Foundation and at the Institute was clandestinely passed on, perhaps in garbled form, to someone who scented a quick profit rather than to someone more interested in biowarfare. If either is the case, we need to know exactly what he did tell them."

And you need to be able to understand the answers, Lisa thought. *Which is where I come in—and why you're willing to overlook Judith Kenna's reservations about me. Chan's the only other person with my advantages, and he's not turned up yet. He's also not British.*

"Have you heard the tape of my conversation with the burglar?" Lisa asked the MOD man.

Smith shook his head. "DI Grundy let me in on the summary he'd received from an officer at the scene, but that's all," he said.

"I thought it was just bullshit at first," Lisa said slowly, "but it's becoming clearer. The intruder said that Morgan Miller didn't give a damn about me—that whatever he'd promised me, I'd end up with nothing. Either they were assuming that Morgan had already confided in me as to what he was taking to Ahasuerus and the Institute of Algeny, or they were fishing—trying to figure out by provocation whether I knew. Hell and damnation! I never thought to check whether they'd taken the wafer out of the answerphone. Of *course* they did. That may even have been what they were after, although they had to take the rest in case I'd changed it or backed it up . . . they must have figured they had to cover the possibility even though they weren't sure that Morgan had called me."

"Which he hadn't, had he?" Smith prompted, presumably to secure his own peace of mind. "He hadn't actually told you anything at all."

"Nothing at all," Lisa confirmed grimly, wondering why not. Surely, if Morgan *had* made any kind of groundbreaking discovery, he'd have been avid to share his triumph, desperate to bounce the idea off someone who understood not merely the nature of his work, but the philosophy behind it.

Or would he?

Suddenly the whole hypothesis reverted to the semblance of a house of cards, too frail to survive the least disturbance. As she'd tried to impress on Mike Grundy, nobody stumbled across longevity technologies, or anything of comparable value, *by accident*. Morgan Miller's Holy Grail had always been another kind of vessel entirely. He'd always been far more interested in *methods* of transformation than in the manipulation of particular genes. There were likely thousands of geneticists worldwide who had been looking into the genetic bases of aging for half a century—how could one man working on something entirely different stumble across something they couldn't find with a directed search?

"There must be other areas of concern that the two institutions have in common," Lisa said speculatively. "We shouldn't get hung up on the seemingly obvious until we've actually talked to them."

"You need some sleep," Smith said. "My people still have work to do here, not just in Miller's office and lab, but in Burdillon's too—we're not about to jump to any conclusions without covering all the ground. We also have to complete our background checks on the institutions before we move in on them. Chief Inspector Kenna says that you can't go home yet, and there's no point in challenging her ruling, so I want you to check into one of the hotels close to the campus and get your head down. I'll be in one called the Renaissance, I think. Take a pill if you have to. I'll pick you up when I'm ready."

Lisa was about to protest, but she knew that the feeling of wakefulness prompted by the new information wouldn't last. If she'd been sleeping properly for the last few weeks, it wouldn't have done her much harm to miss out on a single night's sleep, but she hadn't actually had a *good* night's sleep for as long as she could remember. She really did need to crash out, even if she had to take a pill to put her away and another to bring her around again. "Okay," she said finally. "I'll book into the Renaissance. It has delusions of grandeur, but a bed's a bed."

"Good," said Smith. "With luck, this whole thing will be unraveled by this time tomorrow." He didn't sound as if he meant it, and Lisa could understand well enough why he wasn't expecting overmuch luck. He worked for a government with its back against the wall. If the opposition were the EU, or the USA, or even representative of the kind of private enterprise in which the megacorps indulged, Smith would be working from a position of severe disadvantage.

On the other hand, Lisa thought as she moved toward the door, *if it really is someone at Ahasuerus or the Institute of Algeny who has set this farce in motion, there might be hope. Common sense suggests that fringe organizations of their kind ought to be even less competent than the police or the Ministry of Defence.*

She had left the room before she realized that she didn't have her car, and would either have to walk to the campus gate or beg a lift from a friendly policeman. In the circumstances, the friendly policeman seemed to be the better choice, even if his friendliness might wane slightly when she explained that she couldn't tell him anything of what had passed between herself and the man from the Ministry.

In the event, Mike Grundy had sufficient tact not to ask her what Smith had told her. He knew well enough that everything he couldn't get directly from the man from the Ministry was being deliberately withheld, and that it wouldn't be diplomatic to go after it, even in the privacy of his own car.

The journey to the Renaissance Hotel was only a few hundred yards, but it was long enough for Mike to voice concerns for Lisa's safety.

"I could post a uniformed officer outside," he suggested.

"When he could be doing something useful? Don't be ridiculous, Mike. It's broad daylight. If they're crazy enough to come after me again—and I can't believe for a moment they are—they're going to wait until they have at least minimal cover."

"They're crazy enough to incinerate half a million mice," Grundy pointed out. "They could be crazy enough to do *anything* if things aren't going their way. Amateur terrorism always looks good to the amateurs in question while it's a plan on paper, but once the dreamers start acting it out, it always spins out of control."

"It's too complicated to be amateur terrorism," Lisa told him, figuring that it was safe to say that much. "They want something, and they're not going to do anything that will blow their chances of getting it. They won't turn rat until they're cornered, and we haven't even got near them yet."

"I could take you to my place," he suggested. "I owe you, remember."

"And your place is a fortress, is it? They walked straight into mine. I'm safer in the hotel, Mike. It's a public place, full of human eyes and ears as well as the electronic kind."

He conceded defeat readily enough as the Rover drew up on the hotel's forecourt. "We'll get them, Lis," he said as she fumbled at the car door with her left hand. "We'll find Morgan, and we'll get him out." It was pure bravado.

"Thanks, Mike," was all Lisa could say when she finally got the door open. "We'll talk later."

As it turned out, she didn't have to take a pill. The nights she had spent lying fretfully awake, unable to relax into sleep, had been spent in a very different context. Relaxation was no longer necessary; exhaustion had taken control. She didn't even undress; the moment she was in her room, she had only to throw herself on the bed to pass swiftly into unconsciousness.

EIGHT

Lisa was unaware of having dreamed, or even of time having elapsed, when she was awakened by the ringing of the phone beside the bed. At first she had not the slightest idea of where she was; it took five seconds of bewildered confusion to get her mind back into gear and reconnect her with her memories of the long night and painful dawn. Even then, her reflexes made her reach for the phone with her right hand, and the torn skin between her thumb and forefinger sent a stab of pain into her brain as she flexed her fingers in preparation for the grab.

She overrode the warning and picked the handset up anyway, but transferred it to her left hand as soon as she had rolled over.

"Yes?" she said.

"Peter Grimmett Smith, Dr. Friemann. I've got a car to take us to Ahasuerus. I've brought you some breakfast. Five minutes, okay?"

"Okay," she said.

She didn't have a toothbrush or a comb, and her unsmart outer garments were not only bloodstained, but showing clear signs of long wear. There wasn't much she could do about any of that; it was the inevitable penalty of clinging too hard to twentieth-century habits. She washed and tidied herself as well as she could, then went down to the lobby to meet Peter Grimmett Smith.

"Better not check out," he told her. "You might need the room again."

"Maybe," she admitted. "But I'll also need to go home at some stage, unless Mike Grundy or Steve Forrester can delegate someone to bring me some stuff from my wardrobe and bathroom. I'll need my car too."

"You can phone one of them later," Smith said as he led her out to the car. "You really ought to invest in some smarter clothing—that tunic's ruined."

His own outer clothes, Lisa noted, were only shaped in an old-fashioned way; the fibers were brand new, as avidly active as anything on the market. Only something as paradoxical as gray power, she thought, could create a market for living fibers that maintained an appearance so staid as to seem more fossilized than dead.

The car was a sleek gray Jaguar with tinted windows. The driver's window was wound down to reveal a young blond woman with eyes so pale as to seem almost colorless. Smith introduced her as Ginny. As soon as she and Lisa had exchanged nods, Ginny closed the window again, to seal herself away from the eyes of the world.

Smith opened the rear door for Lisa before going around to the other side of the car. The tray built into the back of the front-passenger seat was down; there was a cup of black coffee slotted into it beside a bag containing a flaccid croissant and an over-iced Danish pastry. The cup and the bag were both made of active fibers, though, so the coffee was still hot and the food was warm.

Lisa checked her wristwatch. She had slept through the remainder of the morning and well into the afternoon; it was far too late to be eating breakfast, but she was glad that Smith hadn't attempted to provide lunch. She had lived alone all her life, and had long since given up hope that food technology would ever deliver a satisfactory prepackaged meal. She went to work on the food, glad of the simultaneous hit she obtained from the caffeine in the coffee and the sugar in the Danish pastry's embellishments.

As the Jaguar pulled out into traffic, the computer sounded a discreetly mellow-sounding bell, but the screen didn't flash up any warning messages; it was obviously programmed in a more sensitive way than Mike Grundy's.

"Get lost," the driver muttered, presumably addressing the driver in the car behind, who must have reckoned that she should have let him pass first. In several American states, so rumor had it, whole families had been shot to death for less, but British drivers were famed for their restraint. Few of them carried anything more lethal than a pepper spray for self-defense in road-rage incidents.

"Chief Inspector Kenna seems to favor the hypothesis that this is all due to some lunatic fringe group," Smith told Lisa. "I've tried to ease her away from that point of view, but I can't share my own suspicions while there's a possibility that Miller's in possession of a secret with security implications. She's no fool, though, so she's keeping in mind the chance that the seemingly amateurish aspects of the assault on your flat are a calculated smoke screen of disinformation. In any case, we should be careful not to lose sight of the possibility that she might be right. If the target *is* the university's Department of Applied Genetics and what it stands for, rather than Morgan Miller, our involvement in the investigation might be one of the things the perpetrators would like to highlight in a list of imagined crimes against nature and humanity."

Lisa was still busy eating and didn't particularly want to reply, but there were questions she had to ask. "Has Chan turned up?" she said.

"He's alive and well," Smith assured her. "He was in Birmingham last night, but he called in as soon as he picked up his messages. He said he'd be here as soon as possible."

Lisa was surprised by the shock of relief that coursed through her. She hadn't been consciously aware of the level of her anxiety. She wasn't in the least reconciled to the possibility of losing Morgan Miller, but even if worse came to worst, there was some small solace in the fact that Chan was alive and well.

"He'll help," she said. "If anyone knows what Morgan's been up to lately, it's Chan."

"I have someone waiting to talk to him as soon as he arrives," Smith confirmed.

Lisa realized that she hadn't the faintest idea of where the local office of the Ahasuerus Foundation was, but the fact that the Jaguar was powering up the access road to the westbound artery suggested that it was in the Bristolian sector of the cityplex. There didn't seem to be any urgent need to inquire further.

Smith hesitated slightly before introducing the next topic of conversation, but only for show. "You and Miller," he said abruptly. "More than colleagues? More than friends?"

Lisa nodded, unable to do more until she had washed down the last of the pastry. Handling the cup was awkward because the holder was at the right-hand side of the tray and she didn't want to test the wounded skin on that hand again.

"What about Burdillon and Chan?"

Lisa blinked slightly at that one. "Ed and I have been friends for a long time," she said. "Nothing more. My department occasionally puts some work his way, but not recently, so I guess our friendship has become a trifle dormant. I still see Chan once in a while—just as friends. It's difficult to describe in conventional terms the relationship Morgan and I have nowadays. I haven't seen him more than half a dozen times in the last three years—maybe less frequently than I've seen Chan."

"But you were very close at one time?"

"We still are, even if it doesn't look like it—as close as we ever were. Neither of us ever wanted to get married, and neither of us ever thought of the other as the great love of our life, but that doesn't mean that I don't care deeply about getting him out of this in one piece, or that I wouldn't take this business personally even if they hadn't paid a call on me too."

"I've listened to the tape now," Smith said. "That part you drew my attention to—what do you make of the insistence that Miller never cared about you, and that any promises he made were false?"

"Exactly what I wondered then," she said. "That the idiot with the gun doesn't know the first thing about Morgan Miller. Morgan doesn't make promises he can't keep—and he always cared about me as deeply as I always cared about him."

"But he didn't tell you what he was taking to Ahasuerus?"

"No, he didn't," Lisa said, becoming tired of having to repeat it. She had been waiting for an opportunity to turn the conversation around, and she didn't give him time to slip another question in. "So what, exactly, is Ahasuerus? Why are we going there first?"

"It's nearer," he said, answering the second question. "That may be why Miller went there first. Ready accessibility might have been the primary motive for him selecting both institutions from a longer list of candidates, given that he obviously didn't want to discuss what he had over the phone. Unfortunately, our background check hasn't turned up much more than the information that's freely available on the Ahasuerus website. The Foundation was set up by a man named Adam Zimmerman, who made billions out of the financial crisis of 2025. What the website doesn't say, of course, is that he helped to engineer and direct the crisis—he was just a mercenary, hired by the megacorps to do their dirty work, but he seems to have had an agenda of his own. He's dropped completely out of sight, and there's a rumor that he's been frozen down, but it's easy enough for a man with that sort of wealth to hide, even in today's world, and to manufacture disinformation by the yard. It's possible that Ahasuerus is a front, but everything we and Interpol can gather suggests that it's a bona-fide research sponsor, financing and collating information on longevity biotech and SusAn techniques. At any rate, it seems distinctly less shady and somewhat saner than its apparent rival for Miller's affections. Dr. Goldfarb wouldn't discuss Morgan Miller over the phone, understandably, but when I told him what had happened, he seemed anxious to help us. I'll be keeping an open mind, of course."

"Of course," Lisa echoed. She knew as she said it that it wasn't enough to maintain the change of subject if he wanted to go back to it, and he clearly did.

"What about Miller and Burdillon?" he asked. "How close were they?"

For a moment, she wondered if Smith were asking whether Morgan and Ed had ever been lovers, but that idea was too bizarre. "Certainly not enemies," she said. "Perhaps not even rivals, although there's bound to be an element of that within a department. Not close friends, though. If Morgan had a hot secret, I think he'd confide in Chan before he would in Ed Burdillon—and in me before he would in Chan."

"What about vice versa?"

"You think it might have been something of Ed's that Morgan was taking to Ahasuerus? No—he'd never do that, even if he didn't like what Ed was proposing to do with it. He's a man of principle."

"That's not quite what I meant," Smith was quick to say. "Given that Miller *is* a man of principle, and trustworthy, might Burdillon have asked for his help on work that he'd been commissioned to do, if time were pressing?"

Lisa looked at Smith long and hard before replying. "What work might that be?" she asked finally.

"Urgent work," Smith parried. "Might Burdillon have co-opted Miller, if the need were there and his expertise fit the bill?"

"Yes," Lisa said, having considered the hypothetical question with all due seriousness. "If Ed were up against a deadline and needed help, he'd have asked Morgan first, Chan second—and I suppose he might have instructed both of them not to tell me about it. So what was Ed doing for the war effort that might have required urgent assistance?"

"I'm not a biologist," Smith said defensively. "I don't even know what the words mean, but have you ever heard of antibody packaging?"

"Yes," Lisa admitted. "I have."

"Did Miller ever mention it to you?"

"Only in a general way—long before the war that we aren't supposed to call a war actually broke out. We always discussed ongoing developments, breaking news. I take it that we're not just talking about the salvation of the banana republics?"

"What?" Smith was obviously telling the truth about not being a biologist. He probably didn't even bother to read the science pages in the newspapers. *The war effort really must be soaking up a lot of time and expertise,* Lisa thought, *if the Ministry has to put someone like Peter Grimmett Smith in charge of an investigation like this.*

"One of the earliest applications of genetic modification was the production of so-called plantibodies and plantigens," Lisa told the Ministry man. "Way back at the turn of the century, engineers began transplanting genes that produced antibodies and antigens into plants. A lot of the early experiments used tobacco and potatoes, because they were the best hosts for the mosaic viruses that were then the vectors of choice for ferrying DNA into plant cells. Attention soon switched to bananas because bananas are naturally packaged and eaten raw, so the fruit could be used as a carrier of antibody-cocktail oral vaccines. Genetically modified bananas helped wipe out most of the major tropical diseases between 2010 and 2025. That was when the phrase 'packaged antibodies' was first bandied about. It has slightly different connotations in a biowar context, but the basic principle's the same."

"I don't follow," Smith confessed.

"You're presumably familiar with the theoretical protocols of biological warfare," Lisa said, although she was testing the limits of Smith's ignorance, not making any such presumption. "Anyone planning an assault using pathogens as weapons needs to make sure not only that they can be efficiently delivered to the target and that they will then have the desired effect, but also that they won't rebound. The aggressors need to immunize their own personnel against the spread of infection—but if they do that too openly, or too far in advance of the attack, they risk blowing their cover and attracting retaliation. Mass immunization programs are difficult to hide, and once the immunization has been implanted in everyone who needs to be defended, it's out there in the world just waiting to be analyzed and synthesized by the intended objects of the aggression. I'm no expert in strategy, but I assume that tactical difficulties of this kind have been primarily responsible for the fact that the only confirmed uses of biological weaponry during the last twenty years have been intranational, either by terrorists like those lunatics who carried out the Eurostar attack or by political elites aiming bioweapons at their own troublesome underclasses.

"Like most biological-warfare research, antibody packaging has a certain amount of general medical significance, but the main reason people have remained interested in it is that it might provide a way to disguise defensive measures taken in advance of biological warfare. At its most elementary, the idea is that a domestic population can be clandestinely immunized against a bioweapon by secreting antibodies in a locally distributed product that wouldn't normally be suspected as a carrier."

"And beyond the elementary?" Smith prompted.

"In theory, at least, there are more subtle ways to tackle the problem. You could, for instance, use surreptitious vectors to import dormant genes capable of producing antibodies into tissue cells that normally have nothing to do with the immune system, but that could—if and when necessary—be activated by a switching mechanism broadly similar to those that already exist to determine which genes are expressed in which kinds of tissues. Effectively, it's a calculatedly cumbersome system, which splits the process of infection resistance in two. No antibodies show up in advance of the bioweapon's launch, but as soon as it's launched, the launchers can distribute the trigger to their own personnel without it being obvious to any onlooker that it's a defense mechanism."

"Isn't that overcomplicated?" Smith asked dubiously.

"Of course it is," Lisa agreed. "That's the whole point of biowarfare. Sneaky is best. But if I were planning World War Three, I probably wouldn't approach the problem that way. I'd probably be looking at smart fibers and second skins. If I were on the Containment Commission, I'd be looking to issue the population with some *very* smart suits." She was looking hard at him, trying to gauge his reaction, but he was spooky enough to have an efficient poker face.

"Morgan Miller was once an expert on retroviruses, I believe," he said, abruptly changing tack.

"A long time ago," Lisa agreed. "In the early years of the century, retroviruses were the vectors of choice for transforming animal eggs stripped from the ova of slaughtered livestock. Morgan's search for an all-purpose transformer focused on that kind of carrier mechanism until 2010 or thereabouts, when anti-viral research moved into the next phase. Don't be misled by the AIDS connection, though— not all retroviruses were bad news even back then. The ones Morgan worked with were constructive. I doubt that he bothered to keep library specimens in living mice, in Mouseworld or anywhere else, although he may have had a few frozen down and he'd have kept full sequence data for any novel types he put together. Is there some particular reason that the MOD is interested in retroviruses?"

She didn't expect an answer to the question and she didn't get one.

"We have all his publications from that era, of course," Smith said. "What we don't know is how much work he did that was never written up."

"All university staff wrote up everything they could in those days," Lisa assured him. "Publication wasn't just the currency of promotion back then—it was the high road to grant funding. The patent wars confused the situation, of course, but once the intellectual-property situation was clarified, he'd have put everything on the record that would go."

"Including failed experiments?"

"There's no such thing as a failed experiment," Lisa told the MOD man wryly. "Those experiments also serve the cause; they merely confirm the null hypothesis. But everyone has runs that get fouled up and are quietly dropped from the record, and everyone has the kind of dull results that they always mean to write up when they've nothing better to do, but never quite get around to because something better always turns up in time. Then again, there are the incomplete sequences—sets of data that need a little something extra to cover all the angles and make them genuinely meaningful. Sometimes it's so difficult to block off the last few holes in a story that doesn't have much of a punch line anyway that it hardly seems worth the effort. So, yes—even though Morgan would have put everything on the record that was fit to be put, he probably had all kinds of results that never got that far, including sequences for all kinds of viral transformers—retros and every other kind of artificial we've classified. But the idea that any one of them might be a recipe for a powerful bioweapon, or a defense against one, is the stuff of crude melodrama. It Ed Burdillon was working on some new method of antibody packaging for you, and Morgan was helping him, I'd have to say that that's far more likely to have attracted unwelcome attention than his old work on retroviruses."

"I see," Smith said unconvincingly. "You do understand, Dr. Friemann, that all our biowarfare research is purely defensive."

"Of course I do," Lisa agreed, taking care not to sound too sarcastic.

"Could a defense mechanism of any kind that would fit under the rubric of antibody packaging be short-circuited? If an enemy knew how the antibodies were to be packaged, but didn't know exactly what was to be included in the package, could the whole system be attacked? Could one, for instance, deploy a virus to attack an entire antibody-packaging system?"

"Maybe," Lisa said, "but we're getting into deep hypothetical water here. Unless you care to tell me exactly what it is that Ed Burdillon was asked to do, and why your bosses think that Morgan's particular expertise might have had a special bearing on the problem, I can't make a useful judgment."

Either Smith didn't know the answer himself or he didn't care to tell her yet—which didn't surprise Lisa in the least. "We're here," he said as the Jaguar swung into the entrance of an underground parking lot.

While the vehicle paused at the booth outside the opaque screen that covered the entrance to the lot, Lisa had time to look up at what appeared to be a perfectly ordinary office building. Whatever kind of ID the blond driver was holding up to the security guard at the barrier must have impressed him, because he saluted as he pressed the button that raised the screen, then waved them through.

"Let's see what Ahasuerus has to tell us," Smith said as he reached across to open Lisa's door for her, even though her left hand would have been perfectly adequate to the task.

nine

The building into which Lisa and Peter Grimmett Smith ascended was indeed perfectly ordinary, at least by the standards of recent construction. The elevator from the parking lot took them only as far as the lobby atrium, where they had to pass through a metal detector before being allowed to approach the reception desk. The edge of the circular desk was surmounted by a transparent wall made of some chitinoid substance that glittered eerily as its curves reflected the light of the high-set mock chandeliers.

Smith passed a smartcard through a narrow slit in the wall. The bored teenage girl who accepted it fed it to her station with the world-weary air that was currently de rigueur among what the tabloids called "slaves of the machines."

"That's okay, Mr. Smith," she said after consulting her screen. "Dr. Goldfarb's waiting for you. Take elevator number nine. This afternoon's code is 857. Thank you for your patience."

Lisa tried to remember when "Thank you for your patience" had replaced such vapid formulas as "Have a nice day" in the standard lexicon of programmed social interaction, but she couldn't put a date on it. Patience had been in such short supply for so long that the mantra might have come into use at any time between 2001 and 2030.

The principal design features of the high-rise had, of course, pre-dated the establishment of the Containment Commission by some twenty years. Their ostensible purpose in the 2020s had been to offer protection against the ever-present menaces of client rage and employees inclined to "go postal." Unfortunately, the equipment of such edifices with "fortress hearts" had quickly demonstrated that the quality of a fortress is only as good as the people and systems manning it. It hadn't taken more than a couple of years to reveal the many kinds of chaos that could be created in such a building by a systems crash, and only a couple of years more to reveal how much worse such chaos could become if it were boosted by active malice.

Arguments had raged for years as to how much better each new generation of "foolproof software" really was—until the advent of new plagues had brought about a sudden reversal of public opinion as the millions of people who had to work within the carcasses of these monstrosities suddenly realized the advantages of careful isolation. The building housing the West-of-England office of the Ahasuerus Foundation was probably host to more than a hundred different megacorp groups and close to a thousand human employees, whose chances of picking up even so much as a common cold within its walls were negligible. Even the fiercest plague war was highly unlikely to touch inhabitants of institutions like this one, provided they kept their cars clean and their clothes smart. It also helped if they lived alone.

No wonder the world is overfull of workaholics, Lisa thought as the elevator smoothly carried them up to the thirty-first floor. While conversation was suspended, she took the opportunity to ring Mike Grundy and ask for news. He reported that Chan still hadn't checked in and that his own attempts to see Ed Burdillon at the hospital had been thwarted by Smith's men. He also confirmed that her flat was still out of bounds. Lisa asked him to transfer her car, some clean clothes, and a few other essentials of everyday life to the Renaissance. He promised to see to it.

"Did your people get anything useful from Ed Burdillon?" she asked Smith when she'd returned the phone to her belt.

"Nothing useful," Smith told her, so glumly that it had to be true. "We passed the clothes he was wearing to Forrester—let's hope he can come up with something."

The elevator car was capable of sideways movement through "unmanned corridors," as well as vertical movement in its shaft, so it eventually delivered them direct to a door that was supposedly unreachable by any other means.

Dr. Goldfarb was a little man in a dark-blue suit. The suit was as smart in the new sense as Peter Grimmett Smith's, and considerably smarter in the old sense. Although the texture of Goldfarb's skin implied that he was five or ten years younger than Smith and Lisa, he was wearing gold-rimmed spectacles that would not have looked out of place in a Dickensian costume drama; either he was something of a poseur, Lisa deduced, or he was untreatably phobic about lasers.

Goldfarb ushered his visitors through the reception area and into his station-packed inner sanctum. He seemed to be in sole charge of the office at present, although there were two chairs in each section. He politely offered both the chairs in the inner office to his visitors, but Smith declined and Lisa thought it best to do like-wise. It was as if none of the three wanted to offer any of the others the psychological advantage of standing.

"I'm afraid that I really can't offer you much help," Goldfarb said, securing his quasiDickensian image by rubbing his hands together to emphasize his helplessness and his regret.

"This is both a police matter and a matter of national security," Smith informed him coldly. "I understand that you need to operate a policy of strict confidentiality, but Morgan Miller's life may be in danger. We need to know exactly what he told you."

"Oh, yes, of *course*," Goldfarb was quick to say. "I've been in touch with New York, and they agree entirely that we must cooper-ate *fully*. The problem is that Professor Miller really didn't give me any significant information when he visited. I've made a tape of our entire interview for you, but I fear that you won't find it very useful."

As he spoke, he picked up a wafer from the console to his left and held it out to Lisa. Lisa accepted it, then glanced at Smith to see if he wanted it passed on to him immediately. When he made no sign, she put it in the breast pocket of her tunic.

"Thank you," said Smith.

"I'm not trying to hide anything," Goldfarb insisted, although no one had insinuated by word or gesture that he was. "Professor Miller came here primarily to ask me questions about the organization.

He'd read our mission statement and had made what seemed to me to be a reasonably comprehensive study of the research projects we currently sponsor, but he seemed slightly anxious about certain unfortunate rumors that have circulated in the tabloid press. . . ."

"I presume that what you mean," Peter Grimmett Smith observed, although he didn't inject any measurable sarcasm into the statement, "is that he wanted to make sure you're a real research institute, not a bunch of crackpot conspirators."

Goldfarb actually blushed, but he didn't go so far as to wince. "If you want to put it so crudely," he conceded. "Professor Miller was anxious to ascertain that we would make responsible use of any data that he might pass on to us."

"But he didn't tell you what the data in question might be?" Smith asked. Lisa didn't think much of Smith's interrogatory technique, but he was severely handicapped by his reluctance to ask the questions he actually wanted answered. To introduce the topic of antibody packaging would be recklessly indiscreet.

"As you'll see for yourself when you look at the transcript," Goldfarb murmured defensively. Lisa realized that one reason why Smith hadn't taken the wafer from her was that he was signaling to Goldfarb that he knew perfectly well that the transcript could easily have been doctored and didn't consider it worth the silicon and rare earth it was printed on. "All he said," Goldfarb added when he realized that Smith and Lisa were waiting for him to go on, "is that he'd been trying to solve a seemingly intractable problem for nearly forty years, and that although he'd failed, he thought he ought to make his data available so that other researchers wouldn't have to repeat all his wasted stratagems."

"That doesn't make sense," Lisa said immediately. "I've known Morgan Miller for thirty-nine years, and I've followed every step of his quest to solve the problem of developing a universal transformation system. Even if he hasn't published every last detail of his failed attempts, there's nothing esoteric about the work. Anyway, why should he think that an organization like yours would be interested in his records? He's never done anything specifically relevant to longevity research or suspended-animation techniques."

"Really?" said Goldfarb, who seemed genuinely surprised. "I must admit that isn't the impression he gave me. When you look at the transcript—"

"What *is* the impression he gave you?" Smith butted in.

Goldfarb hesitated, but only for a moment. "Well," he said, blushing again, "I did get the impression that the data to which he referred *was* directly relevant to the core element of our mission statement."

"The extension of the human life span?" Smith was quick to clarify.

"The fostering of human emortality," Goldfarb corrected him. Glancing sideways at Lisa, he added: "That's emortality with an 'e.' Our founder disliked the word 'immortality' because he thought it implied an inability to die no matter what, whereas—"

"I know what emortality means," Lisa said through slightly gritted teeth. "I'm a scientist, not a community policeman—and I've known Morgan Miller well for nearly forty years. Are you suggesting that Morgan was engaged throughout that time on some clandestine line of research that he never even *mentioned* to me?"

Goldfarb shrugged. "I know nothing about the circumstances . . ." he began, but trailed off in evident confusion, unable to decide where the sentence ought to go.

"But you're definitely telling us that whatever this line of research was, it was unsuccessful?" Smith put in. "According to what he told you, he only wanted to save others from wandering up the same blind alleys, not knowing that they'd already been checked."

"That's what he told me," Goldfarb agreed hesitantly. It didn't need a psychologist to spot the implied "but."

"And what did *you* tell New York?" Smith demanded.

Goldfarb didn't reply. He and his superiors had obviously agreed that he had a duty to override the issues of confidentiality that were relevant to his conversation with Morgan Miller, but Smith's question presumably went beyond that decision. "It was just an impression I got," the little man said defensively.

"We've already taken note of the fact that you're the kind of man who forms a lot of impressions," Smith said rather intemperately. "What did you tell New York?"

"*Nothing,*" Goldfarb insisted. "It's just . . . I'm trying to *help* you here . . . it's just that scientists nowadays have got into the habit of playing their cards very close to their chests. Miller came here fishing for information, and I wasn't entirely sure that he'd have bothered doing that if his results had been as uniformly negative as he said they were. I told New York that I thought he was probably keeping something up his sleeve."

Goldfarb was blushing again, having obviously considered the possibility that it might have been his "impression" that had prompted Morgan Miller's kidnapping. It didn't seem very likely to Lisa, but in a crazy world, it sometimes didn't need much to trigger precipitate responses.

"That was rather irresponsible, don't you think?" she put in.

"There's also the possibility that he'd missed something," Goldfarb retorted, shifting his ground uncomfortably. "Scientists don't always have a clear view of the implications of their own results, especially if they haven't exposed them to any kind of peer review. I told New York that I thought Miller might be uncertain about the causes for his failure, and that he might want someone else to take a look at his results in case they could pick up something he'd overlooked. He did seem . . . well, *frustrated.* As if he were annoyed with himself for not having solved what must have seemed at first to be a minor obstacle, even after all this time. There was something about the manner of his approach that suggested *desperation.*"

"That's ridiculous!" Lisa said, unable to contain her annoyance. "You may think you're a good judge of character, Dr. Goldfarb, but the person you're describing isn't Morgan Miller, and the Morgan Miller I know never gave me the slightest hint that he was working on any kind of longevity technology. None of this rings true. I don't have a clue as to why he came to you, but if he really said what you say he said, in the way you say he said it, then he must have been playing a part. He was spinning you a line, maybe because he wanted to find out something about Ahasuerus—or *you*—that he couldn't find out without trickery."

Lisa saw that Smith was frowning, and realized that Mike Grundy would probably have been blazing mad if she'd gone off like that during one of his interviews. She knew she shouldn't be throwing speculations of this sort at a witness—but everything Goldfarb said had needled her.

"How good is your security, Dr. Goldfarb?" Smith asked, abruptly changing the subject.

"Oh, the very best," Goldfarb assured him, seemingly glad that the subject had been changed. "Our founder was a systems expert, thoroughly versed in methods of encryption, and he knew as well as anyone what damage can be done when confidential information becomes available to people who want to use it for their own ends."

Such as precipitating stock-market crashes, Lisa thought.

"So nobody outside your organization could possibly have obtained a copy of the text on the wafer you've just given my colleague?" Smith followed up. "Even though it's been to New York and back, and even though you've recently produced a decrypted version?" *Unless, of course,* Lisa added silently, *it was deliberately leaked, here or across the pond.*

"Nothing's absolutely certain," Goldfarb admitted cautiously, "but I have to say that it's very unlikely. At the very least, we'd surely have some indication if our systems had been hacked. We have *very* good alarm bells."

As if on cue, a bell began to sound. Goldfarb spun around as if he'd been burned, but he relaxed almost immediately when he realized that it wasn't an alarm at all. It was Peter Grimmett Smith's phone.

Smith scowled, turning his back to take the call.

"I thought for a moment that something had crashed downstairs," Goldfarb said to Lisa, as if to establish the fact that he was not listening in to Smith's conversation. "It seems to happen more frequently with every week that passes. It's all that newspaper talk about 'slaves of the machine'—nobody with half a brain wants to do basic inputting and negotiation anymore in case they get stuck with a reputation as an idiot, so we get stuck with actual idiots minding reception and the parking facilities. They're always pressing the wrong buttons and getting flustered because they can't work their way out of the error maze. Believe me, Dr. Friemann, *our* alarms *never* ring, and nobody in this office has ever been accused of contributory negligence. If Morgan Miller was kidnapped because of anything he told me—which I find very difficult to believe, in view of its vagueness and negative tenor—the kidnappers must have picked it up somewhere else. You *might* try the Algenists in Swindon; I believe Professor Miller was also checking them out, although I can't imagine why."

The words "pot," "kettle," and "black" floated unbidden into Lisa's mind, but she resisted the temptation to extend the thought. Ever since Judith Kenna had begun to hunt for evidence of the twentieth-century habits Lisa had allegedly failed to transcend, she had been trying to update her stock of clichés.

Smith turned around again. "It's Ginny," he said. "Chan Kwai Keung's at the booth outside the lot. He must have followed us out from the Renaissance. He wants to talk to you, Lisa. He says it's a private matter that he's not prepared to discuss with anyone else until he's cleared it with you."

Lisa could hardly help but infer that whatever Chan had to say, it must have an urgent bearing on Morgan Miller's kidnapping—but she had no more idea than Smith of why Chan couldn't have told the police, or the MOD man Smith had instructed to talk to him.

"I'd better go down," she said.

Smith obviously resented being dragged away from an interview he didn't consider to be complete, but it was equally obvious that he wasn't about to let Lisa talk to Chan without being there to hear what was said. He turned away again, although all he said into the mouthpiece of the phone was: "Tell the guard to let him in. We're on our way—we'll be there in five minutes."

"I'm sorry," said Goldfarb, "but I really don't think there's anything else I can tell you."

"That's okay," Smith said insincerely. "We'll take a look at the transcript while we're on the road to Swindon, and if there's anything we need to come back for, we'll contact you by phone."

"I'll call you an elevator," Goldfarb said, reaching out to make good his word. His eagerness to be rid of them would be understandable, Lisa thought, even if he had a conscience as pure as—

She swallowed the intended reference to driven snow, cursing at the necessity of censoring her private thoughts.

The elevator had arrived at the door of the outer office by the time Goldfarb had ushered them out of his little empire. Goldfarb didn't actually push them into it, but the little man's hands were fluttering with ill-restrained impatience. "I do hope you find Professor Miller before any harm comes to him," he said anxiously. "A terrible thing—and Edgar Burdillon hurt! Terrible! A man held in the greatest respect throughout *our* organization, I can assure you."

"Did Miller mention Burdillon when he came to see you?" Smith asked, pausing on the threshold of the elevator.

"No," said Goldfarb. "At least, I don't think—"

The bespectacled man was still in mid-sentence when the door slid shut and the elevator slid sideways toward its shaft.

A *universal transformer* might *be as useful to researchers in the longevity field as any other,* Lisa thought as they descended. Was it possible that Morgan had been talking about the main line of his research, albeit from a slightly odd angle? The transformer he never found might have been even more useful to people determined to give humankind a hefty shove up the evolutionary ladder. If Morgan *had* been talking to Goldfarb about his own Holy Grail, and someone misunderstood. . . . Maybe he'd recently seen some results obtained by one of the researchers sponsored by Ahasuerus that connected in a nonobvious way with what he'd been doing for the last forty years—something that made him see some of his former results in a new light. Maybe his old hopefulness had been stirred up again.

She abandoned the train of thought when she noticed that Peter Grimmett Smith was frowning. His mind was still on Chan Kwai Keung, and Chan's insistence on speaking to Lisa. All the suspicions Smith had generously set aside in order to make use of her expertise had obviously been reawakened. He looked like a man who was wondering whether he might have made a serious mistake. Given his age, he must be in the same position relative to compulsory retirement that Lisa was, and he probably had an equally thin margin for error.

Lisa wished that she'd had more sleep and that she didn't feel so ragged. Despite the smartish dressing, her right arm had begun to ache all the way from the elbow to the palm of her hand.

Fortunately, Smith still remembered the code when the elevator reached its destination on the ground floor. The teenage receptionist hardly glanced at them as they crossed the lobby to the other elevator; she was busy with her computer, making a great show of concern, although the dullness of her blue eyes gave the lie to her performance.

"Do you think he was lying?" Lisa asked Smith, hoping to distract his attention from more embarrassing possibilities. "Goldfarb, I mean."

"Difficult to say," Smith replied, catching his lower lip with his teeth as he put on a show of bringing the question into focus. "The trouble with organizations like Ahasuerus is that they're a law unto themselves. They think they're above petty national concerns. If Miller *had* given them something they considered valuable, I'm not at all sure that they'd tell us what it was just because the poor devil has been kidnapped. They'd be more likely to hire some fancy mercenary group to go after the kidnappers for them—but we've had no indication yet of any such move, and even if Ahasuerus's private enclave of the net is as secure as Goldfarb thinks it is, there isn't a mercenary outfit in these parts whose communications are any more solid than a sieve."

"And if he *isn't* telling the truth," Lisa said, "why make up such a peculiar story? Why take the trouble to tell us that whatever Morgan wanted to give him, it's forty years out of date? And why throw in all those impressions? It's not the kind of smoke screen I'd have—"

She broke off as the elevator stopped and its twin doors parted.

"Oh, *fuck*!" she breathed.

Directly ahead of them, about fifteen meters away, the body of Peter Grimmett Smith's driver lay supine on the concrete, unconscious or dead. There was an obscenely large gun in her outstretched right hand, pointed in the direction of a yellow Fiat that was skewed across the entry.

If appearances could be trusted, the Fiat had been shunted into that position by a black Daf van, both of whose doors were yawning wide. The huge screen shielding the entrance to the parking lot had almost completed its descent a couple of meters behind the van.

Chan Kwai Keung was standing beside the Fiat, having apparently exited the driver's seat in some distress. There was blood on his forehead and naked fear in his face as he stared at a black-helmeted figure who was pointing a gun almost as large as Ginny's at his chest, from little more than arm's distance.

TEN

Peter Grimmett Smith was obviously a senior spook, who had presumably been desk-bound for many years, but he must have known more active days and he hadn't lost the reflexes instilled by his early training. No sooner had he seen the body of his driver than he threw himself forward, leaning low in anticipation of plucking the gun—which Ginny had presumably failed to use to any significant effect—out of her limp hand.

Lisa understood, of course, why Smith had felt compelled to go for the gun. He was unarmed, and the person who had felled the driver would know that, because he or she would know he would not have been allowed to carry a gun into the lobby. Smith had no idea of how many adversaries he might be facing, but he did know that once he got a gun in his hand, he would be no mean opponent.

Unfortunately, he was by no means the only one who knew that and understood its implications.

As Smith went for the gun, the black-helmeted figure who had Chan covered immediately turned in order to take care of the new hazard. As the gun fired, Lisa winced reflexively, but the sound was nowhere near as loud as she had anticipated.

The MOD man was already reaching out to snatch up the gun, and the shot that had been fired at him *almost* missed—but almost wasn't good enough. The impact wasn't sufficiently powerful to bowl Smith over, but it made him lurch and stagger, and his extending hand failed to pick up the weapon.

Lisa hadn't been able to see the dart flying through the air, but she saw its red fletchings as soon as it lodged in the muscle at the back of Smith's lower leg. She registered the fact that the missile was non-lethal, but only in passing. The intention at the forefront of her mind was to get out of the way before the black-helmeted figure fired again.

Chan Kwai Keung obviously had the same idea. As soon as the gun had swung away from him, he dived to his left, determined to put the body of the Fiat between himself and the shooter.

Lisa went to her own left. There was a gray Datsun parked on that side of the elevator doors, no more than a couple of meters away, and she dived toward it, ducking down as low as she could to ensure that her whole body would be shielded the moment she was in front of the hood. It was a wise precaution, because a second shot sounded from the direction of the attendant's booth, far louder than the first. The window of the Datsun's passenger seat exploded into a host of tiny shards.

"Lights!" howled a distorted voice, twisted as much by anguished urgency as by the device set to disguise it.

That was a real bullet! Lisa thought. *If it had hit me. . . .*

Only twelve hours had passed since the time she had been forty years in the police force without ever having had a gun pointed in her direction. Now she had been shot at twice, and although she was fairly certain that the first shooter had aimed to miss, she wasn't at all sure about this one.

The first time, she had been curiously detached from the whole business, incapable even of participating fully in her own pain, but twelve hours had made a big difference. This time, she was abruptly consumed by a sickening wave of pure terror.

If we don't have what we need, the first shooter had told her, *we'll be back, and then. . . .*

They didn't have what they needed. They couldn't have, because she hadn't had it. So now they were back, in a mood less generous than before. It was crazy, of course—completely crazy—but that didn't mean that the danger facing her was any less. Quite the reverse, in fact.

There was a delay of three or four seconds before the parking lot's strip-lights went out. That left enough time for Lisa to peep over the Datsun's hood and see Peter Grimmett Smith make a second attempt to grab Ginny's pistol.

He succeeded, but the dart in his leg had discharged its cargo of relaxant poison and the leg was already useless. He couldn't balance himself to fire, and his body betrayed him as he tried. By the time he had swiveled the weapon to point at the shooter, his target was on the move, chasing after Chan Kwai Keung. Smith began to topple before he could adjust his aim.

Lisa guessed that Chan must have used the cover provided by the Fiat to roll under one of the vehicles parked on the far side of the area, because the black-helmeted figure couldn't seem to find him.

Is that a man or a woman? Lisa thought as she ducked down again. The figure wasn't tall, but it was very solid, with a body-builder's muscles. If it *was* a female body, it had to be the body of a Real Woman. Whoever had shot the telephone out of her hand had been every bit as solid, and every bit as aggressive, but if that had been a Real Woman too, it couldn't possibly have been the one she knew best. Whatever else Arachne West might have said to her, she would never have addressed Lisa as "You stupid bitch." She had never thought of the woman as a friend, but Arachne had seen things slightly differently.

The overhead lights went out before Lisa gave in to the temptation to sneak another look. With the strip-lights off too, she knew that her sense of sight would be useless for at least three minutes. Although the lot wasn't entirely dark—there were horizontal ventilation slits set high in the walls, and some daylight filtered through, but her eyes would need time to adapt. She had to presume that the shooter had wanted the lights out because her dark helmet was equipped with some kind of infrared sensor that would make living bodies stand out like beacons.

Lisa knew that if the second shooter had the same equipment, as well as a gun that fired real bullets, she and Chan were in real trouble. She reminded herself that although the shooter in her apartment had made some ugly threats, all the bullets fired had been directed at inanimate targets. When Ed Burdillon had walked

in on the Mouseworld bombers, they had only used their heavy
artillery to cover him while they knocked him out and then
dragged him to safety. So far, these lunatics had tried hard to avoid
killing anyone—but they'd never have come back for a second bite
at the cherry, especially in broad daylight, if they weren't desperate. Their carefully laid plan must have gone wrong. They hadn't
found what they wanted at Lisa's apartment, or on the equipment
they'd stolen from Morgan's house, and Morgan himself presumably hadn't told them what they wanted to know. They were not as
scrupulous today as they had been the night before—and the shot
fired at her as she dived for cover behind the Datsun had been far
too close for comfort.

Lisa cursed herself for the weakness of her body and spirit alike.
She was too old, at sixty-one, for playing cat-and-mouse with killers.
Her bones were too fragile, and the shock of fear that had gripped
her made her feel utterly helpless.

She scrambled along the body of the Datsun and huddled
behind the rear wheel. She guessed that whoever had shot at her
must have fired from the attendant's booth, and would probably
have left it as soon as the lights went out, intending to edge along the
wall against which the cars were parked. She had noted that the car
beyond the Datsun was a Renault with an overgenerous wheelbase,
and she rolled beneath it. That placed her in deep shadow, from
which she could see nothing—but in which she could not easily be
seen, even by someone with a body-heat sensor. Unfortunately, she
knew, the advantage would probably be temporary. Whoever was
inching along the wall would soon start peering beneath the vehicles,
knowing that they provided the only available hiding place.

Lisa shut her eyes and concentrated her attention on listening; if
their assailants had boots as smart as their black clothing, they
wouldn't be making a lot of noise, but they couldn't move silently.
She tried to summon up a picture in her mind's eye of the exact spot
in which Peter Grimmett Smith had fallen, and the probable disposi-
tion of his limbs. Had she a chance of getting to the gun that had

fallen from his hand before the enemy could get a clear shot at her? If so, could she judge the position of either shooter well enough by sound alone to get off a good shot of her own? It might not be necessary to hit anyone—the mere fact that she had a gun and was capable of using it would surely make them cautious, and should make them seek cover.

Her right arm was alight with pain from wrist to elbow. When she had rolled over, she had pressed the cuts between her body and the concrete floor, and the sealant hadn't been laid on thick enough to provide a protective cushion.

She swore at herself, commanding herself to focus, and to stop complaining.

She decided, having given due consideration to the plan, that if she tried to go for Smith's gun, she would make an absurdly easy target. The sensible thing to do was to try to put more distance between herself and the elevator door. If the person who was coming after her was moving slowly enough, she might actually be able to reach the exit gate at the far end of the lot. If she could only raise the screen . . .

It was not to be. As she rolled across the gap separating the protective chassis of one vehicle from its neighbor, she finally heard the give-away scrape of cloth against brick, and the gun that was firing real bullets sounded again, close enough this time to leave her ears ringing.

The adaptation of her eyes was set back too, by the sight of the muzzle flash and the vivid spark that soared from the concrete not five centimeters from her face as the bullet struck the ground and ricocheted away.

"Cool it!" screeched a distorted voice, which must have originated from the far side of the lot, although it blended with the gunshot echoes rebounding eerily from the walls.

"Have you got him?" was the only response—a totally unnecessary one, given that the shooter with the dart gun hadn't fired, as he or she surely would have if Chan had presented a target.

Despite the aftereffects of the echoing shot, Lisa heard her own pursuer drop awkwardly to the ground, presumably using the butt of the gun for temporary support as he or she fell into a prone position no more than a couple of meters away. Lisa knew that she had to get out of the confined space beneath the car if she were to avoid a shot that could hardly miss, so she scrambled forward desperately, not caring about the fact that she would expose herself fully to the shooter with the dart gun. If she had to be taken out, she figured it was far better that it should be done by a dart than by a bullet.

As soon as she pulled herself to her feet, she set herself to run across the open space between the lanes, hoping she could see well enough to throw herself into the space between two cars and obtain a measure of cover. She could see a little better now, but the world was full of shadows.

She heard the dart gun go off as the other shooter fired at her, but she felt no impact. As soon as the body of another vehicle offered her protection against another shot from that direction, she concentrated on putting something solid between her body and the enemy who was firing real bullets.

This time, there was no pursuing shot. Was that because the advice to cool it had been heard and heeded? Or was it just that the shooter with the real gun knew exactly where she was and was moving in for the kill?

For the kill. The unspoken words echoed in Lisa's skull, sending forth new ripples of panic—but no shot came.

Lisa dared to think that she might make it after all if she resumed her stealthy flight toward the exit door—and the distinction between deep and light shadow was becoming a little clearer now. She couldn't *see*, exactly, but she wasn't blind either. She began to move once more—but then the dart gun went off yet again, and this time she did feel an impact.

The strike was in the upper part of her left arm, and it didn't feel like a prick or a stab. It was as if some mildly boisterous acquaintance had struck her lightly with his fist, in a perfectly friendly fashion—but that was an illusion. Lisa knew immediately that the glancing nature of the blow wasn't good news. The muscle relaxant with which the dart was tipped had to be powerful if it had felled a man of Peter Grimmett Smith's mass within seconds. Although it might take as much as a minute for her veins to carry the less than full dose far enough to immobilize her, and a further two minutes for enough of it to reach her brain to render her unconscious, she was finished— and with two searchers to evade, Chan Kwai Keung's chances of getting away would be minimal.

Then she heard an almighty crash, far louder than the gunshots that had preceded it.

Startled, she turned and lifted her head. The movement made her dizzy, but she was still conscious, and true sight was abruptly returned to her.

The plastic doors closing off the entrance to the parking area had imploded. A black van, somewhat larger than the Daf that had rear-ended Chan's Fiat, was hurtling through them, its headlights ablaze. A voice was already blaring from an invisible loudspeaker: "Put down your weapons *now!*"

It wasn't a cityplex police van. Cityplex police vans were white. It could be Special Branch, Lisa thought, or even more spooks from the MOD. Whoever it was, though, they had to be on her side, not the side of the black-clad assassins.

As she began to feel faint, the first retaliatory shot rang out. She saw the black van's windshield respond to the impact; it was crazed, but not shattered. The result of the shot became irrelevant in any case when the new arrival cannoned into the back of the Daf, whose forward lurch sent Chan's yellow Fiat spinning. The noise was appalling.

The Fiat's windows weren't as resilient as the big van's. Shards of plastic seemed to fly everywhere. The shooter with the dart gun was briefly silhouetted against the glare of the headlights, running but seemingly going nowhere.

Lisa just had time to think "Wow!" before the dizziness blurred her vision irrevocably. Even then, she didn't lose consciousness. She tried with all her might to stand up, but her body wouldn't obey, and the only result of her determination was that she stumbled sideways. The concrete rose up to smash itself into her shoulder, but she was hardly aware of the fact of the pain, let alone the intensity of the feeling.

Hey! she thought. *This stuff has its advantages. I could get used to this state of mind, if only . . .*

It seemed, somehow, to be terribly unfair that she never got the chance to finish the sentence. Her pain had disappeared. Her fear had disappeared. Even the burden of her years seemed to have disappeared, but she didn't have time to savor her immunity from all harm. She finally fell, precipitously, into unconsciousness.

ELEVEN

The first thing Lisa remembered after waking up was that the last time she had awakened, she had had been unable to remember where she was, because she had been forced to check into the Renaissance Hotel instead of going home. For a moment or two, therefore, she assumed that because the bed on which she was lying was definitely not her own, she was back in the hotel. This conviction lent moral support to her reluctance to open her eyes, but her attention was soon claimed by the awkward awareness that her mouth was *very* dry. That seemed odd—she couldn't remember drinking any alcohol. What on earth could have happened to render her so thirsty?

When she finally remembered the circumstances under which she had gone to sleep, and the fragment of a day that had preceded it, she had no alternative but to force her sticky eyes open. She tried to sit up, but she got only halfway and had to lean back on her elbow.

She found herself staring into the capacious features of a brown-eyed man she had never seen before.

He waited for her to realize, as she tried to raise herself, that she was wearing only her not-so-smart underwear—at which point she snatched up the sheet she had been trying to cast off.

She glanced around at the room, which was small and low-ceilinged, its walls papered with off-white anaglypta that probably dated back at least to the 1990s. The abundant but desiccated autumnal foliage visible through the wood-framed window, eerily lit from within, suggested that she was in an upstairs room overlooking a tree considerably older than the wallpaper. The bed had a tubular-steel frame whose brown paint was flaking off, and the chair in which the brown-eyed man sat was a pine kitchen chair whose cherry-red woodstain was equally eroded. She certainly wasn't in a police station.

Night had obviously fallen again, but there was no way of knowing exactly how long she had been unconscious.

A large hand extended a cup toward her that was full of a warm brown liquid, at which she stared suspiciously.

"It's tea," explained a deep voice.

"I don't drink tea," she said, contradicting herself by taking a tentative sip. "And I wouldn't take sugar if I did," she added, grimacing.

"Drink it anyway," the brown-eyed man advised. He was wearing a smartsuit made from the same fabric as Peter Grimmett Smith's but cut in a contemporary style. Its quiet elegance made Lisa all the more conscious of her own lack of clothing and the fact that her undershirt was far from smart in any sense of the word.

She drank some more tea, figuring that the only thing that really mattered, given the circumstances, was its wetness. It moistened her mouth and moderated the intensity of her thirst. Then she said, "Who are you?"

"The man who saved you from abduction by two crazy women. Abduction—or worse," he replied. He obviously knew that she was a police officer, and felt obliged to establish his moral credentials in case she felt—as she was surely entitled to do—that wherever she was it was not the place she ought to be.

"Crazy women?" Lisa queried.

"You didn't know they were women? Or was it that you didn't know they were crazy?" He was trying to make a slight joke, but she wasn't in the mood.

"Those matte-black one-pieces aren't the most figure-flattering garments in the world," she pointed out. "Who *are* you—and what were you doing crashing into the parking area like that?"

"You can call me Leland," he said in an offhand manner calculated to suggest that it probably wasn't his real name, first or last. "We were paying a call on someone in the building. We figured that something must be wrong when we saw the security guard unconscious, hanging halfway out of the hatchway. It seemed to be our duty as honest citizens to ride to the rescue."

"It probably was," Lisa conceded. "But you must have checked the ID in my pouch, so the fact that you've brought me here makes you guilty of obstructing justice, as well as abduction and unlawful imprisonment, so you can cut the honest-citizen crap. Why did you take my clothes?"

"They were dirty and torn," Leland told her. "Even smart fabric wouldn't have been able to cope with all that rolling around on the concrete, and there were some old bloodstains too. Your belt wasn't clean either—police personnel really ought to be more careful about pollution, especially the metaphorical kind. Intruders in the night don't just take things away, you know."

"They bugged my belt?"

"I've cleaned it—but if you've said anything you shouldn't have in the last eighteen or twenty hours, you'd better start thinking of ways to limit the damage. I think I can find you a shirt and some slacks to wear until your own clothes have been cleaned—Jeff's, not mine. He's more your size. He was with me in the van; you owe him for the rescue too." The man still seemed amused. Lisa didn't have time for a mental run-through of all the conversations of the early morning and late afternoon, but she was fairly certain that her own ignorance would have prevented her from giving away anything of real value to Morgan's kidnappers.

"Where am I?" Lisa asked. "Why aren't we at East Central Police Station?"

"Well, that's a long story," Leland told her. "I admit that I fell prey to temptation—but I honestly believe that you might thank me for it. I thought we might be able to scratch one another's backs. No pressure at all, of course—you can have your phone back at any time, and call whomever you want, so there's no question of unlawful imprisonment or obstructing justice. It wasn't me who shot you, but you did get a whiff of the gas we used against the shooters, so I felt obliged to render what first aid I could. If you feel that you have to cry for help right now, I'll just fade quietly way, leaving you here with the two women. I'd understand your determination to play by the book, in spite of your personal involvement. On the other hand, if you happened to decide that you'd rather have a word with the people who tried to shoot you *before* their lawyers get involved—or if you'd simply like to listen in while I have a word—I'd understand that too."

"Where am I?" Lisa repeated stubbornly.

"A little way out in the country," Leland said. "Not far from the cityplex. You could be back home inside an hour, by car—ten minutes if they care to send the MOD helicopter. There's nothing of much interest happening back there, though. Here's where it's at, for the moment. I really do think that we could help one another, and that you and I stand a better chance of figuring this thing out together than either of us would have if we followed separate lines of investigation. If your first priority is to get Morgan Miller out in one piece, I could be a lot more useful than Kenna's blindfolded plods or Smith's third eleven spooks. What do you say, Dr. Friemann?"

Lisa's head was still aching, and the tea hadn't yet quenched her thirst. She didn't want to make any decisions just yet. She made a show of inspecting the sealant on her arm and hand. The old wounds hadn't been reopened, but she noticed a new graze on her elbow. Her upper left arm, where she'd been darted, was much uglier but it didn't hurt at all. Leland, or his friend Jeff, had sprayed sealant on it.

"Who are you working for?" she asked.

"Can't tell you that," he replied unapologetically.

"Who were you going to visit when you interrupted our little melodrama?"

"Goldfarb, of course. We don't know much more than you do, so we were following the same trail. Really lucked out, didn't we? All we had to do to crack the case was smash down the door. The crazies had already kayoed all three of you, so it was just a matter of picking up the bad girls and getting the hell out before the cityplex police arrived. Your response times stink, by the way."

He hadn't mentioned Chan, Lisa noted. Maybe he didn't know that Chan had been there. He obviously thought the "bad girls" had been after her, and hadn't realized that the pulverized Fiat had anything to do with the case. Maybe Chan was still loose, still carrying whatever item of information he had that he wanted to confide to her and her alone.

"Try to see it from my point of view," the big man urged. "I had to take the opportunity to grab the two women, and I couldn't resist the temptation to bring you along too. Technically, as you've carefully pointed out, it's illegal, but we're on the same side. We both want Morgan Miller out, and we're both *burning* to know why he was snatched in the first place. As proof of my good intentions, I'm prepared to give you the one bit of valuable information I have that you don't, without asking anything in return but a little of your time. Want to hear it?"

"Go on," said Lisa, making no promises.

"Smith's got his knickers in a twist for nothing. The project Burdillon was working on is redundant. It never mattered a damn whether he succeeded or not. The government spent so much time dithering that the war arrived before they were halfway ready, but my guys were always ahead of the game. They already have the product, and they'll be the ones who'll determine its distribution. It's quite possible, of course, that the crazy ladies didn't realize that and thought it might be salable, but if that's so, the whole thing is a storm in a teacup of no real significance. If it were something else of Miller's—something unconnected with the war work—I'd be as puzzled as you are by the fact that he doesn't seem to have confided in you. If *that*'s so, there must be a *very* good reason for it, don't you think?"

It was a tricky question, and Lisa thought about it for a full minute before replying. She had finished the tea and was desperate for a refill, even though she didn't drink tea. "I think this whole stupid affair is a comedy of errors either way," she said eventually. "If it's not Morgan's recent work that sparked this off, then Goldfarb, or his opposite number in Swindon, must have put two and two together and made twenty-two. Someone *might* think that Morgan has stumbled across some kind of longevity treatment, and the rumor may have been exaggerated as the whisper was passed on, but I can't believe there's anything really there. If Morgan says he failed, he really did fail."

"There are no failed experiments in science," Leland told her sardonically. "Just experiments that don't give you the answer you were looking for. Sometimes that's because you're asking the wrong question."

He doesn't know Morgan Miller, Lisa thought. *Morgan was always careful to ask* all *the questions, even if he couldn't answer them.* "So who are the crazy women working for?" she asked.

"I don't know," he confessed. "It's not the Leninist Mafia, or any gang of biotech bootleggers that *we* know about. It looks like an ad hoc conspiracy, hastily flung together. Even in this game, appearances aren't always deceptive."

"And why should you know more about the Leninist Mafia or biotech bootlegging than *we* do?" Lisa challenged, trying to imply that her "we" included the MOD as well as the police, although she didn't know the first thing about Special Branch ops, let alone Peter Grimmett Smith's secret business. Although her warrant card identified her as a forensic scientist, she figured that her interlocutor couldn't know for certain that she wasn't attached to Special Branch and hadn't done any significant work on bootlegged biotech.

Leland hesitated before saying, "Well, there are no prizes for guessing that I'm private security, nor for figuring out that I probably wouldn't be on the case if I weren't in something like the same line of work as you. I might as well come clean, though, and admit that busting everyday pharmaceutical counterfeiters is more my sort of thing than a weird mess like this. You know I can't tell you who I work for, but you also know what that means."

"The megacorps," Lisa said. "I suppose they don't like to be called the Cabal?"

"As far as I can tell," Leland informed her wryly, "they *love* it. But that's by the by. The question is: can we work together, or are you going to go after me for loading you in back of the van with the other two? Even though the girls aren't mafia, they're bound to have lawyers. If I'd left them to be taken into custody, the local plods would have done everything by the book—and by the time you'd woken up, you'd have had to sit twiddling your thumbs while the MOD hammered out some kind of deal to persuade the captives to sell out their pals. You ought to be grateful to me for expanding your options."

"I'm not going to make myself an accessory to torture," Lisa said sharply.

"Of course not," Leland replied soothingly. "If I were going to try anything of that sort, I'd make very sure you weren't involved, for my sake as well as yours. In this instance, we don't have time—the trouble with obtaining information under duress is that you have to be able to check it out and take punitive action if you've been sold a pup. However crazy these two are, they know that we're in a race against the clock. They'll feed us bullshit if they can, especially if we play the bully. We'll have to work a little more creatively. It won't be easy—but I figure that the two of us might have a better chance than either one alone."

"You haven't tried to question them by yourself?" Lisa asked skeptically.

"They're still asleep," he told her. "There wasn't time to be subtle back in the car lot—I had to hit them with the gas. I figure they'll be awake at any time now, but it might be as well to let them consider their situation for a little while. Their clothes weren't nearly as badly damaged as yours, but I took them anyway. They're very modern girls—smartskins, no underwear. They're tightly secured, each in a different room. They'll be feeling *very* vulnerable."

"I can't be a party to this," Lisa said, without much conviction.

"That's a shame," Leland told her. "I'll be talking to them anyway—the only result of your staying out of it will be that our chances of getting what we need are reduced—and you'll remain ignorant of anything I do manage to find out. Do you really want to pass on your best chance of finding out where Miller is in time to get him out alive?"

Lisa could only reply to that with a censorious glare, but Leland wasn't the kind of man to wilt before a dirty look. She knew he was right, and that the two would-be assassins were far more likely to let something slip in their present circumstances than they would be if they were subjected to due process under the protection of PACE 2, with their lawyers at their elbows. She also knew that he was trying to curry favor by letting her in on the interrogations—a favor whose acceptance might be dangerous. Making herself an accessory to an illegal interrogation could easily turn out to be the next best thing to handing her head to Judith Kenna on a silver platter, careerwise. Mike Grundy had suggested that cracking the case might be exactly what the two of them needed to stave off compulsory retirement for a few more years, but the *way* it was cracked might be even more important in that regard than merely getting a result.

In the end, it all came back to Morgan Miller and the need to get him out of whatever mess he'd contrived to get himself into. How much did she have to lose? The fact that Kenna was out to get her anyway increased the danger of not playing by the book—but how much should she care, at her time of life? If she wasn't prepared to be reckless now, when would she ever be?

"So what are you waiting for?" she asked the big man. "Get me those bloody clothes. And something else to drink."

Leland grinned as he took back the empty cup. "Don't worry," he said. "I'll cover your back if you cover mine. All we have to do is make sure that the good end happily and the bad unhappily. As long as the story works out, it won't matter a damn whether there really is an immortality serum or not."

Lisa waited until he had fetched the clothes, a bunch of bananas, and another cup of tea before telling him that the legendary Adam Zimmerman hadn't approved of the word "immortality" because it implied an inability to die. "In the business," she said as she regarded the bananas with a suspicious eye, "we prefer the term emortality, with an 'e.'"

"They're ordinary supermarket fruit," Leland assured her. "Standard dietary supplements. No therapeutics, let alone psychotropics. I'm paid to hunt down bootleggers—I don't rip off their stock."

The shirt and slacks he gave her were loose, but not absurdly ill-fitting. When she'd achieved a better state of modesty and a fuller stomach, he handed back her belt, pouches and all. It was an obvious gesture of good faith. She could have summoned help within two seconds, using two fingers; he wouldn't have been able to stop her. If they were way out in the wilds of Somerset or Gloucestershire, it might take so long for help to come that he and his friend Jeff could be five miles away by the time it arrived, but he'd have to be very clever indeed to avoid the consequent chase, and he probably wouldn't get anything out of his captives in the meantime. Lisa didn't bother to take the phone out of its holster.

"Had you checked out the Institute of Algeny?" she asked.

"Not yet." The abruptness of the answer suggested there might have been no need—perhaps because the information that had been handed down to him had originated there. Perhaps, Lisa thought, Goldfarb's disdain for the Algenists hadn't been a mere matter of the pot assuming that the kettle was black.

"If Morgan did have something valuable," Lisa observed, "the fact that he was talking to supposedly nonprofit organizations implies that he wouldn't have wanted it to fall into the hands of your employers."

"Or Mr. Smith's," Leland pointed out.

"Morgan wasn't the government's biggest fan," Lisa agreed, "but he did know that there's a war on. If he'd thought the MOD could use whatever he had, he'd have given it to them. I still think this is all a wild goose chase."

"You're probably right," the big man conceded. "But if there are any wild geese to be caught, I want to be the one who bags them, and if there aren't, I need to be able to convince my employers of that fact. If I can't, I could be out of a job. Then, if you decided to turn vindictive later, I could be in a very deep hole indeed."

"Strangely enough," Lisa said grimly, "I think I know exactly how you feel. If this doesn't go well, we could both end up regretting that we ever met."

TWELVE

They looked in on both prisoners before attempting to bring either of them around. The first was in the bedroom next to the one where Lisa had been lodged. She had reddish-brown hair, severely cut into a styleless bob, and sharply delineated features flecked with freckles and moles. She was older than Lisa had expected, though not as old as Lisa herself. Lisa paused long enough to examine the tenor of the muscles in the arm that rested on top of the blanket covering her naked body.

"Metabolic retuning and artificial steroids," Leland opined, but Lisa shook her head.

"Hard work, mostly," she said. "Carefully calculated diet, obsessive exercising, strict denial of all cosmetic and quasimedical aids. She's a Real Woman."

"I don't go for the muscular type myself," Leland observed.

"Real Woman with a capital R and a capital W," Lisa said.

"I thought they'd gone the same way as all once-fashionable causes. Died with the so-called third phase of feminism, didn't they? Before my time, of course."

And beyond your interest, evidently, Lisa added silently. She said, "The movement broke up, but its core members stayed loyal to its ideals, some of them even more so than they had been before. They still have a voice within the radfem ranks, and they still command a lot of respect in an elderly statesman kind of way."

"We already knew they were radfems," Leland observed in a neutral tone—but he was looking at her thoughtfully, as if there was something she wasn't telling him.

"Did we?" Lisa countered.

"You saw the tapes of the university bombers," he came back.

"You shouldn't have," Lisa reminded him. "They were supposed to be a secret between the police and the Ministry of Defence."

"And the campus security patrol," Leland pointed out. "How many holes does a sieve need? You don't know her, I suppose?"

"I don't think so," Lisa told him.

"You don't *think* so? What's that supposed to mean?"

"It's supposed to mean that there's something vaguely familiar about her. It might just be the type, of course—I've met more than a few Real Women in my time, and I wouldn't necessarily recognize this specimen if we'd met ten or twenty years ago. Maybe I've seen her working out at one of the gyms I've used. Either way, I can't put a name to her."

"But if she were local, you'd have mutual acquaintances? All part of the same old-girls' network?" He said it as if he thought he'd put his finger on a useful connection, but he didn't follow it up. It would be easy enough to check out local women who'd once been self-declared members of the movement. Arachne West's name would come out on top of the heap—but that didn't mean that Arachne was involved, or that it would be easy to locate her if she were.

Lisa was still smarting from the insult of the "old-girls' network" remark when she walked into the downstairs room where the second captive was secured, although she knew she was displacing emotional energy from a slowly growing anxiety that her personal involvement with this mess might not have begun, and might not end, with Morgan Miller. Fortunately, there was no danger of any further embarrassment. She recognized the second prisoner immediately, and knew that she was the real prize—the linchpin of the whole conspiracy.

Stella Filisetti was less than half Lisa's age, and at least twenty years younger than her companion. Her pale hair was of medium length and silky, and her body was possessed of the peculiar combination of softness and solidity that was still the sole prerogative of authentically young women. She had not yet reached the point of decision regarding the use of such artificial aids as metabolic retuning, calorie-depleted food, indwelling scavengers, and epidermal rejuvenation.

Stella had been carrying the real gun, Lisa realized; it was Stella who had come within inches of killing her. It probably was not Stella who had called her a stupid bitch and taunted her with Morgan's indifference, but it must have been Stella who had supplied the script.

"It's Morgan's current research assistant," she informed Leland.

"Ms. Filisetti," he said, to show that he was up to speed.

"Suspect number one," Lisa confirmed. "The only one close enough to have taken a good long look at his continuing experiments and his stored data. The only one close enough to have gotten ahold of the wrong end of an awkwardly placed stick. She had the means to get the bombers into Mouseworld and almost certainly knew the codes that let the kidnappers into Morgan's house." *But not,* she reminded herself, *the codes that let the burglars into my flat.*

"We don't know for sure that she got ahold of the wrong end of the stick," Leland reminded her dutifully. "We have to work on the hypothesis that it might have been the right end."

"You might," Lisa demurred. "I'm not under contract to deliver the elixir of life to *my* employers. All I have to do is free Morgan Miller before he gets hurt. For that purpose, the hypothesis that this is all some stupid mistake will do very well indeed."

Leland didn't bother to point out that if Miller really had nothing to give away, accounting for his exploratory visits to Ahasuerus and the Algenists wouldn't be easy. He was more concerned to usher Lisa out of the room before Stella Filisetti woke up and heard them talking. He wanted to conserve the element of surprise.

Morgan must have been playing a game, Lisa thought. *He was laying down a false trail, dangling a lure—and it worked, far too well. Why on earth couldn't he have let me in on it?*

Leland stood aside to let her precede him into a surprisingly capacious, if rather bare, kitchen, where a short and wiry man with a dark complexion—presumably Jeff—was seated at a hectically stained pine dining table, circa 1995. Lisa guessed that the table must have lost its initial polish shortly after the turn of the century, and that Jeff had never had any to lose.

As Leland and Lisa sat down, the other man politely rose to his feet, waiting for instructions. Leland told his subordinate to wake the prisoner in the downstairs room, advising him to do it gently and to give her a mug of tea, with lots of sugar. Jeff nodded. He filled a mug from the teapot that sat in the middle of the table and spooned three sugars into it before nodding to Lisa and departing.

"Okay," Leland said when Jeff had closed the door behind him. "You know her. That puts the ball in your court. How should we play it?"

It wasn't an easy question to answer. Lisa was slightly surprised that it had been asked. She had assumed that the plan was fairly simple: they would say what they had to say in order to elicit a response—any kind of response to begin with—and if Stella wouldn't let anything slip, they would become gradually more provocative. Then she realized that Leland was testing her in exactly that progressive fashion: all Mister Nice Guy to begin with, slowly tightening the procedure to shake something loose from *her* cabinet of curiosities.

"She's a rank amateur," Lisa observed, feeling no compunction about reiterating the obvious. "She'll be scared, but she must have gone into this knowing she'd eventually be caught. Professionally speaking, this was a suicide mission. Crazy—but not *just* crazy. The motive must have been powerful if it not only moved her to this kind of recklessness, but allowed her to draw so many others into the conspiracy, including at least one Real Woman."

"Right," said Leland. "The rest probably know by now that they can't hold out long, even if they thought differently to begin with. They must want to get the information to friends elsewhere before the net closes on them, but they obviously don't have it yet. Why else would they come after you a second time? Miller's holding out, or feeding them lies, and they haven't found what they want on his computers or your wafers. That's good—panic is always healthy in an interrogation situation. If I were to offer Filisetti a big enough bribe and a way out of the back door, do you think she'd sell her friends down the river?"

"How big a bribe?"

"Think of a number. What she'll eventually get, if anything, will depend on what she has to sell. As to what we can offer—the sky's the limit."

There was no point in insisting that what Stella Filisetti would eventually get was at least ten years if Lisa had any say in the matter. "She's not stupid," she said instead. "She's not going to believe you if you offer her a million euros. In fact, our principal problem is going to be persuading her that anything we say can be trusted—and persuading ourselves that anything she says can be trusted. As you've already pointed out, people desperate to buy time will come out with any old bullshit."

Leland sighed. "All the effort that went into the Human Genome Project," he said, "and we still have no trustworthy truth serum. Call that progress?"

Jeff returned. "She's very woozy," he reported. "Might be better to catch her before she's collected herself."

"Oh, well," said Leland. "I guess it's play-it-by-ear time. Come on."

Lisa took a quick peek through the kitchen curtains as she followed Leland back to Stella Filisetti's bedside, but there wasn't much to be seen through the reflection of the lighted room. The absence of any discernible lights outside suggested that they were quite a way from the cityplex, but she already knew that. There was a faint animal odor in the corridor, but the suggestion that they were in an old farm laborer's cottage could have been misleading.

Woozy or not, Stella Filisetti recognized Lisa immediately, and her eyes grew wide. She looked around as if unable to reconcile Lisa's presence with the surroundings. The fact that one of her wrists and one of her ankles were secured to the head and foot of the bed by smartfiber cords must have told her that she was not in police custody, even if the godawful carpet and matching curtains hadn't.

"Hello, Stella," Lisa said, unable to deny herself the satisfaction. "How does it feel to be such a lousy shot?"

The younger woman didn't reply, although her eyes certainly reacted. Lisa moved a straight-backed wooden chair to the side of the bed and sat down, her face no more than a meter from Stella Filisetti's. Leland remained standing, showing off his intimidating bulk.

"This is how it is, Stella," Lisa said, improvising furiously. "For me, this is a personal matter, for reasons you'll understand perfectly. For my friend here, it's business. He wants to bribe you and I want to cause you pain, but we both want Morgan Miller and we're prepared to settle for that. If anything happens to him that you could have prevented by talking to us sooner, you're going to answer to me as well as to the courts—and I can guarantee that it won't be a comfortable ride." She really had intended to start out gently, but it wasn't so easy to play nice while she was staring into the unrepentant face of the person who was responsible for this whole sorry mess, who had compounded that offense by trying to shoot her.

"You can't do this," the younger woman said, with little conviction.

"Yes, we can," Lisa retorted, figuring that she might as well go with the flow now that she had turned on the tap. "You know full well that anything that could motivate you to pull off this crazy stunt has to be important enough to motivate us to do what it takes to prize it out of your hands. It's driven you to the brink of committing murder, although I doubt that you had any inclination in that direction beforehand, so you can imagine well enough how far it might drive us. It's time to give it up and save yourself—and we can arrange that too. Just tell us what we need to know while there's still time and you can walk away."

"I don't know where Morgan is," Stella replied swiftly. "They thought it best that I didn't, just in case . . ."

Was it too glib? Lisa wondered. It would, after all, have been a sensible precaution to keep Morgan's location secret even from their own field troops—but these conspirators had not so far shown much sign of being sensible people. Even by the standards of a crazy world, they seemed seriously deranged.

"I don't believe you," Lisa said when she'd paused long enough. "The stupid thing is, Stella, that your scruples have led you astray. It was all a scam—a trap. Morgan seems to have fallen into it too, but he always did like to be out there ahead of the field, didn't he? Never a team player, alas, even while he was playing for the greatest team of all in the cause of progress. Heroic individualists can be so seductive, don't you think? Well, of course you do. I know exactly how you feel, because I've been a victim too—for forty years. Imagine that! I know *exactly* how you feel, Stella, because I've been up and down the same escalator half a dozen times. I know *exactly* how seductive Morgan can be, and exactly how deceptive—but I love him anyway. I always have. I love him enough to do whatever's necessary to save him from his own recklessness. So I'd be very grateful if you could just tell me where he's being held. It's over anyway. You must see that. You don't have the data, and time's already run out."

All the time she had been speaking, Lisa had been moving her face closer to Stella Filisetti's, flaring her nostrils slightly and widening her eyes so that the whites would be visible all around the irises. As mad acts went, it lacked all subtlety, but subtlety didn't seem to be an issue anymore.

It didn't work. It wasn't, as far as Lisa could judge, that the younger woman didn't seem convinced. It was more a matter of the conviction being woefully insufficient to break her resistance.

"Okay, Dr. Friemann," said Leland, his voice lowered almost to basso profundo. "That's enough of the threats. I warned you, didn't I? Now get the hell out of here so I can have a sensible conversation with the young lady."

Lisa winced inwardly, not so much at the "young lady" bit as at the realization that Leland had obviously learned his good cop/bad cop routine from classic movies that Stella Filisetti had probably seen and laughed at while she was in her teens. Lisa had no alternative, though, but to keep on going with the flow and hope that the oldest tricks were still the best. She stood up and stalked out of the room, closing the door behind her before pausing and gluing her ear to the ancient hardboard panel.

"She's upset," Leland explained to his prisoner, his deep voice clearly audible through the door. "She doesn't understand modern commerce. The police tend to have a very jaundiced view of the way the economy works—but that's necessary to the way they play their role. They're obliged to regard most forms of private enterprise as evil, and they don't have to recognize or face up to the fact that if they weren't *necessary* evils, they wouldn't exist. Personally, I'm a pragmatist. No ax to grind. To me, it's just a matter of fixing a price."

"It's not for sale," Stella Filisetti told him. Her voice wasn't powerful, but the words were quite distinct. "If you think it could be, you don't know what you're talking about. She's lied to you."

"She? You mean Dr. Friemann? Why would she do that?"

Lisa bit her lip, but reminded herself that Leland had to know that this was a ploy even older and more hackneyed than his own. Being helpless, the only chance Stella Filisetti had was to sow dissent in the opposition ranks.

"Because she wants it for herself. She's taken the long way around, but she knows what it is and she wants it. We have proof of that."

"What proof?" Leland wanted to know.

"Check your records, megacorp man. It's in the freezer."

What's in the freezer? Lisa thought, knowing that Leland must be wondering exactly the same thing.

"If Dr. Friemann already knows," Leland said, "the secret's already out. What harm is there in letting me in on it too?"

"It's been buried too long already," the higher voice said, becoming slightly shrill as hysteria sharpened its edge. "She's helped to keep it under wraps—but we're not going to let it stay buried. It doesn't matter what you do to me. I can't tell you where Miller is. We had to make certain of that."

"Everything's for sale, Stella," Leland told her—but Lisa could hear the puzzlement in his voice. "It's just a matter of finding the right price. The only question you have to ask yourself is whether you'd prefer to deal with a good customer or a skinflint."

"If that's what you think," Stella responded, "then she's definitely lied to you. God only knows what game she's playing—I certainly don't—but she and Miller have kept this thing between themselves for forty years. In my book, that's a crime against humanity. If you want answers, ask her."

That, Lisa thought, *had* to be acting. It had to be a bluff, no matter how convincing it sounded.

"I have asked her," Leland said. "She's convinced me that she doesn't know why Miller was taken. If you want to convince me otherwise, you'll have to give me more than mere abuse. It might be as well to remember that I'm the only thing standing between you and a long jail sentence. I'm the only one who can get you out of this."

"I don't have to convince you of anything," the young woman told him. "In fact, I hope you're right. I hope Miller *did* keep it secret, even from her. If it *is* true, however unlikely that may be, she's going to be extremely pissed when it does come out. Anything she wants to do to me, she'll want to do to Miller ten times over. If she thinks hell has no fury now, wait till she finds out what *scorn really is!*" The way the captive raised her voice implied that she knew perfectly well that Lisa was listening, and that she was talking to both of her interrogators, determined that if she couldn't drive a wedge between them, she could at least sow a little unhealthy confusion.

"I'm sure that's right," Leland said, having carefully lowered the volume of his voice, perhaps to imply that he was prepared to deal confidentially. "My people are pretty sure that she doesn't know—although I might be able to change their minds if you explain to me why you think otherwise. So why don't you let me in on the secret, so that we can figure out exactly what it might be worth?"

"To you," Stella Filisetti replied, not bothering to whisper, "it's not worth a damn thing. And that bitch outside the door, whether she's a rat or just a fool, probably isn't going to profit from it now. To us, it's worth *everything*. More than anything the law can throw at us once we've given it to the *right* people. So you and Friemann can go fuck yourselves—or each other, if you have the stomach for it. You're getting nothing out of me. Even if I knew where Miller is, I wouldn't tell you. You can hurt me as badly as you like, but all you'll get is wasted time."

Leland was silent. His script had been blown apart. *If Stella's lying,* Lisa thought, *she's much better at it than her amateur status suggests. If she's playing a game, she has far more skill than the average panicky interrogatee. If there really is a riddle to be solved, it isn't going to be easy to unravel, even though it doesn't need a genius to figure out what it must be that she thinks Morgan has discovered.*

After a further minute, Leland emerged from the room and closed the door behind him. "Better let her consider her situation for a while," he murmured. "Could be that the other one will be a little saner. After all, she's never screwed your crafty boyfriend."

His tone was neutral, but Lisa could tell that Stella Filisetti had got through to him. Whatever trust Leland had had in her had evaporated. From now on, she was a suspect in his eyes too. She wondered whether it was time to call for help, but decided after a moment's hesitation that duty could wait a little longer. After all, Leland could be right. The Real Woman presumably hadn't ever screwed the aforementioned crafty boyfriend, and even Lisa had to admit that that might make her just a little bit saner than someone who had.

"But this time," Leland added, "it's my turn to go first."

Second Interlude

DISTURBING SYMPTOMS

The dog riots of 2010 were the closest Lisa ever came to "frontline policing." She was called to the university to serve as an adviser to the chief inspector, David Kenneally. What she had in mind as she traveled out in one of the vans was a cozy situation way behind enemy lines, from which she could offer expert judgment as to the wise deployment of the uniformed officers. Kenneally had other ideas; although he had taken a training course in Advanced Negotiating Skills, he did not feel that what he had been taught was particularly relevant to the situation.

Presumably, the chief inspector would have felt far more confident if a lone gunman had taken hostages, or if some overstressed undergraduate were sitting atop the biology building threatening to jump, but Lisa had little sympathy for his plight. If Advanced Negotiating Skills didn't cover ugly mobs whose members had studied strategy and tactics by watching videotapes of cult activity in Jerusalem, Tokyo, and New York in 1999 and 2000, what on earth was the use of them in the twenty-first century?

"Why me?" Lisa asked when Kenneally told her he wanted her right beside him when he went to meet the notional leader of the demonstration.

"You know more about their concerns than anyone else on my staff does," he informed her.

"Only because I was once what *they*'d call a professional torturer," Lisa pointed out. "I even used to practice my dark artistry on this very site. I never worked with dogs, but I think the temperature out there's already a little too high to encourage nice distinctions. Right now, they're not likely to concede that being a mere mass murderer of mice is the next best thing to saintly innocence."

"We won't have to discuss your credentials with the demonstrators," Kenneally informed her dismissively. "You have seen this videotape they're up in arms about, I take it?"

Lisa had to admit that she had. "The voice-over is a pack of lies," she said. "Okay, so the dogs in the first sequence are more than a little disoriented, and maybe more than a little distressed, but there's no way their symptoms were caused by prion proteins or by any prion-producing autoimmune reaction. The labs have mouse models of classic CJD and at least three of its variants, but nobody makes dog

models of *any* human disease. The second lot are *not* being injected
with immunosuppressant viruses for the sake of germ-warfare
research, and the puppies being gassed in the final sequence are being
put down humanely in order that researchers can study the development of a disease that kills thousands of pets and working dogs every
year, with a view to finding a cure. Nor are any of the dogs British-
born—ever since the 2000 ban on the breeding of domestic dogs for
research purposes, the university has imported the very few dogs it
needs from France. The tape's pure black propaganda from beginning to end."

"That's exactly what I need, you see," the chief inspector told
her. "The calm voice of sanity."

"But they're not going to listen to the calm voice of sanity," Lisa
told him. "That's not the way this kind of game is played. Even if the
students who routinely use the building are steering clear, there's
bound to be somebody out there who'll recognize me and tip them off.
To them, I'll just be one more vivisectionist plugging the party line.
Believe me, sir, they hate police scientists almost as intensely as they
hate company-funded research workers."

"You speak their language," Kenneally insisted.

"Maybe—but with an inflection that immediately marks me as an
enemy," she protested. "You might as well ask Chan to talk to them."
Chan was also in the van, as was one of the campus security guards.

"Dr. Friemann's right," Chan put in. "If it is not safe for me to go
out, it is not safe for her."

"But Dr. Friemann is a police officer," Kenneally pointed out.
"For her, it's a matter of duty."

Chan called Edgar Burdillon on his mobile phone and told him
what the chief inspector was planning to do, but Kenneally was no
more impressed by Burdillon's objections than he had been by
Chan's.

"If you go out to talk to them, they will turn it into an argument,"
Chan said to Lisa. "It will add fuel to the flames. Far better to
stonewall them. If the chief inspector's men can hold their position,

the gale might just blow itself out. If you provoke them, you will definitely end up having to deploy riot shields and mount baton charges."

"It's not my decision," was all that Lisa could say in reply.

"With all due respect, Dr. Chan," Kenneally said, "I think I know more about keeping order in this sort of situation than you do. I helped to police dozens of political demonstrations and labor disputes while I was in the Met between fifteen and ten years ago. I even faced down the Countryside Alliance a time or two."

"The Countryside Alliance went to bat for the privilege of killing things," Lisa pointed out tiredly. "They weren't possessed by anything like the kind of righteous fervor that has these people in its grip."

In the end, of course, the chief inspector prevailed. He was the one with the privilege of issuing orders. Kenneally and his reluctant scientific adviser sallied forth, valiantly hoping to slay the dragon of extremism with the lance of moderation.

The crowd outside the main entrance of the building was about two hundred strong, but at least three-quarters of them had only come along to watch. They weren't being proselytized particularly fiercely and for the moment, they weren't part of the mob per se. The Animal Liberation Front and its allied organizations had bused in some two dozen agitators to swell the ranks of the local hard-liners, most of whom were local only in the sense that they lived somewhere in the cityplex. Being the easternmost campus of the Combined Universities, this one had attracted far less public attention in the past than those closer to the old Bristol city center, but the videotape that some insider had cobbled together with the aid of a miniature camera had brought the facility into prominence in spite of the fact that what the tape actually *showed* was negligible without the highly imaginative and completely mistaken voice-over. Having come into the eye of the public, however, the campus was not to be allowed to slip out again without a fight; that had become a point of principle ever since the ALF's nuisance tactics had started winning battles.

Chief Inspector Kenneally was a hardened twentieth-century man;

he hadn't adapted to the reality of the new millennium. He still believed in arbitration and compromise, but his opponents here were only interested in forcing concessions—and if they had to batter a few policemen to do it, they were ready to face the consequences. The jails were so overcrowded that they would be out on amnesty in a matter of months.

The leaders of the demonstration went by the cod-revolutionary pseudonyms of Eagle, Jude, and Keeper Pan. Keeper Pan was the only female. All three had voices trained to carry, and none was given to speaking if he or she could shriek instead.

When Chief Inspector Kenneally tried to assure the three of them that he could assuage many of their anxieties concerning the nature of the experiments in which the department's dogs were involved, they assured him that he could not. When he denied that any dogs kept by the university had ever been infected with brain-damaging antibodies or artificial viruses, they told him they had heard such apologetic lies a hundred times before, and invited him to deny that the pups that had been seen to die in a gas chamber were really dead.

"I can't do that," he admitted, "but my colleague Dr. Friemann will be pleased to explain to you exactly what kind of research is being conducted, and what benefits are expected to flow from it for thousands of household pets and working dogs."

Thanks a lot, Lisa thought as the hostile gazes of the three liberationists swung around to study her face. Eagle's face was doubly shielded by blond dreadlocks along with face paint that split his features into black and white, but his blue eyes were penetrating. Jude's warpaint was less flamboyant, and his dark eyes seemed less threatening, but Keeper Pan must have been even paler of complexion than Eagle when she was not in uniform, and the pinpoint pupils in her brilliant turquoise irises seemed particularly sinister.

"Just as her colleague Dr. Goebbels would have been happy to explain exactly how the death of the victims *he* sent to the gas chambers would benefit the mass of humankind," Eagle informed the chief inspector from the side of his mouth. "Murderers are never short of excuses."

"My job is to catch murderers," Lisa pointed out, figuring that while she was in the spotlight, she might as well try to do the job. "Not to mention rapists, thieves, and animal abusers. I analyse DNA—not just human DNA, but plant and animal DNA. I can tie a suspect to a crime scene by means of the grass stains on his shoes. I can identify the individual nest from which eggs have been looted and the individual tiger whose organs have been ground up to make quack medicines—and I've done both those things, for the Royal Society for the Protection of Birds and the World Wildlife Fund. I'm not the enemy. Biologists are not the enemy."

"Biologists who murder animals in the name of experimentation *are* the enemy," Jude retorted. "They're the enemy we're here to fight, the enemy we're here to stop. Biologists who create whole new species whose sole reason for being is to suffer from horrible diseases are *the enemy*. Biologists who make new kinds of viruses for use as weapons of war are *the enemy*. Biologists who play with immunosuppressants and prions as if they were toys are *the enemy*. They're the enemy that has to be defeated if we're to live like truly *human* beings. They're the enemy that has to be defeated if we're to live *at all*."

His oratorical technique was good. If he hadn't been trained, Lisa thought, he'd certainly put in some practice. As far as the people who'd come only to be bystanders were concerned, he was winning hands down.

"The vice-chancellor has agreed to set up an internal inquiry to look into all the allegations made by the person who made the tape," Kenneally said, obviously figuring that it might be best to bring the discussion down to earth again. "He's also offered to let you have a seat on the committee as well as to send delegates to give evidence. That's generous, I think—"

"Generous!" echoed Keeper Pan, her high-pitched voice cutting through the stormy air like an ancient factory whistle. "One place in a ready-made committee! One vote against a ready-made majority! One voice against a chorus! One honest witness against a team of stooges! Inquiry's just another word for *stall*. We don't want an inquiry—we want immediate action and a public guarantee that all animal experiments will be abandoned for good. We want it *now*." Perhaps, Lisa thought, Jude and Keeper Pan practiced their rabble-rousing techniques after sex, just as she and Morgan Miller had always practiced the art of clinical rhetoric.

Even Kenneally knew that Keeper Pan's last cry was the cue for a chant, and he tried to get in the way.

"That's not possible," he said, raising his voice to make sure everyone could hear him. "That simply *isn't possible*."

"Yes, it is," Eagle shouted back. "It's not just possible, it's *easy*. All you have to do is let the animals go."

Half a million mice! Lisa thought. *Well, maybe we should. Give them the half-million mice, and the cats—not to mention the rabbits—and let them carry their prizes away, while smooth-talking them into refraining from killing one another. If only Ed and Morgan had a pride of lions and a flock of lambs! How these fools could educate us then in the art of the possible!*

That was when the eggs started to fall on the police line. The "Rioters' Handbook" on the net advised all demonstrators to start with eggs, because eggs were messy without threatening real injury. The tactic was supposed to put the police at a PR disadvantage, because passing out riot shields in response to half a dozen eggs would always look like overreaction when the videotapes were studied. Every policeman and newsreader in the land had read the "Rioters' Handbook," of course—but that didn't make the gambit any easier to counter.

Kenneally didn't hesitate. He signaled for a second line of officers to move in front of the existing line, so that the men with the helmets and shields could be seen to be protecting their defenseless colleagues. As soon as the shields were in place, however, the hail of eggs intensified, smearing the sheets of transparent plastic with an opaque mess. At least one in ten of the eggs was rotten, and the stench of hydrogen sulfide filled the air. The volley was aimed primarily at the helmetless officers, but Lisa and Kenneally were too close to the line to avoid it—and there was no further point in their staying put, given that Eagle, Jude, and Keeper Pan had melted back into the crowd. Lisa didn't wait for an order before turning on her heel and running back to the command vehicle.

As if her flight were the cue that the demonstrators had been waiting for, a hundred voices took up Keeper Pan's suggested chant—and the hundred increased as the bystanders began to join in with the fun.

As soon as he was back in the command vehicle, hot on Lisa's heels, Kenneally ordered up the reserves. He instructed them to move into flanking positions, formed up for a baton charge.

"What kind of gas?" a uniformed inspector demanded.

How nice to have a choice, Lisa thought. *Once upon a time, it all had to end in tears, but now we have an entire spectrum of specialist smokes.*

"No gas!" Kenneally told him. "They're just kids, mostly. Let the batons give them pause for thought, then move forward—walking, not running. No head-breaking."

If only the demonstrators had been working to the same sporting assumptions, all might have been well—but the new kinds of gas were advertised on the net, and the best efforts of His Majesty's Customs & Excise were inadequate to prevent deliveries to eager customers. The reservists hardly had to take up their formations when the gas grenades began to break them up again—and when they charged, they *charged,* raggedly but with violent effect. If they refrained from head-breaking, it was only because their training had taught them well enough the tactics of jab-and-slash. They went for bellies, balls, and kneecaps, and cut down the opposition with far more effect than random blows to hard heads could ever have achieved.

The protesters didn't panic, but the bystanders did—and somehow, the least-careful bystanders now seemed to be in the front lines to the right and the left, if not yet in the center.

Lisa and Chan observed the chaos dutifully from the command vehicle, each with a conscientiously clinical eye.

"You were right, Miss," the security man observed, as if it were cause for surprise.

Lisa knew long before the official announcement came, twenty-four hours later, what the outcome of the riot would be. The university authorities undertook to comply with the spirit as well as the letter of the 2000 Act, banning all current and future experiments on dogs, unconditionally.

The ALF claimed yet another famous victory, and wisely refrained from returning to the fray on behalf of the rats and mice. Eagle and Jude were arrested but released without charge; Keeper Pan was the only real catch among those against whom there was sufficient video evidence to bring charges of assault. Under her birth name, Pamela Hardiston, she was sentenced to three months' imprisonment, but was removed from Warminster Open after seven days on medical grounds. She was credited with five more weeks of theoretical jail time at the Royal United, served under the joint supervision of Group Four and Bristol Cityplex Social Services, before being released on parole.

Lisa had faced at least a hundred perpetrators of serious crimes in various courtrooms before she finally ran up against one, in 2019, who was crazy enough to swear that he would come back and kill her when he was released. She was mildly surprised that it had taken so long, given the extreme reluctance of the vast majority of serious offenders to accept any responsibility for their own deeds. It always seemed to be *somebody* else's fault, and police scientists in general were no less unpopular among the criminal classes than detectives, but detectives received far more threats of vengeance—though not, of course, as many as innocent bystanders who happened to be eyewitnesses and therefore seemed to be universally regarded as legitimate targets.

The man who broke precedent by threatening Lisa was a serial rapist named Victor Leverer, who appeared utterly convinced of his innocence of any wrongdoing in spite of his frequent use of a knife. He seemed to regard the fact that none of the slashes he inflicted were mortal—even though some of them were far from trivial—as proof of his loving intent, and he offered an impassioned speech in his own defense in which he claimed that the minority of his accusers with whom he had actually had intercourse had been more than willing, and that the only reason they had subsequently turned against him was that they had been pressured by lesbian radfems convinced that all heterosexual intercourse was rape. Lisa, he claimed, was at the core of a radfem conspiracy, and she had fabricated the evidence linking him to those incidents in which he still denied any involvement at all. Strangely enough, there was no detectable pattern to his loudest denials—they were not the most serious assaults, nor the accusations whose evidential support was weakest.

"Don't worry about it, Lis," Mike Grundy said after the judge had delayed sentence so that a psychiatric report could be compiled. "He's just putting on a mad act before he goes to the shrink. It's only a ploy."

"The problem with that kind of ploy," Lisa told him glumly, "is that the people who try it sometimes fall for their own patter. If he pretends hard enough that I'm the Antichrist who stitched him up on behalf of Lesbians Incorporated, he might end up believing it, and even if the shrinks tell the judge to throw the book at him, he'll be out in seven—ten at the most. That's plenty long enough for the grievance to fester, but not so long that I needn't worry about it till I'm old."

"These things never come to anything," Mike told her. "Real life's not like TV and the movies. He'll have other things on his mind once he's sent down. He'll forget all about you inside of a year."

"Real life is getting more like TV and the movies every day," she countered with a sigh. "Where else can people find their role models now that the family's completely broken down and nobody reads books anymore?"

"The family hasn't broken down," he assured her. "And people still read. It's only TV that says otherwise."

In Mike Grundy's view, he and Helen still constituted a family of sorts in 2019, even though he'd accepted Helen's decision not to have children. On the other hand, while Mike and Helen were alike in hardly ever opening a book for other than strictly functional reasons, Lisa was a committed reader.

"Well," she said philosophically, "I suppose it goes with the territory. I suppose anyone who retires from the force without accumulating a whole football team of ugly monsters who've threatened to chop them into little pieces at the first opportunity obviously hasn't made sufficient impact on the Empire of Evil."

Oddly enough, it was the fallout from the Leverer case that first brought Lisa into contact with the Real Women, whose movement was still visible and fairly buoyant. She had often seen members of the clique working out in the gym she had been using for the last seven months, and had taken note of the fact that they were becoming gradually more numerous, but it wasn't until Leverer's threats hit the headlines that any of them tried to recruit her, or even to test out her credentials as a fellow traveler.

Two of them approached her one evening as she came out of the showers after finishing her routine.

"Lisa Friemann?" said the taller of the two—a dark-eyed woman who had taken the trouble not merely to shave but to permanently depilate her head. "I'm Arachne West. This is Della Vertue." Arachne West's shorter companion, whose still-abundant hair was flagrantly dyed a peculiar shade of blue-black, nodded. "We read about what happened in court."

"It happens," Lisa said. "Nothing to worry about."

"Maybe not," the bald woman said, "but it reflects on us all when people begin spouting that kind of hate. There are too many willing ears about. You live alone, don't you?"

Lisa blinked. "What makes you think so?" she asked warily. She was trying to edge away and terminate the conversation, but the two Real Women followed her into the dressing room.

"We haven't been digging," Arachne West assured her. "No reason why it should be a secret, is there? We can give you some numbers, if you like. Support, in case of trouble." She held up a small card, but Lisa could see only one phone number on it.

"I'm a police officer," Lisa said disbelievingly. "I've *got* support."

"Yeah—but sometimes there's support, and then there's support. We have policewomen in the movement, and they don't always seem to feel that their male colleagues are as supportive as they might be. Things do change, but they change slowly, and appearance doesn't always match reality."

"I'm fine," Lisa assured them. "Really."

They should have gone away then, but they didn't. "You really should get rid of those dead clothes," Della Vertue observed. "It makes good sense to keep up with the technology—for the sake of safety, not of fashion."

"What do you mean?" Lisa asked, taken somewhat aback by the woman's presumption.

"We live in a plague culture," Arachne West informed her. "You can steer clear of pricks, but steering clear of STDs is harder. Soon everyone will need a whole second skin."

"But not yet," Lisa pointed out.

"Soon," the bald woman repeated with perfect confidence. "Health is our most precious possession, and it gets even more precious as you get older. Keeping fit is only part of the answer. If you'd like to come to a meeting, we'd be very glad to see you. If you want to talk in private, that's okay too. Call me."

Lisa accepted the makeshift card but she didn't call. The sin of omission didn't offend Arachne West sufficiently to make her stop greeting Lisa when she saw her in the gym, often taking time out to exchange a few friendly words, but the Real Women didn't press their case any harder than that. They never offered to supply her with any body-building advice, but they presumably figured that a genetic analyst probably had access to any legitimate somatic modifiers she might need or desire.

In the course of the next couple of years, Lisa's chats with Arachne West grew gradually longer. Although she always thought of the Real Woman's theories and ideals as slightly crazy, she couldn't help but find them intriguing and mildly amusing.

"You might think that we protest a little too much," the strong-woman told her, "but that's because you haven't realized the depth of feeling that's wrapped up in the continuing backlash. Feminist analyses of the mechanics of male domination didn't just serve to educate women. They also educated men in the sly art of holding on to their most cherished privileges while making slow concessions in other areas. The iron fist wears a velvet glove nowadays, but it's still an iron fist. When it comes to the crunch, it's all about power, and men aren't going to let it go easily. This is one cold war that won't end in collapse and surrender."

"Oddly enough," Lisa told her, "I know a man who says much the same thing."

"Don't be beguiled by that kind of tactical honesty. It's a gambit. Never underestimate male hatred of womankind, or the lengths men will go to in serving that hatred. Know your enemy—and fear your friend."

"I value my male friends too much to fear them," Lisa said dismissively, "and I'm not entirely convinced that you have sufficient experience of the male of the species to qualify you to tell me to discount my own."

One of Arachne West's better points was that she was capable of laughing at barbs of that kind. "You're a treasure, Lisa," she said. "I bet your friends think so too. I hope you'll never be disappointed. But you really should get rid of those old clothes. Think smart, lady—*always* think smart."

"You might be eager to acquire a second skin," Lisa replied, "but I'm not. Too claustrophobic."

"It's a claustrophobic world," the Real Woman reminded her. "Crowds are germ Utopia, and the whole world is one big crowd struggling to get through the aisles of the Megacorp Mall. Smart insulation is the only thing that can keep you safe in the conflicts to come."

"Claustrophobia isn't just a matter of crowding," Lisa said, quoting Morgan Miller. "It's also a matter of continuity. Nobody panics in a crowded elevator while it's moving, but when it stops . . ."

"Not relevant," Arachne informed her loftily. "All continuities come to their end. When crowd fever finally comes your way, little Lisa, you'll need those smart fibers for a shield—all the more so if you haven't got us to back you up. Invest now, and keep on investing. It's the only way."

In time, though, Arachne West seemed to give up on Lisa, and as the Real Woman movement waned, her attendance at the gym dropped off. Lisa didn't miss her much, because she figured that she'd already heard all her best lines, but she did recognize the loss as one more stage in a developing pattern of isolation. Some of the things Arachne had said about her existential inertia continued to rankle, and when Victor Leverer's release date rolled around, she paused more than once to wonder whether the backup she had on call was really the best available.

Fortunately, Leverer never came looking for her. The next woman he attacked was a mere slip of a thing, not yet out of her teens, but she was also a member of the ALF and she had studied the "Self-Defense Handbook" as carefully as the "Rioters' Handbook." She cut his hamstrings and his Achilles tendons with his own knife and he didn't walk again until the NHS got to the very bottom of the waiting list for new-generation prosthetics.

Lisa never had any confrontational dealings with apocalyptic cultists or hobbyist terrorists. She was occasionally called upon to sift through the debris of an explosion in search of complex organic material, but she never turned up any evidence that was crucial to a prosecution. No amateur biological weapons—or, for that matter, amateur chemical weapons—were deployed in the vicinity of the Bristol cityplex while she was stationed there. She was co-opted to assist with the investigation of the London Underground incident of 2019 and the Eurostar incident of 2026, but her part in each operation was minor and she was not required to appear at either trial. For her, therefore, what the tabloids called "the creeping chaos" remained part of life's background. It seemed ever-present on the TV news and in newspaper headlines, but it never became personal. It was a mere phenomenon, and as such, could be discussed in a perfectly dispassionate manner with everyone she knew.

TV researchers and tabloid reporters sometimes visited Mouseworld in search of a hook on which to hang their latest story, but they received no encouragement from any of the staff. Chan Kwai Keung would not repeat in their presence the kinds of argument that he was still, on occasion, prepared to lay before Lisa.

"Of course the world continues to mirror Mouseworld," Chan told her in the aftermath of the Eurostar incident. "How could it be otherwise? The cities continue to mock us by setting an example that is by no means good but is nevertheless measurably better than our own. The H Block continues to pile up its tangled record of failed experiments, obsolete stratagems, and forgotten secrets. Morgan's incessant declarations about the redundancy of the entire operation ring more true with every year that passes—and the same emotional sickness resonates in the hearts of millions of people. It is as ludicrous an oversimplification to group all the tiny explosions of wrath together as symptoms of stress disease as it is to regard them as facets of a mysterious chaos emanating from the depths of Hell. The violent effects may be depressingly similar, but the motive forces are much more various than anyone will allow."

"Failed experiments, obsolete stratagems, and forgotten secrets?" Lisa echoed.

"Precisely," he said. "How else can the majority of people see themselves nowadays? How else can they explain their unhappiness, their loneliness, their futility? Accelerating progress robs them of expertise and wisdom more rapidly than education can equip them, leaving them intellectually and imaginatively stranded from the moment they reach adulthood, castaways whose plight can only deteriorate. How can they help hating a world that treats them with such casual abandon? How can they bottle up their frustration indefinitely, when they can see only too clearly that there is no possibility of rescue or relief?"

"Who are the *we* that your *they* excludes, Chan?" Lisa wanted to know. "Are we the citizen mice, adapted to intolerable circumstances? How do *we* get by without going postal?"

"I wish I could say with greater certainty that we are," Chan said dolefully. "But I fear that only habit makes me speak in terms of they rather than an all-inclusive we. Even you and I would surely be reckoned failed experiments or obsolete stratagems were we viewed by a coldly objective eye."

"You and I never view one another, or anyone else, with any other kind of eye," she answered dryly. "And no, I wouldn't call either one of us a failure, or judge our skills as obsolete. We do good work, and we do it well. We may not be close to defeating the forces of chaos as yet, but we're certainly doing our bit to hold them back."

"You don't believe that," Chan told her bleakly. "It's the mask you must maintain at work, and it may well suit you to leave it in place even when you leave, but you know in your heart of hearts that the world is going from bad to worse and that our contribution to its decay is a mere matter of ritual. I used to believe that I could make a difference, not by virtue of any unique ability of my own, but as part of the great biotechnological crusade. I recognize now that the best that crusade can hope for is to assist in the rebuilding of civilization after the collapse."

"I don't believe you believe *that*," Lisa retorted. "You've spent too much of your life in one place, working alongside the likes of Morgan Miller. If you're going to wallow in the same pathological Cassandra Complex, you'd better school yourself to take the same perverse delight in prophecies of doom as he does. You can't convince me that you're as crazy or malevolent as the people I labor to put away. You're one of the sanest men I know, and one of most morally upstanding. You're not one of *them*, and never will be. Modesty is one thing, but drastic underestimation is another. And the fact remains— if the world *is* to be saved, biotechnology is the means that will save it. The crusade has to go on. Even Morgan says so."

After conversations of that nature, it was always good to return to the company of innocents like Mike Grundy, whose underlying faith in the cause had never been dented, even though the wellspring of his old cheerfulness had gradually dried up.

"We're victims of our own success," he said on the day the Eurostar plague leaders were found guilty and sentenced to life. "The prisons are overflowing because we've become so bloody good at catching the evildoers. The advancement of your kind of forensics and the rapid spread of invisible eyes and ears has made it extremely difficult to plan any kind of successful premeditated crime and almost impossible to get way with any unpremeditated act of violence. At the moment, the situation seems absurd, because people haven't yet managed to adjust their behavior to take account of the certainty of getting caught, but that's temporary. As soon as everybody gets it into his head that he can't get away with it anymore, the incidence of criminal behavior is bound to fall—and once the trend starts, it'll go all the way. If we can just hang in there, we can usher in a whole new moral order."

Lisa had no difficulty in playing devil's advocate to pessimism and optimism alike. "We're victims of our own success, all right," she said. "With the aid of mouse models, oral vaccines, and gene therapy, we've wiped out all the premature killers except the ones cooked up in labs to steer around the defenses. We've never been healthier, never so long-lived, never so crowded, never so *old*. But gray power isn't really wisdom, is it? It's inertia. The rights of the aged mostly translate into the right to be stuck in one's ways, to rail against anything and everything new, to see everything as a threat. I could get nostalgic for the days when most of the people we put away were young, because it was at least possible to hope that they might change—but your new moral order will have to be built from the bottom up, and the demographic structure of today's world is way too top-heavy."

"It isn't the old who are committing the crimes," Mike said. "The average age of offenders may be rising steadily, but that's because it started out so low."

"No, it isn't the old who are committing the crimes," Lisa agreed, "but it's the old, by and large, who are provoking them—and, increasingly, striking back. When they begin to figure that it might be a good idea to get their retaliation in first, the shit really will hit the fan, and all the invisible eyes and ears in the world won't inhibit them. The Eurostar plague merchants weren't just amateurs, they were idiots. When somebody decides to do the job properly, we'll certainly see the beginning of a new moral order—but not the kind *you* have in mind."

"You still spend too much time with Miller and the other old witches cackling around their cauldrons at the university," Mike told her, unaware that he was ironically echoing what Lisa had said to Chan. "You should have cut that umbilical cord long ago. We're in the real world, and we have to tackle practical problems in a practical way. So do the people we're trying to control—and in the end, they'll accept that. They have to."

"Unfortunately," Lisa said, "they don't. That's why we keep picking up the pieces—and why every year that passes delivers more and more pieces to our doorstep."

"We still have to keep picking them up," Mike insisted. "What other choice do we have?"

"None," she admitted. "But having no choice is no guarantee that we'll win in the end."

"You're beginning to sound like Helen," Mike told her glumly. "Or she's beginning to sound like you. She used to be so optimistic, so *brave*, but now . . . it's far worse being a social worker, of course, than being in the force. When we send them up, we chalk up another victory, and every year brings more, but that's just another beginning as far as Helen's people are concerned. What's winning, from her perspective? All she can ever do is to try to hold back time, and in the end, she always loses."

"She could move on," Lisa pointed out.

"So could we," Mike countered. "Even if we've both hit our limit promotionally, we could move sideways—but we don't. We keep plugging on, willing prisoners of routine. Helen's the same. She's losing her courage as well as her convictions, but she's no quitter. Not at work."

"Citizen mice," Lisa said quietly.

"What?"

"That's how the mice adapt—the ones that do. They accept the conditions of adversity. They accept the narrowing of their personal space. They accept the loss of their reproductive drive. They accept that the only thing to do is to stave off disaster and keep staving it off. They accept that there's no virtue in being a competitive rat when competition only leads to ulceration and cannibalism and insanity."

"We're not mice, Lis. We're people."

"I know that," Lisa told him, "but we have the same problems as mice, and some of us find the same solutions, while we look for all the others that we need and can't quite find."

"The bloody Cassandra Complex," Mike observed in disgust. "Sometimes, you know, I could almost wish that you'd joined the Real Women when you had the chance. Arachne West and her chums might have been crazy as well as ugly, but she wasn't as *miserable* as Morgan Miller and the comic-book Chinaman. Helen's still in touch, I think, if you want to change your mind."

"Citizen mice don't change their minds," Lisa told him. "They just keep on going with the flow."

"Until it ends."

"Until it ends," she agreed.

PART THREE
The Morality of Algeny

THIRTEEN

The second captive was wide awake and wary by now. Jeff had taken no chances with the smartfiber bonds that secured her right hand and her left foot to the steel frame of the bed, but it was a collapsible bed and she could probably have broken it into pieces if she'd cared to exert herself. She hadn't. She was still sipping meekly from a mug of tea when Lisa and Leland came in, but she set the mug down on the low formica-topped table that Jeff had placed conveniently close at hand. The way in which she looked up at her captors suggested that she had a better appreciation of the hopelessness of her situation than Stella Filisetti did, but her features were stubbornly firm.

"Okay," Leland said without preamble, "this is the situation. My name's Leland. I think you know Dr. Friemann, even though you've never been formally introduced. Not unnaturally, she's eager to bring in her police colleagues and the MOD so you can be properly charged, tried, convicted, and put up for the next ten years or so, but she's also anxious about the safety of Morgan Miller. I've managed to persuade her that we might get to him sooner if we make a deal with you, and she's agreed to delay calling in her colleagues until we've explored that possibility. Time is pressing, and your window of opportunity won't stay open for long. We've already had a chat with Ms. Filisetti, and to be perfectly honest, I can't imagine how any sane and reasonable person—I'm prepared to assume for the moment that you can be included in that category—could possibly get involved in any scheme based on information obtained by a person like that. You must suspect by now that you've been led up the garden path right into the compost heap and that your only chance of getting out of this with your life intact is to dump the imbeciles who got you into it. So how about it?"

Lisa watched the Real Woman's reaction carefully. The offer had to sound good, but only if the woman thought Leland could be trusted. For her own part, Lisa thought Leland could be trusted about as far as you could throw a feather into a headwind, but she still hadn't called for help. Anything he got, she wanted to have too.

"I can't do that," the woman said flatly.

"Yes, you can," Leland said mildly. "Hasn't this thing gone far enough out of hand? It's only a matter of time before one of your gun-toting friends shoots somebody dead. Amateurs, eh? I bet you were with the snatch squad that collected Miller—the only part of the operation that went smoothly. Did he get a chance to warn you that you were wasting your time before you put a dart in him?"

"Since you're so concerned," the woman replied, "I suppose I ought to take the opportunity to warn you that you're wasting *your* time."

"That operation in the garage was a real farce, wasn't it?" Leland said sympathetically. "You probably figured that in advance—but you did it anyway. Under orders, I suppose. I know how *that* works, believe me. You take a job that looks simple enough, but then the others start to screw up and you wonder whether you should ever have got involved. Then they start improvising, and you know you should get out, but you're already in and things are moving forward . . . it's all fouled up, hasn't it?"

"Has it?" The Real Woman's tone was guarded, but Lisa had the impression that she would really have appreciated an honest answer to that question, even if she couldn't afford to believe it.

"Your friends didn't even take the time to do a thorough search of Lisa's files before they started panicking, did they?" Leland went on. "They *could* have snatched her last night, but they didn't. The plan's all fucked up, isn't it? What you did today was worse than improvisation—it was pure desperation. A gut reaction conditioned by fear. The fear was justified, by the way—the whole thing's fallen apart. Someone like you can't afford to stay with people like that, no matter what kind of prize is at stake—if there *is* a prize. Apart from Miss Filisetti, nobody really believes that there is. Dr. Goldfarb doesn't. The people who matter at the Ministry of Defence don't. Lisa doesn't—and Lisa's in a far better position to judge than Stella Filisetti, who's only been screwing Miller for a matter of months. Given Miller's age, he probably figured he had to work extra hard to get her interested and spun her a line about dark secrets. Maybe he was too modest. After all, it's not as if Filisetti's a real radfem—or even a Real Woman—is it?"

The woman's eyes weren't looking into Leland's anymore. When she had first turned away—when Leland referred to "a gut reaction conditioned by fear"—she had fixed her gaze on the wall, but now she was looking directly at Lisa, and not because the frayed anaglypta was simply too horrible to contemplate for long. Her manner was doubtful, as if she were trying to decide whether the stories she'd been told about Lisa could possibly be true. Leland obviously took due note of her uncertainty.

"Lisa's no traitor," he said, his deep voice sounding surprisingly soft. "Grimmy Smith didn't entertain the slander for a moment—he had her seconded to the MOD inquiry. He didn't know, of course, which cause she was being accused of being a traitor to, but he knew it wasn't true. Even Lisa didn't know, when your colleague took time out to spray the word on her wall, what kind of betrayal she was being accused of—but now that we do know, we all can see that it's absurd. She's done far more for the feminist cause than Stella Filisetti ever did. She's a police scientist, and she's never been tempted to join half-baked rival organizations like yours, but that doesn't mean she's not sympathetic to the same ideals. Think about it. If your support hadn't been preempted and you met them both without any preconceptions, who would you be more likely to trust—Friemann or Filisetti?"

Lisa felt a sinking sensation as she realized that it wasn't going to work. It might have worked, given that the Real Woman had probably heard Arachne West's account of Lisa as well as Stella Filisetti's, but that wasn't the only consideration. The Real Woman had deduced that Lisa hadn't bothered to correct Leland's misapprehension about the reason for the Real Woman's presence in the garage. She had taken that as evidence that Lisa was playing her own game, and that she was untrustworthy from every point of view.

"You didn't get it, did you?" the Real Woman said to Lisa. "He didn't give it to you."

"What didn't we get?" Leland asked. "Who didn't give it to us?"

"Chan," the captive said. "He's still got the backup."

Lisa steeled herself against an anticipated stare, but Leland was too good an interrogator to be thrown.

"We don't need it," Leland said. "The important thing is that you don't have it and can't get it—and that's why the sensible thing for you to do is to give up everything you do have. If it's enough, you can walk away. Filisetti's the only one who's tried to kill anyone—and that was personal. Give us Miller and you're clear. I guarantee it."

The woman was obviously hesitating, carefully weighing up everything Leland had said—but not, Lisa realized, because she was contemplating acceptance of Leland's offer. She was trying to work out the state of play, and she had no intention of turning rat.

But why not? Lisa thought. Everything Leland had said sounded perfectly reasonable, even though he hadn't managed to infer from the Real Woman's sarcastic observation that Chan had been in the parking lot or that he'd been the actual target of the ambush. Lisa could understand why Stella Filisetti might not have been impressed by any offer to let her off the hook, but this woman wasn't personally involved in the way Stella was. No matter how far out her political views might be, or how intense her paranoia, she must see that she had been dragged into deep water without adequate cause.

In the end, the Real Woman merely shook her head. "You're both working for the Secret Masters," she said. "You just want to keep it for yourselves. You know the collapse is coming—hell, it's already begun. To you, it's just the inevitable unraveling of the tragedy of the commons. Not to us. You intend to be the seed of a New Order—well, so do we, and we have a very different idea of what that New Order ought to be. If people like me don't do anything, the crisis won't simply kill us all—it'll put people like *you* in power for ever and ever. Your threats don't mean a damn thing while the whole damn world is trembling on the brink. You can lock me up and throw away the key. I won't be any worse off than the billions who'll be scythed down by hyperflu and its successors, or starved to death in the aftermath of the pandemic. At least I'll have gone down fighting for something I believe in. It's not a choice between trusting Filisetti and Friemann—it's a choice between trusting the people who stand shoulder to shoulder with Filisetti and the people whose company Friemann keeps. People like *you*, Mr. Leland, and the Ministry hack, and Morgan Miller, the Neanderthal neo-Malthusian. We're fighting for the future here, and we're not going to give it up until we're all dead, even if what Miller told us turns out to be true. I'm giving you nothing—not even name, rank, and serial number."

Leland was astonished, and Lisa couldn't blame him. Everything Leland knew suggested that his ploy should have worked. On the other hand, everything *she* knew suggested that the crazy sequence of crimes should never have happened at all. Even if Stella had convinced others that Morgan had what she presumably thought he had, they must have suspected all along that it was a mere mirage, and the failure of the operation should have convinced them all. The Real Woman must be nursing an exceptionally powerful hatred of Leland's employers if she wasn't prepared to play ball "even if what Miller told us turns out to be true."

What Morgan must have told his kidnappers, of course, was that Stella had got it absurdly wrong—and he must surely have been able to explain to them exactly how and why she had got it wrong. But what, in that case, had Chan been so anxious to deliver to her? Stella Filisetti had obviously jumped to the conclusion it was the backup that hadn't been found among Lisa's possessions—but she'd never have been commissioned to collect it herself if her companions had been fully convinced. Stella must have been the prime mover in the conspiracy, but she obviously wasn't giving the orders. So who was?

Arachne West? Lisa couldn't believe that. Arachne was too careful, too methodical.

While she was thinking, Leland had stood up and moved to the door, but he waited there for her to follow. Lisa signaled her consent with a slight nod and he led the way down to the kitchen. Jeff wasn't there, and Lisa couldn't hear any sounds of movement from within the cottage.

"Well," Leland said as he opened the refrigerator and peered unenthusiastically into the lighted interior. "I guess that's one own goal apiece. At least we know what we're dealing with now."

"Do we?" Lisa queried.

"They have to be Millenarians," he said as he shut the fridge door and slumped down at the table with a can in each hand. "The end of the world is nigh, and anyone who wants to be saved has to follow the recipe, no matter how crazy. Anyone who stands in the way is an Antichrist in the direct employ of the Devil." He offered the right-hand can to Lisa. According to the label, it was Szechuan pollen beer—highly nutritious but difficult to stomach. She shook her head and he shrugged, abandoning it on the tabletop so he could use his right forefinger to crack the seal on the other can.

"What she actually said," Lisa pointed out, "is that you and I are working for the Secret Masters. Which we are—you directly, me indirectly, at least as long as I let this farce continue. And she could well be right about the impending pandemic too. If the release of hyperflu was the first strike in a biowar—and nobody seriously thinks otherwise, no matter how closely we guard our tongues—then the war probably will kill billions rather than millions, and social structures really will collapse all over the world. Even if the Containment Commission can come up with measures that work, Britain is too closely integrated into the global economy to withstand the aftermath."

"I already told you we have that covered," Leland reminded her uneasily.

"So you did," Lisa agreed. "But you also told me that the Cabal, not the government, would see to the distribution of the defense mechanism. That's exactly what the Real Woman's afraid of. She finds the idea of your friends selecting the survivors even harder to bear than the idea of ecocatastrophic collapse."

"My point exactly," Leland came back. "She's a Millenarian. The end is nigh, the New Order is yet to arise. You heard her. Filisetti must have found out about something Miller had fed in—or was intending to feed in—to Burdillon's defense work. They want the antibody-packaging system for their own people. They probably came back for you because they thought they could use you as a lever to make Miller give it up, but the real key is Chan if he has the only backup not securely stashed on university or Ministry premises. How it must have burned them up to have to leave Burdillon behind at the university when they made their getaway! You were right—it *is* a wild goose chase. Whatever new wrinkle Miller brought, or intended to bring, to Burdillon's inquiry, it can't be as good as ours. We don't need it—but that doesn't mean I can let it go. If it's really out there, I need a copy. A copy will do, but I can't go back empty-handed. Got to justify my fee. I need to find Chan. We need to get Miller out too, of course, but I need to find Chan as well. Got to cover all the angles."

Lisa was tempted to tell Leland, merely for the sake of honesty, that he had jumped to the wrong conclusion, but she contented herself by asking a question. "Was she right when she said that the megacorps regard the biowar as the inevitable unfolding of the tragedy of the commons?"

"Always the tragedy of the bloody commons," Leland muttered. "You'd think we'd have forged a new cliché by now. Even the megacorp buccaneers who'll fight the Hardinist label till they drop believe in *that* one. You've read the essay, I suppose?"

"Oddly enough," Lisa confessed, "I never did. Morgan explained the thesis to me, of course—and I did read *The Ostrich Factor*."

"That's not so popular in the ranks of the so-called Secret Masters," Leland told her. "That's why half of them refuse point-blank to describe themselves as Hardinists. They *hate* the Russell Theorem. Remember the Russell Theorem?"

Lisa remembered the Russell Theorem well enough. Given that two other Russells were numbered among Morgan Miller's favorite sources, Morgan had always taken great care to point out that the Russell approvingly cited by Garrett Hardin was a different one: Bertrand Russell. What Hardin had called Russell's Theorem was the proposition that social solidarity could be maintained only in collective opposition to some external enemy, and that any world state would inevitably fall apart for lack of one.

"Why should the men who engineered the crash of '25 hate the Russell Theorem?" Lisa asked, curious.

"Because they're One Worlders through and through, of course," Leland said. "They're happy to use Hardinist cant to justify the big steal—*Oh, no, we aren't taking over the world because we're greedy bastards who love being richer than anyone can imagine; we're merely humble and dutiful souls who've accepted the responsibility of protecting the ecosphere from the tragedy of the commons*— but now that they have the world in their pocket, they don't want to hear any argument that says they'll never be able to hold it together. Some people, of course—including our guest, apparently—reckon that the men behind the coup *are* the common enemy of the remainder of mankind, and there are some among the world's new owners who think that perception, however mistaken it may be in objective terms, might actually serve their purpose. Why else do you think they disseminate such terms as '*Secret Masters*' and '*Cabal*'?"

"Well," said Lisa, "to judge by what we just heard, it's working."

"Far too well," Leland agreed, cracking open the second can of pollen beer. Lisa felt a momentary pang of regret as she swallowed and found her mouth still dry, but she told herself that she needed to keep a clear head if she were to stay abreast of the game.

"Personally," Leland continued, "I prefer the lunatics who just sit on mountaintops waiting for the flying saucers to come and carry them away to the new world. The ones who want to plant their own New Order in my backyard are a royal pain in the arse. Utopian socialists, Gaean freaks, pretend radfems . . . they're all the bloody same."

" 'Pretend' radfems?" Lisa queried. "Are you assuming that the radfem thing is just a cover—an overlay to conceal their real political interests?"

"You heard the woman," Leland reminded her. "How did it sound to you?"

"Not quite as crazy as it sounded to you, obviously," Lisa admitted. "But then, I had heard most of it before, from other Real Women. To me, she sounds like a classic case of the Cassandra Complex—someone who believes she's seen the future and can't stand the frustration of knowing she can't do a damn thing about it. Someone who'd jump at the chance to make a difference, however slight. Maybe the person she's taking orders from has filled her with a certain charismatic fervor, but it's nowhere near as crazy as waiting for Jesus to arrive in a flying saucer. She's not looking backward to ancient prophecies and obsolete commandments. She's looking forward. I ought to call in the troops, by the way—I've already delayed too long."

"That's okay," Leland said. "Jeff should have everything packed by now and the engine running. Do you have any suggestions as to where I might start looking for Chan?"

"He's back from Birmingham," Lisa said guardedly as she took her phone from its holster. "It shouldn't be too difficult to track him down."

"No, it shouldn't," he said contemplatively—and then his expression changed. Lisa's fingers froze before touching the buttons that would summon the cityplex police. Leland looked at her, reproachfully as well as quizzically.

"He was there, wasn't he?" he said softly. "They were after *him*, not you."

Lisa hesitated for a moment, then shrugged. "He was there," she admitted. "Chasing after me. I don't know what happened to him—he probably skipped out through the hole your battle wagon made as soon you started lobbing gas grenades around. By now, with luck, he'll have given over whatever he's got to Smith."

"I really would have appreciated it if you'd seen fit to mention this before," Leland complained, although his tone had as much admiration in it as resentment. "But I can understand why you kept it up your sleeve. You will remember, I hope, that I played fair with *you*—and if you ever need a job, get in touch. I can fix it."

Lisa couldn't help feeling flattered. But Leland *still* had a hold of the wrong end of the stick. Did she really want to work with someone like that? Her fingers relaxed again, and she picked out the number of Mike Grundy's mobile.

"Help yourself to the stuff in the fridge," Leland said as he moved to the door. "Once they turn up, you'll be as busy as I will—no time to snack. Wish me luck."

"You don't need it," Lisa assured him, not really caring whether he did or not.

FOURTEEN

Leland had left Lisa's outer clothes behind, draped over the banister on he upper floor. They'd been washed, but not pressed. The black smartsuits the women had worn were there too, and their guns and helmets were in the kitchen cupboard. Lisa didn't see any point in changing out of Jeff's slightly ill-fitting shirt and trousers, even though she figured there had to be a clever bug lurking in one of the buttons. They'd almost certainly sneaked one into her own outfit too.

As soon the van had driven away, she went back to the downstairs room where Stella Filisetti was secured.

"A police vehicle is on the way," she told her prisoner. "It'll be about twenty minutes. We're in the Mendips somewhere east of Winscombe. Sorry I can't let you take a longer look at the view—it's the last you'll see till you're my age, so you'd better make the most of it while they're loading you up. Morgan might visit you if the prison's not too far away, but I wouldn't bank on it. Your friend reckons that it'll be as good a place as any to sit out the end of civilization as we know it, but I'm not so sure. If you really did spot something in one of the library models that nobody else had noticed in forty years, you must be pretty good. It's a pity to let ability like that go to waste, but it can't be helped now. Who do you think will get the big prize— Leland or Peter Grimmett Smith? Either way, I suppose it'll end up with the Secret Masters. If you'd only let Morgan alone, he'd probably have given it to Ahasuerus. Your intervention will almost certainly have the effect of bringing in a worse result than the one you'd have had if you'd let well enough alone."

"You can drop the act now," the younger woman told her, although she surely wasn't naive enough to think they were safe from electronic eavesdroppers. "I know you know, because I know Morgan. He wouldn't have kept it from you. From everyone else maybe, but not from you. He trusted you to see it his way. And you did, didn't you? You even consented to grow old—but I know how you kept your options open. You can fool that idiot cowboy, and your second-string boyfriend, and the secondhand spook from the MOD, but you can't fool me. I know you know, so I know exactly how desperate you are to get Morgan back—but you can't have him. There's too much at stake."

"Maybe I don't need him," Lisa suggested blandly. "Maybe I already have everything I need. Maybe the only thing your friends will accomplish by killing Morgan is to make me the sole custodian of the big secret. It's not on any of the wafers or sequins you took from my desk, but that doesn't necessarily mean that I don't have it hidden."

"Maybe you do," Stella agreed. "Maybe the time will come when *you*'ll have to make up your mind what to do with it, without Morgan to seduce and tyrannize you. Maybe then you'll realize that we're in the right. You had radfem sympathies yourself once, I understand. If it hadn't been for joining the police force, you might have been one of us."

Lisa continued staring out the window for half a minute longer, but then she turned to look down sternly at the woman on the bed. Instead of responding to Stella Filisetti's provocations, she said, "You tried to shoot me. The original plan was not to let anyone get hurt, but you were shooting to kill."

"Was I?" was Stella's only riposte.

Lisa watched the half smile that spread across the younger woman's lips. It looked like a smile of satisfaction. Even though Stella's shot had missed, she was pleased that she had tried. She wasn't going to admit it while eavesdroppers were hanging on her every word, but she didn't care whether Lisa knew. Lisa felt compelled to retaliate. "What do you mean, 'second-string boyfriend'?" she asked abruptly.

As she'd intended, the question took Stella entirely by surprise.

For a moment, the younger woman hesitated in confusion, obviously unsure as to whether or not she'd made a mistake, and whether or not it was recoverable. "The detective inspector," she said, smoothly enough but rather belatedly. "You're screwing him, aren't you?"

"Who told you?"

The hesitation was minute, but perceptible. "Nobody," she said. "We've been keeping a close eye on you. We know far more about you than you might think."

"The keys to all my locks, for instance," Lisa retorted. "Were you the one who sprayed 'Traitor' on my door? I know you weren't the one who shot the phone out of my hand, because you couldn't shoot that straight, but you could have been the furtive one who went through my desk so ineptly. Or were you at the university, making sure that the mice were all burned up? That was pointless, by the way—a stupid, meaningless gesture. You should have been content with the ones you'd already sneaked out, the ones whose absence you were trying to cover up. Torching the room was sheer mindless vandalism. Surely you could have covered your tracks without burning the cities and nearly killing poor Ed Burdillon."

"The cities had gone on far too long," the woman told her coldly. "They were a living lie. The Crisis is already here, and the population of all the real cities on Earth is about to take a steep fall. You know it, I know it—and everyone involved in the making and distribution of hyperflu certainly knows it."

"Is that why you burned them?" Lisa asked, unable to believe it. "Because they were a *living lie*?"

"Weren't they always supposed to be a parable? That's how Morgan puts it, at any rate. Well, now they're a parable of the coming holocaust. That's why we did it."

Lisa didn't believe her. Presumably, Stella had persuaded her fellow conspirators that it was necessary to destroy the H Block to cover up the fact that some mice were missing, and to prevent them from being identified. They had burned it to prevent anyone who investigated from figuring out which ones had been removed by surveying the remaining DNA patterns. Did that mean there might be other library specimens tucked way in a forgotten corner of some other institution's Mouseworld? Probably not—but it wasn't something to discuss out loud in any case, given that Leland was bound to be listening. The longer it took him to figure out what this was really about, the more time Lisa would have to find Arachne West and persuade her that she had to let Morgan go.

"It's not too late," Stella Filisetti told her. "You could still throw in your lot with us. If we don't manage to get the data files, you might turn out to be the last hope of the cause. I know how you kept your options open when Miller first discovered the emortal mice. They're still open. It's not too late to change your mind."

"I could say the same to you," Lisa pointed out—but she turned to look out the window as she heard the distant wail of a siren. The bright headlights and the stroboscopic blue flash of a police cruiser were just visible on the road that wound through Chew Valley, several miles to the north. The headlights flickered as they were briefly interrupted by leaf-laden trees. The leaves were all brown by now, but they were still awaiting the Atlantic front, whose swirling winds would whip them from the branches.

Then Lisa caught sight of the internally lit helicopter that was moving effortlessly past the car, fifty or sixty meters overhead. She calculated that it would arrive several minutes earlier. Peter Grimmett Smith had obviously decided, after waking up from his enforced nap, that time was now far too pressing to permit him the luxury of road travel. In any case, he probably wanted to make sure that Lisa talked to him before—and perhaps instead of—reporting to her own people.

"You've stepped over the line here," Stella Filisetti whispered. "You should have made that call an hour ago. They'll throw you out of the force. How old are you, Lisa? What choices have you got?"

"I'm working for the MOD at present," Lisa told her. "I have all the latitude I need—and all the information I need, thanks to your slack mouth. It's over, Stella. I'll have Morgan out before noon."

"Bitch," the younger woman said in heartfelt fashion.

"And you," Lisa murmured.

She went outside to meet the helicopter. The air was cold but still—there was mist in the meadow on the other side of the dirt road that led to the cottage. The cottage looked larger from the yard, but that was because the shadow gathered about the lighted windows was exaggerated by the steep pitch of the tiled roof.

As she'd expected, Peter Grimmett Smith didn't even bother to step down. He merely held the helicopter door open, inviting her to climb in before the rotor blades slowed to a halt. She ducked reflexively as she did so, although she wasn't tall enough to be in any danger.

Mercifully, the helicopter wasn't one of those with a transparent cupola; its cabin was wide and deep and its sides were reassuringly opaque. The pilot was Ginny, but Lisa didn't have time to ask after her health before Smith bundled her into the second rank of seats.

"Radio the Swindon police," Smith instructed his dutiful chauffeur. "Tell them that one of their cityplex colleagues needs a clean suit of clothes. Tell them to have it ready at the landing pad."

"Size twelve," Lisa put in. "Ten if the goods are U.S.-originated. Did Chan make contact again?"

"No, he didn't. Who shot me?" Smith obviously had his own agenda, and wasn't about to be sidetracked. As soon as Ginny had made the call, the copter raised itself from the ground again. The downdraft from its wings scattered newly fallen leaves in every direction, but the blizzard vanished into darkness as they gained height. It was surprisingly quiet inside the cabin, although the thrum of the motor rotating the copter's blades extended an uncomfortable vibration throughout the body of the craft.

"She wouldn't give us a name," Lisa told him. "Steve Forrester will find out, as soon as he can get a DNA sample. The other one was Stella Filisetti. She shot me too, by the way—I didn't wake up until I was tucked up in the cottage. The men in the van came to our rescue, but they didn't quite manage to arrive in the nick of time."

"And who were they?" Smith demanded.

"The one in charge told me his name's Leland," Lisa told him. "Mike Grundy will be checking out the van as we speak, but it'll probably be a dead end. Leland's just a fly attracted by the stink. Working for the Cabal, he says—but that might be garbage. If he's just a chancer, he's not important; if he *is* working for the emperors of private enterprise, we might as well let him play his hand. If he finds Morgan before we do, so much the better. That's why I thought it was worth giving him some rope to play with instead of calling in as soon as I woke up. Why are we going to Swindon?"

The helicopter was moving rapidly through the night, but Lisa had lost her sense of direction. The lights below could have been Paulton, but she wasn't sure.

"Why not?" Smith asked. "Have you got a better idea?"

Lisa didn't want to go to Swindon, and she did have a better idea—but she didn't want to tell Peter Grimmett Smith what it was, especially while she was wearing Jeff's bug-infested clothing.

"We've missed our appointment," she stalled. "Surely they'll have locked up and gone home."

"Someone's waiting up for us," he assured her. "Did you and this Leland fellow get anything useful out of the two women?"

"Only bullshit," Lisa told him. "Leland thinks they're some kind of secret cult freaked out by signs of the apocalypse. He thinks they may be after something Morgan contributed to the project that Ed Burdillon had put his way—the defense work you sounded me out about while we were on our way to Ahasuerus—but he's not sure."

"You don't agree," Smith was quick to observe.

"I don't believe they're apocalypse freaks. I suspect they're exactly what they seem to be: radical feminists. Leland didn't even know a Real Woman when he saw one, and when I told him what she was, he figured that he might be able to excite her disdain for Stella Filisetti because she's prettier and hasn't cultivated her muscles. I think I annoyed her by failing so utterly to understand where she was coming from." She was speaking as much for Leland's benefit as Smith's, on the assumption that he was still listening in as he headed for the cityplex in the hope of picking up Chan's trail.

"You'd have to explain it to me too, I'm afraid," Smith said unenthusiastically. "But not now. We've more important matters to deal with."

The niceties of post-backlash feminism obviously interested him as little as they interested Leland. Lisa had to remind herself that Smith, like her, had been born in the late twentieth century and had been delivered by maturity into the midst of the so-called backlash. Like Leland, he took it for granted that people he didn't agree with were all essentially alike. Lisa knew better—and she suspected that the internal politics of twenty-first-century feminism might have a significant bearing not merely on the motive for Morgan Miller's abduction, but on its ultimate outcome.

Real Women hadn't seen the stalling of the feminist cause as an unfortunate failure of a crusade to win equality of opportunity and reward. For them, as Arachne West had taken great pains to explain, the battle had always been a straightforward power struggle. What men had surrendered in the late twentieth century was no more than a series of palliative concessions, intended to blunt the force of female complaint and produce the illusion that progress would continue to be made if only women could be patient. The Real Women weren't interested in inching toward equality; they wanted to take as much ground as possible as quickly as possible by any means available—and they didn't see any virtue in stopping when the balance was even. They wanted the upper hand, although they didn't have any illusions about the difficulty of taking it. That tied in to their unbounded enthusiasm for "natural physical culture."

Although the movement's brief popularity had passed by 2035 at the latest, the remaining Real Women still saw themselves as units in an army of conquest. Other feminists might see them as misfits unable to compromise with the demands of the moment, but that only made it all the more remarkable that the Real Woman had been fighting shoulder to shoulder with Stella Filisetti—and that Stella had had the gun that fired real bullets. The conspiracy whose out-lines had now been revealed was, Lisa knew, far more remarkable than Leland or Peter Grimmett Smith could imagine.

"We need to find Chan," Lisa told Smith. "They may go after him again."

"We have people on that," Smith assured her. "So has Chief Inspector Kenna. Dr. Chan's behaving rather irresponsibly, I fear. Professor Burdillon should never have admitted him to the research program."

"According to Leland," Lisa told him, "the project was and is redundant. He says that the princes of private enterprise already have a method of protecting their clients from the effects of plague war. Presumably, the only reason they haven't advertised it already is that they're letting paranoia inflate demand. It's nice to know that all those Mexican, Nigerian, and Cambodian kids are dying in a good cause, isn't it?"

Peter Grimmett Smith was staring at her, but it wasn't the thought of millions of Third World children dying for lack of a defense that had startled him; it was the thought that the megacorps hadn't deigned to inform his government of the fact that they had the means to save whomever they wanted to save from the war that wasn't officially a war at all.

"Chan was right all along," Lisa remarked.

"I can't agree," Smith retorted. "This ludicrous insistence on talking to you before he parts with whatever information he has is holding up the investigation."

"Not about that," Lisa said. "About the politics of Mouseworld. He always said that it was a better mirror of contemporary human affairs than Morgan would ever allow, and he was right. No matter how hard we pretended, Mouseworld's cities were always ruled from without, not from within. The imperatives of birth and death, and the conditions in which life had to be lived, were all determined by the experimenters: the Secret Masters. They always had the power to decide how many mice there were, which ones lived and which ones died. The mice only had to find their own stability because the experimenters refused to intervene—which they could have done at any time, according to their merest whim or most careful long-term strategy. Sound familiar?"

"It sounds *irrelevant*," Smith told her.

"Unlike the Institute of Algeny, I suppose," Lisa said. "I think we'd get to the heart of the problem a lot faster if I could talk to an old friend of mine—Arachne West." She figured it was safe to say that much, even with Leland listening in. As soon as Mike Grundy saw the Real Woman at the cottage, he'd remember Arachne, and he'd start looking for her. Leland would find out about that soon enough, if he cared to. But Lisa wasn't about to say any more, for the present. Now didn't seem to be the right time to inform Peter Smith—or anyone else—that she had a shrewd suspicion as to who might have recruited Arachne and her loyal troopers to assist in the kidnapping of Morgan Miller, or that she had formed a plausible hypothesis as to why that person thought the discovery that Miller might or might not have made was worth killing for.

"Arachne West will have to wait," Smith informed her brusquely. "I have a trail of my own to follow, and I may need your advice again."

"Okay," said Lisa, knowing there was nothing she could do about it. "So we go to Swindon first."

She couldn't help resenting the digression, but she knew she had to make the best of it. The quicker they got through the interview with the Algenists, the sooner the helicopter would be on its way westward again. In the meantime, she had to take the opportunity to reconsider her own long-term strategy as carefully and profoundly as she could. She had to figure out exactly whose side she ought to be on, if her guesses turned out to be correct, when the cracked plot finally fell apart. That would be a lot easier, she supposed, if she could only work out what Stella Filisetti had meant when she claimed to know how Lisa had "kept her own options open." The one enigma her guesswork hadn't even begun to unravel centered on how she was supposed to prove she had known all along what this uproar was all about, when she hadn't known at all.

If the radfems believed, however mistakenly, that Morgan Miller really had stumbled onto a technology of longevity that worked only on females, why would they think that she would have had to do anything to keep her options open?

FIFTEEN

The night through which the helicopter soared was clear of cloud, but the light pollution was too intense to allow the stars to be seen. The moon was three-quarters full and the pink stain cast on its face by the intervening atmosphere seemed slightly sinister, as if it were an extension of the vale of shadow that hid the invisible crescent.

The vibration that crept into Lisa's limbs from the polished plastic upholstery seemed to be growing more intrusive with every minute that passed. Although she had relaxed into her seat with some relief after the constant tension of the interrogations in the cottage, Lisa felt that she was already back on the edge of experience. She began to wish she had taken advantage of Leland's invitation to raid the fridge at the cottage. Hunger was now adding to the confusion of troubles by which she was beleaguered, although not as much as exhaustion was.

Peter Smith finally thought of asking Lisa how her hand and arm were.

"They're okay," she assured him. "Leland gelled the dart wound. I'll be able to peel the sealant off my hand tomorrow, and I should be able to use it normally. I could do with some sleep, though—some real sleep, that is. My usual insomnia seems to have deserted me in my hour of need. I don't know why, but knockout drops don't do the trick. I woke up just as tired as I was before I fell unconscious."

"I know the feeling," Smith admitted. "We'll fly back to the Renaissance as soon as the Algenists' spokesman has given us his side of the story. I'm beginning to wish I'd taken a couple of hours out this morning, while you were resting."

Lisa resented the implication that she'd wimped out when she'd accepted Smith's offer to take time out from the investigation, but it wasn't worth challenging. "Why all the urgency to get to the Institute of Algeny?" she asked.

"I'm using the helicopter because I'm reasonably confident that it isn't bugged," Smith said, misunderstanding the import of her question. "At least I was reasonably confident until we took *you* aboard."

"You mean that the car *was* bugged? You had it swept?"

"As per routine," he said. "We'd picked up two plants that weren't there when we left the Renaissance—one obvious, one camouflaged. Presumably planted by the same person. If the first one was there to attract our attention so we wouldn't look hard for the second, the second could have been there to stop us short of looking *really* hard for a third."

Lisa knew that Leland had had the time, the opportunity, and the motive to rig the car after staging his flamboyant rescue, but she also knew how dangerous it was to jump to conclusions.

"And you think the Algenists are involved?"

Smith sighed. "I don't know," he confessed. "But the background check makes them look exceedingly fishy. It seems to me that they're the people most likely to have grabbed Morgan Miller."

"Why would they do that? He went to them."

"The fact that he went to them could have convinced them that he had something valuable. If he then decided to take it to Ahasuerus instead of handing it to them—and it seems to me that if he did *any* kind of proper background check, that's what he'd have decided to do—they might well have figured it was time to take matters into their own hands."

It didn't sound at all likely to Lisa, but that was the emerging pattern of the investigation. Everyone who looked into the matter seemed to be seizing on different details—details that reflected the particular tenor of their own innate paranoia. *Am I any different?* she wondered. *Am I seeing it the way I do because that's what tickles my idiosyncratic fancy? Are we all so terrified by the impending crisis that we're grasping at straws, all equally blinded by fear?*

"What makes you think the Institute's not what it seems?" was all she dared say.

"Once we deepened our own background check, I could see why Dr. Goldfarb was so offended by the fact that Morgan Miller put Ahasuerus and the Algenists on the same list. Adam Zimmerman's grandparents emigrated to the States in the 1930s, fleeing Hitler's persecution of the Jews. The Foundation's mission statement contains some very strong injunctions against releasing results that might be useful for military purposes or for political oppression. The Algenists' website makes similar protestations, but if you look back in time far enough, it becomes fairly obvious that algeny's intellectual forebears were firmly in the Nazi camp. The parent Institute of Algeny in Leipzig was previously a branch of the German Vril Society, which claimed descent—falsely, one presumes, but no less significantly—from the Bavarian Illuminati. There are similarly remote historical links to Theosophy, the racial theories of Count Gobineau, and something called the World Ice Theory. Does any of that ring a bell with you?"

"No," Lisa confessed.

"Nor to anyone else alive and sane, I suspect. Apparently, there's more than a linguistic analogy connecting algeny to alchemy. Vril was an occult force invented by some nineteenth-century British novelist; it was enthusiastically taken up by a number of continental occultists. Nowadays, although its current mission statements still refer in approving terms to Nietzschean moral reconstruction, contemporary algeny has cleaned up its intellectual act considerably, but if Miller bothered to do any digging, his investigations would have revealed the rotten core beneath the shiny surface."

Lisa had no idea of what to make of all this. It sounded almost surreal, and completely irrelevant—but she reminded herself that her own far more modest inferences had sounded equally irrelevant to Smith. "If they really are crackpots from way back when," she said warily, "where does their money come from?"

"Switzerland," was the terse reply.

Switzerland had long been a world leader in the arcane art of money laundering—which grew more arcane with every year that passed. Ordinarily, "money from Switzerland" was a euphemism for the "Mafia," which had controlled up to fifty percent of GDP in the post-Communist nations at the turn of the century. During the last thirty years, following the example set by the organizations on which they were modeled, much of that wealth had been rechanneled into legitimate businesses, and the organizations had revamped their image considerably. Some had remarketed themselves as a new breed of revolutionary communists—hence the term "Leninist Mafia"—who were deeply and sincerely concerned with issues of social and economic reorganization. Despite their much-publicized opposition to "Imperialist Global Parasitism," the Leninist Mafia did not seem to have fared any worse during the worldwide economic upheavals of '25 than its alleged counterparts in China.

"So now you think they're gangsters pretending to be crackpots," Lisa said skeptically. "And you think they kidnapped Morgan because they got the same impression as Goldfarb—that he was deliberately underselling whatever it was he had."

"It's a possibility," Smith said defensively. "There's also the apocalyptic angle to consider. You said this Leland character inferred from what the women told you that they were apocalyptic cultists. Did he have any particular group in mind?"

"No," Lisa said. "Do you?"

"The women didn't mention the Ice Age Elite by any chance?"

"That's just post-Millennial folklore," Lisa said. "The Real Woman started sounding off about the Secret Masters and the seeds of a New Order, but those were the only phrases she used."

Lisa remembered talk of the Ice Age Elite being bandied about during her years as a research student, but she couldn't remember Morgan Miller ever having dignified their existence with an opinion. When the years 1999 and 2000 had come and gone, everyone gifted with common sense had expected Millenarian cults to wither away, or at least to be effectively mothballed until 2029 or 2033, the two dates most widely touted as the two-thousandth anniversary of the crucifixion. Ever perverse, however, several of the most vocal cults had refused to go away, and their tales of impending woe had grown ever more fanciful. One such tale had fixated on the anxieties expressed by some scientists that global warming might subvert the ocean-circulation mechanism sustaining the gulf stream, abruptly precipitating a new Ice Age.

The contemporary myth of the Secret Masters hadn't really come into its own until the crash of '25, but earlier versions had been around long before that, and one of its earliest twenty-first-century manifestations had been the idea that the greenhouse effect was being deliberately stimulated, with the intention of causing an Ice Age. The Ice Age Elite were the plotters allegedly responsible for this scheme. They were said to have made elaborate plans to survive the ecocatastrophe in comfort. Accounts of their motives were widely various, ranging from the suggestion that they were Gaean altruists determined to save Mother Earth from further rape, to the proposition that they intended to buy up all the ruined real estate in the northern hemisphere, whose overlords they would become when they eventually unleashed the biotech that would end the Ice Age as abruptly as it had begun. Little had been heard of the Ice Age Elite since 2025, presumably because the Cabal was now widely believed to be in the process of achieving their alleged aims without having had to go to the trouble of precipitating an Ice Age.

"The problem with folklore," Smith told her, "is that it wouldn't qualify as folklore if there weren't people who believe it. Admittedly, Ahasuerus isn't called Ahasuerus because its founder believed in the myth of the Wandering Jew in any simple sense—in fact, if the rumors of his present whereabouts can be trusted, he'd be more accurately considered to be the ultimate Sedentary Jew—but the Institute of Algeny is different. It wasn't set up from scratch, so it still carries a certain amount of ideological baggage left over from who knows when. Its interest in future human evolution is closely linked to ideas of apocalyptic notions of destruction and transformation. You say that this Real Woman used the words 'New Order'?"

"Yes," Lisa admitted, "but it's a perfectly commonplace phrase."

"Maybe it is," Smith agreed, "but the Real Women were great enthusiasts for physical culture, weren't they? Very militant too, I believe."

"They weren't Nazis," Lisa said firmly. "I think you might be letting your imagination run away with you."

Smith obviously resented that comment, perhaps because it had a little too much accuracy in it for comfort. "Why did Leland take you along with the two women?" he asked sharply. "Even if it hadn't been obvious that you weren't one of them, he had only to glance at your ID. Why didn't he leave you behind with Ginny and me, to sleep it off in the parking lot?"

"I think he wanted to explain himself," Lisa told him judiciously. "He wanted a quick word with the ambushers before turning them in, but he didn't want us to think they might have been spirited away by their friends. He doesn't want us chasing after him with the same fervor we're devoting to the task of trying to find Morgan Miller. He'd rather we thought of him as an ally. He took me with him so I could bear witness to his good intentions. He might, of course, have fed me a complete pack of lies."

"But you think he was on the level—or as near to it as a man of his type ever is?"

"Probably," Lisa admitted, thinking that Smith was a pompous fool whose attitudes, instincts, and modes of expression were so twentieth-century as to be almost beyond belief. "While we're still searching for Morgan, we can use all the help we can get, and whoever he's working for, Leland does seem to be running a parallel investigation. If I'm right and this whole thing is some kind of silly mistake, it probably won't matter who he reports to."

"And if you're wrong?"

Lisa looked away, feebly pretending that the view from the window had attracted her attention. The helicopter had already begun its descent and the lights of Swindon were displayed beneath her, their brightness and variety testifying that the town was booming, as it had been for half a century. It had owed its first spurt of growth to the fact that it was the halfway point between the original termini of the Great Western Railway, and it advertised itself nowadays as the bridge between the two great cityplexes of England—a claim that excited a certain amount of resentment and scorn in the Birmingham metropolitan area and United Manchester. At the moment, it looked more like an island than a bridge; the threads of illumination connecting it to Chippenham and Reading seemed as frail as spidersilk in comparison to the blaze emitted by the glittering hub where the leisure spots of the town's twenty-four-hour society were clustered. Lisa blinked her eyes, fighting tiredness.

"If I'm wrong," she said, as much to herself as to Peter Smith, "and Morgan really has stumbled onto the kind of technology that can create some kind of a New Order—without bothering to tell me about it—the government doesn't stand much chance of keeping it secret from anyone Leland might be working for, although the reverse might be a different matter. I still think the Ice Age Elite is a silly myth, but if there really are people in the world who are anxious to set themselves up as inheritors of post-Crisis Earth, our job is to make sure they don't get away with it, whoever they are. Isn't it?"

"Of course it is," Smith answered—as he would surely have done even if he hadn't been under the assumption that Leland had planted camouflaged bugs in Lisa's clothing. He was, after all, a loyal servant of king and country. If he couldn't be trusted to put matters of duty above personal considerations, who could?

SIXTEEN

There was a uniformed policeman waiting for them at the helipad. As soon as Smith descended from the craft, the man handed him a plastic bag, which he immediately passed on to Lisa.

"Change in the helicopter," he commanded. "Put your belt and wristwatch in with the old clothes." Lisa hesitated, wondering whether to raise an objection, but Smith was right. If Leland had planted anything, it was as likely to be in her belt or watch as in Jeff's shirt and trousers. If she had to be phoneless for a while, she had to be phoneless. She moved back to the second rank of seats so that she'd be shielded by the first, although she felt slightly shamed by her obsolete modesty.

It wasn't the first time she had ever put on one of the new garments, but she had found the previous tentative trial so uncomfortable that she had decided to stick with her "dead clothes" for a while longer. Now she wondered why she had reacted so negatively. Was she as much of a dinosaur as Peter Grimmett Smith? Of course not. She was a scientist, supposedly immune to the reflexive "yuck factor" that governed initial reactions to so many new biotechnologies. In a sense, her own response had had an opposite cause; she had always thought of the new fabrics in terms of "fashion," because that was the lexicon the advertisers had used in order to push it, and she had always resisted the idea of being a slave to fashion, valuing newness for its own sake. Now, if the suspicions raised by Smith's clumsy inquiries could be trusted, the advertising lexicon was about to undergo an abrupt change.

What Arachne West had told Lisa on the occasion of their first meeting didn't seem quite as paranoid now as it had then. Now it was perfectly obvious to anyone with half a brain that the new global culture was a plague culture, and that smart clothing would soon have to be seen in terms of personal defense—not antibody packaging in the traditional sense, but in a significant new sense. Soon enough the first questions anyone would ask salespeople about the clothes on their racks would concern the quality of their built-in immune systems and the rapidity with which they could react to any dangerous invasion of the commensal bodies within their loving embrace.

The garment Lisa was struggling into wasn't uncomfortable in the sense that ill-fitting clothes could be—although the way it hugged her flesh so cloyingly was slightly disconcerting—but it was worn without underwear and followed the contours of her body so carefully that she felt unusually *exposed*. She hesitated before dropping her belt into the plastic bag along with the clothes she had discarded, eventually retrieving her personal smartcards and tucking them into one of the pockets of her new suit. The smartcards ought to be clean, she reasoned, and it was one thing to be phoneless, another to be keyless and creditless.

Ginny reentered the copter just as Lisa finally let the belt drop in the bag. There was a conspiratorial gleam in the younger woman's eye. She extended a gloved hand over the back of the front passenger seat, opening the palm to display two small white tablets. Lisa met her gaze suspiciously.

"It's going to be a long night, Dr. Friemann," Ginny said. "You need to stay alert." Her free hand also came into view, clutching a plastic bottle filled with turbid fluid. "Fortified GM fruit juice," she explained. "Calories, vitamins, ions . . . everything you could possibly need. The boss told me to give it to you." Plainly, the boss hadn't mentioned the side order of pep pills.

If only, Lisa thought as the comment about everything she could possibly need echoed in her skull—but she accepted the pills into her right hand and took the bottle in her left. She swallowed the pills and washed them down thoroughly.

"Keep it," Ginny said. "Drink the rest on the way."

Lisa nodded and followed the pilot out of the helicopter. She handed the plastic bag to the policeman who'd met them. "Better have them swept," she said. "Tell the lab to be careful not to damage the goods—if the equipment is state of the art, it'll probably come in handy. Send the proceeds back to the East Central Police Station."

The officer nodded.

"The next generation of suitskins will probably have sweepers built in," Ginny observed as she slammed the helicopter door. "The police will have to adopt smart-fiber uniforms then."

Lisa hadn't heard the term "suitskin" before. She'd only heard smart-fiber ensembles called "smartsuits." She had to admit, though, that the one-piece she was now wearing did feel rather like a second skin. As the fibers of such garments accumulated more faculties, their quasisymbiotic relationship with the body's own outer layer would become increasingly intimate as well as increasingly complex. The suits currently used to hook up to virtual-reality apparatus were much bulkier, restricted in their use to dedicated spaces, but the gap between organic and inorganic microtechnology was closing all the time.

Sometime within the next fifty years, it would be possible to talk of nanotechnology as having arrived rather than merely anticipated, and the bridges between the organic and the inorganic would be multitudinous. Even the best suitskins imaginable would be external technology, though: overcoats for ordinary people. Even gut-based nanotech would be external in a technical rather than in a topological sense. One day, if Algenists and other champions of evolution toward the superhuman got their way, none of it would be necessary. True overpeople presumably wouldn't need overcoats to protect them, not from the elements or from all the hostile viruses that bio-armorers could devise.

"That's better," Smith said as she joined him in the elevator that would take them down to ground level. Lisa had already noted that however smart the fibers of her new suit might be, it was perfectly staid in cut and color. It hugged her figure tightly on the inside, but on the outside, it was shaped like a conventional jacket and trousers, and she didn't suppose that its almost-black color would look significantly brighter in daylight than it did beneath the soft yellow lights of the elevator cab.

A patrol car was waiting for them. The driver switched his blue flashers on before setting forth into the traffic, but it didn't accelerate their progress to any noticeable degree. The city streets were surprisingly busy, and the drivers of the other vehicles evidently didn't feel under any obligation to get out of the way. Their onboard computers would be storing up instances of "contributory negligence" with the usual alacrity, but nobody seemed to care anymore. The improvements in road safety wrought by the '38 Road Traffic Act had proved as temporary as the achievements of all its predecessors.

Lisa finished off the dregs of the drink Ginny had given her. It had taken the edge off her appetite, but the pills hadn't kicked in yet and she was still engaged in a constant struggle to remain fully alert.

Unlike the Ahasuerus Foundation, the Institute of Algeny had not leased office space in an ultramodern building. Its governors had gone to the opposite extreme, buying a house in an upmarket residential area—which still looked like the private houses that surrounded it. The fact that its walls and gates were topped by razor wire didn't seem at all unusual, given the similar levels of paranoia manifest by its neighbors. The tree-lined street in which it was located was obviously home to people who valued their privacy and took the business of property protection very seriously indeed.

After being admitted to the house, Smith and Lisa were ushered into a room that could have passed for an ordinary suburban living room had it been equipped with a homestation, although the mock-antique furniture was the kind usually advertised on the shopping channels alongside discreetly cabineted, twentieth-century TV sets. It wasn't until they were seated that their host introduced himself.

"Matthias Geyer," he said. "Delighted to meet you, Dr. Friemann. There are Friemanns in my family—perhaps we might be distantly related." His accent was smooth and melodious, but quite distinct and deliberate.

"I doubt it," Lisa said.

"But the ancestor who bequeathed the name to you never bothered to Anglicize it," Geyer pointed out. Lisa wondered whether he was trying to recruit her as a potential ally, or making a point for Peter Grimmett Smith's benefit.

"No," she admitted. "He never did."

Matthias Geyer was taller and slimmer than Dr. Goldfarb, but he wasn't as tall or as angular as Peter Grimmett Smith. He was better looking and seemed considerably younger than either of them, although Lisa thought she detected signs of cosmetic somatic engineering on his cheeks and neck. If so, he was probably a forty-year-old determined to preserve the appearance of his twenty-five-year-old peak rather than a thirty-year-old devoted to clean living. He offered his guests a drink, and when they declined, he suggested that they might like something to eat, given that they must have missed dinner. When they declined that offer too, he bowed politely in recognition of their sense of urgency.

"I'm very sorry to hear that misfortune has visited Professor Miller," he said, now addressing himself—with what must have been calculated belatedness—to Peter Grimmett Smith. "I will, of course, do anything I can to assist his safe recovery. I would be devastated to think that his contact with our organization had anything to do with his disappearance."

"But you do recognize the possibility?" Smith said swiftly.

"I fear so. What he told me was inexplicit, but he was clearly attempting to use an element of mystery to engage my interest. I could not say that he was dangling temptation before me, but he did go to some length to hint that when he spoke of negative results and blind alleys, he was not telling the whole story."

"And that's what you reported back to Leipzig, is it?" Smith asked.

"I am not required to report back to anyone," Geyer informed them loftily. "I make my own decisions. Ours is not a centralized organization, like the Ahasuerus Foundation. Nor has it any principal base in Germany. We have come a long way from our roots, Mr. Smith—in every way."

Lisa wondered whether Geyer knew what they had been talking about in the helicopter. Even if there had been no other bug but Leland's, it was possible that Leland was working for, or with, Geyer—but Geyer's defensiveness was natural enough. He must have known that Smith would have made a comprehensive background check on his organization, and what it would have revealed.

"What was it that Miller was trying to sell you?" Smith asked, unwilling for the moment to be sidetracked into a discussion of the Institute's shady origins.

"He made it perfectly clear that he was not trying to *sell* me anything," Geyer corrected him. "He wanted to make a gift, of results accumulated over four decades, concerning a series of experiments he had conducted on mice and other animals."

"What other animals?" Lisa was quick to put in. Nobody else had mentioned other animals, and it was a long time since Miller had been involved with the creation of transgenic rabbits and sheep.

"Dogs, I believe," Geyer replied.

"Dogs?" Lisa echoed skeptically. "The university hasn't used dogs as experimental animals since the 2010 riot."

"What *kind* of experiments?" Smith asked, impatient with what seemed to him to be an irrelevant digression.

"Professor Miller was calculatedly vague," Geyer said apologetically. "He was insistent, however, that the work had a direct bearing on our core endeavors. He expressed concern that if our researchers did not know what he had tried to do and failed, they might waste years of effort following the same sterile path. It had once seemed such a promising line of research, he said, but had disappointed him grievously—and by virtue of its time-consuming nature, he could no longer carry it forward himself."

"Time-consuming nature?" Smith queried.

Geyer raised his hands helplessly. "Given that he also contacted the Ahasuerus Foundation," he said, "I could hardly help drawing the inference that he was speaking of a technology that would permit the extension of life, but he did not say so in so many words."

"But that *is* one of your so-called core concerns, isn't it?" Smith's suspicion that Geyer was being evasive was painfully obvious.

"One of them," Geyer readily conceded. "The founder of the Ahasuerus Foundation was rather narrowly interested in the possibility of human longevity, apparently assuming that human nature could be changed in that single respect without unduly affecting its other components. We have always taken the view that a more general transformation is desirable, of which longevity would not necessarily be the most important aspect."

"You're more interested in breeding a master race than in simply helping everyone to live longer," Smith said, not bothering to employ the kind of inflection that would have turned it into a rhetorical question.

Geyer's expression hardly changed, but Lisa put that down to stern self-control in the face of naked offensiveness. The pills were taking effect now, and she felt a certain tautness and tone returning to the muscles of her limbs and face. She hoped that the dose wouldn't prove too great. She needed to have her wits about her; it wouldn't do any good to be wide awake but too wired to maintain a proper balance.

"If you'll forgive me saying so, Mr. Smith," Geyer said smoothly, "that's the kind of observation one never hears anymore outside of England. Here, as in Germany, there is hardly anyone now alive who first learned to understand the world while Adolf Hitler was still in power. In four years' time, a whole century will have elapsed since the end of World War Two. It's time to put away the old insults, don't you think? The purpose of the Institute of Algeny is to fund research in biotechnology that will assist the cause of human evolution."

"Point taken," Smith said easily. "I take it that you'd rather I was equally careful to avoid the use of such terms as *übermensch*?"

"Yes, I would," Geyer said equably.

"Even though your own publicity material describes algeny as a Nietzschean discipline and *Thus Sprach Zarathustra* as one of its inspirational documents?"

"Even so," Geyer conceded with the ghost of a smile.

"Not that you have anything to hide, of course," Smith persisted.

"Nothing at all," Geyer said. "I am merely trying to save time. Our aims are widely misunderstood, and clearing up misconceptions can be a vexatious business. It is true that a few of our intellectual antecedents harbored some very strange hopes, but in the days when there was no technology available to carry forward their aims, they had little alternative but to place optimism above practicality. Now that technology has replaced superstition, we have shed the delusions of the past. Professor Miller did not seem to be confused or dismayed by the kind of slanders that have occasionally been leveled against our organization, and I find it difficult to believe they are relevant to your inquiry—unless you believe that mere contact with us might have been enough to inspire his kidnapping by political extremists." Geyer seemed to find that possibility amusing, implying by his attitude that the suggestion was absurd.

"I believe that's possible," Smith said doggedly. "Has your Institute ever had any links with a movement whose members call themselves Real Women?"

"No," Geyer said, still manifesting slight but rather contemptuous amusement.

"But you've heard of them?"

"Yes. We have nothing against what they refer to, rather oxymoronically, as natural physical culture. I suppose they might have regarded our endeavors as a kind of unnatural physical culture, but I'm not aware that they ever singled us out for particular criticism."

"You're using the past tense," Smith pointed out.

"My impression is that the feminist movement no longer has any meaningful existence, as a movement," Geyer said. "If I'm mistaken, I apologize. Is this really relevant?"

"It is if Morgan Miller has been kidnapped by Real Women," Smith answered sourly.

Geyer turned to look at Lisa again. "You must have discussed Nietzsche with Morgan Miller, Dr. Friemann," he said. "Perhaps you could advise your colleague that he is taking the wrong inference from his citation in our charter."

"I'm not so sure that he is," Lisa replied. She felt strangely calm now that the effect of the pills was no longer manifest as a disturbance. "I haven't read your charter myself, and I never had the privilege of hearing Morgan's views on Vril—or, for that matter, on your particular brand of algeny. If it was a recent enthusiasm of his, he's more likely to have discussed it with Stella Filisetti, his current research assistant. Did he mention her contribution to his experiments, by any chance?"

"I don't believe so," Geyer said. "He gave me to understand that he had begun this work before or shortly after the turn of the century. If so, he'd have been far more likely to credit you as a contributor, don't you think?"

"Did he?" Lisa inquired. She could feel a smile tugging at the corners of her mouth, and wondered how long it had been since she had last smiled.

"I fear not," Geyer admitted. "He implied that it was a sideline to the research on which his early reputation was based—an unexpected spin-off. Perhaps he was reluctant to discuss it with his colleagues until he'd made more tangible progress."

"You just told us that he'd hinted to you that he *had* made more tangible progress," Lisa pointed out.

"Perhaps there came a time, quite recently, when he reviewed his results and began to wonder whether they were as disappointing as they had seemed at the time," Geyer suggested.

"We need detail, Herr Geyer," Lisa said. "We need to know precisely how this hypothetical research was supposed to make a contribution to the cause of human evolution. If it wasn't a failed life-extension technology, what was it?"

"I wish I knew," Geyer said, exuding sincerity with practiced ease. "The puzzle becomes more intriguing with every hour that passes. He did not tell me. But if I were to answer as an Algenist rather than as a mere witness, I would point out that one cannot alter one aspect of human nature without altering others. A man who did not age, and who might live forever if he did not die violently, would differ from you and me in many subtle ways, Dr. Friemann, and perhaps in some not so subtle. Ancient romances of the elixir of life could sidestep such questions, but serious scientists cannot. If someone came to you with a supposed elixir of life, Dr. Friemann, you would be bound to ask the awkward questions, would you not? How, exactly, does it work? What, exactly, are its side effects? There are unintended consequences in everything we do, are there not?

"If Morgan Miller had told me in so many words that what he wanted to give me was a technology that would allow people to live longer, those are the questions I would have asked him—but he did not tell me what he had discovered, or why it had not lived up to his expectations, or why his attempts to overcome the problem had come to nothing. If the people who have abducted him had not asked those questions beforehand, they have acted precipitously, perhaps at the risk of bitter disappointment. If they had asked them but had jumped to the wrong conclusions, the depth of their disappointment will be all the greater. Do you see what I mean?"

It was impossible to be certain, of course, but Lisa thought she could see at least part of his meaning. If Matthias Geyer had reached the same tentative hypothesis that she had, he'd had more time to think about its implications, with fewer distractions. Smith's reference to Real Women hadn't seemed to come as any surprise to him, which reinforced Lisa's suspicion that Leland and the Institute of Algeny were hand in glove—but while Leland had seized upon the apocalyptic aspects of the Real Woman's speech, Geyer might have taken the same view as Lisa as to its actual import.

However clever Geyer might be, though, he didn't know everything that Lisa knew. He had no way of matching her guess as to the identity of the person behind the kidnapping. All he could do was to sit around and wonder why Morgan had thought his quest a *partial* failure—which would surely have driven him to the same hastily formed conclusion that Ms. X must have reached: that if Morgan had discovered a method of life extension that worked only on women, he would have immediately gone to work to find a way of making it work on men too. But surely, Lisa thought, neither Matthias Geyer nor Ms. X knew Morgan Miller as well as she did—unless, of course, she was a mere fool where Morgan Miller was concerned, and always had been.

"No," she said. "I don't know what you mean."

Geyer flashed her a ghostly half smile that might have been a calculated reflection of her own. "Perhaps I'm not entirely sure what I mean myself," he said. "Algeny encourages the use of the imagination—the everlasting intellectual struggle to transcend the mental limitations imposed on us by the idols of the theatre and the tribe. I deeply regret what has happened. I feel sure that Morgan Miller was an Algenist at heart, and I wish he had come to us forty years ago for assistance with whatever line of research it was that frustrated him so deeply. If you ever come to feel that your vocation in forensic science has run its course, Dr. Friemann, I hope you will consider the possibility of seeking employment with us. We need people of your caliber."

Lisa remembered Leland's assurance that he could fix her up with a job. She had thought at the time that he was merely trying to suggest that her decision to overstep the legal line wouldn't cost her too dearly, but now she considered the possibility that the Algenists really were enthusiastic to recruit her because of what she might know about Morgan Miller's stubbornly secret research. She had to control an impulse to laugh at Geyer's temerity. Peter Smith's expression of disapproval was a sight to behold.

"If you'll forgive me, Herr Geyer," the tight-lipped man from the MOD put in, "I must insist that we stick to the point at issue. Do you have a tape of your interview with Morgan Miller?"

"I'm afraid not," the Algenist replied. "It's not our policy to tape confidential conversations. I really am trying to be helpful, although I apologize for digressing so far as to tell Dr. Friemann that we value expertise like hers. You have my word that if there is anything I can do to facilitate Morgan Miller's safe release, I shall certainly do it—but for the time being, I cannot see anything I can more usefully do than urge you to return forthwith to more profitable lines of inquiry. I have told you all I can."

No sooner had Geyer finished speaking than Peter Smith's phone rang. It seemed an uncanny echo of what had happened at the Ahasuerus Foundation. "Yes," Smith said, putting the phone to his ear.

Whatever was said didn't seem to lighten his mood. His spirits had already become fractious, but the call seemed to darken them even further. When he put the phone away again, all he said was: "Very well, Herr Geyer—we'll leave it there for the time being."

Lisa rose with an alacrity she could not have contrived an hour before, no matter how impatient she had become. Smith obviously didn't want to say anything in front of Geyer that could be construed as an indiscretion, so she didn't ask any questions. It was, however, left to her to thank Matthias Geyer for his assistance. Unlike Smith, she thought that he probably had been as helpful as he could, in his own way.

When they were back in the police car, with the gates of the Institute firmly closed behind them, she asked Smith what had happened.

"They've identified the Real Woman," he said. "Cross-connecting her records with Filisetti's revealed what seemed to be a promising network of mutual contacts, but the moment your people got to work on it, they found that it was hopelessly confused by a smoke screen. Someone's been busy corrupting the files, and the corruption extends into the heart of the police net."

"Oh," said Lisa. She had not anticipated this, but now that the information had been laid before her, she could see that it was not in the least astonishing. "What kind of smoke screen?"

"The statistical sort threw out a substantial list of names," Smith told her glumly, "but the top three, at least, appear to be somebody's idea of a joke. Guess whose name is number one, even though she didn't even recognize the woman in question?"

"Mine," said Lisa, her heart sinking slightly as she realized that this might look a lot worse than Stella Filisetti or one of her confidantes spraying the word TRAITOR on her door. Even so, she couldn't help adding: "And I bet I can guess who numbers two and three are too."

"Go on," Smith invited, trying hard to pretend that it wouldn't make him any more suspicious than he already was if she happened to guess right.

She went ahead anyway. "Chief Inspector Judith Kenna," she said, "and Mrs. Helen Grundy."

"Spot-on," Smith confirmed. "I suppose I ought to be grateful that they had no way of knowing I'd be sent down from London, or they'd have put my wife's name in as well." He didn't sound entirely convinced of that.

"What about Arachne West?" Lisa asked.

"She was on the list too," Smith confirmed. "Farther down, of course—but near enough to the top to assist the theory that her name's one of those that the smoke screen is trying to conceal, not part of the smoke screen itself. It's only a matter of hours, of course, before the disinformation is eliminated. By dawn, or shortly thereafter, we'll know for sure who our enemies are and be able to begin tracking down their current whereabouts. Once we can start making arrests, we'll be able to ascertain Morgan Miller's whereabouts soon enough."

Lisa considered telling Smith that she already knew who Smith's so-called enemies were, and that she already had a plan for ascertaining Morgan Miller's whereabouts, but she decided against it. Until she knew beyond a shadow of a doubt that she didn't want to be one of those so-called enemies, she had to work alone—or almost alone. There was one person to whom she still felt a limited sense of obligation, although it wasn't going to be easy to give him fair warning without compromising her temporary advantage in the game of hide-and-seek.

"I need some sleep," she said. "If I'm to be of any use to you when the disinformation is eliminated, I have to get my head down."

"So do I," he said. "We'll go straight back to the hotel—but as soon as the sun comes up, we'll have to move on."

By daybreak, Lisa thought, *I'll have moved already—and with luck, you won't catch up with me until I have all the answers I need.*

SEVENTEEN

As soon as Ginny had eased the helicopter into the air again, Peter Grimmett Smith rounded on Lisa. "Okay," he said. "So tell me—what was all that about? You were practically flirting with the guy."

"As a matter of fact," Lisa informed him frostily "it was he who was practically flirting with *me*. He seemed to feel that you were a trifle hostile and that I might be more sympathetic. Wasn't that the point of my being there?"

"Of course," Smith conceded ungraciously. "But you have to remember that he's a suspect. He could be the one who had Miller kidnapped."

"I doubt it. He's infinitely more likely to be the one who set Leland loose—indirectly, if not directly. He had no reason to think that Morgan would prefer Ahasuerus to the Institute, given that Morgan doesn't have your knee-jerk response to the mention of Nietzsche and that Morgan never suggested there was any kind of competition going on. When he heard about Morgan being abducted, though, he must have had a sudden anxiety attack that something so nearly in his grasp might be snatched away before he even got a chance to find out what it was. He was probably on the phone to Leland within minutes, although he might have checked with Switzerland first."

"That doesn't mean he's on our side," Smith reminded her sharply. "The fact that you and this Leland character seem to have embarked on some kind of conspiracy—"

"That's bullshit," Lisa was quick to put in. "I'm happy to let Leland follow his own priorities while freeing Morgan is number one on his list, but I'm under no delusions as to whose side he's on. I'm in no sort of conspiracy with anyone. The only reason Geyer was eager to talk to me was that he didn't like the way you were talking to *him*. You were right to cut it short when the new information came in. Once you've purged the data relating to Stella's contacts, the true guilty parties will be easy enough to identify. The priority now is making sure they don't do anything too stupid when they're cornered. They haven't killed anybody yet, but they've come close enough to suggest that Morgan may still be in a mortal danger."

"That's not the only issue," Smith said grimly.

It is for me, Lisa thought. But that was because she wasn't yet prepared to believe that whatever Morgan had taken to Goldfarb and Geyer had had any military or commercial value.

The lights of Swindon were fading into hungry darkness as the helicopter reached its cruising altitude, but Lisa looked in vain for any hint of dawn on the horizon they were fleeing. For the first time, she felt the lack of the personal equipment she had abandoned to the plastic bag when she had been forced to change her tainted clothing. She had lost contact with the patient cycle of the hours; the pills that had banished her fatigue had disconnected her from any sense of passing time.

She had to raise her head over the top of the front seat and scan the red lights of Ginny's instrument panel in the hope of catching sight of a clock face or digital display. When she finally found one, she was startled to observe that it was five to four, twenty-four hours to the minute since the panic had set in. A single day was all it had required to crack and bruise the veneer that sixty-one years had ingrained upon the surface of her life. It was undoubtedly the most eventful day she had ever lived—but while she watched, the display changed.

It was now four minutes to four, and a new day had begun: a day that would likely wrench the cracks apart, turn the bruises into bloody wounds, and shatter to smithereens everything she had patiently made of herself.

"It's not just a matter of identifying the ringleaders," Smith added, following his own train of thought into the tunnel of silence. "We need to know how wide the conspiracy extends. If Stella Filisetti did remove a number of mice from the university, they might already have been split into several different consignments and moved out of the cityplex. We need to cover the Institute and Ahasuerus, of course—but how many other possible destinations are there, and how many potential couriers? They obviously want the data as well as the animals, but losing the animals might be a serious breach of security in itself. It's a pity that mice are so small."

"If they weren't" Lisa pointed out drily, "Mouseworld would never have been a possibility." Smith was right, though; unless Stella could be persuaded to tell them exactly how many mice she'd taken and how they'd been dispersed, it would never be possible for the MOD to be sure they'd plugged the leak. Without a record of exactly how the mice had been transformed and how they had fared, it would be a long and difficult process to work back from a DNA analysis to the production of a new transformer.

"But you're right, of course," Smith said, switching to a conciliatory tone with all the subtlety of a charging hippopotamus. "Our first priority is to liberate Morgan Miller, and if Herr Geyer is trying to do that too, he's not our enemy—at least not for the time being. I might have misjudged him—but you have to admit that his organization merits suspicion. What did you mean about my 'knee-jerk response to the mention of Nietzsche'?"

"That's what Herr Geyer seems to think," Lisa was quick to say, conscious that it would benefit her to be a little more diplomatic. "He seemed to assume that you hadn't quite understood the relationship between algeny and Nietzschean morality. He probably thinks your interpretation of the term *übermensch* is a little on the vulgar side."

"So educate me," Smith said acidly. "What does *he* think it means?"

"Nietzsche's idea of the overman was rather vague," Lisa told him, "but he would certainly have been horrified by the subsequent usurpation of the idea by the Nazis. Nietzsche seems to have thought of overmen—and he did mean *men* in the narrow sense, although I hope that modern Algenists are more generous—as intellectuals and creative artists, definitely not swaggering oafs in jackboots. Nietzsche's critique of moral systems is complicated, but one of its fundamental observations is that the old moral systems tend to see good in negative terms, as the absence of manifest evils like hunger, pain, injury, and death. That was perfectly reasonable in societies so primitive that they were perpetually assailed by all the ills that made even human life nasty, brutish, and short—but it no longer makes much sense in advanced societies that have the means to oppose the elementary evils and drastically reduce their role in everyday life.

"Nietzsche thought, and Morgan Miller agreed with him, that there comes a point in social and personal evolution at which one has to stop thinking of good merely as the absence of manifest evil— the so-called 'ethics of the herd'—and begin thinking of good in positive, active, and creative terms. It's a fundamental tenet of algenist philosophy that instead of merely trying to insulate ourselves from suffering, we have to start thinking about what we actually want to *make* of ourselves. We have to stop being content to be merely human and decide exactly what kinds of superhumans we intend to become. Nietzsche would have agreed with Morgan that the two most obviously mistaken models are political tyrants and plutocrats—and I think Herr Geyer would like us to believe that his Institute of Algeny takes the same view."

"Does it?" Smith wanted to know.

"You're the one who commissioned the background check."

The MOD man curled his lip skeptically. "What about the other stuff?" he asked. "That crack about the elixir of life not being as simple as fantasists made out. He seemed to be trying to make a point."

"He was," Lisa admitted, and hesitated only briefly over the question of how honest she ought to be in explaining her interpretation of the point in question. "As far as I could judge, he was suggesting that finding ways to live longer would be futile if we continued trying to live in the same old way. That's why he was rather contemptuous about Ahasuerus. If Adam Zimmerman really has had himself frozen down until his Foundation can find a way to make him emortal, Herr Geyer might concede that the man's an enterprising and ingenious coward, but would nevertheless find his cowardice deplorable. I daresay that he said much the same to Morgan in the course of the conversation he was too scrupulous to tape—and he seems to think that he struck a chord. Herr Geyer presumably wants to believe there's more to Morgan's imperfect discovery than the possibility of extending the life span—but that might be wishful thinking on his part. He might have been misled by his optimism into mistaking the actual import of Morgan's reservations."

Smith thought about that for a moment or two. "You mean that if Miller has discovered a way of extending the human life span, it may have some unfortunate side effect that renders it less than wholly desirable. Like the Struldbruggs in Swift."

Lisa was mildly surprised by the literary reference, but all she said was "Yes." She had gone as far as she was willing to go—but it was far enough. She looked out the window again, but there was still no sign of first light. *How can dawn be dragging its feet*, she wondered, *when time is racing at such a headlong pace? Have I somehow cut myself adrift from order and continuity?*

"I think what Dr. Friemann means, sir," Ginny put in, her voice only slightly muffled by the loose-set mouthpiece of her helmet, "is that it might work only on females. That would explain the radfem motivation."

Lisa didn't know whether to curse the pilot silently or congratulate her audibly, but she settled for saying: "It's a possibility—but even if that's so, it might be far more complicated. That's why Geyer was so keen to stress that you can't change one aspect of human life without changing others, sometimes unpredictably. But we can't forget that this is about what Morgan's kidnappers *think* he's got, not what he actually *has* got. There might be a world of difference. I may be foolishly naive, but I cannot believe, even for an instant, that

Morgan could have made a discovery of this magnitude without telling me—or, indeed, anyone else."

"But we don't know that he didn't tell anyone else," Ginny pointed out, carried away by the flood of her own ingenuity. "Dr. Chan obviously knows *something*—and it seems to be something he's reluctant to confide in us before he's explained it to you."

Not just a pretty face, Lisa thought. *But if you're right, Ginny darling, and Morgan really does have a technology of longevity whose only downside is that it doesn't work on people with balls, whose side will you be on come the time when the fat lady sings?* Aloud, she said: "I still don't believe it. Chan wouldn't keep something like that from me anymore than Morgan would. We go back a long way."

"As friends," Smith reminded her.

"As friends," she echoed. The words obviously meant more to her than they did to Peter Grimmett Smith—but the real question was how much they meant to Chan. *Where the hell is Chan?* she wondered. *And what kind of stupid game is he playing?* The sky was brightening again, but it was only the lights of the cityplex looming up in the west, far more perverse than any natural sunrise.

"This is all rather fanciful," Smith complained. The tone of his voice suggested that he didn't think much of Ginny's hypothesis, and not because of Lisa's lukewarm endorsement. Ginny was, after all, only his driver—and Lisa was a woman on the wrong side of middle age. He didn't have the same imaginative reach as the flirtatious Matthias Geyer did, and nothing like the same imaginative reach as Stella Filisetti and Arachne West. Perhaps that was a virtue, given that Stella Filisetti's imagination seemed to have carried her away to ludicrous extremes, and allowed her to persuade at least half a dozen otherwise sensible individuals that her runaway paranoia *might* be justified. Could she have been so effective if the world hadn't been trembling on the brink of plague war? Maybe not. But the world *was* on that edge, and the knowledge that the men who controlled global commerce—and it probably *was* men, in the narrow sense—had a solution ready for the marketplace wasn't as much of a comfort to Lisa as it might have been to Peter Grimmett Smith.

"We'll find out the whys and wherefores soon enough," Lisa told him, trying hard to sound as if they weren't important enough to warrant much expenditure of intellectual effort. "What we need to do is make sure that we're ready to act when your people have sorted out the good data from the bad. We need some sleep. I do, at any rate."

She saw Ginny's helmeted head turn halfway, as if the pilot intended to favor her with a long, hard stare—but the gesture was never completed. Ginny's eyes went back to her instrument panel, and her lips remained sealed.

"Imagine how I feel," Peter Grimmett Smith complained, evidently of the opinion that he'd had the harder day. "You're right, of course—we all need to get our heads down for a while. I was right to insist on seeing the Algenist tonight, though—and however crude and vulgar my understanding of Nietzsche may be, I don't think they're the kind of people who ought to be entrusted with whatever Morgan Miller has discovered . . . if he's discovered anything at all."

"They probably think the same about the Ministry of Defence," Lisa couldn't help observing.

"What's *that* supposed to mean?" Smith asked impatiently.

"Merely that *our* primary interest is national security," Lisa replied, knowing that it would be wise to reemphasize the fact that she was still on Smith's team. "That's our sworn duty, and Geyer has to respect it—but he undoubtedly imagines that he's serving a higher cause, not merely because it's global rather than parochial, but because it's progressive rather than conservative."

"Pie in the sky," was Smith's immediate retort. "If he thinks we can simply forget about the old evils and move on, he's sadly mistaken. Hyperflu is coming fast, and worse things loom in its wake. Our first priority—and for the time being, our *only* priority—is to protect as many of our own people as we can from the murderous kind of chaos that's already taking hold in the poorer parts of the world. Unless Morgan Miller's hypothetical discovery bears on *that* problem, we're all wasting our time here."

Again Ginny's head jerked, as if she were going to look around—this time, presumably, at her boss rather than at Lisa—but she thought better of it, perhaps because she was already being guided into her final approach.

"That may well be true," Lisa said, her voice firm, although its volume was hardly above a murmur. "In the context of the war effort, this is probably no more than a domestic dispute flared up in consequence of an absurd mistake. I can't see that it's likely to have any defense implications at all. Even if Morgan's problematic discovery has anything to do with antibody packaging—and I doubt very much that it does—it won't allow you to stop hyperflu at the far end of the Channel tunnel. If it could, he'd have been knocking on your door instead of the Algenists', and he wouldn't have waited so long before doing it."

It was impossible to tell whether Smith was prepared to take her at her word, but Lisa was past caring. In his position, she would have reserved judgment, and she assumed that he would do exactly that—but she didn't give a damn. With or without the aid of Judith Kenna's computer crime division, his spooks ought to be able to penetrate the smoke screen laid down to delay the identification of Miller's kidnappers within a few hours, and then they'd still have to track down the culprits. If there was anything to be recovered that might assist the defense of the realm, they'd doubtless recover it in their own good time—but Lisa had her own far more urgent agenda to follow.

"I don't like all this talk of a New Order," Smith said reflectively. "Talk of a New Order always implies that the existing order needs to be swept away. It's a fine line that separates the mere conviction that it's bound to happen from the desire to help it along—and what you've told me about what Geyer might *really* have meant doesn't make me any less anxious about his organization."

"The line may seem fine to you," Lisa said irritably, "but it's firm enough to Morgan Miller, and to every other sufferer from the Cas-

sandra Complex. Knowing that something is certain doesn't anes-
thetize the knower from an acute consciousness of its tragic dimen-
sion. I can't speak for Geyer, or for the Real Women, but the kind of
interest Morgan had in the kind of global society that might emerge in
the wake of the population crisis didn't make him enthusiastic about
hurrying the crisis along. He would have moved heaven and earth, if
he could, to delay the day when the Four Horsemen of the Apocalypse would increase their pace to a gallop. I've no reason to think
Geyer wouldn't do the same. He'd probably argue that we were more
vulnerable to moral criticism because we're servants of the Crown
rather than champions of the entire human race. Even Leland took
time out to give me a little lecture on the virtues of one worldism."

"Just because our primary duty is to defend the Realm, it doesn't
mean we want to see the rest of the world go to hell," Smith told her
a little petulantly. "If we could stop hyperflu everywhere, we would.
We didn't start this war, and we're not interested in saving just our
own people—but charity begins at home."

"It's not me you have to convince," Lisa told him soothingly.
"You don't even have to convince Herr Geyer if you don't want to.
But he isn't dangerous just because he doesn't see things the way you
do. Nor are the great majority of the Millenarians, or groups like the
Real Women. They're no more likely to spawn mad bombers and
random shooters than the rest of the population—maybe less, to the
extent that their ideologies provide some sort of safety valve. I've
caught a lot of murderers in my time, and although the ones I've
encountered are a skewed sample, because all the people with real
motives can usually be identified and arrested without requiring my
kind of voodoo, they're mostly loners unable to conceive of any
escape from their own tortured predicaments. Conspiracies like the
one that formed to snatch Morgan Miller are rare exceptions—and I
can't believe they're enemies of the state, no matter what kind of
rhetoric they employ. If Stella Filisetti knew Morgan as well as I do,
she'd never have set this snowball rolling."

"But you'd have to think that, wouldn't you?" Smith observed, employing all the delicacy and sensitivity he'd displayed when he had blithely suggested to Herr Geyer that the Institute of Algeny was a neoNazi organization. "If only to save your own self-respect."

"Yes," she admitted, to herself as well as to him. "Maybe I would, even if I were wrong. But I'm not wrong. I do know Morgan Miller better than anyone else does, and I know that if he had what Stella Filisetti thinks he has, he wouldn't have buried it and he wouldn't be trying to dispose of it under the table to Ahausuerus or the Algenists."

"I can't assume that," Smith told her flatly, "and as a member of the police force, neither can you."

"I know," Lisa conceded reluctantly.

The helicopter was settling gently into the space reserved for it in the university's parking area. It was only a few hundred meters from there to the Renaissance Hotel, where Smith's car was waiting. It wouldn't matter much whether it was still harboring a bug or two, Lisa thought; there weren't any more questions that Peter Grimmett Smith could profitably ask, and even he was tired of asking unprofitable ones. The conversation lapsed as the copter settled onto the tarmac and the three of them made their way to the other vehicle.

The silence allowed Lisa the luxury of a brief period of mental relaxation before Ginny pulled into the Renaissance parking lot. It required only a single unobtrusive sideways glance to reassure Lisa that Mike Grundy had done as he was asked and had brought her own car to the hotel. She collected her room key from reception and without any comment, accepted the bulky package that was handed over at the same time. She went up to her room, where she stayed close to the door as she took out the keys to her car, listening closely all the while for sounds of movement in the corridor.

As soon as she was reasonably sure she would be unobserved, she slipped out again and headed for the service stairs. She didn't need to go through reception to get back to the parking lot, and there didn't seem to be anyone watching as she slipped into her car and started the motor. No one followed as she drove away into the night. Dawn had still not fully come, but it could not now be far off.

lthough she had no watch to keep time with, Lisa's impression was that it took less than ten minutes to get back to Number 39—but she might have been wrong, given that her onboard computer didn't register a single offense or an instance of contributory negligence. She parked the car in the school playground, where her intruders had left their vehicle before making their own surreptitious approach to the building, and she let herself in with a minimum of noise. She tiptoed up to the second floor, then knocked softly on the Charlestons' door.

Unfortunately, soft knocking didn't do the trick. She had to knock harder, then harder still. In the end, though, she heard footsteps within the apartment and repositioned herself so that she could be seen through the glass peephole.

John Charleston must have recognized her immediately, but when he opened the door, it was only by a crack.

"Lisa?" he said anxiously. "What's wrong?"

"Nothing," she said as reassuringly as she could. "I need to use your phone."

"Why? What's wrong with yours?"

"It's a crime scene upstairs," she told him. "It hasn't been cleared for entry yet, and I don't have my mobile. It won't take long."

He was still suspicious—for which she couldn't blame him, given that her real reason for not wanting to use her own phone was that she feared that the call might be overhead—but he unchained the door so she could slip through.

He was wearing a dressing gown that was so dead as to be slightly malodorous, but she didn't make any comment. He indicated the phone and then stood still, making no move toward the bedroom from which he had presumably emerged. Martha called from within to ask what was happening.

"It's nothing," he replied. "Go back to sleep."

Lisa tapped out the number of Mike Grundy's mobile. As soon as he replied, she said, "It's Lisa, Mike. Are you free to talk?"

"Sure," he said uneasily.

"Meet me where we had the run-in with the red Nissan yesterday," she said. "Your car's computer logged it, in case you don't remember. Soon as possible, okay?"

"What—" he began.

"*Okay*," Lisa repeated insistently.

He got the message. "Okay," he said, and immediately rang off.

She wasn't off the hook yet. John Charleston had heard every word. Before he could open his mouth to ask her what it was all about, though, she lifted a finger to her lips. "Police business," she said in a stage whisper. "If anyone asks, I was never here."

"Oh," he said unenthusiastically. "Yeah, I guess." He might have said more, but his gaze suddenly moved upward as he fixed his stare on the ceiling.

Because Lisa lived in the topmost apartment, she had never quite realized how loud a creaking floorboard might sound beneath the lath-and-plaster ceiling below it, at least in the dead of night. She felt a sudden chill of fear, not so much because she thought she was in physical danger, but because she foresaw that her plan might have to be recalculated yet again. If the radfems had come back for her, that might be convenient, in a way, but if she were to convince them that she meant business, she really ought to be the one to make the approach. As Leland had shrewdly observed, anything said by a captive under duress was likely to be bullshit, and likely to be construed as bullshit even if it were the sober truth. Allowing herself to be taken prisoner might provide an easy route to the heart of the matter, but it would seriously hurt her chance of taking control once she got there.

"Shit," she murmured

"I thought—" Charleston began.

Lisa hadn't any time to waste. "Have you got a gun?" she asked sharply.

"A gun?" he spluttered. "That would be—"

"Just give me the gun, John," she said, dismissing any objections with a casual gesture of her wounded hand. "I need it."

He had to go into the bedroom to remove it from its hiding place. Citizen mice always kept their illicit guns in the bedroom, because the fear that moved them to arm themselves was that of waking up in the dead of night—as Lisa had done little more than twenty-four hours before—to find intruders in their home.

"It's just a dart gun," Charleston explained unnecessarily as he handed it over. "Certified nonlethal. Everybody's got one."

"It'll do," she assured him in a whisper. "Close the door behind me, *very* quietly, and stay close to it. If you hear shots, or if I don't knock on your door again inside five minutes, hit Redial and tell the man I just spoke with to get over here as fast as he can. Whatever happens, you stay here. Okay?"

"Okay," he said with soldierly alacrity.

As soon as the door had closed behind her, she moved lightly up the stairs. She held the gun in her right hand, rather gingerly because the sealant between thumb and forefinger was starting to denature and it had become slightly sticky. She used her left hand to sort through her smartcards. She would still have to punch in the two combinations once her card had gone through the swipe slot, but she figured she could do that quietly enough. With luck, whoever was in her apartment wouldn't know that he or she had company until Lisa actually opened the door.

If the light was on, she would have to keep moving while she assessed the situation, making herself as difficult a target as possible. If not, she would have to flick the switch with her left hand while keeping the gun at the ready, and then—

As soon as the door had opened by the merest crack, she knew the light was on, and she moved rapidly to her left as she pushed her way in, raising the gun to point it at the chest of the man who was rising from the armchair with an expression of startled horror on his face.

But she didn't fire. The continuing effect of the pills had combined with her adrenaline to boost her sky-high, and she felt well and truly wired, but she still had the presence of mind to freeze her finger on the trigger.

Instead of firing the darter, she raised her left forefinger to her lips in an urgent gesture, imploring silence.

Fortunately, Chan Kwai Keung had always been quick on the uptake, and he must have been expecting her for hours. He stifled his cry of recognition and nodded eagerly, to show that he understood. Lisa used the barrel of the gun to beckon him to the door, and she closed it behind them as quietly as she could. Then she shook her head and pointed downstairs. Chan nodded again.

As soon as they reached the third-floor landing, Lisa knocked on John Charleston's door. When he cracked it open, she thrust the gun through the narrow gap.

"It's okay," she said. "All sorted out. No cause for alarm."

"Can I still keep it?" he asked tremulously—meaning, of course, the illicit gun.

"Keep what?" she replied generously.

Charleston wasn't quite as quick on the uptake as Chan, but he was quick enough. "Oh," he said feebly. The direction of his gaze switched to Chan's face. "Right. Thanks. You're okay now?"

"Fine," she said. "Neither of us was ever here, okay?"

"Absolutely," he assured her.

Lisa waited until she'd eased the car out on the road again before turning to Chan and saying: "What the *hell* do you think you're playing at?" The adrenaline should have abated by now, but it hadn't. The pills had thrown her entire system out of kilter, and she was locked like a crazy lemming or a snowshoe hare on the verge of a nervous breakdown. She was on the edge, and she wasn't going to get off until she had seen the affair through to its bitter end.

Chan winced at the rawness of her tone. He seemed genuinely chastened. "I am very sorry," he said, punctilious in his diction even now. "I did not know what to do for the best. I thought you would know, so I tried . . . I really had no idea those crazy people would try to snatch me the way they snatched Morgan. I was naive, I suppose—but that made me all the more anxious. As soon as I got out of the parking area, I ran like the wind. At first I expected you home in a couple of hours. Then, when you failed to turn up, I thought you must have been shot. I did not know what to do."

"How did you get in? Those locks are supposed to be unhackable."

"You should change your pass codes more often," Chan chided her, "and your smartcard needs to be at least twice as smart as it is. But that is not important. Where have you *been*?"

"*That*'s not important. What's important is why you're playing silly cloak-and-dagger games while there's a full-scale crisis on. What on earth have you got to hide?"

Dawn had turned to daylight now, but the light was gray and cold and utterly unwelcoming. It was less than a week to All Hallows' Eve, but the weather should still have been relatively benign. This was like a return to the old days, before the greenhouse effect really took hold—but that was no reason for the dead not to hold to their calendar and keep to their graves. The world had no right to be turning topsy-turvy.

"They bombed Mouseworld," Chan said in a whisper. "If it had just been Morgan, and Ed . . . but when I was told they had bombed Mouseworld, that was when I knew it had to be my fault. It had to be that crazy old experiment, not the ones we were doing for Ed Burdillon. If it had only been the work we were doing for Ed . . . but how did they ever find out?"

"I don't have the time, Chan," Lisa said sternly. "You'll have to do better than this. *What* crazy old experiment?"

"It was my idea," he was quick to say. He continued so rapidly as the car sped along Wellsway toward Entry Hill that Lisa wondered whether her hearing had somehow gone into fast-forward. "I had to let Morgan in on it, but it was entirely my idea. We had to do it secretly, even if it meant breaking the law, because the department would never have given us permission. Mouseworld had become a sacred cow, untouchable—but that was pointless, do you see? As soon as all four populations had stabilized, there was no further point in the replication. If they had continued to behave differently, it would have been a different matter, but they did not. And there was so much more that might be done! Four cities: two experimental samples, two controls. What an opportunity! How could we let it go to waste? But the Departmental Committee could never have agreed. If there had ever been a majority to concede the principle, it would have fallen apart as soon as the question was raised as to which of countless imaginable experiments should be carried out. The only way that progress could be made was for one or two individuals to do what needed to be done *in secret*. All mice look alike among so many . . . and the people keeping track had ceased to do anything but *count*. It was so easy, Lisa, so very easy."

Lisa felt completely numb. Time ceased to race and became suddenly still. So it was not unthinkable, after all, that Morgan had kept a secret from her for forty years—and not unthinkable, either, that Chan had kept it from her too. But even that revelation was marginally less shocking than the other. Morgan Miller and Chan Kwai Keung had subverted the Mouseworld experiment! They had taken it over, for their own secret purposes, without telling anyone what they were doing, or why. For thirty or forty years—presumably ever since the so-called "chaotic fluctuations" of the zero years—the four cities of Mouseworld had been running *their own* experiment instead of, or at the very least alongside of, the one they were supposed to be running. What kind of deception was that?

"*What* experiment?" Lisa demanded tersely. She hadn't time to digress.

Chan went on, speaking faster than he had ever spoken before, at least within earshot of Lisa. "I had developed a new and unprecedentedly versatile system of antibody packaging. It was not *very* closely akin to the new method Edgar Burdillon has been helping to test, but it was sufficiently close to make us uncomfortable when Ed asked for our help with his new project. I am sworn to secrecy regarding that new project, of course, but I think that the broad outlines of the old experiment, at least, can be divulged without breaking that oath. I would not have you told at the time, because you were a police officer and it would have put you in an awkward ethical position, but if this is why Morgan has been kidnapped . . . well, it must suffice to say I thought I had devised a new and better approach to the problem of antibody packaging, and that I had high hopes for its utility. The world was still rife with natural infectious diseases in those days. I could not have been so optimistic had I come across it twenty years later, when the vast majority of those evils had been defeated by other means. I thought it an elegant method, but it involved importing a cumbersome package of new DNA into the superficial tissues of any carrier. The mouse models I constructed in order to study the efficiency of the system and its various side effects thrived, but there were certain ambiguities of effect that made me regret deeply that I could study them only in isolation, in interaction with one another. In order that the efficacy of the system could be *properly* tested, I needed to discover how the models would cope with a more realistic context. Do you see what I mean?"

Lisa turned left into Bradford Road, wondering why they had made so little progress. How much time was actually passing while the cracks in the surface of her being widened and spread? *Did* she see what he meant, or was it only the false kind of intuition she sometimes experienced in dreams?

"I see," she said. "Knockout mice are perfect models of genetic-deficiency diseases, but the efficacy of antibody-packaging systems can only be assessed in the context of a whole population—ideally, a population under stress. And there you were, spending hours every day in a room whose four walls showed stable populations under stress, all of them running smoothly in the same ancient groove. So you decided to convert two of them into experimental populations by introducing your own transformed mice to see how they would get on."

"Only one," Chan said. "I wanted to split the replicates two and two, but Morgan insisted that my intervention should be minimal. I introduced the transformed mice into Paris. Technically, it was a criminal act in that it bypassed the university's Ethics Committee as well as the Departmental Committee, but I thought it criminal in a higher sense that the Mouseworld experiment had been allowed to stagnate. I insisted that you be kept out of it, Lisa, because I knew you could not countenance any such argument in your professional capacity, but I hope you can see that my conviction was deep and sincere."

"Cut the crap and tell me what happened to the fucking mice," Lisa instructed him brutally. Bradford Road was giving way to North Road and her rendezvous with Mike was only a few hundred yards away. Her onboard computer still had not registered a single offense.

"They died," Chan said in a hurt tone. "They could not survive among the citizen mice. The reason, I believe—"

She hadn't time to listen to speculation. The fact was all that mattered. "So the experiment failed? It was a complete bust—and *please* don't feed me that crap about there being no failed experiments in science."

"It was a failure," he admitted. "It did not seem significant at the time, when Morgan and I were trying so many different things, but—"

"But when Ed Burdillon roped you into testing *his* new antibody-packaging system, you couldn't help wondering whether it would run into exactly the same problem. So you—and I do mean *you*, in the narrow sense—were thrown into paroxysms of doubt as to whether you ought to confess to your ancient crime, on the off chance that it might save the Containment Commission from pinning all its hopes on a nonstarter. Except, of course, you couldn't quite figure out who to confess it *to*—and when the lunatics who snatched Morgan also took the trouble to torch the evidence of your ancient crime, you *really* got your knickers in a twist. And that, to cut a long guilt trip short, is when you finally thought of me." The junction of North End Road and Ralph Allen's Drive was visible now, and she could see Mike Grundy's car, parked and waiting.

"I thought you would know what to do," Chan said lamely. "I did not."

"For a certified genius," Lisa said angrily, "you truly are completely fucking stupid. I really used to look up to you, you know?" She was extremely annoyed with herself, because she knew this was a bad time to be fighting back tears of frustration and disappointment. It didn't make her feel any better to know that neither Peter Grimmett Smith nor Mike Grundy would have had the faintest idea of what she was on the verge of crying about. The only person who could possibly have understood was Morgan.

"Yes," Chan admitted miserably. "I know."

"I wish I had time to figure out exactly what the hell you're talking about, and whether it matters," she said as she brought the car to a lurching halt at the junction, "but I don't. I have to spring Morgan, and I only have a couple of hours to do it in. So I'm going to hand you over to Mike, and he'll take you to Peter Grimmett Smith. You tell Smith *everything*, except maybe where you saw me last. You can give him my apologies for not being there to translate your explanations for him, and for not being there period. But tell him it really is for the best that I do this now and do it alone. Tell him I'll be in touch as soon as I can, and that if I haven't returned by nightfall with Morgan in tow, we're probably both dead."

"Do you mean that?" Chan asked anxiously.

"Yes, I do," she said, although she really wasn't sure, given that her internal weather was crazy lemming through and through and that she couldn't really be sure of anything anymore. "And although it won't be *all* your fault, you certainly won't have helped. Now *come on.*"

Third Interlude

HUMAN RELATIONSHIPS

By the time she'd been at her new university for a fortnight, Lisa had figured out why Morgan Miller didn't wear a lab coat. It was, as she'd instantly suspected, far more than any mere absentminded omission or some petty desire to stand out from the crowd by refusing to accept its uniform.

In Morgan Miller's view, Lisa eventually deduced, wearing a lab coat implied that being a scientist was a kind of job: something that one put on and took off according to a circadian rhythm of work and leisure. He refused to give tacit license to any such implication. It also suggested that the clothes worn underneath it were more precious than the coat itself, requiring protection from the vicissitudes of laboratory life. Morgan Miller regarded clothes in an icily utilitarian light; he bought his outfits as cheaply as possible, and was not above shopping at market stalls and charity shops. If one of his shirts or a pair of flannel trousers were stained by a laboratory accident, he simply threw them away. He never wore a jacket. Nor did he ever wear T-shirts or jeans, even though it would not have been a violation of his utilitarian principles, because he considered such garments to be key components of the image projected by uncommitted students.

In the course of the first few weeks of their acquaintance, Lisa became as fascinated by her new supervisor as she ever had been by any male of the species. She never deigned to consider the hypothesis that the fascination in question might be classifiable as "love," because she did not consider herself to be the kind of person who might be vulnerable to the horrible indignities of falling or being in love, but that only made its intensity more fascinating. After her own admittedly peculiar fashion, Lisa was as committed a utilitarian as Morgan Miller, and she viewed the fascination that Miller exercised upon her in a conscientiously cold light, as something that would assist her learning.

Lisa's friends and relatives had, of course, always assured her that she was merely a slow developer, and that she would begin to believe in love as soon as the feeling first took hold of her, but she had never taken platitudinous advice seriously and her response to her supervisor could not change her mind. She had always retorted, in the face of such obviously misconceived advice, that "love" was merely a species of psychological dependence, cultivated as much by anxiety as hormonal flux. She had no intention of becoming dependent on Morgan Miller, who was probably not a dependable person in any other respect than the purely professional.

Her observations to date had suggested to her that other women fell in love purely because they cared too much about what men thought of them, suffering adrenaline rushes whenever they thought they were being ignored or insulted: rushes that were not chemically different from those they felt when they became the focus of attention or received a compliment, but which they interpreted very differently when sensation became thought. Lisa cared only about what Morgan Miller thought about her ability as a scientist, and she construed his occasional compliments and insults as mere witticisms of no personal consequence.

He obviously liked that in her, but it was equally obvious that he was far too wise a man to fall in love, especially with a putative soulmate.

Love, in the opinions to which Lisa held firm at the age of twenty-two and Morgan Miller at the age of thirty-four, was merely a matter of self-conditioning and of learned helplessness. Neither of them wanted anything to do with it.

Sex, of course, was a different matter—so different that they wasted little time in courtship before leaping into bed together.

Morgan Miller explained to Lisa, in dribs and drabs, that he had made an irrevocable decision never to get married. This was not so much because he considered his vocation essentially monkish—although he did have a distinct ascetic streak—but because he could see no virtue or purpose in the institution of marriage other than to provide protective cover for children. He was the kind of man who felt obliged to practice what he preached, and it would have been a flagrant violation of his neoMalthusian credo to bring more children into a world that was heading for a population crisis, so there was no earthly need for him to get married. To do so, even if he made his intentions clear to his intended spouse, would have constituted a misrepresentation of sorts. Even a long-term monogamous relationship

without benefit of ceremony would have been a compromise reeking of
bad faith. He had, of course, taken the precaution of obtaining a
vasectomy, by courtesy of the local Marie Stopes Clinic, but that had
not been sufficient to clarify his peculiar conscience, so he explained
to Lisa with all due alacrity that he did not intend to enter into a long-
term relationship with her, and would terminate their arrangement if
ever it seemed likely to become habitual.

Lisa, at twenty-two, could not imagine that she would continue to
see Morgan Miller once she had obtained her doctorate and committed herself completely to some newly hatched state-of-the-art police
laboratory, so she had not thought the assertion worth exploring, let
alone challenging. She was, however, prepared to tease him about the
firmness of his resolution not to maintain the presence of his own precious genes within the great human pool.

"You don't believe in positive eugenics, I take it," she felt free to
observe after they had consummated their purely utilitarian relationship for the third time, nineteen days after their first meeting. He was
the proud possessor of an exceedingly capacious bed whose cast-iron
frame and carved head- and footboards must have dated from the
Edwardian era, when presumably it had been designed to accommodate a whole family. It was pleasantly situated near the neatly net-
curtained southwest bay windows of an equally venerable detached
house on the gentler slope of Beacon Hill. It was the ideal venue for
idle conversation in the late afternoons of autumn, and Lisa was
already looking forward to the sultry evenings of summer.

"I don't believe in taking genetic determinism to absurd lengths,"
Miller told her in response to her question. "I'm an undistinguished
specimen, physically speaking, and the quality of my mind has far
more to do with my education than any genes I might have inherited
from two parents, one an accountant, the other a primary-school
teacher. I have, of course, deposited an abundant sample of my semen
in a convenient gene bank, in case the world should ever feel that it
needs more of my kind, but I am content to leave that decision to
those who come after me. It is entirely possible that I shall accomplish

far more by winning converts to the cause of algeny than by spreading fertile semen far and wide."

"What's algeny?" Lisa asked, as he had clearly intended her to do.

"The true scientific successor to alchemy. Chemistry never had the same objectives, and the fact that inorganic chemistry evolved so much faster than the chemistry of life distorted subsequent opinions as to the nature of the alchemical enterprise. Algeny is the science-based art of practical evolution: the constructive use of our new-found genetic wisdom. I am trying hard to popularize the term, as are a few other enlightened souls, but we have made little progress as yet."

Such pillow talk as Lisa had been involved in before meeting Morgan Miller had tended to the monosyllabic, and she definitely preferred the new kind, even while recognizing the absurdity of its contrived pomposity.

"So you won't be volunteering for the first experiments in human cloning?" she prompted, electing to stick to her own agenda rather than feed him the cues that would allow him to ride his own hobbyhorse comfortably into the neatly framed sunset.

"I shall not," he confirmed, accepting her drift for the moment. "Edgar Burdillon might, but Edgar has ambition, as you've doubtless noticed. If he thought it might further his career . . . but in all likelihood, he lacks the necessary narcissism. I'm no admirer of conspiracy theories, but I strongly suspect that long before Roslin's favorite sheep was unveiled to the world five years ago, there was more than one rich narcissist in America who had already commissioned his employees to carry forward the task of duplicating him with all possible expedition. There's no fool like a vain fool, and American fools are currently the vainest of the vain. Not that I have anything against Americans per se, of course—the USA produces the world's best-educated and most highly accomplished scientists, even if it has to import most of the raw material from the Far East. Its native stock has, alas, been temporarily ruined by feminism."

"I don't see how," Lisa retorted—a little acidly, because she considered herself a feminist and could not abide the contemporary fashion that led so many women of her generation to refuse the label.

"Not intentionally, of course," he said, smiling as if the tenor of her response had scored him a point in some mysterious game. "Indeed, it might be more accurate to say that it is the reaction *against* feminism that has secured the unfortunate and unintended consequences. The fact that more and more American women have become scientists during the last thirty years would not have been problematic had they simply been absorbed into the prevailing culture of science, but the growing resentment against them felt by their male colleagues and the consequent closure of ranks has resulted in the emergence of a distinct cultural divide. In England, which is nowadays among the last nations to be overwhelmed by the tide of cultural progress, we still speak of the two cultures as a way of contrasting science and the absurdly misnamed humanities, but the only genuine culture is scientific and technological, and the only meaningful cultural divisions are those that develop within science."

"I see," Lisa was quick to say, anxious not to be forced back into a purely submissive role, meekly accepting of his penetrative wisdom. "You're talking about holism versus reductionism—holism being seen as metaphorically female, with an emphasis on consensus and conciliation, while reductionism is metaphorically male, on account of being individualistic and imperialistic. But every geneticist knows that it's a false dichotomy—and even if it weren't, I can't see how it's spoiled a whole generation of American scientists."

"That's not what I said," Miller pointed out. "What I lamented is its present effect on the raw material of science: the brains of the young. In recent years, far too many feminists have been sidetracked into compiling what they imagine to be a feminist critique of science and technology, criticizing their supposedly excessive masculinity—and however nonsensical such critiques may be, they have had their influence on educational practice and evaluation. It won't last, of course—feminists will realize soon enough that they have been tricked."

"Tricked? By the great secret conspiracy of male chauvinists?"

"Where large numbers of people have identical interests, no conspiracy is needed to make them act in concert," he replied, taking such evident delight in his cleverness that Lisa almost suspected him of applying a peculiar kind of intellectual algeny, by means of which he was assiduously weaving the residual pleasure of their recent sexual activity into something more purely intellectual. "The victories that feminism has won in the economic arena have not been without their cost, and consciousness-raising works both ways. The same arguments that alerted women to all they had been unjustly denied also alerted men to the fact that they would have to adopt different tactics if they were to ensure that they were to continue to maintain even a fraction of their former advantages. Their strategy was obvious: they had to persuade women to cherish at least a few of the chains of their former bondage. Their greatest victory to date has been the acceptance by so many women that what they *really* wanted to advance was the cause of *femininity*, with all its inherent softness, modesty, and thirst for affection.

"Unfortunately, that has meant that far too many of the young women currently determined to make a career in science embark upon that career without a suitably abrasive attitude of mind. What is worse, many of them flatly refuse to acknowledge the desirability of acquiring such an attitude. Many of the best recruits to American science, in consequence, come from the poorer countries, whose citizens all know perfectly well that life is warfare and that the powerless can gain power only by usurping the privileges of the powerful."

Lisa conceded privately that if there really had been points at stake, Miller would have scored at least nine for technical merit and another eight for artistic impression. She thought she knew him well enough, even on such short acquaintance, to suppose that he not only meant every word of what he said, but also believed she ought to know it too, if she were to be educated in all the fields of his expertise.

All she said in return was: "Isn't that kind of hard Darwinism deeply unfashionable nowadays?"

"Certainly," he said. "Especially in America. Creationism is, by contrast, quite fashionable there. Nowhere in the world is the impending end of civilization anticipated with such naked glee, especially among people determined not merely to see their neighbors perish, but to assist them in the perishing."

"Very masculine, survivalism," Lisa observed. "Creationism too."

"Very," Miller agreed. "Backlashes always tend to the extreme, and to the ridiculous. We shall see a great deal of extremism and absurdity before we die, my darling. We shall see backlashes against backlashes, and a human world drowning in its own uncontrollable adrenaline. We are of the generation that will be privileged to take part in the first lemming year of humankind, no matter how the rags and tatters of femininity may rail against it—but we ourselves do not have to be lemmings, any more than we have to be Calhounian rats or Mouseworld mice. We have the vocation of science to serve our needs. We can be bystanders—not innocent bystanders, I admit, but bystanders nevertheless—provided that we maintain the abrasiveness of our minds and are not so reckless as to give hostages to fortune by having children."

In subsequent conversations, of which by far the majority were held in less comfortable arenas, Lisa heard Morgan Miller's prognosis of the current crisis in human affairs at much greater length, and in infinitely finer detail. She listened to his rhapsodic analyses of the possible scope of the imaginary art of algeny. She bore witness to his careful sifting of the aphoristic philosophy of Friedrich Nietzsche. She patiently tolerated his speculative investigations of the strategy and tactics of the biological warfare that would supply the means by which World Wars Three and Four were bound to be fought. She helped him to discover and expand the unique pathology of his peculiar Cassandra Complex.

Lisa had always thought herself to be the last person in the world to resent the lack of romance in a sexual relationship, but Morgan Miller certainly tested her limits in that regard. From the very beginning, she regarded him as a challenge to—and perhaps the ultimate test of—her own ideals and principles.

In the beginning, at least, she was proud of the way in which she coped with him. She honestly believed she was adapting him to her own purposes while he was adapting her to his. Theirs, she thought, was an honest contract for the pleasurable use of one another's sexual parts, and no sort of marriage at all.

Later, she began to doubt herself, and when that happened, she had perforce to doubt him too, but for a year and more she was convinced that the two of them had the whole art and science of human relationships well and truly licked.

She slept with Chan Kwai Keung too, but only twice. It was not that he was in any real danger of falling deeply in love with her, but the intricacy of his mind would not let him treat their sexual intercourse superficially. It made him more introspective and self-doubtful, and that was not the effect Lisa wanted to have. Morgan Miller was by no means incapable of self-doubt, but it required a far more powerful stimulus to bring it out in him.

She never slept with Edgar Burdillon, although she spent almost as much time with him on a day-by-day basis as she did with Morgan, because he had at least as much to teach her about laboratory technique and biomolecular analysis. She found him more comfortable company than Morgan or Chan, and did not want to prejudice that ease of association by undue complication. No matter how abrasive a mind became, it still required comfortable refuges, and Ed Burdillon became one such refuge, all the more valuable to her because it was part and parcel of her working environment.

If she'd had to guess, in the summer of 2003, Lisa would have correctly estimated that Ed Burdillon would one day be head of the department, and that Morgan Miller would still be working alongside him, but she would have taken it for granted that Chan and she would both move on.

If she had been asked, in the summer of 2003, what it would signify if she and Chan were still around in 2041, she would have judged it evidence of failure, indolence, or cowardice.

If she had been invited, in the summer of 2003, to estimate the

year in which the world's population would finally peak and the great
collapse would begin, she would probably have said 2040, although
she would have hoped secretly that the estimate might be ten or
twenty years too early.

Morgan Miller's lectures on the neoMalthusians were fun—maybe the
best fun available to Lisa outside of his bed during the winter of
2002–3, which turned out to be the worst of the zero years—and she
actually began to relish the prospect of lending him assistance by
supervising the supportive seminars in the following academic year.

Although, Miller, as a confirmed lover of aphorisms, was prepared to borrow telling phrases from the likes of Paul Ehrlich and
Garrett Hardin, his actual teaching drew far more heavily on the
hard data that had been patiently collated by Claire and W. M. S.
Russell in *Population Crises and Population Cycles* in order to add
statistical detail to their accounts of humankind's previous flirta-
tions with extreme population density. Each such flirtation had been
facilitated by a great leap forward in agricultural science or technologies of irrigation, and each one had its own idiosyncratic features
by courtesy of its specific social context, but the raw numbers always
told the same story. Case by case, from China and "monsoon Asia"
through the Near East and Europe to Mexico and the Andes, Miller
followed the Russells' analyses of the rise and fall of civilizations in
terms of the ecological impact of their numbers, bringing all known
history and a substantial fraction of prehistory into a single, over-
arching frame.

The tide of figures was irresistible, and by the time Miller began
to speak to his students about the predicament of the modern world,
there was no room left for doubt that the crisis of contemporary civilization was new and unprecedented in only one significant respect:
the fact that it was global.

"The numbers are larger than they have ever been before, of
course," he said with awesome casualness, "and the technological

efforts that have permitted their inflation have been bolder than could ever have been conceived in any earlier era—but the only truly significant difference is that the impending collapse, which we cannot avert, but only postpone, will not be localized. We shall not be making a little desert, or laterizing the soil of a single plain; we shall be laying waste to the entire world. The survivors will hate and despise us for it. We shall seem far worse in their eyes than the conquering hordes of Attila the Hun or Genghis Khan, because we are motivated not by dreams of glory, but by cowardice and willful blindness. They will be right to hate and despise us, because we know what we are doing, and will not refuse to do it. They will know that we had a choice, and that what we chose to do was to destroy the world. Our gift to the children whose presence will bring about that destruction is a poisoned chalice from which billions will drink premature death. How can they help thinking of us as perverse as well as evil? Why should they?"

The seminars supporting the lectures were not, of course, as lively as Morgan Miller hoped. In that respect, at least, he was a poor prophet, misled by residual optimism. The audiences were thin, and most of the students who actually bothered to turn up spent their time meekly waiting to write down what he said, in case they needed to reproduce it in an essay or a final exam.

Lisa rarely bothered to write anything down at all. She had never made any conscious concession to tradition or ritual, and her policy was never to make a note of anything that could be looked up on the net or in a library. Life was too short.

"It might not be as bad as you suppose," she once suggested to Miller, though not in any public arena. "The traditional Malthusian checks are making new progress in their long war of attrition. The poor are starving in ever-greater numbers now that compassion fatigue has firmly set in, and the war business is booming. Even the bacteria are striking back now that they've developed immunity to so many antibiotics, and global warming is increasing the violence of the weather by leaps and bounds. Maybe the rate of increase will level off at a sustainable level."

"Too little too late," was his gloomy retort. "Medical science is far too efficient to let the bacteria catch up. The war business is far too businesslike. Compassion fatigue is localized. We have no reason to think that the existing population can be sustained in the long term."

"But you admit that the same advances in biology that underlie medial science will transform the war business," Lisa pointed out. "As the territorial imperative gradually overwhelms us and sends the whole world crazy, we'll surely have the weapons we need not merely to reduce but to manage the population. You and I might be on the side of the angels in terms of what *we* do with DNA, but Porton Down is less than fifty miles away."

"It'll be too little too late," Miller insisted. "In any case, the last people who ought to be in charge of demographic management are generals and politicians. In time, no doubt our children's children might make the kinds of social adjustments that the citizen mice of Mouseworld have made—but like the citizen mice of Mouseworld, they won't be able to do it until they've been through at least one population crash, and maybe more than one. With luck, I'll be a very old man by the time I see my nightmares coming true—but you're twelve years younger than I am. You stand to lose that much more than I do."

"I'll go down fighting," Lisa said flatly.

"I know you will," he replied.

It was the first real compliment he had paid her. Unfortunately, it remained the best for far too long.

If Lisa had been asked, in the summer of 2003, whether she really intended to go down fighting, she would have said "Yes" and said it very firmly—but if anyone had asked her to specify exactly what the fight would entail, she would have been unable to do so.

She knew even then that there was bound to be a fight of some sort, but she could not tell who or what the enemy might be with whom she could actually become engaged.

When she completed her work at the university, she moved to a brand-new lab facility that was only two miles away, but it was like stepping into a different world.

The rapid advancement of forensic science since the advent of DNA fingerprinting and its importance in supplying evidence for criminal prosecutions had necessitated a radical overhaul of its institutional structure. The lab into which Lisa moved was part of a series of experiments attempting to discover by trial and error the ideal relationship between the CID's operations and the evidential analysts. It had been placed in the same building, and every plausible measure had been taken to ensure that scientists and policemen would become parts of a single tight-knit community. The intention was a noble one, and the hazard proved in the long run not to be a total loss, but for those abruptly thrown in at the deep end and required to make the dream come true, it was a taxing challenge.

The police force was not a happy organization in 2005. For ten years and more, it had been bruised and battered by attempts to root out corruption, institutional racism, and institutional sexism, and its officers were all too well aware of the fact that one of the most widely publicized effects of the introduction of new methods of scientific analysis had been to expose numerous cases of wrongful conviction in which police evidence had been shown to be manufactured. The siege mentality adopted by the police in response to seemingly never-ending criticism of their attitudes and methods ensured that a large minority among them—perhaps even a majority—saw the arrival in their staff operations of a legion of laboratory workers as an invasion of potential fifth columnists. Everyone recognized the necessity of working together, and everyone recognized that the new partnership was capable of delivering considerable rewards, but the necessity was tinged with bitterness and the rewards seemed, in the beginning, to be the rations of Tantalus.

In spite of her own best intentions, Lisa found that she had to cling hard to the relationships she had formed at the university in order to provide some relief from the constant stress of her new workplace. She continued to seek what solace she could in the arms of Morgan Miller, but exposing her new troubles to the commentary of his abrasive mind made her feel as if she were trapped "between the devil and the deep blue sea." She often found it more restful to see Ed Burdillon or Chan Kwai Keung on a purely platonic basis. Their advice was worthless—Burdillon suggested she immerse herself more fully in her work and focus her attention on the quest for promotion, while Chan wondered whether she might not be a great deal happier if she returned to the groves of academe in order to climb the postdoctoral ladder to tenure—but they were unfailingly sympathetic.

Unfortunately, Lisa was well aware that her continued reliance on old friends was part of her problem rather than any kind of solution. She had to form new relationships within the station, not merely with the laboratory staff alongside whom she had been set to work, but with the officers whose Herculean labors she was supposed to be supporting. She certainly did not want to embark upon any new sexual relationship—within the police force, such liaisons were generally considered to be unhealthily incestuous—but she did need to set up productive and satisfying professional alliances.

It was in this context that her acquaintance with Mike Grundy was forged and tempered.

When she first met him, in 2006, Grundy was a detective constable who had relocated after a sideways move from the uniformed branch. He was hardworking, cheerful, and laid-back. He was not particularly handsome, but he made up for this with a natural charm that made him easy to like. He enjoyed his work enough to be unworried about the necessity of making upward progress through the ranks. Having had no education in science to speak of, he was fascinated by the apparent miracles that the lab workers could perform in regard to fibers and stains, and fascinated by the lab itself, which seemed to him to be a kind of wizard's cave. He loved to be invited to look down a microscope or to inspect some intricate pattern inscribed in gray gel by patient electrophoresis. And he laughed at Lisa's jokes.

He didn't always understand the jokes, but he laughed at them anyway. He soon became her favorite source of puzzles, and she in her turn became his favorite consultant. Without actually intending to, they began to rely on one another, not merely for constructive assistance, but for all the kinds of reassuring strokes that made the routines of everyday life more comfortable. They never dated, and rarely saw one another in any kind of one-to-one situation, but whenever they were in a crowd, they gravitated together to form a distinct subunit.

If Mike Grundy was ever jealous of Morgan Miller—or, for that matter, of Chan and Burdillon—he never gave any sign of it. His sexual interest was routinely attracted by women much prettier than Lisa, and any flirtatiousness in their relationship was understood by both parties to be purely superficial. Once their friendship was solid and comprehensively defined, in fact, Mike frequently used Lisa as a useful source of advice on the management of his love life. Once he had grown used to seeing her as an expert, he tended to assume that her expertise was far less specialized than it was. He had such awesome faith in the linearity of her intelligence that he seemed to expect her to know everything he didn't, or at least to be able to form a more reliable impression than his own. This did not, however, prevent him from disagreeing with her on various issues of personal importance. One of them was marriage.

"You're wrong about there being no point in marrying if you don't intend to have children, Lis," he told her, while using her as a shoulder to cry on the first time he had made an unsuccessful proposal, in 2012 or 2013. "People aren't programmed for the solitary life. They're gregarious, and families—even if they're just couples— are the real units of society, not individuals."

"It's a common argument," she informed him loftily. "The couple as the atom of community—a hydrogen atom, one presumes. But which partner is to become the proton and which the mere orbiting electron? During courtship, it's the men who buzz around the honey pot—but once the ceremony's over, they expect the roles to be reversed, taking it for granted that they'll be the nuclei around which their wives will helplessly circle. I can see why men like the idea—but I think I'd rather be a free radical."

Mike had no idea that the metaphor had become disastrously

mixed, although none of her university friends would have allowed her to get away with it. Even Ed Burdillon would probably have begun rhapsodizing about the analogies to be drawn between the waywardness of human passion and the counterintuitive wonders of quantum mechanics, but Mike Grundy's intellect was cut from coarser and more utilitarian cloth.

"That's *so* twentieth century," he protested. "In fact, it borders on the Victorian. Modern marriage isn't a matter of domestic slavery. Everybody works nowadays, if they can. Modern marriage is more like a business partnership."

Lisa did not like to seem trite, and flatly refused to consider the obvious jokes about sleeping partners, shareholdings, and dividends. "Partnership creates unnecessary obligations," she said instead. "The modern trend is toward freelance consultancy and free-floating labor."

"Not in our line of work," he pointed out. "The consulting detective was a literary conceit, like the lone scientific genius making monsters in the basement."

"Those are all surprisingly stubborn conceits," Lisa observed, "but not as stubborn as the love story. You don't feel obliged to fit your working life into the mold formed by TV cop shows, so why feel obliged to fit your private life into the mold of the kind of paperback pulp you'd be ashamed to display on your bookshelves?"

"Given the number of crimes of passion we have to deal with," he said, "that's ridiculously cynical."

"Given the percentage of crimes of passion that fall into the thoroughly modern categories of road rage, phone rage, and store rage, it would be ridiculous to take any other view."

"That's frustration, not passion."

"All passion is frustration, Mike. Sexual frustration is no different, physiologically, from all the other kinds of stress that eat away at the lining of your gut and pile pressure on your clogged-up arteries. The trick is to deal with it without letting the adrenaline run wild. If you can't do that, your natural cheerfulness and charm will leach away by slow degrees, until you turn into a middle-aged grouch—just like all the other senior officers."

It wasn't intended as a prophecy, but it proved all too true. Mike Grundy's cheerfulness and natural charm did indeed diminish with every decade that passed and every promotion he gained. The fact that he got stuck at DI didn't save him, any more than impact with her own glass ceiling saved Lisa from adding the last few twists to her own brand of bitterness. Mike got married too, to his precious Helen of Troy: an unambiguously lovely girl he always considered to be that little bit too good for him.

It was an opinion that the Helen in question inevitably came to share, as Lisa could have prophesied but never did. Where Mike Grundy was concerned, she felt obliged to keep her Cassandra Complex on a tight rein—and she sometimes wished in later years that she had kept it under even slightly tighter control in her relationship with Morgan Miller.

There were times, during the early phases of Mike's marriage, when Lisa doubted her own judgment of that institution, and she was by no means glad when the passage of time eventually proved her right.

Although they had more than enough in common, Helen Grundy and Lisa never got on well after the marriage. It would have been an exaggeration to say that Helen ever hated Lisa, but that probably had more to do with a policy decision to consider her too contemptible to be worthy of hatred than any lack of passion. In hydrogen-atom terms, Helen had no intention of being switched from a nuclear to an orbital role by any mere ritual. Having given herself in marriage, she expected to become and remain the center of her husband's existence, and she was intolerant of any distraction beyond the demands of duty. From the very beginning, Lisa could see that Helen was far more career-minded than Mike, and that his lack of impetus in that regard would develop into a nasty bone of contention, but she never told Mike. At least, not in so many words. He would not have believed her, and he would have resented the prediction.

He would have resented it even more when it eventually came true, but the fact that Lisa had never actually spelled it out enabled her to remain sympathetic and steadfast when disaster finally struck.

Helen Cornwell, as she was before her marriage, was a hospital social worker at the Royal United, which had recently been combined with the nearby Manor Hospital into one of the country's largest healthcare institutions—exactly the kind of institution that a burgeoning cityplex needed. Her duties ranged from abortion counseling to surgical aftercare, and she was constantly under pressure to extend herself even further; she worked hours that were just as long and often as unsociable as a detective's, and had found that as injurious to her personal relationships as did any policeman.

Helen first encountered Mike Grundy in the context of a delicate series of child-abuse inquiries, and was initially quite comfortable with his friendship with Lisa. The rapid expansion of genetic counseling at the interface of medicine and social services provided them with a ready-made topic of conversation, although Helen never took aboard Mike's certainty that Lisa was a ready font of infallible information regarding the fallout of the Human Genome Project. As Mike and Helen drew closer together, however, Helen made a concerted effort to draw their atom of community away from all rival attractions.

At first, Lisa had tried to defuse Helen's anxieties, going out of her way to assure her that she was no threat to their partnership, but her attempts to form as close a friendship with Helen as she had with Mike were always doomed.

Helen was the kind of feminist that Morgan Miller deplored: a die-hard subscriber to the notion that science and technology were ideologically polluted with the worst kind of masculine ambitions. She was overfond of analogies representing contemporary ecological crises as the aftermath of a "rape of the Earth" that had begun with the Industrial Revolution. She also took far too much notice of propaganda that saw the entirety of genetic science, and the Human Genome Project in particular, as a "Frankensteinian bid" by the male of the species to usurp essentially female prerogatives of reproduction.

Lisa attempted to undermine these opinions with as much subtlety as she could muster, but she couldn't entirely control the temptation to excoriate them with a Milleresque fervor. She even tried to soften that kind of blow by crediting the most scathing observations to Morgan Miller and delicately refraining from lending them her own wholehearted endorsement, but the tactic never worked.

"Your problem, Lisa," Helen said to her with treacly concern, on the last occasion when Lisa attempted a full-scale conversion, in 2024 or 2025, "is that you've sold out. You know deep down that that's what you've done, but you can't bear to face it—so you cover it up with all these layers of dismissive arrogance and barbed sarcasm. You'll never be happy until you can be reconciled with your own conscience, and you'll never achieve that unless you can tear down the walls of false consciousness you've erected in your psyche."

"It's kind of you to lend me your expertise when I'm not one of your clients," Lisa replied as mildly as she could, "but I'm happy as I am, and joining the police—for me as well as for Mike—was more a matter of buying in than selling out. We all have to do what we can, in our different but complementary ways, to hold society back from the brink of chaos."

"I've heard you say many a time that nothing can stop us from going over that brink," Helen pointed out sweetly. "Too many children in the world. Masculine science does love its simple explanations, doesn't it?"

"Even if a fall is inevitable," Lisa replied, "it still makes sense to delay it as long as possible. When the collapse begins, good policing will be even more essential than it is today—and science offers the only hope we have of getting the parachute open before the fall becomes a fatal crash."

"The only remedy we'll ever have against disaster is the capacity to treat one another with courtesy and charity," Helen informed her.

There was no point in contradicting Helen's ready assumption that courtesy and charity were essentially female virtues—or, indeed, in denying most of her other assumptions. She was not the kind of person to admit that she might be fundamentally mistaken, and for all her feminist philosophizing, she certainly couldn't allow the possibility that a plainer and older woman might have the advantage of her. So Lisa gave up trying to be a friend to Mike and Helen alike, and contented herself with maintaining half a friendship with Mike alone.

It was not so great a loss as all that, especially while she still had Morgan Miller, Ed Burdillon, and Chan Kwai Keung. Or so it seemed, until the day when *everything* fell apart.

PART FOUR
The Miller Effect

ike Grundy had pulled the Rover off the road, blocking the driveway of a house on North Road. Lisa left her own car on the roadway, even though traffic was beginning to build up and she was sure to get in the way of vehicles filtering out of Hadley Road into the left-hand lane of North Road. As if suddenly uncertain of his purpose, the detective stopped in his tracks when he saw Chan emerge from the passenger seat, flattening himself against the fender as horns began to blare.

"It's okay, Mike," Lisa said.

Grundy waited by the Rover while they made their separate ways to stand side by side confronting him. The expression on his face was troubled, but the trouble was a mere mask pasted over a deep-seated exhaustion.

"Sorry, Mike," Lisa said. "I needed to see you. Now I need you to take Chan in for me. Don't expect any brownie points for it. Nothing we do from here on in is going to save either one of us. We're too badly soiled. It's not our fault, but we're finished in the police force."

Mike looked at her curiously, but all he said was: "Nice suit. Where's your belt?"

"I had to put it in for cleaning," she said. "I don't suppose you've had that old wreck swept recently?"

"As a matter of fact," he told her, half turning to look down at the roof of his car, "our noble leader ordered a check on all vehicles as soon as it was obvious that the station had become leaky. You can never be a hundred-percent certain, of course, but I think I'm clean. If you can say the same, no one is listening in on us."

"Good," she said. "It doesn't make a lot of difference at this stage, but it would be nice to have the moment to ourselves. I've no time to spare so I'll just say what I need to say. Helen's involved in Morgan's kidnapping. She probably thinks she's in charge, but if she ever actually was, her authority must have grown pretty shaky by now."

The disbelief inscribed on Mike's features was a sight to behold, but he didn't contradict her. Instead, he let the thought linger for a moment while he studied Lisa's face for signs of insanity. He was shaking his head slightly, but it was as much confusion as denial. In the end, all he said was: "What makes you so sure?"

"It first occurred to me when Stella Filisetti referred to you as my 'second-string boyfriend.' There's no way she could have got that from Morgan, or from university gossip—and Judith Kenna certainly didn't tell her. It explained how the kidnappers got the passwords that blacked out our end of the 'plex, and how the intruders got through my locks so easily, but I wasn't absolutely sure until Smith told me about the contact search he ran on Stella and the Real Woman. If the threads leading to all three of the leading names had been planted, it would have been a meaningless joke. Two of the spoilers had to have been added to prevent the third name from standing out like a sore thumb—and I'm reasonably certain that the chief inspector didn't do it. I'll lay odds that you didn't change your passwords to the police systems after the split, and that you wrote down the pass codes to the locks at my flat somewhere that someone who knew your habits very well could easily find."

Mike considered the catalogue of clues for a moment or so, nobly refraining from making any comment on the circumstantiality of the evidence.

"Okay," he said finally. "Why?"

"Stella found something, maybe in Mouseworld and maybe in one of Morgan's computers. Whichever one it was, it made her check the other, and she found confirmation. She put those two together with a further two from Morgan's trips to Ahasuerus and the Institute of Algeny, and made far more than five. She'd probably confided her suspicions to her radfem friends already, but the fact that Morgan was talking to Goldfarb and Geyer spooked them sufficiently to take action. They may have a handful of hobbyist terrorists along—that's probably where they got the weapons, the accelerant they used in Mouseworld, and the idiotic posing—but they're not really an organized gang. Even if they've managed to get Arachne West on the team, as seems probable, they're still the rankest kind of amateurs. Unfortunately, that doesn't make them any less dangerous. When the computer team clears out all the disinformation, Smith and Kenna will move a whole task force against the couriers carrying Stella's stolen mice, but I figure that I have at least a couple of hours to try to get Morgan out quietly before the shit hits the fan. That's what I'm going to do, while you ferry Chan to the Renaissance."

"You didn't answer the question," Grundy pointed out quietly. "What could Filisetti have found that turned a woman like Helen into a master criminal?"

"I don't know for sure," Lisa confessed, "but my guess is that what she thinks she found is evidence that Morgan discovered a means of extending mammalian life spans that works only on females. She thinks he's been sitting on it for up to forty years, trying to figure out a way of making it work on males too. She thinks that because he had failed to do that, he was planning to hand it over to some organization that would carry on the work while maintaining the same kind of secrecy. When she confided all this to her radfem friends, they presumably ran the same background checks on Ahasuerus and the Algenists that Peter Smith ran, and came across all the same tabloid legends. Both institutions are rumored to have exotic secret agendas—but who isn't nowadays? Ahasuerus is said to have been set up specifically to find a means of conferring emortality upon its illustrious male founder, Adam Zimmerman, and the Algenists are misunderstood by their severest critics to be trying to create a Naziesque master race. You can see how that sort of bad press might raise radfem hackles."

"I can easily imagine Helen getting excited about that kind of thing," Mike admitted wryly. "In fact, I don't have to imagine it. Imagining her as a criminal mastermind dispatching gangs of assassins and bombers is a different matter, though."

"They think I'm in on it," Lisa added, shivering in a sudden gust of cold wind. "They think I've known all about it since day one, but that I've kept quiet. Stella and Helen have convinced themselves that I've been prepared to go along with Morgan's plans in return for a promise that I'd eventually be paid off with the treatment, thus betraying the sacred principles of sisterhood. That's why they sprayed 'Traitor' on my door and tried to shake me up by telling me that Morgan never really intended to cut me in. Can I go now?"

Grundy was still dubious. "I'm no fan of Helen's nowadays," he said, "but this is way beyond her. She might conceivably be involved, but she can't possibly be the one behind it."

"She's more than involved, Mike," Lisa told him, hoping she'd read that part of the puzzle right. "This whole thing's been too *personal*. That's partly down to Stella, but only partly."

"That doesn't make sense either," he objected. "We live in crazy times, but—"

"It's not just the crazy times," Lisa told him, determined to put her point across quickly so she could move on. "The sense of impending doom that Containment and the undeclared war have cultivated undoubtedly helped to shove them over the edge, but they're taking it *very* personally. Stella Filisetti doesn't know Morgan the way I do, and I doubt if she can relate to his way of life the way I could. She feels let down because he didn't change into Mister Right the moment he started screwing her. She's magnified that sense of betrayal into something much greater. And Helen doesn't know *me* the way you do. She didn't understand what happened after she threw you out, any more than she ever understood that we really were *friends*. She was all set up to believe the very worst of me. They've inflated their personal frustrations into a much grander paranoia—a conviction that something immensely valuable is being withheld from them by people they know. They think they're being left to die while less worthy acquaintances are plotting to survive the impending catastrophe and come through it with a secure position in the pockets of the rulers of the new world. Hell, even Peter Grimmett Smith of the MOD is a sucker for tales of the Secret Masters and the Ice Age Elite.

The only difference is that he's either too shrewd or too contemptuous to believe that someone like me could ever be a part of that kind of conspiracy. Stella isn't. Nor, alas, is Helen."

"If you say so," Grundy conceded reluctantly. "But even if you're right, it ought to be me who goes after Helen, not you."

"It has to be me, Mike," Lisa told him. "It's because I know Morgan better than anyone else does that I *know* this farce is founded on a colossal mistake. I'm the only one who can convince the radfems of that fact. Morgan obviously couldn't."

"Maybe no one can," he suggested.

"Maybe not—but I don't have time to argue, Mike. I have to go now."

Chan had already moved to Mike's side. He was waiting, with a meekness so exaggerated that it was almost insulting, for further orders. Mike looked sideways at him, as if reading a message from his slumped shoulders and sleepless eyes. "I suppose you have considered the possibility that they might be right, Lis?" he said finally.

That one was too important to leave unanswered, but all Lisa said was "Yes."

Of course she'd considered the possibility that Stella really had found what she thought she had—but she'd rejected it. If Morgan Miller had discovered a life-extension treatment whose only deficiency was that it worked only on women, he wouldn't have kept it entirely to himself. Even Helen Grundy and Stella Filisetti didn't think that badly of him. They thought badly enough of Lisa to believe she'd conspired with him to keep it quiet, but they hadn't been able to suppose that Morgan would simply let her grow old and die with all the rest. Even they accepted that if Morgan Miller had drawn up a list of his own personal Ice Age Elite, she would be on it.

There had to be something else: something that Stella Filisetti had missed; some obstacle that Morgan had stumbled over, that had carried on bruising his shins for forty years.

Lisa wanted to tell Mike that she was deeply sorry he had been caught up in it, and sorry that his ex-wife's meddling would surely torpedo his attempts to cling to the vestiges of his career. She wanted to commiserate with him because her own career had been similarly blighted. She wanted to tell him, in the most heartfelt manner she could contrive, that it might all be for the best, because they should never have allowed themselves to sink so deeply into the ruts that had somehow consumed their lives. She wanted to try to convince him that they had been good citizen mice for far too long, putting up no resistance to the shrinkage of their personal space, refusing to get excited about the stultification of their options. She wanted to ask him whether it was really all bad to be a Calhounian rat, raging against the injustice of circumstance. She wanted to assure him that everything might still work out for the best, not merely for themselves, but for the world.

But she had no time.

Even if it had all been true, she had no time.

"Okay," Grundy said when the silence had dragged on and on to the limits of bearability, even though it had lasted no more than ten or fifteen seconds. "Go."

"You have to go first," Lisa told him, "but you'll have to leave your mobile with me. I need to use it."

Chan had already moved around the Rover to the passenger door. Lisa's final demand was a trifle excessive, but Mike didn't have to ask why she wanted the phone. He simply nodded and handed it over before turning on his heel and opening the driver's door. He glanced back only once before getting in and slamming it shut. Then he drove away, so fast that his onboard computer had to be flashing red warnings. Lisa pressed the automatic-dial button on Grundy's phone and then hit 1.

The surge of relief she felt when Helen Grundy answered on the second ring with a monosyllabic "Yes?" hit Lisa like a tidal wave. She knew how utterly foolish she would have felt had she been unable to make that crucial contact.

"It's Lisa Friemann, Helen," she said, her voice sounding so leaden in her ears that she could hardly recognize it as her own. "We need to talk."

On another occasion, under different circumstances, Lisa might have found something to savor in the silence that followed, knowing as she did what a heady cocktail of shock and fear must have prompted it. On this occasion, she was content merely to wait for a further response.

"What are you doing with Mike's phone?" Helen Grundy asked, confirming Lisa's suspicion that a call from any other instrument would probably have been blocked out.

"Mike's not here," Lisa said. "I sent him away. I'm alone. This is between you and me."

"Well?" Helen said after another pause for thought. "What do you want?"

"It's a matter of hours now, Helen. The computer people are working on the corrupted phone records. It'll take them a while to figure out the obvious, but they'll do it. The computers will leave a safety margin before they feel a hundred-percent confident of the link between the Real Woman we arrested with Stella Filisetti and Arachne West, but Smith has people searching for her already. It won't matter how well hidden you are or how quiet you can keep—your blackout didn't last long enough to make your movements untraceable. Even if it takes a small army to intercept the couriers carrying the mice, they won't get away."

"I don't have the faintest idea of what you're talking about, Lisa," Helen replied stubbornly. "Just put Mike on, will you?"

"Mike knows everything, Helen. For the moment, he and Chan Kwai Keung are the only two who do know—but as I said, it's a matter of hours. Going after Chan was a mistake, by the way. His guilty conscience was reflecting on sins of his own. I can see why Stella and her friend jumped to the wrong conclusion, but it really was a masterpiece of bad judgment."

"I don't understand why you're telling me all this," Helen said. The ambiguity was so neat that Lisa felt free to assume that the other woman had regained most of her composure.

"I'm trying to make it clear to you that you no longer have anything to lose by talking to me, and maybe everything to gain. I want to make you an offer."

"An offer I can't refuse?" Helen countered, although the attempted wit rang hollow.

"I don't blame you for thinking I must be involved," Lisa said. "It was a perfectly natural assumption. I don't blame you or Stella for refusing to take my denials seriously. If I can't understand why Morgan never let me in on his little secret, how could you? I wouldn't blame you for thinking I must be lying now. If I were in your position, that's exactly what I'd be thinking. But consider this, Helen. In a few hours, everyone else will know what I know. I could tip them off right now if I wanted to heed the call of duty. I could have called Judith Kenna, Peter Grimmett Smith, or the mysterious Mr. Leland instead of you, and then I could have gone back to the Renaissance Hotel to sleep all day, knowing that I'd wake up to find the whole thing tidied up—and I'm certainly tired enough. For the first time in months, I'm tired enough to do exactly that. My job was as good as lost already, but the moment I phoned you instead of Smith, I made absolutely certain that I'm finished. Careerwise, the fact that I'm talking to you now is suicide."

"It sounds more like madness to me," Helen Grundy observed, still careful not to commit herself to any recordable admission that she knew what Lisa was talking about.

"Maybe," Lisa admitted. "But the fact is, I want to *know*. I want to know why every initial assumption I made about this case has proved false. I want to know why I was so ludicrously mistaken about the nature of my relationship with Morgan Miller that I was unable to believe he'd kept a secret from me for all these years. I want to know why he never gave me the opportunity to be the kind of traitor you and Stella Filisetti think I am."

"I don't see how any of this concerns me," Helen Grundy said, a faint trace of contempt creeping into her voice.

"Use your imagination, Helen. You haven't got anything tangible out of Morgan. You haven't found anything on the hard disks of his old PC's and you haven't found any backups among the wafers and sequins you stole from my apartment. All you've got today is what Stella managed to put together before she told you that if you didn't act quickly, you'd never get another chance, because her spying activities were bound to be uncovered. You can't get anything you can trust out of Morgan, because he knows as well as you do that it's just a matter of hanging on till rescue comes. If I know Morgan only half as well as I thought I did, I'd guess that he's been feeding you bullshit by the ream ever since you picked him up, and I'll bet a million euros to a bent bingo token that it would take an army of scientists thirty years to sort out fact from fantasy.

"I presume that you and Arachne and the hard core of the sisterhood are more than willing to accept martyrdom for the cause, but I know that you'd be willing to risk anything to get what you want before you go down—to get something you can broadcast to all the other sisters. But you have only one chance of getting that, because there's only one person who has the moral clout necessary to demand the truth from Morgan Miller and get it. In brief, Helen, you need me.

"It wouldn't have done you any good to lift me when you lifted Morgan, because I'd have been just as stubborn and just as inventive in stalling you, and I guess there must have been quite an argument about whether it was safe to leave me on the outside to help with the investigation. My guess is that it was my old acquaintance Arachne who persuaded the team to go for the bug option—which might have been a valuable information feed if Mr. Leland hadn't stuck his paranoid oar in—but that doesn't matter. The point is that it was the right choice, albeit for the wrong reasons. I'm ready to help you, Helen. I'm ready to do what you can't, and demand the truth from Morgan because I want to know, before my life goes down the toilet with all of yours, *exactly* what it is that's flushed me away.

"I need to know, Helen. It's the one thing left that I really do need. And the beauty of it is that from your point of view, it's cost-free. You have nothing left to lose, and any chance to win is worth taking."

It had been an exhaustingly long speech, and she was shivering in the night-born cold that the sullen morning light hadn't yet contrived to banish, but Lisa felt more alive than she had for many a year, and it certainly wasn't Ginny's pep pills that were responsible. She was prepared to go on if she had to; Helen might still need time to think about it, and in a situation of this kind, it was best to keep piling the pressure on until something gave.

Fortunately, something had already given. "I can't trust you," the other woman said pathetically.

"You don't have to," Lisa said. "Your worst-case scenario is that you might be arrested two hours early. I can't guarantee that even I can get anything out of Morgan—after all, whether you believe it or not, he's been keeping me in the dark for the best part of forty years—but at the very least, you'd have an extra hostage to bargain with. I have my car. You name the time and the place—but make it soon. If there aren't enough sisters where you are to constitute a quorum, somebody had better make an executive decision."

"Bitch," was Helen Grundy's reply—but she said it offhandedly, with no real feeling. Lisa was confident that it hadn't been Helen who'd shot the phone out of her hand or sprayed "Traitor" on her door, but she now figured that Helen, not Stella, must have been the principal shaper of the burglars' script.

"We don't have time for insults," Lisa said. "Where? When?"

Whether Helen was alone or not, the executive decision was made. "The mall straddling North Parade Road, where the old recreation ground and cricket field used to be," she said defeatedly. "There's a shop called Salomey on the ground floor, just to the right of the Johnstone Street entrance. Come to the dressing rooms. Come on foot, alone. You have ten minutes."

"I'm too far away. Make it fifteen."

"Break the speed limit and leave the car on a double yellow. You have ten." Helen rang off.

TWENTY

Lisa had no watch to tell her the time, but it was obviously too late now to do the run into what had once been the Bath city center in ten minutes. The morning rush hour was already well underway. The onboard computer, roused from quietude by the parking offense she'd committed on North Road, logged six more manifest offenses and four instances of contributory negligence. Its muted voice was still beeping plaintively about parking regulations when she abandoned it, but she figured she made it to the Recreation Ground Mall within a couple of minutes of the deadline she'd been given.

Lisa didn't expect that her tardiness would make any difference; Helen's imposition of a time limit was a meaningless gesture, born of the desire to pretend that she still had some degree of control over the situation. Lisa left Mike Grundy's mobile in the car, having switched it off after the call to Helen.

She was not surprised to discover that Salomey was a clothing shop, specializing in ultrasmart costumes for ultrasmart women. A notice on the automatic door informed customers that THIS IS A WOMEN-ONLY SHOP, but that wasn't unusual nowadays. The special intimacy of smart fabrics had given birth to a new modesty, and had brought a backlash in favor of privacy that had drawn many new kinds of social boundaries.

The Real Woman who watched Lisa from the purchase desk as she crossed the smart-carpeted floor to the dressing room looked completely out of place. Even if she hadn't been so powerfully built, she would have stood out simply because she didn't look as diffident as the younger sales assistants obviously fighting boredom while they waited for opening time. A clock on the wall told Lisa that the time was now eight thirty-five.

The woman waiting in the dressing room wasn't a bodybuilder, but that didn't detract from the frank hostility and meanness of her gaze.

"Strip," she instructed.

Lisa peeled off the smartsuit supplied by the Swindon police. She braced herself for yet another dose of censorious advice about her style sense, but was pleasantly surprised for once. The one-woman reception committee gave her naked body the once-over with some kind of sweeper before handing her a brand-new outfit. It was a smart, dark-red one-piece, far more expensive and stylish than anything she'd ever have dreamed of buying. Had she not been so ruthless in excising all twentieth-century clichés from her vocabulary, it would have made her feel like mutton dressed as lamb.

The woman to whom she'd given her old one-piece took it away. It was another, even younger woman who came in to peel back the carpet, exposing the trapdoor set in the floor of the room.

"You got me dressed up like *this* and you want to take me down into the sewers?" Lisa asked, feigning astonishment.

"You can walk through a sewer in a Salomey outfit and come up as lovely as a bird of paradise and as fresh as a golden rose," the woman told her, straight-faced. "It says so in our catalogue."

"That's a relief," said Lisa as she lowered herself into the opening, searching with what seemed to her to be stockinged feet for the rungs of the ladder. "In my day, birds of paradise still existed in the wild, and freshness standards were set by daisies—but everything's artificial these days."

It transpired, however, that the well beneath Salomey did not lead to the sewers at all. It led to a dimly lit, stone-clad tunnel that extended in a southeastern direction. To begin with, the tunnel was conspicuously clean and obviously new, but its storeroom-lined walls gave access within a hundred meters to brick-lined spaces of an ancient cast.

Lisa remembered the days when permission had first been granted for the construction of the mall, and she tried to recall the controversies that had raged around the project. There had been a convent on the north side of North Parade Road, she remembered. Deconsecrated and sold off by the cash-strapped Church Commissioners, it had briefly become the site of a rescue dig by archaeologists from the university before its crypt had been abandoned as a supposedly untouchable enclave within the stockholding cellars. Once out of public sight, the place had obviously fallen prey to the combined forces of economic convenience and the new privacy.

"The crypts of a nunnery overlaid and overlapped by a shopping mall," she said to her guide. "You brought Morgan Miller to face the feminist inquisition in the cellars of a bloody nunnery." This, she thought, was a decision that had Arachne West's stamp on it.

"Quiet," her guide instructed, although the command was pointless. If Lisa had still been carrying some kind of bug, the people listening in to it wouldn't have required any verbal cues to help them figure out where she was.

The doors in the various sections of the cellar complex were far more modern than the brickwork that contained them, and they bore fancy combination locks. The guide conducted her through two of them before coaxing open a third. She waited outside to close it again once Lisa was inside, but Lisa wasn't entirely convinced of the impregnability of the inner sanctum to which she was admitted. There was probably more than one way in, and there were probably too many people who knew the codes.

There was no sign of ancient brickwork inside the cosy cell. Its walls had been coated with some kind of artificial plastic, a pale green in color. Against one wall there was a semicircular desk; its generous size took up slightly more than half the available space, effectively reducing the rest to the status of a short, curved corridor. There was yet another inner room on the far side, similarly secured with a certified-unhackable double lock.

There was no one seated behind the desk to monitor the various screens mounted therein, but Arachne West was sitting on top of it. She was still bald, of course, but now that she was in her late forties, the baldness looked almost natural. What didn't look natural was the velvety-black Salomey outfit she was wearing. It should have been highly polished synthetic leather, Lisa thought, or some kind of paramilitary uniform. Arachne wasn't so much mutton dressed as lamb as lion dressed as kitten, but the effect was just as false.

"My mother always told me it was dangerous to talk to policemen," the Real Woman said, "but kids never listen, do they?"

"The advice was bad," Lisa told her. "You should have ignored it entirely. Where's Helen?"

"I told her she ought to try to make a getaway before she's installed on top of the 'Most Wanted' list. It was good to have the excuse—she'd become a liability since we had to make it clear to her that she wasn't running the show anymore. So why was Mama's advice bad?"

"If you'd come to me when Stella and Helen first persuaded you that Morgan had something worth stealing," Lisa told her, "we could have avoided every sad act of this ridiculous farce. I could have talked to him for you."

"You'd been talking to him for thirty-nine years," Arachne pointed out. "I was on your side to begin with—I thought Stella and Helen might be letting personal matters affect their judgment—but in the end, I didn't think I knew you well enough to know for sure which side you'd be on when the chips were down. You never let me get that close. You always kept me at arm's length."

"I was never convinced that you didn't have designs on my body," Lisa said. "What clinched the crazy deal? What's this *proof* Stella thinks she has of my complicity with Morgan's allegedly unholy schemes? You must have figured out after you bugged my belt that I don't know a damn thing."

"You had your ovaries stripped, and the eggs frozen," the Real Woman told her unhesitatingly. "There didn't seem to be any reason for you to do that unless you were in on Miller's grand plan. Stella had her own account of why he gave up on the dogs, which seemed plausible enough to those of us who remembered the old ALF riots. Did you know that Helen Grundy was the social worker responsible for the woman convicted after the riot at the East Central campus way back in '15? Do people still say it's a small world, or is that too twentieth century? Pure coincidence, of course—but that's the whole thing in a nutshell, isn't it? If you stick around long enough, the coincidences accumulate. Nobody can tell anymore what's significant and what's not. Once the dogs were off the menu, Stella said, Miller had to use mice or human embryos. She reckoned that your eggs might be supplying him with raw material as well as giving you the chance to save up for the big payoff. As for the bugged belt—you might have been running a double bluff. People who know they've been tagged can turn the leak to their own purposes, if they're clever enough. You're a cop, after all. You're paranoid, I'm very paranoid, Stella and Helen are *extremely* paranoid. When the whole world turns paranoid, everybody begins to see things that aren't there— especially conspiracies."

"But you, Helen, and Stella really are a conspiracy, aren't you?" Lisa pointed out. "How many others are involved? At first I thought eight or ten, but now I'm beginning to think forty or fifty."

"You have to fight fire with fire," Arachne West informed her solemnly. Beneath her slowly fading musculature, there seemed to be a twentieth-century thinker—but how could that be, when Arachne wouldn't have been more than eight or nine years old when the century turned?

Maybe, Lisa thought, *it's the century itself that won't die, having embedded its clichés far too deeply in the very fabric of social thought. On the other hand, perhaps the people who lived in twentieth-century England spent just as much time berating themselves and one another for a host of leftover Victorian attitudes that weren't at all what they seemed to be.*

"We're wasting time," she pointed out.

"I know," the Real Woman replied. "Sometimes I think that's all we've done for the last twenty years while everyone just waited for the war to break out. Now it has—and are we ready? Are we hell?"

Lisa knew that the "we" in question wasn't just the two of them, or the Real Women, or the entire population of radfemdom, and it might even include a few males of the species.

"According to Leland, private enterprise is ready," Lisa told her. "Whatever containment measures the commission finally recommends will be irrelevant. The lovely people who brought you the kind of fabrics you 'could wear in a sewer and still come up as lush as a golden rose' have their new season all planned out. Suits that protect you from the plague—in all its myriad forms—will be the next big thing. You don't have to contain the evil germs if the people can contain themselves. You needn't worry about hidden eugenic strategies, though. Private enterprise will sell to anyone, provided they have the money. And who doesn't, when it's your money or your life? There may yet be a little worm in the bud, unfortunately."

"What worm?"

"I didn't have time to get the whole story, but Chan's already tested some kind of versatile antibody-packaging system in the only kind of context that really counts. It didn't work. Maybe the suitskin system will screw up. You can never change just one thing, you see, and you can never tell how far the unanticipated consequences will extend."

"Stella told us about the war work Miller was doing for Burdillon," Arachne admitted. "She thought that was what had finally persuaded him to give up on the other thing."

"Can I go in now?" Lisa asked. "I'd rather like to get it over with before the guys break down all the doors and start blazing away in every direction."

"He really didn't tell you anything at all, did he?" the Real Woman said wonderingly. "And you never thought to go digging, the way Stella did. You could have winkled it out forty years ago, if you'd only thought to look. Lisa the policeman, scourge of all the murderers and Leverers in Bristol, overlooks the crime of the century on her own doorstep! What a fool you must feel."

"Okay," Lisa conceded ungraciously. "I'm a fool. It's way past time to repair my sins of omission. Do I get to see him now?"

"Be my guest," the bald woman said tiredly. "You'd better change his dressing before you start, though. The anesthetic's probably worn off and you won't get much out of him while he's all racked up. That was Helen's idea—but if and when the time comes, I won't be trying to duck responsibility on the grounds that I was just an innocent bystander."

Arachne's tone had changed. The last vestiges of graveyard humor had vanished. Her pale eyes were still locked on Lisa's stare, but it wasn't a competition. The Real Woman knew how badly this whole operation had screwed up, but she wasn't looking for a way out. She was just seeing it through to its end.

Lisa accepted the medical kit and water bottle that Arachne hauled out from behind the desk, along with the smartcard that would complete the deactivation of the inner room's locks, provided the code numbers had already been loaded.

"I hope it isn't too painful," the bald woman said. "Unlike the loose cannon, I never had anything against *you.*"

Lisa wasn't certain whether Arachne was talking about the sight that would greet her when she passed through the door, or the truth that would finally be told once she got to interrogate Morgan Miller.

"I can take it," she said, figuring that the reply would do in either case.

Arachne West swung her sturdy legs over the desk and slipped into a seat behind one of the screens. Lisa had no doubt that it was a position from which the Real Woman would be able to see and hear everything that transpired in the cell where Morgan Miller was confined. She didn't mind. There had been far too many secrets for far too long. It was high time that everything was brought out in the open.

She passed the smartcard through the swipe slot, and the door obligingly clocked open. She went through it and closed it behind her.

It was as if she were closing the door on all sixty-one years of her carefully accumulated past.

TWENTY-ONE

The cell was gloomier by far than the anteroom. The bare brick had been carefully preserved here in all its brutal simplicity. The temperature seemed to have dropped by five degrees as Lisa crossed the threshold.

Morgan Miller was lying on a tubular-steel foldaway bed not unlike the one in which Leland had installed Stella Filisetti. He wasn't secured to the frame by smart cords, but that was because he wasn't in any condition to do anything as stupid as attacking his captors. The sleeve of the unsmart shirt he was wearing had been ripped from shoulder to cuff to expose his right arm, which was folded very carefully across his chest, exposing a long series of burns that looked as if they had been etched by a blowtorch. Some kind of dressing had been applied to the wounds, but the synthetic flesh hadn't been able to bond properly. It had mopped up blood and other fluids that had leaked from the wounds, but its capacity to metabolize them had been overloaded. Even its painkilling capabilities had been overstretched.

When he first caught sight of Lisa, a hopeful gleam came into Morgan's eyes, but it dwindled almost immediately to a mere ember of endurance. Even the benign mental chemistry of hope could be converted by injury into a source of pain.

Lisa knelt beside the bed and opened the medical kit. She drew off the useless pseudoskin as carefully as she could—not quite carefully enough, to judge by Morgan's ragged breathing—and substituted a generous helping of gel. Only then was Morgan able to open his eyes again. He seemed to have been utterly drained of all physical resources—a considerable indignity for a man who had fondly imagined that he was as fit as a flea. It was an effort for him to raise his head and take a few sips from the plastic bottle.

"Shit, Morgan," Lisa murmured. "Why didn't you just tell them what they wanted to know?"

"What kind of fool do you take me for?" he whispered as he let his head sink back again. "I told them *everything* before they even turned the flame in my direction. I told them the absolute truth—but they wouldn't believe me. I found out a couple of hours too late that the only way to deal with torture is to tell the fuckers what they want to *hear*, not what they want to know."

"Shit," said Lisa again. She had never felt so helpless.

"I *told* them you didn't have anything to do with it," Miller said, urgency raising his voice. "They weren't in a mood to take my word for anything. If I'd said that two plus two was four, they'd have got out their calculators."

"It's okay, Morgan," Lisa said. "I'm here of my own free will. I came as soon as I figured out which of my old friends and acquaintances were involved. The cavalry won't be far behind. The farce is almost over. Arachne's people were panicked into precipitate action, but they've calmed down now. We'll be okay."

"It was a mistake," Morgan said. "That little fool Stella guessed half the story and didn't have the imagination to look for the twist in the tail. I told them the truth, but they started burning me anyway, and they kept right on no matter what I said. I had to try something else, and when that didn't work . . . by then, I wasn't in any condition to come up with anything they might find convincing. I tried, but . . ."

"It's okay, Morgan."

"They still won't believe it, Lisa. Your being here won't make any difference. They won't believe that I did what I did for the reasons I did it. They're too paranoid."

"There's a war on," Lisa reminded him. "The fact that the government won't admit it yet only makes it that much more terrifying—and the fact that the MOD is ten or twenty years behind the new cutting edge of defense research doesn't help. If you know why Chan's versatile-packaging system was a nonstarter, you're in a better position than I am to guess whether the new systems will fare any better, but the likes of Helen Grundy and Arachne West don't have any reason to believe that they're high on anyone's list of defense priorities. They're entitled to their paranoia—and it wasn't just Stella's prying that made you into a plausible target. You should have told me, Morgan. This farce has trashed my life. All the gray power in England couldn't save me from the scrap heap now. Whatever it is, *you should have told me.*"

"I know that now," he said. He was speaking a little more comfortably; the painkillers administered by the smart dressing had restored what remained of his equilibrium. He was even able to raise his head from the pillow again and prop himself up on his left elbow. "The smartsuit's a mistake, though," he added. "It's nice, but it's not *you.*"

"You wouldn't know," she said bitterly. "So concentrate on what you do know. Stella and Helen might not have been able to recognize the truth when they heard it from your lying lips, but I can. Tell *me* the truth. Explain to me how come I've known you for thirty-nine years without ever being able to see what a sly hypocrite you are."

"I'm truly sorry," Morgan said, letting his voice fall to a whisper again. "But Chan was right about *that*, if nothing else. You were a police officer. It wouldn't have been right to let you in on anything that would have compromised your integrity. Maybe it was only a technical offense, but it was an offense nevertheless. You were so entranced by that stupid experiment that I was never sure of how you'd react to the news that I'd already subverted it. As time went by, it became harder and harder to confess that I'd been keeping the secret for so long. I never told Chan either—and he was too trusting to ever suspect that the real reason I wouldn't let him introduce his experimental mice into two of the mouse cities was that I'd already introduced mine into London and Rome. Anyway, there really are secrets so nasty that the only safe place to keep them is the one between your ears."

"But you offered to give it to Ahasuerus and the Algenists. You couldn't trust Chan or me, but you could trust Goldfarb and Geyer?"

Morgan sighed. The furrows on his brow bore witness to the force with which her arguments were striking into his conscience. "It's *science*, Lisa. It was always a matter of time. Eventually somebody else was bound to come up with the same gimmick, with the same built-in mantrap. I spent forty years trying to iron out the bug—*forty years*, Lisa. I wasn't prepared to let it out with the two sides of the coin so tightly welded together. I wanted to knock out the defect first—but I never could. I had to pass the work on to somebody else. I might have given it to Chan if he hadn't become so heavily involved with Ed's defense work, but the one thing I daren't risk was handing it over to the MOD while the whole world was gearing up for war. If peace had ever broken out . . . but you and I know well enough that there's *always* been a war on, and always will be till the big crash finally comes. I thought that if I could just figure out how to eliminate the downside, it would all be good . . . and it seemed so *simple*, so . . . Lisa, you have *no idea* of how sorry I am. I thought I could straighten it out, but all I did was fuck it up. I had no idea it would take forty years, and if I'd ever dreamed that forty years wouldn't be *enough* . . ."

"Pull yourself together, Morgan," Lisa said, surprised by her own coldness. "Anyone would think you were still under torture. Just tell me the truth, from the beginning. I don't know anything, remember—and like poor little Stella, I still can't figure out why even a misogynistic bastard like you would want to keep a longevity treatment quiet just because it only works on women."

Morgan actually contrived to laugh at that. "If that's all you've figured out," he said, "I can understand why you're so pissed."

"So tell me all of it," Lisa said impatiently.

"Okay," he said, settling back onto the pillow. "Here goes—*again*. It started in 1999, three years before I met you. It was locked up tight in my skull before you ever clapped eyes on me, and it would have taken a lot to break the seal, so don't be too hard on yourself for not being able to. The production of transgenic animals was in its infancy then—even sheep could make headlines. Almost all successful transformation was done mechanically, using tiny hypodermics to inject new DNA into eggs held still by suction on the end of a micropipette. It was ludicrously inefficient, and everybody knew it was just a stopgap, that some kind of vector would soon be devised that would make the whole business cleaner and sweeter. Viruses were the hot candidates—nature's very own genetic engineers. The first mass transformations of eggs stripped from bovine wombs in the slaughterhouse had just been carried out with retroviruses, so everybody knew that it was possible, but we needed viruses that were better equipped for the job than anything nature had. Nature's viruses have their own agenda, and a talent for turning nasty. Everybody with an atom of foresight knew in 1999 that it was only a matter of time before artificial viruses could be developed that would specialize in our agendas, but nobody knew for how long . . . and that was only half the problem.

"It was difficult in those days to build up self-sustaining populations of transgenic animals. Cloning technology was in its infancy, and experiments with sheep, cattle, and pigs were limited by the long life cycles of the animals. In 1999, the vast majority of transgenic strains were mice, simply because mice have such a short breeding cycle. They were the only livestock we had that was prolific enough to allow us to use the bacterial engineer's favorite tactic—transform a few and kill the rest. Plant engineers were still shooting new DNA into leaves from guns, selecting out the few dozen successfully transformed cells from the thousands that were destroyed or unaffected with herbicide, then cloning away like crazy—but you can't regenerate a whole animal from a handful of cells, and even if you grow a transgenic animal from a transformed egg, you still need another exactly like it to mate it with before you can start a dynasty. Sex—the root of all the world's frustrations—was the animal engineer's great stumbling block.

"Mice were a lot more convenient to work with in '99 than anything bigger, but they were far from perfect. The process still took too much time, and it was all very hit-and-miss—but when I read about the mass transformation of bovine ova by retroviruses, I figured it was a method that could be taken to its logical extreme."

He paused, but Lisa wasn't about to play guessing games now that the tale was underway. She contented herself with a mere prompt. "Which was?"

"Well, I figured that if you could transform eggs stripped from a slaughterhouse organ, you ought to be able to transform them in situ—in the ovaries of a living animal. At first I figured that the best kind of living animal to use was a fetus—because eggs, unlike sperm, aren't produced continuously throughout an animal's lifetime. By the time a female animal is born, she's already lost most of the egg cells she had when her tissues first differentiated, and she keeps on losing them before and after she reaches puberty. Not many animals survive to menopause, of course, but humans display the far end of the spectrum. A woman your age has no viable eggs left at all, having lost all but a tiny few before she ever reached breeding age."

Unless, of course, Lisa thought, *she had her remaining stock taken out while she was in her twenties and stored in liquid nitrogen.*

"What I tried to do," Morgan went on, "was to introduce retroviruses into pregnant mice, aiming them specifically at the eggs within the fetal ovaries. The idea was to secure a vast collection of ready-transformed pre-oocytes, which could then be extracted from the aborted fetus. It would have been authentic mass production, on a time scale measurable in days rather than weeks, let alone the years it takes to bring transformed sheep and cows to adulthood. You can see what a boon a system like that would have been to my search for the ideal addressable vector.

"Unfortunately, it wasn't as easy as it sounded. Nature's genetic engineers are unreliable slaves—they have their own agendas, and a lot of those agendas are what the man in the street calls diseases: colds, colics, and cancers. The womb has it own agenda too. It has a system programmed into it, and when you have wombs within wombs, things can get very complicated. I couldn't get effective transmission across the placenta. I had to switch my attention to newborns, although it seemed like a terrible waste. So many eggs have already gone by the time a mouse is born, and the rest are dying in droves day by day. I thought it might at least be possible to do something about the latter problem, so I modified my retroviruses yet again, incorporating a control gene that was supposed to stop the oocytes from committing suicide.

"That one worked. In fact, it worked far better than I'd hoped. In coupling it with the rest of the package, I'd somehow contrived to produce a synergistic effect—one of those million-to-one shots of which I'd always been so flagrantly contemptuous. When you have a hundred thousand genetic engineers trying out hundreds of novel gene combinations every year, though, the laws of probability will give you a million-to-one shot every month. Mine was the only one I ever got in forty years of trying, but it was a big one.

"In those days, we were only beginning to get used to the first principle of genetic engineering—you can never do just *one* thing—so I hadn't figured multiplicity of effect into my plans, let alone synergy, but they sure as hell came out in my results. Do you ever come across genetic mosaics in your police work?"

"Occasionally," Lisa confirmed. Mosaics had first attracted attention when biologists contrived to fuse the embryos of two different species. The first sheep/goat hybrids had been produced in the 1990s, and the revelation had prompted people to wonder how often the same thing happened in nature. Whenever a single fertilized egg divided into two to produce identical twins, the result was obvious, but when two fertilized eggs fused to produce a single individual, there was no easy way of telling that the resultant individual was a mosaic. Until DNA analysis came along, there was no way of knowing how many cows in the barn or people walking the streets were actually patchworks of two distinct but closely related genomes. Human mosaics were even rarer than pairs of identical twins, but a world of nine billion people had to contain millions. Lisa had run across half a dozen human mosaics while conducting DNA analyses in the police lab.

"In that case, you probably know that animal mosaics were often created mechanically back in the 1990s. It was an early alternative to cloning that lost fashionability when nuclear-transfer techniques improved. The mosaics I created with the aid of my trusty retroviruses were a kind that nature had never contrived, though. My retroviruses produced a strain of mice whose egg-filled ovaries became benign cancers—not merely benign in the accepted sense that the cancers were harmless, but in a much stronger sense. The transformed eggs became capable of fusing with one another to produce zygote-like bodies that then began to grow, but not like fetuses, and not like commonplace tumors. What they did was to emit a slow but steady stream of new stem cells that could be—and were—distributed throughout the body and gradually integrated into the organs of the mothers. The mothers became, in consequence, a complex mosaic. Their complexity didn't show up readily in the kinds of DNA analysis that Ed and I taught you to do, because the sum total of all the pesudozygote types was delimited by the original female genotype. I didn't figure out exactly what was happening for quite a while, and I might have missed it altogether if I hadn't started working with newborns, but that made it obvious enough that something very weird was happening.

"The long and the short of it is that the process of mosaic reconstruction stopped the aging process in its tracks. The transgenic mice were rejuvenating themselves. Initially, of course, that did my specimens more harm than good because the newborns, which remained newborns by virtue of their new power of self-renewal, couldn't survive the interruption of their developmental processes. They died of superabundant youth. Once I'd figured out what was going on, though, I soon found out that the retrovirus could also be used to infect adults. Although the effects were variable, some of the inoculated adults were stabilized by the transformation. Their life spans were dramatically extended—and I'm not talking thirty or forty percent. In time, I found that a substantial minority were living ten or twenty times as long as their parents. A few lived a hundred times as long—and the current record holders were still extending the multiplier two days ago. Were the angels of wrath telling the truth when they said they'd torched Mouseworld?"

"Yes, they were," Lisa confirmed.

Morgan Miller sighed again, but this time there was an element of theatre in the sigh. "It was a long time, of course, before I was convinced that even a few of the mice were authentically emortal, but the cream of the crop has stayed stable, fit, and healthy for forty years. A few were sterile, but not all. The real champions didn't cannibalize all the fused oocytes; every now and again they gave birth to litters of daughters. Most of the offspring failed to develop, like the newborns I'd transformed myself, but a few grew to maturity before stabilizing. The selective regime progressed by degrees to the inevitable terminus: a population of emortal female mice whose daughters were likewise emortal. It took time, but when the potential's there and the regime is stern, natural selection is no slouch.

"Long before I was convinced they were authentically emortal, I'd begun introducing the mice to the cities, for exactly the same reason that Chan wanted to introduce his augmented specimens: to see how they'd fare in a stressful and competitive situation. Mine did a little better than his—obviously, or Stella would never have found the transformed mice—but not *that* much better, and not for a long time. When you came along in 2002, I only had half a dozen potentially emortal mice, and nineteen of the twenty offspring they had so far produced had died paradoxical deaths of superabundant youth. By the time I moved on to experiment with other species in '09 or thereabouts, I had a hundred adult mice and the survival rate among the new litters was up to one in three. Even then, you see, I couldn't be *sure* they'd live significantly longer than normal. If I had been, I might have told you . . . maybe.

"It was all so gradual, so uncertain, so surprising. You should be able to imagine how tentative my conclusions were when I first knew you, how much more needed to be done before I could be confident. Stella came in on the hind end of things, when everything was set and fixed, and she never tried to imagine how it must have been in the long and confusing beginning. All she saw, when she tumbled to what was going on in London and Rome, was a secret that I had kept for forty years. And all she cared about was the obvious—she and her friends didn't pause long enough to wonder whether there was more."

"They discovered that you'd found a technology of longevity," Lisa said. "A technology that might be just as applicable to humans as to mice if the retrovirus could be tweaked. A technology that you had discovered at the turn of the century, and didn't tell anyone else about until 2041, at which point you approached Dr. Goldfarb and Herr Geyer: both male, and both representative of secretive institutions with hidden agendas. I can understand why Helen Grundy, Arachne West, and other assorted backlash theorists thought that all their worst nightmares had come true. I can even understand why they started using the blowtorch when you tried to persuade them there was a catch that made it all worthless. There *is* a catch, isn't there?"

"Oh, yes," he said. "The catch to end all catches. I thought I might be able to work around it somehow, but I couldn't. Maybe no one can."

"An army would have stood a better chance than a lone hero," Lisa pointed out. "That's what science is supposed to be all about, isn't it? Many hands make enlightenment work."

"An army might have," Morgan agreed. "What worried me was that an army might have liked the problem better than the solution. What's good for mice isn't necessarily good for humans—or dogs, come to that. We found out soon enough, way back at the turn of the century, that mouse models of human diseases had their limitations, because mice can tolerate some conditions that humans can't. Mice may seem primitive and stupid to us, but there are some things they can tolerate that cleverer and more sophisticated mammals can't."

"Like emortality?"

"Like rejuvenation. People our age think of rejuvenation in

terms of getting back to twenty-one and staying there forever. But what if the stopping point isn't twenty-one? What if the stopping point is one? My survivor mice got past the point at which they were producing offspring that stabilized at a *physical* age estimable in days, but body and mind each have their own aging processes. Mice are creatures of instinct, Lisa—they're born with ninety percent of what they need to know hardwired into their brains. The little they need to learn can be learned over and over again without too much inconvenience. Even a rat needs to be cleverer than that, and a dog needs to be *much* cleverer. You might not be able to teach an old dog new tricks, but a young dog has to be able to learn a lot and hold on to it all. The problem with the kind of rejuvenation my mice go in for is that it rejuvenates the brain as well as all the other parts of the body. It wipes out learning almost as fast as the learning goes in.

"What my retrovirus produces, even at the farthest end of the selection process, is emortal mice that are physically mature but mentally infantile. By introducing them into the Mouseworld cities, I eventually managed to prove that mice can live like that, even among their own mortal kind, because they can keep on learning the things they need to learn over and over again. The catch is that they're probably the most advanced creatures that can."

"The dogs," Lisa said remembering. "The dogs on that stupid video the ALF circulated. Their voice-over claimed that the first lot they showed had been primed to produce an autoimmune reaction modeling mad cow disease, but they hadn't. I knew they hadn't—but I never thought to find out what *had* been done to them. They were yours, weren't they? Another project you hadn't referred to the Ethics Committee—another breach of the law. You'd rejuvenated them—and the rejuvenation had wiped their minds clean of anything faintly resembling a personality."

"If whoever filmed them hadn't been in such a rush to get the product out, they'd have seen far worse," Morgan admitted. "Are you still interested in taking the treatment, Lisa?"

"Emortality and murder all wrapped up in one little retrovirus," she said. "The body lives forever but the human being becomes . . . not quite a vegetable, but not much more than a mouse. A zombie. Worse than a zombie."

"That's about the size of it," he confirmed. "Not that I've tried any human experiments, of course. If I've missed my chance to have my little discovery enshrined in the textbooks as the Miller Effect, I'll just have to take my place in the ranks of the historically anonymous. You can understand now why it didn't seem like a good idea to share it, can't you? Your friends couldn't, and that's part of the reason they wouldn't believe me, but *you* can."

"We live in a plague culture," Lisa said, more for Arachne West's benefit than Morgan Miller's. "Any tuppenny-ha'penny Cassandra with half a brain has been able to see for fifty years and more that World War Three would be fought with biological weapons. These days, even hobbyist terrorists use biological weapons if they can get them, in spite of all the problems they pose, because they're so very *modern*, so very *twenty-first century*. And you've devised a biological weapon that works only on women—a biological weapon that has no rebound problem, provided that it's deployed by uncaring males."

"A nonlethal weapon that would turn most premenopausal women into zombies," Miller added. "Zombies with the minds of mice."

"Oh, shit," Lisa murmured as the corollaries continued to unravel in her imagination. "And *Arachne West* refused to believe that? The perfect Real Woman wasn't cynical enough to think that such a thing could exist? Or that there wouldn't be people queuing up to use it if they knew it existed? Or armies avid to research the possibility, as soon as they knew it *could* be done?"

The irony in Morgan Miller's smile was ghastly. "It's far more probable," he said, his voice sinking back to a whisper, "that what they couldn't bring themselves to believe was that if that was really what I had, I'd kept quiet about it. They thought I was just trying to put them off."

TWENTY-TWO

When Lisa eventually left the room, Morgan Miller stayed on the bed, content to wait. It wasn't like him to be content to wait, but he didn't seem to have the strength left to do anything else. He hadn't been imprisoned very long, and the injuries inflicted by the blowtorch weren't life threatening in themselves, but he was an old man. The shock to his system had been profound.

When Lisa came through the door, Arachne West commanded her to shut it behind her. She obeyed, but not because of the pistol the Real Woman was passing carelessly from hand to hand.

"You didn't ask him the big question," the bald woman observed.

Lisa was mildly surprised, having been more than impressed by the magnitude of the revelations she had obtained. For a moment or two, she thought that Arachne might have "Is it infectious?" in mind, not having been able to follow the details of Morgan's concluding technical discourse about species-specific variant designs and attachment-mechanism disarmament, but then she realized that she was being stupid.

The big question in Arachne West's mind was still: "Where's the backup?"

The members of Stella Filisetti's hastily contrived conspiracy still hadn't found a record of the experiments or a map of the primal retrovirus. They had the mice, and the researchers who eventually obtained custody of the mice would be able to work back painstakingly from there, but Morgan Miller still had at least one neatly wrapped package of vital information stashed away, hidden somewhere among the disks, wafers, and sequins they hadn't been able to remove from his house because their sheer quantity had made it impractical.

"He'll tell me if I ask," Lisa assured the Real Woman, "but we need to work out a deal first."

"Sure," Arachne said, too willingly to be entirely plausible. "Whatever he wants. As you're so fond of pointing out, I've nothing left to bargain with." But she was still passing the pistol from hand to hand.

"It *is* true," Lisa said. "What he told me just now. I'm sure of it."

"It's only a couple of hours since you were equally sure he couldn't possibly have kept a secret from you for the last thirty-nine years," the Real Woman pointed out. "But that's a cheap shot. I know it's true. I was prepared to believe it as soon as he came out with it. It was so horribly plausible—and I mean *horribly* plausible."

"So why did you start burning him?"

Arachne shrugged. "You know how it is with committee decisions," she said. "There's always some stupid fucker who won't fall in with the party line. Collective responsibility always gives birth to collective irresponsibility. It wasn't vindictiveness, Lisa—not on my part, anyhow. If I'd been running the show . . . but you know how the spirit of sisterhood works. Discussion good, hierarchy bad. Result: confusion decaying into chaos. I knew we'd lost the plot the moment he opened his mouth. You know what? I actually think he was right. I think he did the *right thing*, at least up to a point. There really are some things that man was not meant to know. Never thought I'd say that. Could I get anyone else to see it the same way, though? Could I fuck. Crazy times, hey?"

"I don't," Lisa murmured.

"Don't what?"

"I don't think he did the right thing. Not even up to a point. He should have let other people in. Not necessarily me, but somebody. Ed Burdillon or Chan. It's not just collective responsibility that mothers irresponsibility if you don't take precautions."

Arachne West shook her head slightly, but there wasn't the least hint of a smile about her forceful features. " 'Oh, what a tangled web we weave, when first we practice to deceive,' " she quoted. "Always been one of my favorites. So why'd you do it, Lisa? Have your ova stripped and frozen, I mean. That looked *very* suspicious. Could even have got you killed if Stella and the other loose cannons had blasted off a few broadsides." She obviously didn't know how close she was to the truth.

Lisa sat down on the edge of the desk. "It was one of the things I used to debate with Morgan, back in the days when we were as close as close could be. Although he admitted that one of the major causes of the population explosion was the clause in the UN's Charter of Human Rights that guaranteed everyone the right to found a family, he wasn't opposed to it, and he didn't altogether approve of the Chinese approach limiting family size by legislation. What was really needed, he always argued, was for people to accept the responsibility that went with the right: to exercise the right in a conscientious fashion, according to circumstance.

"There had been times in the past, he said, and might be times in the future, when the conscientious thing to do was to have as many children as possible as quickly as possible—but in the very different circumstances pertaining in the early years of the twenty-first century, the conscientious thing to do was to postpone having children for as long as possible. To refuse to exercise the right to found a family was, in his opinion, a bad move, because human rights are too precious to be surrendered so meekly. His solution to the problem had been to make a deposit in a sperm bank, with the proviso that it shouldn't be used until after he was dead.

"I decided, in the end, to do likewise—but there was a slight technical hitch. Donor sperm was easy to acquire and by no means in short supply, but the procedure to remove eggs from a woman's ovaries is much more invasive. Eggs were in such short supply that there was no provision in the contract for the kind of delay clause Morgan inserted. A donation was supposed to be a donation, and that was that—but the bank was prepared to make an informal compromise and agree to leave my eggs on long-term deposit unless the need became urgent. I figured that the principle remained the same, so I settled for that. It had nothing to do with Morgan's emortality research."

"Are you sure?" the Real Woman asked.

Lisa saw immediately what Arachne was getting at. Morgan had persuaded her to make the deposit. The arguments he had used were good ones, but in view of what she now knew, they probably had not been the ones foremost in his mind. Back in the first decade of the new millennium, he must have hoped that all the problems he'd so far encountered with his new technology were soluble. He must have hoped that he might one day be able to make human women emortal—always provided that they had enough eggs left in their ovaries—or eggs available that could be replaced therein.

No wonder it looked so suspicious, she thought. *No wonder Stella Filisetti took it as proof that I knew.*

"Tangled webs," Arachne observed. "Wish I could spin 'em like that."

"You don't seem to be in any great hurry to get the answer to your big question," Lisa observed.

"No," the Real Woman admitted. "As a matter of fact, what I was instructed to do—or would have been if we were allowed to use words like 'instructed'—was simply to keep you here as long as possible. There's no way for me to avoid implication in the kidnapping, or for Helen, but the rest of the girls have scattered to the four points of the compass and they have to figure that they have a chance to get away. How many mice do you suppose Stella managed to get out before the bombers went in? Anybody's guess, isn't it? Your colleagues will intercept a few, but they won't get them all. The committee figured that was the fallback position that we had to protect at all costs. As far as they're concerned, my only utility now is to hold back the hounds as long as possible—which means, the way they see it, preventing you from unleashing the pack prematurely. I'm supposed to shoot you, if necessary."

"And Morgan?"

"Him too. Some of them even think I might do it. I have this tough image, you see. Some people bluster and threaten but never shoot, and some don't but do. Then there are the Stellas, who shouldn't ever be trusted with fireworks at all. We started out with the intention of not killing anyone, and I'd rather finish the same way if I can, but you shouldn't take too much for granted. I have no idea of what I might be capable of if the situation becomes desperate. God, listen to me. *If* the situation becomes desperate! By nightfall, the men at the Ministry of Defence will know that there's a really neat weapon whose specifications are hidden somewhere in Morgan Miller's house. And unlike us, they have all the time in the world to search for it. How many other *men* will get to hear about it, do you suppose?"

"Your people will get at least some of the mice," Lisa pointed out. "Stella and Helen have seen to that. Once they have the mice, it's only a matter of time before they get the retrovirus. It's just a virus. A vaccine can be developed, given time—but it would save time if your people had the gene map."

"It's *all* a matter of time now," Arachne agreed, "and there's never been enough of it. I don't much feel like following orders, given that I'm the one who's left holding the baby. I'd prefer to get a hold of the data, if I can—on any terms you care to offer, although I don't have much to offer now I've already told you that I'm not going to kill anybody. I'd also like a chance to run. I probably won't get far, but sisterhood has its advantages. So—if you ask Miller the big question, will he give you the big answer? And if he does, what will *you* do with it?"

"We might not have time to do anything with it," Lisa pointed out. "By now, Smith's people will probably have purged the phone records. They'll be after Helen and everyone they suspect of involvement. They were already looking for you."

"That'll tie up a lot of manpower," Arachne observed. "Everybody running this way and that, far too busy to stop and count the daisies. I suppose Miller's house is under guard?"

Lisa nodded slowly. "Twice over, probably," she said. "The MOD will have people there, as will the police."

"I'd never get in, would I?" the Real Woman asked. "Even if I knew what I was looking for, I'd have no chance. A police officer who's been seconded to the MOD team would be a different matter. You may be AWOL, but you're still on the case."

"And you're still trying to recruit me," Lisa said, although she knew she was merely stating the obvious. "Even after all these years."

"And you're still playing coy. Why would I have let Helen invite you here if I didn't think you could be turned? And why would you have volunteered to come if you weren't finally ripe for turning?"

"I just wanted to know what the hell was going on," Lisa told her. "I didn't realize you'd already figured it out. If I had—"

"You'd have come anyway. And now you do know what's going on. Even Miller knew the time had come to hand his vile secret on to somebody—but I happen to think that his list of candidates stinks, and the Ministry of Defence is potentially even worse. You and I might find some better guardians, don't you think?"

Another piece of the puzzle slotted into place in Lisa's mind. In Morgan's mind, the most significant thing that Ahasuerus and the Algenists had in common hadn't, after all, been the fact that they each had an interest in longevity technology. It was that both organizations had a fundamental commitment to pacifism. Morgan had been trying to find someone to carry on his work who wouldn't be interested in the weaponry potential of the imperfect retrovirus. No wonder he had been coy about telling Goldfarb and Geyer exactly what he had while he was probing the seriousness of their mission statements.

Why didn't he come to me instead? she wondered. But she knew the answer to that. It wasn't because she was a police officer—although that must have played a part—it was because she was sixty-one years old. At best, she'd have been a caretaker, and he was looking for a long-term arrangement. But now, like Arachne West, she was on the spot and on her own. If she asked him, Morgan would probably tell her where the information was, and if she moved quickly enough,

she might be able to get it out of Morgan's house before Peter Grimmett Smith found out what was at stake and let loose a whole army of
assiduous searchers. She wouldn't be stealing anything except time—
but in a situation where time was of the essence, any margin of opportunity was a valuable commodity. Even if Arachne West was mistaken
in her harsh judgment of Goldfarb and Geyer, there were undoubtedly
other potential recipients of the new wisdom who would be far more
interested in neutralizing its weaponry potential than exploiting it.

Lisa reminded herself that she was sixty-one years old and that
her career was already in ruins. If Arachne West was willing to let
her act, she was still in a position to do so, and even if the big
woman-hunt were already underway, she probably still had time to
play her own hand.

"Are you in?" Arachne West asked her.

"Of course I'm in," Lisa said. "As you so rightly pointed out,
why else would I be here?"

TWENTY-THREE

Lisa could hardly believe the change to which Arachne West was subjected by a conservative Salomey suit and a smart wig. The elaborate superstructure of the suit wrought a remarkable transformation of her mannish figure, while the hairpiece—in combination with a pair of ornamental eyeglasses with tinted lenses—altered the context of her features so drastically that Lisa could have passed her in the street without a flicker of recognition.

"My God," Lisa muttered sardonically. "You could have been beautiful all along—what a waste."

"Clothes maketh the woman, they say," Arachne replied, "but it's all lies. I was always beautiful."

"If Helen and the others have altered their appearance to the same startling extent," Lisa observed thoughtfully, "it won't be easy to pick them out on digicam footage. If they have clever smart-cards—and they obviously do—they might actually get away."

"The police have never fully understood the potential of smart fabrics," Arachne observed. "It's one of the penalties of clinging so hard to institutional masculinity."

The once Real but now conspicuously Artificial Woman led Lisa away through the maze of subterranean corridors that extended beneath the mall. They eventually came to a door that gave them access to the staff's garage. The car in the slot directly to the left of the door was a modest blue Nissan, whose locks sprang open in response to the button on Arachne's key ring.

Before getting into the Nissan, Lisa glanced back at the door that had closed behind them. She didn't like leaving Morgan Miller imprisoned, even with his wounds properly dressed. Arachne had assured her that he would be released whatever happened, but Lisa wasn't certain that the gatekeepers in Salomey could be trusted. Discipline within the ranks of Stella Filisetti's hastily formulated conspiracy seemed to have broken down in the face of adversity, and there might be conspirators left behind who wouldn't take kindly to Arachne West's decision to take matters into her own hands. Lisa had to remind herself that no one had been killed yet, and that anyone who still had ready access to the hideaway would be foolish indeed to break that precedent now.

Arachne eased the Nissan out of the exit on the east side of the mall, turning left on to Pulteney Road. The cloud that had made the early morning seem bleak had been carried away by the west wind. It was not yet noon and the sun was making stately progress from east to south above the invisible expanse of Salisbury Plain. Its strengthening light stained the cloudless sky an unusually deep shade of blue. *Royal blue*, Lisa thought. *Fading to navy blue. Or did navy blue go out with the twentieth century? Even when I was a kid, they'd started calling it Trafalgar blue. What is it now, I wonder.*

"Did it ever occur to you," she said to Arachne West, "that we might both be more paranoid than the situation actually warrants? When you think about it, ultimate weapons of one kind and another have been around for more than a century, but no one's ever been eager to deploy them. Sure, they used atom bombs to finish World War Two—but they hadn't used poison gas in Europe even when whole fleets of aircraft were committed to blitzkrieg tactics. The notions of chivalry and gallantry may have been ninety-percent illusion even in their heyday, but they lingered for a long time in social etiquette. Even hobbyist terrorists have standards. Maybe we're falling prey to the *yuck* factor here—zombie women with the minds of mice! Maybe nobody would want to do it. It's possible that everyone would agree that this is a weapon too dreadful to use."

"It's possible," Arachne agreed. "But if I had the choice, I'd like to have a reliable defense, just in case. Wouldn't you?"

"Maybe there already is one," Lisa said speculatively. "The men who run the global economy may not have have been interested in the same range of potential as the women who run Salomey, but if their messenger boy can be believed, they have smart fabrics ready for deployment that can hold *any* virus attack at bay. Remember what Morgan said about being unable to transform the eggs in ovaries within a womb because he couldn't get it across the placenta? Just because Chan's versatile antibody-packaging system failed, it doesn't mean the newer versions will."

"All that could be true," Arachne admitted as she steered the Nissan carefully around the first of the mini roundabout series that would take them up Sydney Place to Bathwick Street. "We got used to thinking of the future of fashion in terms of second skins, but the return-to-the-womb analogy has its charms. I really would like to believe that even the craziest hobbyist terrorist would think of Miller's retrovirus as an unconscionable horror rather than a neat trick, and that no government on earth would ever countenance its use under any circumstances—but I can't. Morgan Miller didn't believe it either. Okay, so he's way down the dark end of the paranoia spectrum too, thanks to this bee he's got in his bonnet about overpopulation being the ultimate evil—but that's the world we live in, isn't it? Maybe everything will be fine if we just sit back and do nothing, but even if it turned out that way, would you be happy to be set down in history as someone who'd been prepared to sit back and trust everybody else in the world to be reasonable? I wouldn't."

"The people who sit back and do nothing don't go down in history at all," Lisa pointed out. "Their anonymity remains inviolable—but people who make mistakes are always remembered. I don't think Morgan needs to worry about losing the credit for discovering the Miller Effect, because I can't believe that there'll be an eager crowd of alternative claimants. If you and I figure in the story at all, it'll probably be because we've fucked up."

"So who's too paranoid now?" Arachne wanted to know. She turned left onto London Road before taking the right fork to cut across to Lansdown Road. Her onboard computer censured her for not sticking to the arterial road, but she didn't even mutter a reply. "Your boss might call this 'dereliction of duty,' but we know better, and history will side with us. When the final score is calculated, we'll be the heroes. Unless, of course, we somehow end up as zombies with the minds of mice. Then we'll be numbered among the martyrs. Either way, we'll have done what we could."

Arachne parked the car behind the derelict church just above the fork where Lansdown Road and Richmond Road diverged. It was nearly a five-minute walk to Morgan's house, but to go any closer would have risked exposure to the surveillance umbrella.

There was no conspicuous police presence in evidence as Lisa approached the house, but a quick scan of the unmarked cars parked in the street revealed a familiar face: the sergeant who had been in Thomas Sweet's office reviewing the security tapes on the night of the Mouseworld holocaust. Lisa headed straight for him, and he wound down his window.

"Sergeant Hapgood, isn't it?" she said.

"Dr. Friemann," he replied. "I thought you'd gone over to the other side."

Her heart lurched slightly before his smile tipped her off to the fact that he meant the MOD. "Worse than that," she said. "I'm running every which way under two separate commands. Chief Inspector Kenna wanted me to cast an eye over the scene to see if I could help with a list of what's been taken from the house, but this is the first chance I've had. When I haven't been busy getting shot at, Mr. Smith has had me on the go. Can't get into my own place yet—had to buy a new outfit. I haven't even got my belt—I feel half naked without it."

"I heard about you getting darted and carted," Hapgood said. "Some rent-a-cop sticking his oar in, wasn't it? As if we didn't have enough trouble falling over the feet of the Ministry men. Where do they dig these guys up? The Civil Service Senior Citizens' Club?" He realized his mistake almost immediately and said: "No offense."

"None taken," she assured him. "Have you seen Mike today?"

"No. While the suspects are flowing into custody, he'll be up to his eyes. Did you hear about his ex? He got out before she flipped, but that might not be enough to save him. Kenna won't back him if she thinks any of the dirt might rub off on her. You knew the ex, I suppose?"

"Only slightly," Lisa replied. "There'll be plenty of time to be embarrassed about it when we're not chasing our tails so hard. For now, I've got to get through my list of things to do as quickly as I can."

"Do you want me to come in with you?" Hapgood asked.

"You don't have to" Lisa said, "but I'd be obliged if you'd walk to the door with me and introduce me formally to the Ministry men. I haven't met any of them yet except for Smith, and he's not the one who sent me here."

"Sure." Hapgood seemed glad of the opportunity to stretch his legs. "Your new outfit looks okay, by the way—the high street makes the so-called new uniforms look a bit scabby, don't you think? I'm glad I'm in CID." His own suit looked brand new, but it was probably trying to pass itself off as something smarter than it really was. *Shallow people always choose clothes that reflect their personalities,* Lisa thought, *even when they don't realize what they're giving away.*

"It's a bit flashy for lab wear," Lisa countered. "But then, I'm not in the lab, am I?"

Hapgood walked her to the front door and waited until it was opened. The man who peered through the gap did indeed look like some ancient reservist recalled to active service because of the emergency.

"Inspector Friemann, Forensics," Hapgood explained. "She's one of ours. The chief inspector asked her to look around."

"Our own forensic staff has gone over the site," the Ministry man said dubiously.

"The inspector knew Professor Miller. She's better placed than anyone else to assess what might be missing," Hapgood said, letting a trace of resentment show. "It's our investigation too, remember. We're all supposed to be on the same side."

Lisa suppressed a smile. "Mr. Smith co-opted me to help him out at Ahasuerus and the Institute of Algeny," she said apologetically. "I was with him most of yesterday and last night. This is the first chance I've had to get out here."

The door finally swung open.

"Thanks, Jerry," Lisa said dismissively.

"You're welcome," Hapgood assured her, presumably having taken some small satisfaction in exercising his meager authority upon the invaders from London.

"We're very busy," the man from the Ministry informed Lisa as soon as he had reclosed the door.

"That's all right," Lisa told him. "I know my way around. That's the whole point of my being here. I won't get in your way. You'll hardly know I'm here."

It would have been a good deal easier to follow Morgan's instructions if she'd had his study to herself, but that, inevitably, was where the majority of the Ministry men were busy. There were three of them. She had to make a show of prowling around, studying the dust patterns on the desk where Morgan's oldest surviving PC had stood for thirty-some years and pushing objects back and forth to expose similar traces on the unevenly cluttered shelves. Eventually she convinced herself that the operatives engaged in methodically copying wafers and sequins into their own equipment were so used to her presence that they had stopped paying attention to what she was doing, and it was at that point that she began to look for what she actually wanted.

Morgan had never set aside his twentieth-century habits. He had always taken it for granted that although burglars would plunder electronic-storage devices with alacrity, because they were so easily portable, they would never bother with books. He wasn't vandal enough to to make a safe by cutting the centers out of the pages of a book, no matter how disposable the text might be, but he regarded the space within a reference book's spine as the kind of repository that no one would ever think to investigate.

In order to get the wafer out, Lisa had not only to pick up volume *M–Z* of Morgan's *Webster's New International Dictionary*, but to let the pages fall open far enough to get her fingers into the opened crack. The cut between her thumb and finger hadn't bothered her for some time, but the maneuver tested the flexibility of the sealant to the limit. She had to fight hard to maintain the appearance of a purely fortuitous movement. Fortunately, none of the Ministry men paid the slightest heed. The youngest of them was forty-five and the oldest must have been eight or ten years older than Lisa, but that didn't prevent their deciding, consciously or unconsciously, that she was too old to be worth looking at.

When the wafer was safely lodged in a hidden pocket, Lisa continued her charade, dutifully pretending that she really was making a mental list of missing objects. It wasn't beyond the bounds of possibility that Judith Kenna would one day ask her for exactly such a report. She gave the job an extra five minutes before deciding that enough was enough. She didn't bother to announce that she was leaving, although she did favor the man who'd let her in with a slight nod when he looked up to take note of her departure. No one challenged her on the way to the front door. She simply walked straight out—but it seemed unwise to treat Jerry Hapgood quite so loftily, so she walked over to his car.

"I can't give you a lift, Dr. Friemann," he said before she had opened her mouth. "Got to stay here."

"That's okay," she said. "My car's only a couple of minutes away. If you see Mike back at the station, tell him I'll catch him when I can. Have to get back to my other boss now—no rest for the wicked."

"Sure," he said with a tolerantly patronizing smile. Lisa knew perfectly well that nobody of his generation ever declared that there was no rest for the wicked—but what the hell did he know?

She was back at Arachne West's Nissan within four minutes, although she was careful not to look like a woman in a hurry. Arachne West wasn't so concerned about appearances; the Nissan's computer served her with a voice warning and a visual alarm as soon as she pulled onto the busy road. "Fuck off," she replied automatically. Then, to Lisa, she said: "I wasn't sure you'd be back, you know. I really wasn't sure."

"I want a copy for myself," Lisa said.

"I knew *that*," the Real Woman replied. "I want *lots* of copies. Now that the secret's out, we have to make sure it reaches as many of the right people as possible and hope the opposition will keep it under a tighter rein. Do you know anyone who owns a big black van built like a battle cruiser?"

"Oh, shit," said Lisa, swinging around to look through the rear window at the traffic behind them. The van in question had no distinguishing marks, but she knew that its presence on their tail couldn't possibly be a coincidence. "How did *he* get on to us?"

"It's the mercenary, right?"

"I assume so. His name's Leland. Last time he butted in, it was blind luck. I thought I'd got rid of all the bugs he planted on me. So did Smith."

"You probably did," Arachne told her philosophically. "He's put his own watch on Miller's place, of course, and he probably has the details of this car too. He'll have traced Min—she's the one I set to baby-sit Filisetti—before your people did. Mrs. Grundy used her ex's passwords to play merry hell with the police computer, but she couldn't do much about the mall moguls, so Leland's probably way ahead of the crowd. This whole operation was put together in too much of a hurry. It's a pity I had to park the car for so long—it gave him a chance to get to us."

"Sorry," Lisa said. "If I'd left any sooner, even the Ministry's third reserve eleven might have gotten suspicious. We're not going to be able to lose him, are we?"

"Not in this traffic. I daren't even try—I've got so many violations stored up that the watchdog would probably shut the engine down if I made a U-turn or ran a red light. Back on home ground, it might be a different story, though. I'll drop you in Great Pulteney Street on my way back to the parking lot. The crowds will be swelled with lunch-hour shoppers. Run down William Street and turn right to the Pulteney Mews entrance of the mall. Don't mess about—just go straight to Salomey and tell them we're out of rope. I'll dodge into the under-world as soon as I'm out of his sight and join you in the office. Don't wait for me, though. Start copying. I have only three people left on-site, but they're all bona-fide mall staff. They have friends and they know hiding places. Okay?"

"Okay. Leland won't come after us with anything too heavy—he won't even want to use the sleepy gas he deployed at Ahasuerus. While he doesn't know what we know, his first priority is to get information."

"I can look after myself," Arachne assured her. "And let's face it—I really don't look dangerous in this getup, do I?"

"You're too tall to look entirely harmless," Lisa told her. "But that's okay. Just smile at him—and keep the gun behind your back."

They had already come off Lansdown Road into Broad Street, joining the queue for the turn that would take them on to Pulteney Bridge. The black van was two vehicles behind. Lisa could have seen Leland's face if the windows of the van hadn't been privacy-protected, and the fact that he could probably see hers as she turned wasn't reas-suring. Once they had taken the turn, however, it was just a matter of waiting for the traffic flow to carry them through the roundabout and into Great Pulteney Street. Arachne had no alternative but to drop Lisa on the wrong side of the street, but she didn't leave her to stand there while the van caught up; she kept her foot on the brake until Lisa had crossed in front of her.

Unfortunately, bringing the traffic to a halt allowed ample time for the passenger door of the black van to slide back. Jeff must have been driving, because it was Leland who got down. How or why he had decided she was the primary target, Lisa didn't know, but there was no point in pretending she was a shopper. She ran, and was delighted to see from the corner of her eye that Leland's first attempt to dodge through the traffic and follow her into William Street was frustrated. Her view of him was immediately cut off by the corner, but she glanced back again as she turned into Pulteney Mews and saw him lengthening his stride as he rounded the previous corner.

As Arachne had anticipated, the crowds had thickened considerably because of the lunch hour, but no one got in Lisa's way as she raced through the automatic doors and into the side concourse. There was no hope of concealing the fact that she had gone into Salomey, but once inside the store, the racks came to her aid, and she was able to duck out of sight while she made her way to the dressing room. When she took a peek between two pair of trousers hanging on a rack, she saw Leland still poised on the threshold, hesitating—not so much over the injunction on the door as because he was uncertain of whether to go left, right, or straight ahead.

When she reached the dressing room, the guide who'd taken her down into the bowels of the mall before was sitting on a chair, trying unsuccessfully to look bored.

"Trouble," Lisa said. "The man following me is a mercenary. We have to make sure the doors down below are all shut tight."

The woman didn't waste time asking questions. She had the trapdoor open in a matter of seconds, and she lowered it again as soon as she and Lisa had passed through.

"Where's Arachne?" she asked as she led the way to the first door.

"She'll make her own way. The mercenary's hireling is following the car. We'll need couriers, but the first priority is to distract the opposition."

"We'll do what we can," the woman promised. "It's open, but you'd better knock."

The last sentence referred to the door to the anteroom of Morgan Miller's cell, and was spoken as the guide turned on her heel to retrace her steps.

Lisa did as she was told. When she knocked on the door, she was admitted without delay—but she hardly had time to enjoy the swift reflexive surge of relief before she was clumsily struck down from behind.

The blow was glancing, but it had been made by a heavy metal object. Lisa was momentarily blinded by the pain as she stumbled, falling to her knees. Anticipating a second blow, she ducked and scrambled away on all fours toward the inner door, uncomfortably aware that the reaction must seem extremely ungainly to whoever it was that had hit her.

The second blow never came, and Lisa was able to turn around, raising herself to a kneeling position while clasping her hand to the sore spot at the back of her skull.

She found herself looking up reproachfully into the hostile eyes of Helen Grundy. The gun with which Lisa had been inefficiently struck was now aimed directly at her heart.

hat was *that* for?" Lisa complained bitterly. "I'm trying to help you, you stupid cow!"

"Just give me the data," Helen said grimly. It was the tone rather than the content that communicated the wrongness of the situation to Lisa's dizzied brain. She remembered then that Helen was supposed to be long gone, bearing mouse models of useless emortality to some distant destination.

"Do you even know who you're double-crossing and why?" Lisa asked, coming slowly to her feet. "Or have you lost track too?"

"I can't afford to give it away," Helen told her. "I've too much stacked up against me. I used Mike's passwords to hack into the police computer and foul up the precious databases, not to mention stealing the security codes that let us black out half the town. He won't care about the others, but he'll make bloody sure they throw the book at *me*. So give me the wafer, Lisa—or an excuse to shoot you."

"Got too hot for you, did it?" Lisa said. "Arachne did mention that the weaker-kneed members of the team lost their nerve when they figured out exactly what kind of a snake you had by the tail." While she said it, though, she glanced back anxiously at the inner door, wondering just how bad the situation had gone.

"He's all right," Helen said. "I don't have anything against *him*."

"You don't have anything against me either, did you but know it," Lisa said with a sigh. "Arachne has the wafer. I jumped out of the car to draw the head mercenary away while Arachne took care of his henchman. It wouldn't do you any good if I did have it. Leland got as far as Salomey before he lost me, so we're cornered. We just have to hope that Arachne gets away with the goods."

"I don't believe you," Helen said. "Anyway, if it's only the mercenary who's on to you, he can't possibly have enough backup to seal a maze with as many exits as this one has. Give me the wafer, Lisa. It really would be just as nice to shoot you instead—all that's stopping me is the possibility that I might still be able to make a deal. Leland, did you say his name is?"

"He's a pro, Helen. He wouldn't bargain with you if he didn't have to—and he wouldn't have to, even if you had something to sell. Which you don't. All you're doing here is letting your side down and trying to foul things up even worse than they are already."

Helen's wild eyes were growing even wilder. She had obviously realized that Lisa wasn't going to hand anything over, whether she had anything to hand or not. The script that she'd formulated in anticipation of the confrontation had let her down, and she didn't know what to do. In the movies, the people holding the guns always got the respect they deserved, and if the people who were on the wrong end of the barrel were slow to cooperate, the people with the guns simply knocked them about a bit more and rummaged through their pockets and pouches until they found what they were looking for—but Helen Grundy had already cottoned on to the fact that Lisa wasn't going to make any effort to oblige her. She was afraid that if she tried to carry forward the fight with anything less than a bullet, Lisa would win—and no matter what she thought about the amount of pleasure it would give her to shoot her ex-husband's good and loyal friend, she was exactly the kind of person to whom the logic of rational deterrence applied. She was trying to get out of trouble, not deeper in—and she knew, even if she couldn't quite admit it to herself, that she wasn't going to get out. No matter what she did, she was in trouble. She had been reckless in running up her moral debts, and now the account was due for payment.

That, at least, was the way Lisa calculated the situation—so the fact that Helen actually fired the gun caused her considerable annoyance as well as a horrid thrill of pure terror.

Fortunately, the analysis had been fundamentally correct, and Helen had been careful to raise the barrel of the gun before firing, so that the bullet went over Lisa's head and smashed into the lintel above the door to Morgan Miller's prison.

"Leland probably heard that," Lisa observed when her nerves were calm enough to permit speech. "If he didn't figure out where we went before, he will now."

Leland wasn't the only one who had heard the shot. The door through which Lisa had come hadn't closed again, although it had swung back so that it stood ajar. Now it opened wide again, and Arachne West came through it with her own gun raised and ready to fire.

The Real Woman had pressed the barrel of her weapon to the back of Helen Grundy's neck before she realized who it was that she was covering. Her command to drop the gun was overtaken by a disgusted curse, which emerged in a form that was semi-articulate at best.

Helen dropped her gun anyway. She seemed relieved to be required to do it, although she had to know what an admission of failure it was.

"Like some rat or lemming the day after the crash begins," Lisa observed drily. "Running this way and that, going nowhere, lashing out at anything within range. No direction at all. Self-destruction born of panic."

"You haven't even started!" Arachne West accused her.

"No," Lisa admitted. "I didn't even get to start." She reached into the pocket on her thigh and pulled the wafer out, displaying it to Helen Grundy. "Surprise!" she said. But Helen didn't look surprised at all.

Arachne took the wafer and vaulted over the desk to reach the copier that would allow her to duplicate it repeatedly. "I gave the van driver the slip," she said, "but they had a pretty good idea of where we are even before you set up the audible signpost. We still have half a chance while they're trying to make their way through the maze, though. Pick up the gun, Lisa."

Lisa knelt down carefully. She didn't dare duck her head precipitately while it was still aching from the clumsy blow Helen Grundy had given her. She picked up the gun, but took due note of the fact that if anyone came hurtling through the door with heroism on his mind, she would be the first target to attract attention. Arachne had a switch within easy reach that would engage the door's locks, but she hadn't touched it—presumably because the idea of being locked in while the corridor filled with ambushers was even less appealing than the prospect of reckless heroic intervention.

Lisa contemplated asking Arachne to open the inner door, but it was probably safer to leave Morgan locked in. That way, he'd be okay no matter what happened in the outer room if or when Leland and his taciturn friend arrived on the threshold.

Arachne fed the wafer into the computer. She began decanting information onto the local disk before opening the connection to a subsidiary station that would allow her to transfer data slot to slot.

The sound of a slightly muffled explosion made Lisa start. "He's shooting his way in!" she exclaimed.

"He can't hack the locks," Arachne told her, her calmness exaggerated by concentration. "He's in too much of a hurry to be subtle. He's a way off yet."

No sooner had she finished speaking, though, than a second explosion sounded. Alarm bells now began to sound in profusion. The cityplex police would be on their way—but Leland had already pointed out that their response times left something to be desired, and the lunch-time crowds in the mall would be panicking by now. Aboveground, everything would be chaos and confusion.

The alarms weren't loud enough to block out the sound of another door being taken off its hinges. This one seemed very close. Lisa had been aware for some time that Ginny's pills had worn off, but while she was moving, she hadn't lost her momentum. Now that she had nothing to do but stand still, the letdown could no longer be put off. She felt as if a heavy blanket had descended upon her. The sharp pain caused by Helen Grundy's clumsy blow had become oppressively dull and constant now, and she had to clench her left fist tight, digging her fingernails into her palm, to fight the deadening numbness. She still needed help, though—and help came.

"Dr. Friemann!"

The raised voice came from the corridor; it was loud and clear enough to dash any hope that its owner didn't know exactly where they were, and the jolt it delivered to Lisa's slowing heart restored the sharpness of her consciousness so completely as to make the situation seem surreal and hallucinatory.

Lisa immediately eased Helen Grundy to one side and went past her to the doorway. She took the gun with her, but she held it limply at arm's length, pointed at the floor.

She was relieved to note, once she was outside the door, that Leland was alone, and that his own already-raised weapon was a dart gun like the one the Real Woman had been carrying in the parking lot—so alike, in fact, that it was presumably the same one.

Leland looked down at the dart gun apologetically. "Cheap Bulgarian crap," he observed, "but it fires straight enough."

"One copy only," Lisa said immediately. "All the experimental data, plus a map of the retrovirus. You take it and you leave. You'll have everything we have—and as far as anyone else is concerned, you weren't even here."

"I'm not worried about that," he said. "Were you with them all along, or have you been turned?"

"Neither," Lisa told him. "I'm just trying to make the best of a bad situation. You'll have to trust my judgment that it's a good deal. After all, I know what it is and you don't—yet. It is worth fighting for—or against, depending on your point of view—so I'm not going to let you monopolize it. I'll shoot you if necessary, and this isn't a dart gun. If you take a copy and go, nobody gets hurt. It's a good offer, Leland."

"I'm probably a much better shot than you are," Leland observed. "Even with a piece of crap like this. Don't be fool enough to think you can shoot back before the drug takes effect. The dart would knock you over at this range. It might even kill you—do you know how many deaths are caused by supposedly nonlethal weaponry?"

"Of course I do," said Lisa, "but the radfems have three more guns inside and they're *real* marksmen. They consider me expendable. They know they're cornered, but if you hang around too long, the police will be here, and getting all tangled up would be a really bad idea. One copy, and you leave. Go far and go fast."

Leland shrugged. "Suits me," he said. "I'm glad it's you. I'm not sure I could trust anyone else not to hand me a blank." If it was a threat, it was delicately couched.

Lisa, of course, had to trust Arachne West not to hand *her* a blank when she stuck her arm around the door. She passed the wafer she received to Leland without bothering to wonder.

"I'll have to check it in the van," Leland said as he took it. "If it looks okay, I'm gone. As you said, I was never even here." He was already moving back into the subterranean maze. As he disappeared, he called back: "I'll be in touch about that job."

When Lisa stepped back inside, it was a resentful Helen Grundy who asked, "What job?"

"You cost me mine," Lisa pointed out. "Maybe you ought to congratulate yourself for that. If I hadn't been finished in the police force, I might not have been so nice when I phoned you or so pliable when I turned up here. Can Arachne assume that you're back on board now that you have nothing left to rat her out with?"

"If that man works for a megacorp," Mike Grundy's ex-wife observed, "there's no way anybody we can give it to will be able to work through the data before they do. They'll have the weapon before we have a defense, and they'll be halfway up the ladder to a workable emortality treatment before we're clear of the first rung."

"There is no workable emortality treatment, Helen," Lisa informed her quietly. "Not by this route. If forty years of Morgan Miller's ingenuity couldn't get the merest glimpse of a fix, the resources of the vastest megacorp in the world won't turn one up any time soon. He told Goldfarb and Geyer the simple truth. As a way of extending human life, it's a dead end. Our personalities are formed by the closure of synapses, the withering of alternative pathways. Our memories are sculpted, not piled up. Rejuvenation of the brain wipes out everything but instinct. It's a weapon, Helen—that and nothing more. It's not the radfem Holy Grail. It's just a poisoned chalice. I don't believe anyone will ever use it, but I do believe that handing it over to Leland has further decreased the already slight probability. The people he works for are committed One Worlders. When they go to war—if they haven't already—they'll do so with that end in mind. They'll use dirty tricks by the thousand, but I don't believe they'll use this one. It's not compatible with their ultimate aim. If anyone else tries to use it, or threatens to use it, the Cabal will be better placed to put a stop to it than anyone else. Maybe I'm not paranoid enough, but that's the way I see it. Even so, I'll be even happier if those copies Arachne is making are delivered into as many sympathetic hands as possible. A solid defense is the best foundation for any campaign."

"Can you get a job for Mike too?" Helen Grundy asked, using up her last reserves of malice. "He'll be needing one, won't he?"

"He can look after himself," Lisa assured her. "But if I can help him, I will—just as I'll help Arachne. I'll even put in a good word for you, if you want me to."

"Finished," said Arachne West. "Here's yours. Can you stall the cops for us?"

"I expect I can keep them fully occupied for quite a while," Lisa said as she accepted the proffered wafer and tucked it into her thigh pocket. "Go far. Go fast. Try to let me know how it works out for you."

When they had gone, she put the gun down on the desk and moved over to open the door to Morgan's cell.

He should have looked relieved when he saw that it was Lisa coming through the door, but he didn't. He had expected her. He'd had faith in her—but it was too belated to win him any moral credit.

In spite of everything they had done together, and everything they had been to one another, he had never had quite enough trust in her discretion, or in her devotion to the only real duty she had ever recognized.

"You're a smug, selfish, secretive bastard," she said as she went to help him up.

"And you," he muttered reflexively. All things considered, it seemed preferable to a counteraccusation of contributory negligence.

EPILOGUE

When Morgan and Chan had finally finished packing, Lisa went with them to take one last look at the ruins of Mouseworld. The room had been tidied up, as far as was possible, and all the roasted corpses had been removed, but the plastic slag that had once been feeding mechanisms, cleaning systems, ladders, and cage fronts had resolidified into a bizarre work of conceptual art.

"They're not actually going to leave it like this, are they?" Lisa asked.

"Undecided as yet," Chan told her. "It all depends on Ed Burdillon. I told him that a monument of this kind is worth far more to the department, and to the world, than anything that could be put in its place, but this is supposed to be a research-active department, and there is a war on."

"It won't matter," Morgan Miller stated loftily. "When the big collapse really begins, in ten or twenty or thirty years, all this will be lost. Not just the appearance, but the meaning too."

"A pity, if true," Chan opined. "The allegory of Mouseworld was never so apt as it was in the manner and aftermath of its destruction. I always said it was a far better symbol of the world's predicament than you would ever allow, and I was right."

Chan was the only one of the three who could have kept his job if he had wanted to. The university authorities still didn't know about his unauthorized usurpation of the Mouseworld experiment, and probably never would. His only misdemeanor, according to the official record, had been an idiosyncratic but understandable desire to talk to Lisa before he talked to Peter Grimmett Smith. That was little or nothing by comparison with Morgan's self-confessed forty-year history of unlicensed and unrecorded experiments. If Morgan had bothered to state his case to the Ethics Committee and the university senate, he would have faced several dozen charges of gross misconduct and would have lost on every one of them. *Even so, Lisa thought, it would have been very interesting to hear his defense, and it would have been a real education for every undergraduate allowed to listen in.*

She hadn't had the option of stepping down *that* quietly, although neither Judith Kenna nor Peter Grimmett Smith had had the slightest interest in putting her in the witness box in an open court. She had been refused permission to resign before facing an internal inquiry, so she had been forced to undergo the ritual humiliation of listing as many of her sins as she cared to admit, expressing repentance and offering profuse thanks for the leniency of her punishment. She had taken the procedure very seriously, as was only to be expected of such a long-serving officer, and she had taken great care to confess to every peccadillo they could actually prove, even condescending to own up to a couple they couldn't, in the interests of not having them dig too deeply in pursuit of more.

Surprisingly enough, she had played the game well enough to absolve Mike Grundy from all blame except that attached to his carelessness in managing his computer passwords. For that, he got off with a caution. He could have gone back to work, at least for a year or two—so his resignation, like Chan's, really had been voluntary. As Lisa had anticipated, he had no difficulty in looking after himself, and he required no help from her or Leland or anyone else in finding a new challenge.

Judith Kenna had also walked away from the affair without the slightest blot on her reputation. Lisa never heard whether or not Peter Grimmett Smith had been tokenistically censured by the oafs who had thrown him in at the deep end without adequate support, but she hoped that he'd escaped more or less unscathed. Because Morgan Miller declined to give any testimony relevant to the charges of abduction and malicious wounding, the CPS had to drop them, and the specific individuals who had taken part in the raid on Lisa's flat and the bombing of Mouseworld were never conclusively identified.

The only person to serve a jail sentence was Helen Grundy, who had been given three months for vandalism, although she had been released on amnesty after a fortnight. Stella Filisetti had contrived, with the aid of a good lawyer, to obtain release. Lisa assumed that she would be continuing her promising career as a loose cannon, although she had been refused access to her former equipment. Arachne West had never even been arrested.

On the whole, though, Lisa couldn't see that the ending was a particularly happy one. There was no technology of longevity, for women or for men, but there was a nasty weapon that would always be lurking in the background of life, even if it were never actually fired. And no matter how well the measures recommended by the Containment Commission worked, or how cleverly they would be facilitated by the newly resurgent textile industry, Malthus was still right. The world's overabundant population was still increasing, and the longer that situation persisted, the steeper would be its fall when the bubble eventually burst. Everyone in the world who was blessed or cursed with a fully developed Cassandra Complex was still in the endless tunnel, still unable to glimpse the light, still laboring under the curse of helplessness.

Lisa couldn't believe that the biowar defense mechanisms pioneered by the MOD and private enterprise would be completely effective. If she had ever been tempted to believe that, Chan's explanation of why his own revolutionary antibody packaging had failed would have put her right. It hadn't failed because it hadn't worked, but because it had worked too well.

"If our immune systems could work any better than they do," he had told her after concluding his deliberately vague technical summary, "natural selection would probably have ensured that they would. The problem posed by viruses of the common cold and of influenza viruses isn't just a matter of mutation—it's also a matter of mimicry. The most successful diseases hide their DNA in protein coats that reproduce protein-formations already manifest in the body's own structures. If the immune system reacts against them too aggressively, it triggers autoimmune responses far more deleterious than the disease effects of the virus—because the most successful diseases are also discreet. Killing one's host is a very bad survival strategy.

"Colds and flu viruses aren't very effective mimics because their evolution is driven by natural selection—but you can bet your life that the designers of bioweapons are much better at it. Hyperflu is the equivalent of a shot across civilization's bow. The real war won't begin until the autoimmune provocateurs are released—and when they are, any general-purpose responsive system is likely to be turned, producing cures far worse than the diseases. Packaging the systems in clothing rather than in the cells of the body is ingenious, but if the flesh/fabric relationship is intimate enough to allow the systems to work, it's probably too intimate to prevent them from being turned. In the end, the piecemeal solutions will probably be the ones that work best—and best is a relative term. There is no ultimate defense. Plague war is coming, and billions are going to die. Not next year, or the year after, but soon enough."

Lisa had to suppose that it was all true, even though Chan couldn't tell her exactly what it was that Edgar Burdillon had been working on for the MOD, let alone what the fashion industry had waiting for the new season to arrive. So why on earth, she wondered as she turned her back on the ruined room, did she feel so ludicrously cheerful? How could she be looking forward to working for a half-baked organization like the Institute of Algeny? Wasn't that a defeat, no less ignominious by virtue of the fact that it was a fate she would have to share with Morgan Miller and Chan Kwai Keung?

"You must be sorry to be going," she said to Morgan as they descended the staircase together. "This place has been your life."

"No, it hasn't," he told her with customary perversity. "I've lived my life in the privacy of my own skull, and I'll live the rest of it in exactly the same place. It doesn't matter in the least where the props and waste-disposal units are."

"You never cease to surprise me," she said sarcastically.

"I doubt that very much," he countered. "I took the trouble to keep only one thing up my sleeve, and once that became too hot to hold, I became absolutely transparent."

"Arachne West said she thought you'd done the right thing," Lisa remembered.

"I'm not about to return the compliment," Morgan retorted tartly. "My arm still hurts, in spite of all the best resources of modern medicine. Now that the grafts have taken, I'm assured it will heal perfectly, without leaving the slightest scar, but memory's scars don't vanish so easily."

"Well," said Lisa, "if its any consolation to you, I told her I couldn't agree."

The three of them passed through the door that let them out into the parking area, one by one. Then they formed up again to walk abreast to Chan's Fiat. All the crates they had left behind in the labs and offices would follow in due course. Morgan and Chan weren't allowed to export their work, of course, but they had piled up an impressive mass of personal paraphernalia over the years.

"It wasn't a matter of doing the *right* thing," Morgan said, effortlessly picking up the conversational thread. "I didn't have the advantage of hindsight, and all my hopeful anticipations were betrayed by ugly circumstance. But science can proceed only by trial and error, and the errors are as informative as the successes, in their admittedly meager fashion. I may be a smug, selfish, secretive bastard, but at least I can avoid sanctimony.

"Of course I was wrong, in retrospect—but what a world we might have had if I'd been right! What a world we still might have once we've learned the lesson of the impending crisis, and once someone luckier than I has found a means of keeping us forever young without the penalty of eternal innocence. What a world!"

Perhaps that's it, Lisa thought. *Perhaps that's the secret. Even Cassandra could have been cheerful if she had only been convinced that when all the mistakes have been made, honest endeavor and natural selection will see to it that we're bound to get it right in the end.*